The Awakening

A curse, two armies, one trial...

THE FOURTH BOOK
IN
THE THIRTEENTH
SERIES

by

G.L.Twynham

G̱ᴛ

G̱ᴛ
Pul

Dedication

This book is dedicated to:
Chyna, my inspiration.

And in recognition

of

Claudia's Cause

*Creating awareness of brain and spinal tumours
in children and raising money to make
a positive difference.*

*

Visit: www.claudiascause.co.uk

The Thirteenth Series:
The Thirteenth
The Turncoats
Nyteria Rising
The Awakening

Prologue

The Escape

A tall, dark-haired figure made his way down the brightly lit corridor. The nods of approval from his colleagues were a visible acknowledgement of what he had just achieved: capturing the one person he had considered not only a best friend, but the brother he wasn't ever meant to have.

"Twenty-Three Eleven!" A voice from behind stopped him.

He turned slowly, still aching from the fight that had taken place just hours earlier. "What?"

"The Warden wants to see you in his office. Now," a fellow Guard told him.

"Fine." He sighed, changing direction. As he approached the young Guard he could see the spark of speculation in his eyes. "I know my way," he said dryly, trying to deter any attempt at conversation, hoping the Guard was too shy to start the 'Tell me all about your escapades' quiz and clever enough to realise that he was bruised and weary, with neither the time nor patience for frivolous questions.

But the inquisitive young Guard's eyes sparkled and he blurted out, "Is it true you just captured Twelve and the Princess of the Ranswars?"

So he wasn't as shy or as clever as Eleven would have liked. "Yes, but remember, everyone is innocent until proven guilty, so your opinion on these prisoners should stay in your head." He gave the Guard a stern scowl. The young man took the hint and stood back a pace, kicking his boots together in annoyance before heading back to his quarters.

As Eleven passed the teleportation bay, a petite woman in a black suit emerged. Held captive by her tiny hand was a colossal, dark-green creature with three bony arms on each side, each covered in talon-like claws. Its fur standing on end, it grappled with thin air, roaring and spitting deep blue mucus that the woman deflected with her free hand. She held it with the same ease as he would hold a plasma ball.

"Ah, Eleven," she greeted him. "Have you made your paperwork available to me? You know how I like to keep your workload up-to-date."

His expression changed to one of affection. "Yes, Collector. I wouldn't want to get into any trouble."

"Good," she replied, a twinkle in her eye. Nodding farewell, she continued on her journey whilst the creature continued to howl, writhing and struggling in its fruitless attempts to escape.

When Eleven arrived outside the Warden's office, he could clearly hear angry sounds, sounds that were loud enough to carry through not one, but two walls. He found the Warden's assistant sitting at her desk looking at a screen, apparently completely oblivious to the ranting.

"I'm here to see the Warden," Eleven informed her.

She looked up at him. "Bracelet?" she demanded.

He lifted his sleeve, revealing a bracelet, its metal worn and battle scarred. It always served to remind him of how long he'd been a Guard.

She scanned it. "Wait over there. He will want to see you next," she instructed then looked back at her screen.

While Eleven waited, the roar from the Warden's office gradually reduced to a muffled rumble, then slowly petered out. At last, the door opened and out came a shocked looking Extractor, her eyes searching the room for the exit, and the fastest route to it.

"Eleven!" The Warden's voice rang out.

He strode into the office. He'd been here many times in his successful career as a Guard. However, today wasn't a day that he felt any sense of achievement or pride in his work. "Warden." He bowed his head in respect.

"I would like to congratulate you on your successful arrest of the traitors Twelve and the Princess Lailah." The Warden scratched his beard in agitation.

"Thank you." Eleven made his response automatically, feeling numb.

"However, I have bad news." The Warden stood. His thickset shoulders looked stiff with stress and Eleven could see that his hands were still unsteady from his earlier angry outburst.

"Warden?"

A heavy fist slammed down on the desk, which groaned under his strength. "Twelve has escaped!"

Eleven was momentarily too stunned for words. "....But how? We only got here a few hours ago!"

"The Extractor reported that he just wasn't there. Have you ever heard anything so ridiculous?" The Warden sat back down and started to move his hands over the desk, causing charts to appear on floating screens. "An informant seems to think he's here." The Warden touched a dot on the screen, enlarging it. "They call it Earth." He glanced up at Eleven before warning him, "This is classified information."

Eleven nodded, resenting the man's need to remind him of the need to keep this information to himself. "Yes, Warden." He knew his job; he'd been a Guard for over four hundred years.

"There's a complication. We sent one of the Old Ones there; if Twelve finds him, we could have a serious problem."

"What are the chances? And what's our next move?" he asked, already knowing in his heart that he wasn't going to get the rest he'd been planning.

"You're going to Earth. You're going to get Twelve back again. And this time I will extract him myself," he growled.

"Should I take Boden and Hadwyn with me?" He really could do with the backup; Twelve hadn't been an easy arrest the first time.

"No, this isn't a job for the Magrafe." He looked up, saw the tensing of Eleven's jaw, recognised the hard glint in the other man's eyes and quickly added, "However, I will make them available to you if you feel you need them?"

Eleven nodded, accepting the compromise. "Who will be my contact?"

"We have no trustworthy contacts on Earth, so this will be a solo mission. A Judge and his companion have been investigating the planet and have informed me that it's too primitive to be of any danger." The Warden's hands shifted fluidly over the desk, opening new screens faster now. Finally he stopped. "Memorise these co-ordinates."

Eleven inspected the images carefully. "Yes, I have them stored."

"If you have any problems, use them to get back here. You will also need a human name." He pushed more screens to the side. His hand hovered over an image of a man with wings. "You will be called Gabriel. To the humans of the area Gabriel is a messenger from their God. They are more likely to trust a man with such a name. Now go, don't waste another minute."

Eleven knew you were only given a name when it was totally necessary. His companion, Hadwyn, would be disappointed: he took great pleasure in mocking Eleven because he had never been given one. The High Judges believed that it made you more of an individual, and the Prison worked hard to maintain the ethos of the collective.

"Yes, Warden." He bowed once more in respect and turned to leave the office.

"Gabriel." The Warden stopped him. "Bring him to justice or leave him where he dies." His tone was bitter.

Eleven understood that it must have been a hard blow. Losing a Guard was never easy and Twelve had been one of the best Guards on the Prison. This would cause a ripple of questions through the others, and that was not good.

"As you order." The new name would take a while to get used to and as he left, he felt the weight that had been temporarily removed, descend once more upon his shoulders.

He made his way to the Distribution Office to collect his equipment. Showing his bracelet to the mechanic, he was informed that he would require no extra equipment, that the technology on Earth was so basic that the inhabitants would be of no danger to him; his usual weapons would be enough. His biggest concern on Earth would be disease, so he was given a vaccination and enough nutritional supplements to last him for the next cycle.

As he walked back to the very portal through which he had arrived earlier that day, he wondered how Twelve had escaped so quickly. And why Earth? He also thought it odd that Twelve had left Lailah behind, knowing how much he was under her control. That vile Ranswar! He'd known there was something suspicious going on from the minute he'd laid eyes on her.

His Collector was already waiting by her portal; she must have been informed he was leaving. She'd been his Collector since his very first journey. She was stern and liked to do things correctly, but he knew she had a soft spot for him, and his trust in her ability to transport him to the correct co-ordinates was absolute.

"Seems I'm going away again."

"It's not right; you have only just arrived back." She shook her head in annoyance. "Luckily, Earth's a very basic planet. You will make an arrest in no time I'm sure. Have you been to the Mechanics?" As she talked, she opened the shimmering portal in front of him.

"Yes, no need to worry." His lips rose into a crooked smile. "Anything else I need to know?"

"No..." She stood to one side, then held him on the spot with a light touch of her tiny hand, as if in thought. "...Well yes." Their eyes met. "I like the name you have been assigned."

"Thank you. Maybe one day you'll get one." He patted her arm and she let him go. He never ceased to be amazed at the power of the Collectors. They could control beasts far bigger than themselves with no apparent effort. They crafted portals all over the galaxy and yet they remained suppressed by the Prison. He looked back one more time, then disappeared through the portal.

*

His landing was silent; hundreds of teleports had honed his skills. It was night time here and he could see light up ahead. Light created by a fire. He moved through the trees towards it. As he came close the sounds of chanting rang through the woods. Voices seemed to bounce off the trees, echoing back and forth. Silently, he crept to the edge of a clearing and made sure he was hidden from sight. Ahead, he could see a group of people all gathered around a large fire. They seemed so happy. Clearly, Twelve hadn't reached them yet. Then a young woman caught Gabriel's attention. She was dancing, the reflection of the fire skipping burnt oranges and golds across her face and body. He held his breath, watching her spinning. The others clapped their hands to keep her going, the volume and energy rising and rising as they seemed to reach fever pitch. He couldn't take his eyes off her.

Suddenly she stopped. Gabriel realised he wasn't breathing and took a breath that reached deep into his chest. She was staring straight into the woods, seeming to look precisely at him. But that was impossible. He was trained in the art of concealment; there was no way she could see him. She must have spotted something else. He froze, holding his breath once more. She was walking towards him now, her pace unhurried, unworried. Hastily he pulled out his Dellatrax, searching for another life form, something that might have caught her interest. Twelve? His heartbeat quickened slightly, then slowed again when nothing showed on the screen.

She was at the edge of the clearing, almost upon him. Gabriel wasn't sure if he should stun her before she came any closer. He had been trained to deal with prisoners and had no problem with that, but this was an innocent woman.

"Welcome," she called into the darkness. Gabriel nearly choked. Surely she couldn't see him. "You're safe here," she reassured him.

Gabriel felt ridiculous. This woman clearly knew he was there and yet he was still hiding. He needed to find out how she'd spotted him. Was he more visible on this planet? Was it like the time he and Twelve had been on Braltar and the occupants had smelt them from three sectors away? Her face was in shadow and he couldn't see her expression. He needed to make eye contact. What was the worst she could do? He knew the Earth's inhabitants were primitive. He had his weapons; he could take out the whole village if he wanted to. He was the more advanced being.

"Well, you can stay in there all night, but it's going to get cold." She took another step closer to him.

"Stop! Stay where you are," Gabriel warned her.

Immediately she tensed. "Very well, but I am offering a hand of friendship. Your presence does not feel threatening to me. We saw your arrival in the flames of the Goddess Hecate."

"If you saw my arrival, then you will know I'm not here to hurt you. If you leave now everything will be fine." He leaned forward, still unable to make out her face clearly.

"Let's think about this. You're hiding in the woods on my land. These people are my family and the Goddess has told me to come and get you. I don't feel like leaving you there, so I will give you a choice: come out and prove you're not a threat to us, or I'll send the spirit of my dead grandmother in there to drag you out screaming and kicking." She placed her hands on her hips.

Dead grandmother? Gabriel tapped on his Dellatrax. Death on Earth was the same as everywhere else. This was a threat he could not comprehend and he was wasting valuable time with this woman. He stood up and walked slowly towards her. "Fine." She stepped back. A flicker of fear surfaced briefly and was then hidden with the same speed. The light of the fire now played across her profile illuminating her round eyes, petite nose and full lips, framed by waves of dark brown hair that cascaded down her shoulders. Gabriel took a deep breath; never had he been so close to someone so beautiful, so stupidly brave.

"Who are you? And what do you want?" she asked.

"I am Gabriel and I have come from the stars." He pointed towards the sky. His words made no sense; he had never introduced himself in such a way before.

"From the stars?" she almost laughed. They were just feet apart now. "Well, Gabriel from the Stars, my name is Wyetta and this is the village of Mistley. I think you need to come with me." She held her hand out towards him and he looked at it warily. On the Prison physical

9

contact was frowned upon, but she was waiting for him to take it and he felt strangely compelled to do so. As they touched he felt a bolt shoot through his body, like someone had just made his heart beat for the first time. He followed her, powerless, and she led him to the gathering where her companions greeted him with a depth of warmth and trust that he had never received before. They seemed to want to befriend him, without the slightest knowledge of his intentions. This was going to be more complicated than he had expected.

CHAPTER 1

The Arrival

The journey was over, but the destination couldn't have been worse. Val looked around her in disbelief; could this really be happening? The Warden had promised they would go home to her parents. 'No-one will remember you,' had been his parting words. Well, there was *unknown* and then there was *non-existent*, and this situation was definitely the latter.

But if the circumstances they now found themselves in were complicated, they were at least an improvement on the past twenty-four hours when she'd been forced into wearing a ridiculous, pink meringue dress and marrying a crazy blue-skinned dictator called Nathan Akar from the dying planet of Nyteria, with the sole purpose of saving the Prison from becoming a galactic light bulb. It had probably been the shortest marriage in history. Her new husband had been instantly taken away by a stranger, dressed in black metal. His soul consumed by the Interspace, a place where he would be held, suspended in internal and eternal agony – not exactly a dream honeymoon location. And the reward for her bravery? She'd been sentenced to extraction! Not exactly a medal for valour in the face of imminent enslavement. But on Alchany, the law was the law; a hard lesson to learn, and one she wouldn't forget in a hurry.

Belinda, Wendy's mum, had quickly confirmed that they were in the close vicinity of Manningtree. Which, with the appearance of Val's biological mother, Wyetta, waddling over to them with her hugely pregnant belly, was stating the obvious: they'd been abandoned, on purpose or by mistake in 1645, the time and place of Val's birth. Now, huddled miserably together in a field, they were all coming to terms with the *when* and *where* of their new situation, and the fact that, if her history classes had been correct, the latest technology was the fork.

Within the short time they had been there, Fran had asked loudly at least three times, "Have you seen the Horrible Histories programme about the Slimy Stuarts? I watched it with my little cousin. We're all going to be captured, tortured, chopped into little pieces and dipped in tar."

Wyetta, Val's birth mother, had welcomed them, but had wanted to know whom they followed: Cavaliers or Roundheads. Luckily, Jason, who'd paid attention during history class, reassured her that they followed someone called Freeborn John and that the monarchy and religion weren't on their agenda. This seemed to put Wyetta at ease.

Val surveyed her surroundings. The familiar tree line, the looming evergreens that made you feel young and inferior in their presence, the deep, rich scent of summer without any interference from modern-day pollution was all quite overwhelming to her senses. It felt strangely like home.

The Warden had told her she would be free from anyone who had seen her on the TV – she hadn't realised that he meant to send her somewhere without electricity! This seemed a little extreme. This had all become necessary thanks to her psychotic, ex-best friend, Delta's, perfectly timed 'plan-b' appearance on Sky News, so she had to admit that in some twisted way, the Warden had fulfilled his side of the bargain.

No-one here knew them, but she was pretty sure that in 1645, most people didn't know anyone more than five miles from their front doors, unless they were related. Speaking of relations, where were her mum, dad and Daniel?

"So, what brings you to Manningtree?" Wyetta asked, turning her attention to the whole group, her dark brown locks flowing gently around her face.

"We're travellers," Zac told her, his quick response full of conviction. "We've journeyed here from… France." He darted a glance at the others, encouraging them to follow his lead and they nodded in mechanical agreement. He had made it very clear in the few moments they'd had before Wyetta had reached them, that under *no* circumstances should they tell her who they were, or how they'd arrived.

"Well, that's a fair journey. I've heard of France; it's quite a distance from here," she smiled warmly looking them up and down, "and that would explain your unique attire."

"France is two hundred and eighteen miles from here," he pointed to the ground, "exactly." Val sighed. For someone trying to blend in, he stood out like a clown in the Arctic.

Wyetta gave a polite nod of agreement. "We seem to be getting a lot of visitors from far distant lands at the moment. But you must surely realise it is not safe to be wandering around. We're under constant attack. If it's not the King's men, Cromwell's."

Val knew a little about the Civil War, but not enough to understand what the situation must be like to live with. "Have you by any chance seen a small woman with black hair and a white streak, travelling with two men?" she asked. She was sure her parents must be nearby.

Wyetta shook her head. "No, I'm sorry, but we can ask in the village. If they're here, you'll find them I'm sure," she assured her. "You can accompany me there now, that's if you want to. My husband has gone hunting and won't be back for a few days, but I have enough to share. I imagine you must be hungry having come so far?" She offered her hospitality with a smile, resting her hands on her pregnant belly.

"No, we aren't," Zac thanked her.

Jason interrupted. "Speak for yourself!" He flashed a crooked smile at Wyetta. "I'm hungry. Can't remember how long it is since I last ate and if we have to get back to *France*, all two hundred and eighteen miles away," he raised an eyebrow, "before I eat again, I will starve to death." He strode past Zac, completely ignoring his hand signals.

"Jason's right. We need to know if my parents have made it to the village. Let's just get our bearings and something to eat, ok?" Val pulled Zac along as they followed Wyetta.

"Fine, but quickly," he grumbled, checking his watch as he followed the rest along a sheltered path towards a small clutch of dwellings.

Val followed, but kept a distance from the others and quietly observed as her mother pointed out the different houses, explaining who lived where to Jason, who seemed to be completely embracing this crazy experience. His head tipped backwards as he laughed at the description she had given him of one of the oldest men in the village, Tom the Dirty. Val caught a fleeting glimpse of Shane in his face and her heart ached as she thought of her friend who would never again be at her side. Here she was, spending time with one of her two mothers. What must it feel like for Jason to find himself alone at such a young age?

Jason's mum had died when he was very young and his bond with his dad had been like steel. Now that Shane had gone, all he had was them: Fran, two witches, a Hunter and an alien Prison Guard who had managed to get him dragged back in time. That raised yet another question. Was she still a Prison Guard? She assumed she had been given the sack, but she was still wearing her uniform, and she couldn't explain Zac being there, unless he was still her Hunter.

Wyetta stopped outside a small house that Val instantly recognised. "Here is my humble home. Please come in." She pushed open the uneven wooden door to reveal the room Val had been in with Sam the night she was initiated. Sam! Another person she would have to let go of. She sighed. Life was pretty tough at the moment, but it was what it had to be to keep them safe.

"Seems like people's fear of strangers and burglars is very low in 1645." Fran commented, as she walked into the unlocked house. Although, once she had surveyed the room, it quickly became apparent that there was nothing to steal. It contained the sum-total of a small wooden table, a bench, a round black metal pot over a fire in the corner, and an open window. "Well, that answers that one," she muttered, smiling politely.

"Please sit. I have a pottage already cooking. It's not much, but sharing is always more filling than watching others go hungry. Do you have your plates and knives?" she asked as they all congregated in the middle of the room, like visitors at a heritage centre. "I'm sorry. A plate and knife?" Zac's response was full of wonder.

Wyetta pointed to a single plate and knife placed neatly in the centre of the wooden table, then shrugged. "No? Fine. In France you must have far more luxuries than we do here. In England, we take our plate and knife with us on our travels. Wait, while I go and ask some of my neighbours to lend us theirs. Please make yourselves at home."

The door closed on them and Fran moved around the room, allowing her hand to slip over the lumpy walls and gazing up at the exposed underside of the roof that still had the twigs protruding from the simple, smoke-darkened thatch that covered it. Making her way over to the pot she glanced in and let out a hissing sound of horror. "I think there's something dead in there." She turned away, her face etched with revulsion. "If we eat this food we'll catch something. Our bodies aren't ready for this level of hygiene, and don't get me started on what the water could do to us."

Belinda put a reassuring arm around her shoulder. "Well, we don't really have much choice. Heaven knows how long we might be here. Just be grateful we are being offered food of any type. Wyetta is an extraordinarily brave woman to agree to help us."

Zac clasped his hands behind his back as he prowled the room like a caged tiger. "I hope I don't have to remind you all that whilst we are here, you must *not* talk about the future or what will happen to these people. Val, do you think she knows who you are?"

"I don't know. She doesn't seem to be acting the way she did last time I was here. But then I don't even exist yet."

There was an unexpected bang at the door, catching them all by surprise. A man's voice yelled, "HELP WYETTA. HELP!"

Val pulled it open to find a slightly built, middle-aged man, dressed in a brown shirt and tanned trousers. He seemed to be in a state of confusion, forcing his fingers repeatedly through his wispy brown hair whilst shaking his head. Seeing Val's unfamiliar face clearly added to his anxiety. "Who are you?" he demanded, staggering backwards.

"I'm…" She went to answer, but Zac poked her painfully in the back, cutting her off.

"We're visitors from over the sea," he answered for her.

"We're friends of Wyetta's," Val added, hoping this would reassure him they could be trusted.

He searched the group for Wyetta. "Where is she? They've taken my wife."

"She went to her neighbours for some plates. Don't worry; I'll help you find her."

Val made her way towards the pond, which was situated in the middle of the cluster of houses. "Wyetta! Wyetta!" She called repeatedly until, at last, Wyetta's head popped out of a door on the other side of the pond, three wooden plates balanced precariously in her arms. "This man needs you!" Val hurried to Wyetta, the man, Zac and the others now in tow.

Wyetta quickly returned the plates to an elderly woman who was standing in the doorway. "Ben! What's wrong?" she asked, taking both his hands as he started to explain.

"The soldiers came for her this morning. I was out in the field working, and they just took her. I heard her cries and when I caught up with them - they looked like Cavaliers, Wyetta - they said she'd been accused of witchcraft. Something about how she now belonged to Lady Eleanor. What am I going to do?"

"Stay calm, Ben. Did they tell you why they were accusing her of witchcraft?" She started to head back towards her house, pulling what looked like an apron from the front of her dress.

"They said John Trumble's wife was struck down by illness after Daisy delivered some milk yesterday."

Wyetta shook her head. "Don't worry Ben. We'll get her back. Go home and wait."

He nodded. "Thank you." Then, to Val's utter amazement, he kissed Wyetta on the cheek and walked away. Was he seriously leaving a heavily pregnant woman to deal with this?

Wyetta hurried back to her tiny house, followed by the group. She pulled back a cloth cover on the far wall. Behind it rested a cloak on a peg, and, on a rope, three shrivelled frogs. Val caught her breath. She'd seen this cloak before; she'd worn one exactly the same.

"Where are you going? Look at you! You're about to burst. What can you do?" she asked as Wyetta pulled the sackcloth cloak over her shoulders.

"I'm going to get my friend back." She pulled the hood over her head. "Please, wait here till I return."

"Yes, that's a good idea," Zac agreed.

"No, you can't go out there alone. Not in your condition," Belinda objected.

Zac's eye flickered nervously from one face in the group to another. "You know we can't help!"

To his visible surprise, Belinda pushed past him. "I know we can't, but I know what's going to happen if we don't, and you aren't going to stop me from helping this woman. So you had better get out of my way."

Val was shocked. She'd never seen Wendy's mum so adamant about anything, but she agreed. "Wyetta, we'll all come with you."

Zac grabbed her arm, tighter than she had expected. "Be warned, Val, if you change the past, you may regret what's waiting for you when you get back to the future. You're not a Judge, you don't have their powers."

"Zac, I promise we'll try to have as little impact as possible. If you want to stay behind, then do." Val pulled away and joined the group.

*

They followed Wyetta, concertinaing to a halt as they reached the centre of the village. Seeing them approach, the few people outside their homes dispersed. Zac caught up with them, mumbling to himself about how this was a very bad idea. Wyetta raised her arms into the air, and began to chant, "Sorores ad me. Sorores ad me."

"What's she saying?" Val whispered to Wendy.

"I think she's calling her sisters. I'm guessing that's in a witchy way, not her extended family." They exchanged a moment of realisation. The woman that had gone missing *was* a witch.

"Beats a mobile phone I guess," Jason quipped from behind them.

Then to Val's surprise, Wyetta started to walk, with total conviction and at a fair pace, towards the woods. Then they were all hurrying to keep up with her, dodging trees, branches and tall grasses as they ploughed forward. Val was actually grateful to be wearing her uniform as she caught herself on brambles and bushes more than once. Wyetta stopped when they reached the edge of rough dirt road. She lowered her hood, not even out of breath, and crouched down, concealing herself behind the bushes and long grass. "She's over there." She pointed ahead of them.

Val looked across at what she could just make out to be a bridge. She couldn't see anything other than the road and possibly a glimpse of water under the stone-built bridge. Then she heard voices. Quickly, they all crouched down beside Wyetta. "How do you know it's her?"

"She answered my call." Her confident expression never wavered. "See." A group of four men came into view, dragging a woman along the road. She was tied by her wrists to one of the larger men. Each had long hair and a short, trimmed beard and they wore matching outfits of tall, brimmed hats, suede cloaks and knee high boots in various shades of brown and red. Val felt like she had wandered into a history book. "Cavaliers?" Jason asked.

Wyetta nodded, "Roundheads, Cavaliers, they're all the same; they're enemies."

"She's bleeding," Wendy whispered through gritted teeth.

The poor woman had bare feet and was leaving a trail of blood behind her. She whimpered and cried as the men threw her to the ground. "Please believe me, I didn't do anything," she pleaded, trying to rise. One of the men kicked her brutally in the leg and she stayed down, hugging her thighs into her body. Val felt a knot tighten in her stomach, but she had to wait to see what Wyetta's plan was before she went all fiery alien on them.

"What were the orders?" one of the men asked another, who seemed to be in command.

"She gets a special dunking. If she survives, Lady Eleanor wants her." He laughed and slapped the other man with his leather glove. The contact cracked like a whip through the air.

"What's a dunking?" Val didn't really want to ask, but she knew she would find out soon enough.

"They will tie her thumbs to her big toes, and then lower her into the river. If she floats she's a witch and they will surely kill her. If she sinks and drowns then she's isn't, and their God will have been kind enough to take her away." Wyetta glanced behind her, as if checking to see if they were still alone.

"So what do we do?" Val asked.

Zac pushed his way forward. "Nothing, you do nothing," he urged.

"Zac, can you honestly tell me this is ok, that this woman deserves to die?" Val felt shocked and hurt by his actions.

His face softened. "No, but it's her fate," he said, attempting to justify his response.

"It's never anyone's fate to die at the hands of another," Wyetta replied sharply, standing up and stepping out into the open.

"Val, I warn you, if you follow her and change that woman's destiny there will be no turning back," Zac warned.

She knew he meant well, and he was right, but she couldn't ignore her instincts to help another human being. "Sorry, but that's my mother." She turned. "Wendy, stay here with your mum, Fran and Zac as back up. Jason you come with me." Val stood and followed Wyetta, Jason close behind her.

The men were laughing loudly as they tried to tie the woman's toes to her thumbs, too busy to observe their attackers approach. "Arh! I have witches blood on my hand," one man moaned as he pressed his bloodied hand hard onto the woman's cheek, wiping it down her face. "Will it kill me?" he grunted.

"We can only hope it does, for your sake," Wyetta interrupted.

Val watched her mother spin gracefully around him, pulling the sword from his belt. She tensed. Was her mother going to kill someone? She wasn't sure how to react. However, Wyetta moved incredibly fast, shifting around the back of the soldier. Holding the woman to the ground she brought the sword down. Val gasped, but her worries were quickly put to rest as the blade slipped through the rope binding the woman's hands and feet, freeing her.

Val was now level with the group of men, and knew she would need to use her powers to help them escape. She thought her sword would probably draw the least attention. Approaching one of the men, she focused, exactly as Boden had taught her, but nothing happened. "Sword," she commanded extending her hand expectantly. Still nothing. She looked behind her to see

Jason coming in on her left hand side and striking one of them with a solid left hook.

Her mind was now racing. Maybe being sacked from the Prison had stopped her uniform working, but it wouldn't stop her lighting up like a torch. She raised her hand, focusing on creating a ball of fire. Once again, nothing. "What the hell?!" She shook her hands vigorously, flexing her fingers. She was so intent on trying to activate her powers that, for a few vital seconds, she forgot to watch what was happening around her.

"Val!" Jason called out a warning, leaping in front of her and receiving the full force of the man's gloved fist. She closed her eyes and tried to teleport but nothing happened. Then, Jason's body rocked with the impact of the blow, which knocked him back against her and they both stumbled to the ground.

"Cado," Wyetta shouted. "Cado." Each time she called out the word she touched one of the men and they dropped to the ground like swatted flies. She was moving with amazing agility for someone in her condition. Jason pulled Val back to her feet as she again tried in vain to produce the simplest of sparks. Then he was on the move again, grabbing the woman off the ground and lifting her into his arms. Wyetta had wiped the floor with the men, and she, Val Magrafe Saunders, the one with the kick-ass powers, had done the sum-total of nothing but get in the way.

Wyetta joined Jason, leaving all four men motionless on the ground behind her and Val had no choice but to follow them in a walk of shame back to where the others were waiting.

Wyetta placed her hand on Jason's cheek. "Thank you. You're a brave young man."

Jason blushed. "It was nothing."

"Daisy, how are you?" Wyetta asked. The woman in Jason's arms was hardly able to lift her head. She gave a weak smile then closed her eyes.

"My hero." Fran placed a kiss on his cheek. Val was miserably aware that, unarmed, he had done a darn sight more than her, and now she was panicking. As they walked back to the village she repeatedly tried to light a flame, extend her sword, pick up a hint of air to create a whirlwind.

Zac caught up with her. "I'm pleased to see you didn't use your powers; you never know what the effects could have been."

"Nothing's working, Zac. My powers, they're gone. No fire, no sword, and no teleporting." She didn't want the extent of her panic to show to the others, but Zac heard it in her voice.

"What?" He stumbled on a root, and then pulled himself together. "You have changed something. I told you... but no... you wouldn't listen." He threw both hands in the air like an annoyed child.

"No! You said something in the future may change, not now, not this." She felt frustrated with him. "You and your stupid cryptic responses."

His brow broke into deep furrows of annoyance. "Did you think the things you changed in the future by your actions now wouldn't have an effect on you? I don't know why your powers aren't working; we will investigate when we're safe." He walked ahead, too cross to continue the conversation and she was left at the back of the group to make her way back to the village, powerless and confused.

CHAPTER 2

Power

Wyetta led them all back to her house. Its four walls were the only thing they had right now. Jason gently lowered Daisy onto the bench as there wasn't a bed. She thanked him again. She was weak, but extremely grateful for being rescued.

Wyetta handed her a cup of water. "We must hide you. When the soldiers wake up they will come looking for you and until we're sure they've given up, this place cannot be your home. You will go to Jamie's. He can protect you." She rummaged around the fireplace, picking up scraps of what looked like leaves and dried grass.

"Very well. Have you seen Ben? Is he safe?" Daisy asked, as Belinda wiped her bloodied feet with a cloth.

"Yes, he's fine. I sent him home. They won't touch him. The rich need to eat and drink and your husband supplies them with too much to take action against him. Tell me what happened. It's not like you to make a mistake and who is this Lady Eleanor? I haven't heard that name before." From her pocket, Wyetta pulled a bunch of grasses that she had collected during the return journey. Snapping the leg off of a dried frog hanging by the fire, she started to wrap the bunch in rough-looking twine.

"All I know is what I heard the soldiers talking about. There is a woman and they call her the Lady. One man said she's catching witches, but not just one or two. They spoke of hundreds."

"Hundreds?" Belinda quizzed, looking up from Daisy's feet.

"Yes, they also talked about an elderly man. He's also looking for witches and offering a large money reward. They said he's not from around here, seems he travels around with a small child." Wyetta passed her the bunch and Daisy thanked her, placing it in the pocket of her muddied skirt. "They say he can smell out a witch."

"Really? Well I would like to see him sniff me out," Wendy snipped.

Daisy nervously pulled back her matted hair. "You would do well to stay out of their way and off the road. I was just taking some milk to John's wife and the next thing I knew I was grabbed and dragged away."

"Did anyone say what the young child looks like? Is it male or female?" Zac enquired.

Val interrupted. "What if this Lady Eleanor has my parents and Daniel? Did they say anything about an odd-looking group, or a woman with white streaks in her hair?" She knew her mum would trust anyone. At least if Daniel was there he could protect them, but what if he had lost his powers as well?

"No they didn't, I'm sorry, but they did say that the young child was a girl and as cruel as the man, though nothing about her appearance." Daisy tapped her pocket. "Is this for my escape?"

Wyetta nodded. "Take it to Brigit and tell her that you need to become unseen, then head to Jamie's. I will get news to Ben. We will be free from these people soon enough. Jason, please take Daisy to the house on the other side of the pond with the rabbits hanging over the door. You can rest there for now," she instructed calmly. Jason picked Daisy up again and headed off. Wyetta moved around, taking down the few pots she had hanging on the walls. "Could you fetch me some water, the freshest is just outside the village?" She offered a pan to Val.

"Yes, of course." She took it.

"Do you think that's a good idea?" Zac asked.

Wendy let out a laugh. "Are you joking? Val's the safest person here." She winked at him.

"Yes." Val stared back at Zac. "*I am,* and we still need to eat and drink. Don't worry, I'll be fine," she reassured him, heading to the door.

"I will come with you," he insisted.

*

As they walked, Val thought she knew exactly who Daisy was talking about: Flo and Excariot. That could, if unaddressed, become a huge problem, but she was more frustrated at not knowing where her parents were. "I'm guessing you're thinking the same as me about the little girl and the man?" She broke the silence. Zac nodded, fiddling with his watch. "Have you picked up their signals?"

He shook his head. "Like you, I seem to be without power, although I believe it may rain in the next few hours." He waved his wrist around as if trying to grab a signal.

"So your watch doesn't work here. How come Sam's and my father's did?"

"Probably because I am the first Hunter to ever travel back in time," he replied matter-of-factly.

Val paused, then holding his wrist, she stopped him. "Seriously?"

"Hunters never lie." He turned and looked her in the eyes for the first time since their earlier argument. "I may not survive this experience. No-one knows what would happen to a Hunter during time-travel and so I have no reference for the effects on my DNA." He showed her his screen. It was blank.

"Will it kill you?" she asked him bluntly.

"I can't answer that, for any of us."

Her shoulders dropped. "I'm sorry you got dragged into this, but if it's any consolation, I believe everything happens for a reason. If you're here with me then it has to be ok." She tried raising a reassuring smile.

"No, it's of no consolation to me and that sort of irrational logic will eventually get you killed."

Val dropped her fake grin. "Right then, let's get some water. Just keep your eyes open for Excariot, Flo, my parents and this woman, Lady Eleanor. I wonder what that's all about? A woman catching hundreds of witches?"

"Knowing your talent for always being in the wrong place and attracting problems, I am sure we will find out soon enough."

She glared at him for a moment then, reluctant to start another argument, simply walked on.

As they moved away from the familiar path they became more cautious, not knowing what could be behind the next bush. Knowing Val was powerless, tension hung heavy in the air. If she met with Excariot now she knew she wouldn't stand a chance and, like it or not, Zac was right; she mustn't do anything to cause any more problems, not until she had her powers back.

They paused by a small brook. Surely Wyetta didn't mean water from here? Val couldn't even see the bottom. Dipping the pot, she pulled it out, full of dark brown liquid. The pungent odour was enough to make her gag. There must be a source of clean water somewhere. A pump or a well maybe? She'd seen them in films about the olden days. She emptied the pot and walked past the brook, heading towards a dirt road.

As they walked, she wondered about Gabriel. Although she hadn't seen him yet, she knew he was here. Would he know who she was? It seemed wrong to hide their identities, considering Wyetta had just revealed herself as a witch, which led to her wondering why Wyetta had been so unconcerned about letting them see her display of magic in such a turbulent and mistrusting time. Having seen her in action, Val conceded that you would have to be a fool to cross her. So, was she playing them? Or did she sense that Wendy and Belinda were like her? So many questions and still no water.

"Let's join the road." Val took a step towards it when, without any sort of warning she felt a buzzing in the air. Her hand grasped the handle of the pan tighter. "Can you feel that?" she glanced over at Zac.

His gaze shifted nervously from left to right. "No. Feel what?"

She was filled with apprehension. "I don't know. Come on, let's keep moving. Just keep your eyes peeled."

Zak's face scrunched up. "Peeled?"

Val sighed. "Forget it. Just keep a look out."

They still needed water and it was probably just the fact they were wandering around in 1645 that was freaking her out. A few yards further on she noticed something to her left, just off the road. "Over here." She guided Zac towards it. To her joy she was right. Firmly attached to a pole by a rope was a bucket over a hole in the ground. It was all so basic. She would never look at a tap with the same unappreciative eyes again.

"Don't let her touch you, men!" A man's voice barked orders in the distance.

"Chant louder!" Another voice supported him.

Val's pulse went from *on alert* to *out of the stratosphere* in a second. She put the pan down and quickly pulled Zac down into the foliage with her. "Aliens?" she whispered.

"I have nothing." Zac waved his watch at her.

"Come on." She signalled for him to follow her. Keeping low, they cautiously made their way towards the voices. The chanting was now like a dull hum, like bees flying in unison. Val crouched among some ferns, balancing on the balls of her feet, lifting herself up just enough to see what creature was making the noise.

In a clearing stood four nuns, each dressed in elaborate black dresses, large metal crosses hanging from their waists. Small black hats attached to white scarves were wrapped over their heads, tied neatly under their chins. Not the typical image Val would have expected of nuns, yet completely recognisable. The nuns were roped together at their waists, allowing them to make a perfect square. In the middle of this square was a woman, her hands bound behind her back. She was wearing a cloak like Wyetta's. Val could make out her pale complexion and a mass of black tresses. She didn't need any help to recognise that this woman was another witch.

"I said watch her hands." A man prodded the captive with the point of a metal pike, at least two metres in length. Val noticed that he never crossed the ropes. The woman groaned as the spike pushed into her side. She turned, doubling in pain and Val could see that, like Wyetta, she too was heavily pregnant. Val rose up onto her knees, almost toppling over.

"Val," Zac protested, grabbing at her.

"Thanks." She leaned back, opened her hand in the hope something would happen: a tiny blue flame in her palm, anything. But she was still powerless. Without her powers, they would need back-up if they were to attempt to save this woman.

Abruptly the humming stopped. "Why have you stopped?" A stout, bald-headed man yelled at them.

His answer came quickly. A scream escaped the nuns, an ear-piercing shriek that seemed to smash through Val's head. The nuns turned, and she saw that their lips were vibrating at a speed she couldn't imagine was easily achieved. One single word was vomited from their gaping mouths. "WITCH!" they all screamed together, turning to face where they were hiding.

She crouched lower, both hands holding her ears, in a desperate attempt to block out the noise. As she forced herself to look up, she only just caught the scream of horror that rose in her throat. Each nun had two black hollows where her eyes should have been and in each hole she could make out something moving, writhing. She was unsure whether it was maggots or worms, but that was irrelevant; whatever it was, was alive. It was spine chilling, worse than any nightmare she'd ever had.

"Get it." Someone instructed. Four legs in high boots surged towards her. Something grabbed her under the arms and she was pulled into the clearing, still gripping her ears.

"Zac, run," she shouted, but it was too late. Val watched as the butt of a rifle struck him in the head, sending him to the ground, bleeding and unconscious.

Her thoughts darted from flames to helmet to sword, but not one of her powers wanted to help her out of this situation. "Please, we're just travellers from France," she pleaded as they lifted her completely off the ground, then threw her over the rope towards the woman in the centre, who stepped sideways to stop their bodies colliding.

Val hit the ground hard, dust rising around her. She rolled forward and came to a standstill at the woman's feet.

"Stay down," a soldier ordered as the nuns returned to their previous stance, hands folded in prayer and began to chant as if nothing had just happened. Val managed to raise herself onto her knees. "Stay down and shut up," the captive woman ordered.

One of the men came towards the rope. His face was unforgettable. A deep, blood red scar ran from his eye across his cheek down to his jaw. It looked starker because it was framed by long, white-blonde hair, which made him stand out from the others. "Get up witch," he ordered. Then he spat on her. Val turned her face, trying to deflect the worst. She retched and as she bent forward a rope fell over her head.

"Stand up!" he hollered at her.

She rose and the rope dropped to her waist as if she had been lassoed in the old Wild West. It constricted around her, making her gasp for a breath. The man laughed and pulled at it again hoping for the same reaction. Whatever happened to her now, she wouldn't forget his face. He was going to pay.

A shorter, balding man with a thick black beard laughed as she stumbled into a walking pace. "Another one for the Lady. She'll be pleased. This one is interesting. Look at her jester's clothes." They were on the move, one blind nun at each corner, chanting over them. Val looked back at Zac lying motionless in the grass. What was going to happen to her now?

*

The group had been walking in silence for a while. Val had kept her mouth shut as the woman had instructed, but was trying to keep a bread crumb trail in her mind of recognisable land-marks, so she would know how to get back to the others when she managed to escape. The man who'd been pulling her along had grown tired, or bored, and had attached her rope to the nuns.

She wished the others were with her. She was scared. She'd gotten far too used to having her powers, a Hunter, her sword, Jason in her ear, and Sam and the others as back-up, not least the ability to teleport. The Prison had made her rely on being more powerful than the people she was facing, or at least having a good advantage. Here she was, a prisoner with a pregnant witch for company and roped to four of the most hideous looking nuns in history.

"Stand behind me," the woman whispered through gritted teeth, her expression unfaltering.

Val wasn't sure what she was up to, and didn't really know if following the instruction of someone in her position was the best idea. "Why? Who are you?" she whispered back, leaning her head as close as possible.

"My name's Brigit. Now do as I say if you want to live a little longer." One of the nuns turned and Val's stomach flipped as she felt the tension on her rope grow tighter. She contemplated stepping backwards momentarily as Brigit had asked, but they'd tied her so tightly to the nun's rope that she knew they would feel the slightest tug.

"I want to live Brigit, but I can't move back they'll feel it and, no disrespect, but why would I risk my life on the orders of someone who's clearly already been captured and tied up?" Val tried to keep her eyes on the men who were now having a heated debate about somewhere called Naseby, which, for some reason, seemed to be getting them all more and more agitated.

"You need to just trust me and pull," Brigit ordered firmly.

"They'll kill me if I do." Val wasn't prepared to die just yet. Jason and the others back at Wyetta's would surely realise they weren't coming back with the water and send out a rescue party.

"They're going to kill you anyway and if you're waiting to be saved you'd better hold your breath because these people will put us so far underground when we reach that wall up ahead, that no one will ever find either of us again. They will realise what you are and then you're in for a torturous ride, trust me." She glanced across at Val. It was the first time they'd made eye contact and Val held her breath as Brigit's face went from the palest white to a shade of blue she recognised all too well.

"You're Nyterian."

"Yes, I am, and I can sense you're not as human as you look. How do you know about Nyteria?" She faded back to her paler shade of white.

"Oh I've met a few people on my travels. So why Earth?"

A glimmer of angst crossed her face. "I came to escape persecution and imprisonment."

"How's that working out for you?" Val didn't want to seem rude, but it was obvious it wasn't going well.

"Not so good." The woman raised a smile. "But if you trust me and take the risk I'll get you out of here."

"Why can't you get us both out?"

"Our visually impaired friends are keeping me here." She tilted her head towards the nuns.

Val didn't want to engage with them again, but scanned the looming wall. She calculated they had about a half a mile to walk until they arrived. In the centre of the wall was a stone bridge and a raised wooden gate. She could see the silhouettes of several soldiers, carts and horses entering. What options did she have? Zac could still be out cold and how long would it take the others to even realise she was missing? If Brigit was from Nyteria and they were taking this much of a risk to keep her, then she must be powerful. Well, Val hoped she was.

"Ok, let's do it," she agreed. Brigit nodded as Val took a deep breath in and pulled. As she did so, the front two nuns were instantly pulled to a standstill.

"Oi!" one of the men screamed back at them, but she was already behind Brigit.

"What now?" she called through the men's demands for the nuns to do something.

"Hold your hand against mine and whatever happens, don't move." Val pushed up behind her, placing her upturned palm onto Brigit's.

"Don't let the witches touch." One of the men threw a short knife at Val, just missing her head.

"Come on," she encouraged Brigit as something sharp struck her hand. After the initial sting it felt like a dragging sensation, burning under her skin. She wanted to scream with the pain, but the chaos outside the rope was louder than anything she could have mustered. The pain grew in intensity and she began to feel faint. As Brigit continued, the nuns turned on them. Their hollowed-out sockets were the last thing Val saw before she slipped into a dream-like state.

* * *

The small rodent scurried at speed across the shiny transparent floor. Its tail trailing on the ground for balance, it wound with ease through the obstacles in its path. Its destination was the end of the elongated room, where a man sat alone staring out onto a seemingly endless vista of glass walls and floors. The rodent observed his master's half-naked appearance. Every visible inch of his flesh was covered in stark black images, swirling, moving, and alive. From his bald head, the images shifted and moved to his torso, then out towards his arms on their never-ending journey.

"Lovac, what are you doing?" the man asked, sensing the rodent's presence. His deep, rich voice made the tiny creature freeze on the spot. Then it rose onto its hind legs. "Come along, we have very little time," the man urged. It started shaking its head rhythmically, and with each turn, it grew in stature. When it came to rest, it was the size of a small child.

"Little time for what, Master Jarrad?" Lovac sniffed, wiping a run of mucus from his nose onto a furry arm then licking it off.

"The Vari has awoken." He rose, walking towards the glass wall to survey his surroundings. "I've waited for this moment for far too long and today, without warning, it happened." Jarrad span towards his loyal follower, each muscle defined to perfection, a flawless specimen.

"Show me?" Lovac moved tentatively towards his master.

Jarrad pointed to a stark red symbol on his hand. "See this. It's the first new entry to the book of Vari in nine hundred and seventy years."

Lovac's head twitched, in quick, brisk movements, back and forth, allowing the eye on each side of his head to observe the symbol. "But Master, how does this help us?" He sniffed around Jarrad, constantly picking out scents in the air, his nose seeming almost independent from the rest of his face.

"I can interpret a place, a time and a subject from this symbol. I can track this mark to the owner. Then I can find the Writer and I will have the true Vari, and the infinite power and respect that I deserve."

"So where is it?" Lovac twitched in anticipation.

"Earth. 1645 to be precise." He pulled a green jumper over his head, covering the mass of swirling images. "Ready to leave? We're going to change the past," he said, reaching out and patting the small creature on the head.

Lovac flinched under Jarrad's touch. In his mind, a pat could easily turn to a blow. "Yes, Master." He nodded. He knew his place and that was at Jarrad's side.

CHAPTER 3

Relations

'Am I awake?' Val wondered, as her sight started to clear. Her head felt foggy as she squinted and blinked her vision into clarity, revealing a familiar face. "Wendy!" She allowed a moment of relief to wash over her. Then a sharp, stinging pain brought her back to reality, and her throbbing hand.

"Well, that was quite the entrance." Wendy smiled at her.

Val pulled herself up with the help of her friend. "I lost Zac..."

Fran stepped back to reveal her Hunter who was sitting by the fire, strips of dirty cloth wound round his bloody head. "He's fine. We found him staggering back to the village. It seems he's not been attacked with a rifle butt before."

"I see you are able to teleport," Zac said, his voice a little less steady than usual. "Though your arrival was quite unconventional."

"No, I didn't do it! A prisoner helped me escape." She sat up properly now, suddenly remembering the witch's predicament. "Wyetta, we have to save her. She's heavily pregnant, like you. We were being taken towards a huge walled area, some sort of small castle or fortress. She said they would make sure she never made it out. They mentioned the Lady again." Val opened her hand to examine what had caused all the pain. In the centre of her palm, branded into her flesh was the backwards Y with the dot. The exact same symbol she had received in her first tattoo.

"We will. Let me see your hand." Wyetta walked over and gently touched the blistered flesh with her soft finger, pulling up her sleeve to reveal her own tattoo, the one in the drawing Sam had sent Val when she had first met Shane. They were identical. "So, my guardian's premonition was correct. It is you - my daughter." She instinctively wrapped her arms around Val's neck.

Val let Wyetta hold her. Her hair smelt of herbs mixed with fresh grass. It was odd and reassuring. It clearly didn't matter which mother hugged you, it was comforting. "Well, what do I say to that?" She glanced over Wyetta's shoulder to Zac, who had hung his head in despair.

"You must minimise the damage." His hollow, defeated tone showed how perturbed he was. His shoulders slumped miserably.

"I need to know everything about you." Wyetta took Val's face gently in her hands.

"I would love to sit here and tell you all about our adventures, but Zac's right, the more I tell you, the more problems it'll cause us all. You once told me that you had to make the hardest decision of your life for the good of all people. Now it's your turn to trust me when I say that what I don't tell you is also for the good of all people. What I can say is that your guardian's premonition was right, you are my mother, and we've met before, well

G . L . T W Y N H A M

twice actually in real life, but right now we're in so much trouble. We're not from France, were not even from Manningtree, and I need to get myself and all my friends back home to..." Val paused, the craziness was going to move into overdrive, "... the future, and soon."

Wyetta's eyes darted from one person to the other. "How far in the future? You look no more than eighteen."

Val hesitated for a second then murmured, "Nearly four hundred years."

Wyetta exhaled. "Four hundred?!"

"I know this sounds unbelievable, but you have to trust me. We really need to get out of here, but I won't leave until we find a way to free Brigit. I owe her my life." She turned her attention back to Zac. "The woman they were holding was a Nyterian."

His interest rose. "What's a Nyterian doing here?"

"I was hoping Wyetta could tell us? You told Daisy that Brigit would help her be unseen. Is it just that Brigit is a common name in 1645 or were you talking about the same woman who somehow managed to teleport me here?"

Wyetta moved over to the fire, stoking the flames under the pot. "There is only one Brigit I know of, so I'm sure we are speaking of the same woman. She is a great witch, capable of amazing magic. If she has been captured, we must free her."

Val was relieved it was the same woman. "Agreed."

"More information about this individual would be helpful?" Zac enquired.

Wyetta stirred some steaming concoction over the fire. "Brigit came here four years ago. She'd escaped from a prison where she said they wanted to use her as a weapon." Val didn't like where this was going.

"It turns out she was wrongly accused and, because of her powers, she knew they were blatantly lying."

"Did she tell you where this prison was?" Zac's hands went behind his back, his fingers interlocking into his thinking position. Val could see he was on the same wavelength as her. Was the prison Alchany?

"She just said a long way away." She poured a cup of steaming broth and handed it to Jason.

"How did she get here?" Val asked.

"To be honest, I don't think there's much she can't do." Wyetta said, offering a cup to Val.

She declined it politely. "Give me an idea of what that means?" Val felt the bumps on her hand.

"Every witch has a book..."

"...of shadows," Wendy enthused.

"Yes, and in it we write our invocations, Sabbats and things of magical relevance. It's a witch's most precious and secret possession. Brigit has a similar book of magical symbols and incantations, but it's different, unique. What Brigit writes in it comes to pass."

"Like when Wendy goes all white-eyed and sees the future?" Fran asked.

"She means when I get my visions." Wendy nudged Fran.

Wyetta shook her head. "No, what she writes creates the outcome. Her book is called the Vari, and although its power is great, holding many secrets which could turn tides, the true power comes from the act of Brigit writing. So, when she wrote our family symbol on Val's hand she knew it would send her here to me. She created your future. She knew you were my daughter."

"I think I need to sit down." Val sat on the bench. Zac moved closer. This was almost too incredible. How could someone write the future? How did Brigit know who she was? Brigit was like a God in the books of Greek myths or a Super Hero from a comic book. The possibilities were endless and Val was just thankful that Brigit was on their side. "So what are they going to do to her behind the wall we were approaching? Surely she can escape?"

"No one is without weakness. They need to do two things to keep her trapped: make sure she can't write anything- as you've witnessed, even her finger on flesh is enough for her to create her own chosen outcome, and stop anyone getting to her – that can only be done by the most powerful of anti-magic, something like the Sora, but to my knowledge there are none in this country. The last I heard of them, they had settled in Italy."

"I'm just guessing here, but are the Sora gross looking eyeless nuns? If so, I just had a very close encounter with them and I would like to avoid meeting them again – ever!"

"They come in several forms; if they're truly here, then that's very bad news. They're capable of true evil."

"So why has no one from this prison come looking for her?" Zac enquired, almost as if he was asking himself the question.

Surprisingly, Wyetta had an answer. "Because she's never created a new spell. She told me when she arrived that as long as she only taught the existing magic she had already created in the Vari, but never cast another new spell, no one would be able to find her. Although I doubt helping Val was in her plans."

"If you have the same tattoo as Val, what does it signify?" Wendy asked.

"It's a protection spell Brigit shared with me for my baby, to keep us connected." She placed her hand on her stomach.

"That's what you told me, that it would bring me back to you if I was in danger." Val looked at Wyetta's bump. "Zac, you do realise I'm an only child. I am, aren't I?"

Wyetta smiled. "Well, this is my first child."

"Then that's me in there?" She hadn't considered the possibility that she could be in the same room at the same time with herself. Panic was starting to course through her veins. She'd seen movies where you couldn't exist in the same time and space and the squished bodies of the ones who tried it!

Zac frowned. "It's logical. Why didn't we think of this before? You are here with your parents as the Warden promised, at your request. And they had to already be your parents, for you to return to them. It could explain why Sue and Mike don't seem to be here. It also means we are now on a count-down.' He turned to Wyetta, looking truly worried now. 'How many days have you been with youngling?"

"He means pregnant," Val added.

"We think about ten."

"What do you mean, ten?" Belinda asked eyeing Wyetta's large baby bump dubiously.

Zac explained. "Belinda, it takes thirteen days for a Prison Guard to be born, so Val, you have three days to leave this time. The moment you're born, you will no longer exist here as Val Saunders aged eighteen. You have no time to save anyone but yourself."

Jason interrupted. "In English, Zac, what would happen if Val here gets to meet herself?"

"She will cut off her natural time-line, which will cause her to no longer exist in the unmade future."

"I don't understand," Val protested. "I've already lived in the future. How can I no longer exist?"

"Your time will end when you're born. There will be no more. Yes, the past until the moment of your birth will exist in history. Everything you have done until now is past but there will be no future beyond that moment.' Zac paused before adding, "There will be no more Val Saunders."

"Still feeling confused." Jason rubbed his head.

"Imagine your life as a line." Zac took the poker from Wyetta and drew a line in the dirt on the floor. "Beginning and end." He dotted the points on the line. "You, Val, have made your line almost a circle by returning to your point of origin," he turned the poker, making the line on the floor into a circle and almost joining the ends. "If the two ends meet, you will *only* be able to take *one* of the forms present."

"So you're saying that in three days Val or baby Val will have to die?" Wendy asked, sounding panicky. "You can't be serious!"

"Very. And it can't be the baby or Val will stop her own existence and all she has done will be undone. That's why we need to leave here, as soon as possible." He winced, pulling the bandage off of his head to reveal a nasty cut and bump on the edge of his hair line.

"So how do we leave this place? I won't lose anyone else." Jason's voice was tinged with angst, searching for guidance.

But everyone fell silent, a cloak of sobriety falling over them. This was a real problem. Val had only three days to escape her own self-destruction.

"Wyetta, you and the witches sent me to the future before. Surely you can do it again?" From Wyetta's puzzled expression Val immediately knew this was a new idea to her.

"We sent you to the future?" she quizzed.

"That's true." Zac nodded in agreement.

Wyetta shook her head worriedly. "We're powerful, but alone, the coven wouldn't be strong enough to do such magic. We must have received outside assistance."

Val thought for a moment. "Zac, Sam was here when I came back. He helped Wyetta. We need to find him."

"Then that must be our next mission." Zac pushed buttons on his watch.

"Is it working?" Val asked.

"We will have rain in precisely five minutes and daylight tomorrow at 4:35am," he moaned.

*

Val sat in the shadow of the thatched roof, contemplating their predicament and watching the rain Zac had predicted splashing into the pond; at least one thing worked. So far, her new life of anonymity had been a disaster. They were trapped in 1645, she'd lost her powers and had been captured by the Sora and almost handed over to some creepy Lady called Eleanor who had an obsession with witches. But she'd been saved and released by a Nyterian. The irony of being rescued by someone whose people she had just expelled from the Prison, sending them back to a desolate planet and their certain demise, made her feel very uncomfortable. However, somewhere in her gut Val knew she was destined to save Brigit, whatever Zac said. So she had a simple plan in her head: find Sam and then go save Brigit, topped off with a one-way ticket to the future for them all.

She was sure they could do all that in three days. They had plenty of time. Or did they? They needed a real plan, and the one person she knew who would have one wasn't here. Or was he? She only had memories of Sam in the past at the time of her initiation. Had he ever told her that he had known her mother before then?

Her biggest dilemma was that she had usually been dying or been under a great deal of stress when she and Sam had had the *'oh yeah, I took this memory from you'* heart-to-hearts. He had taken so many of her memories that she wasn't sure what had really taken place. This was a side effect of him taking her memory that she would be telling him about if they ever met again. She knew she couldn't afford to waste time trying to find Sam, who may or may not, be due to arrive. And whilst Zac's watch didn't work, they wouldn't be able to pick up the signals of anyone from the Prison.

When Val rejoined the others, Wyetta was kindly offering them dinner: more pottage that resembled a really sloppy risotto. Wendy had turned it down and stuck to some bread. Fran had played with her food, but Jason had eaten his and then the rest of Fran's; he really was starving. Zac had taken a tablet. Val envied him as she watched Belinda move an unrecognisable bone around her plate. It was too small to be from a chicken, and Val didn't have the courage to ask what it belonged to. She knew all too well that food was vital. If she were going to have to fight Jason's way, with no powers, then she would need to keep her strength up.

"Food?" Wyetta offered her a plate.

"Thanks." Val started to eat, pushing her doubts to the back of her mind, but she turned down the cup of water. Its colour alone was off putting and the rancid smell made her wonder how anyone who drank the stuff survived.

As the rain started to pour heavily, she excused herself. Outside, there was a fresh and hopefully clean, supply of water falling from the sky. She reached out her hands, allowing them to fill, then drank what was caught in her palm. Surely rain water was safe in 1645?

The door to the house was open and she listened as Zac chatted with her mother about her powers, seemingly fascinated by the use of herbs, days, stars and moon alignments to create the most amazing outcomes. He asked about Brigit, and if she knew anymore about this person known as the Lady. Wyetta could only tell him that Brigit was a woman who mixed with few and only came to the village if she needed supplies for her work. About the Lady, she genuinely had no information.

The light outside had started to fade and Wyetta explained that there was little chance of doing any more that day. She told them that for several weeks now, soldiers had been waiting outside the local villages in the dark for unwitting victims. She explained that many of the King's soldiers were now in hiding, living in small groups foraging, or stealing money and food. The soldiers they had met earlier were tame in comparison to some of the things she had heard of recently. She reassured them that if they waited until morning, she could get news to her coven and they would at least stand a better chance of getting behind the wall that now held Brigit. Val knew Wyetta was right, but it didn't make her feel any safer.

Having drunk her fill, she rejoined the others who were now huddled together on the piles of straw with which Wyetta had covered much of the floor area. She was weary, but couldn't help trying one more time to light a flame, but nothing. It was official; she was broken. She kept watch as Fran, Belinda and Wendy gradually fell asleep. Jason had removed the burnt-out ashes and then gone with Wyetta to collect some wood, ready for a new fire in the morning. She was struggling to keep her eyes open when she heard a man's voice outside the door. She looked at Zac who was already getting to his feet. He placed his finger across his lips and she nodded.

Climbing over Wendy, she crouched by the wall near the door. Zac positioned himself on the other side. As the door started to open she panicked. The mantra *React first ask, questions later* ran through her head as she leapt up, slamming the door as hard as she could. There was a loud thud followed by a groan as the recipient of the door's full force, unexpectedly found himself full length on the muddy ground. "Oh my goodness!"

Val heard Wyetta's sympathetic exclamation, and knew from her lack of panicked screaming that whoever had been trying to enter the house was probably not an unwelcome intruder. A moment of 'whoops' now ran through her mind as she pulled the door fully open to see a cloaked man lying on the ground. "I'm so sorry." Val knelt down at his side.

He pushed himself up onto his elbows. "And who are you?" He rubbed his shoulder.

"I'm..." She glanced to Zac.

"Damage control," he responded.

"I'm Val." She reached out her hand to help him up.

"What's going on?" Taking her outstretched hand he hauled himself to his feet then brushed himself down. "Why are a Hunter and a Magrafe in my house?"

Val's jaw dropped as he pulled down his hood. Although he was wearing rustic clothes she recognised him instantly. "Gabriel!"

He frowned, seeming distinctly displeased by the situation. "There's no need for you to be here. I'm close to capturing Twelve. Why has the Warden sent you?"

Wyetta entered the mix. "No-one has sent her here. She's our daughter and she needs our help. And you have come home from hunting two days too early," she announced.

"Our daughter?" Gabriel looked at Val in disbelief.

"Yup, that would be me. Your daughter - the Magrafe." She shrugged awkwardly. "Surprise!"

CHAPTER 4

Gabriel

Val felt herself blushing as she released her father's hand. He didn't look much older than twenty-five. "I know this is weird," she apologised.

Gabriel ignored her. "Hunter. Explain what this is about. If you weren't sent by the Warden, then who? And why do you say this Magrafe is my youngling? There are no female Guards," he demanded.

"Gabriel, firstly it is an honour to meet you." Zac bowed his head. "I have watched your arrests countless times."

"Irrelevant! Give me the information that I have requested about this female." He pointed at Val, who was finding it hard to watch her Hunter suck-up so openly. He had transformed from grumpy time-traveller to awestruck fanboy.

"Your youngling *is* the first ever female Guard. She has fought with courage and honour, saving the life of the Warden and most of the Prison. But this has led to our misfortune. She was forced to unite with the leader of the Nyterians, Nathan Akar, to stop him destroying the Prison and the law, as you know, states she must be extracted as the wife of a dictator." As Zac explained,

Gabriel nodded, only giving the odd sideways glance at Val. "But the Warden chose to free her in gratitude for her sacrifice. Val's only request was that she be returned home with her friends and parents. My Guard, your daughter, expected to go back to her home and family in the twenty-first century, but it has clearly not come to pass, and now she is at risk of crossing in time with herself. We must leave this place and return to the future before Val is born. You will understand the implications of our presence here. We are not here to interfere with your capture of Twelve or to report back to the Warden, we are merely seeking a portal home."

Gabriel now brought his attention back to Val, inspecting her silently. "If she is our youngling, then why does she need to go back to the twenty-first century? From what you have said and the facts I have seen with my own eyes," he pulled Wyetta closer to him, "she is half witch and looks no more than a few decades old."

Zac nodded in agreement. "You are correct. Due to circumstances beyond your and Wyetta's control, at a young age she was sent into the future to be protected by two humans – Mike and Sue. I request not to expand on this information under regulation 747707."

"Seriously?" Val exclaimed. She couldn't believe what she was hearing. She wasn't allowed to tell anyone her surname, yet Zac could tell her biological father her life history. It seemed like a hell of a lot of information to her and then, after splurging it all out, he used regulation 747707 on him, which she now understood perfectly since using the Warden's Dellatrax and bracelet together and downloading all the Prison's rules and regulations. To her knowledge 747707 was a warning to Gabriel that

Zac wasn't going to reveal anything more about future events that could jeopardize their mission.

Gabriel agreed. "Request granted, but one last thing, so I can make sure she is who you say she is. Val, show me your mark," he ordered his expression steadfast.

"What mark?" she felt confused. Gabriel lifted his sleeve to reveal a symbol, the exact same symbol that Val had received when she'd been sent unexpectedly to the Prison. The one she had inherited from him, the symbol of the Magrafe. "Oh, *that* mark. Zac, can you give me a hand?" He unzipped her skin-tight suit just enough to expose her shoulder. "Here."

To Val's surprise, Zac's face contorted to an expression of panic. "What is this?" He let out a hissing sound. "Val, what have you done now?"

"What?" she looked down. To her bewilderment the symbol on her arm had once again changed. "No, no, no!" She rubbed at it fruitlessly. "That wasn't what I had; I had one like Gabriel." She spat on her fingers and tried to wipe it off. "Zac, you know what I had. You saw it."

"Val, you need to go inside." Zac was now taking her firmly by the arms, pushing her inside the house. It was definitely an order, not a request.

"Gabriel." She turned to get the attention of her father who was hot on their heels. "Look, Wyetta gave me your bracelet." She fumbled, pulling at her skin-tight sleeve to reveal her bare wrist. The commotion had now woken the others. "Oh my God. Where is it?" She pulled at her other sleeve, but there was nothing. "Jason," she called, grabbing at his t-shirt as he stood up. "My bracelet, it's gone and my tattoo has changed again. What's happening to me?" A sense of panic washed over her. No wonder she had no powers; everything she had been given had been taken away. But why?

Jason pulled Zac's hand from her arm. "Calm down, mate!"

Zac raised both hands in submission. "I do not wish to distress you Jason, merely get Val somewhere safe." He moved in closer to cautiously inspect her tattoo again, and she noticed that his face had become a shade paler. "This is very confusing to me." He shook his head.

Gabriel stepped in. "It's not confusing Hunter. You can see what she is. The question is, if this is new, then how did she get it?"

Jason wrapped his arms protectively around Val's shoulders, but she could feel him trembling. "What do you mean – what she is? How did she get what?" he demanded.

Gabriel was now faced by the whole group who were awake and in a state of increasing confusion. "Please do not be distressed young man; we will give you all the answers. Hunter, can you scan her symbol. Is it functioning yet?"

Zac reached out and placed his watch on Val's arm. They waited as he pressed buttons on the screen, but there was no response. "There's nothing. I have had no signal since we arrived."

Gabriel revealed his own Dellatrax to them. "I wish to scan your arm. If we can get some information then I might be able to tell you what's happening to you, why things have changed, perhaps help you get home." His tone was softer than Zac's and he made a gentle advance holding his hands up, making clear eye contact with Jason and Val.

She looked up into Jason's face, his brow wrinkled, protection written all over it, his broad arms still wrapped tightly around her. "It's ok mate," she reassured him. "He's my father and although I'm freaked out right now, he may have a few answers about why my powers have gone."

"YOUR POWERS HAVE GONE!?" Wendy exclaimed from the back of the room. "Since when? And when were you thinking of telling us?" she demanded.

"I'm sorry Wendy. I was hoping it was just a delayed reaction to the journey, but it seems it's more than that." Val felt bad. The others had seen her as their protector and now that was all gone.

"Goodness me, a trainee Judge." Gabriel acknowledged Wendy. "Anyone else from the Prison here?"

"No, and how do you know she's a Judge?" Jason demanded.

"Her uniform," he replied, giving Jason a reassuring smile, once again moving closer to Val.

Wendy grumbled, nervously wringing her hands. "Yes, I am a trainee Judge, but let's get back to what matters. Can you tell us what's wrong with her?"

"Let's find out," Gabriel replied. Val stepped out of Jason's protective grip and took a step towards her father. She turned her shoulder so he could see her new symbol. "This won't hurt." He placed his hand over her tattoo. His palm was warm but rough and she thought how very similar it was to her dad's. Gabriel pressed the screen of his Dellatrax. They all waited in silence, it was like being at the doctor's, waiting for results. His eyes narrowed and he pressed a few more times.

"Well?" Val's impatience was getting the better of her.

"It seems you're in transformation at the moment and by your reaction you clearly weren't expecting this. Have you had a large surge of power recently?" he asked still tapping away.

Val fidgeted uncomfortably. "When you say power, do you mean like teleporting a couple of hundred aliens across the galaxy or wearing the Warden's bracelet and Dellatrax which caused me to download all the Prison's laws and regulations in one go?" She shrugged; it felt almost embarrassing to say the things she'd done.

He released her arm, his hand lowering to his side. "Are you serious?"

"Yes, she did both of those," Zac confirmed.

Gabriel surprised them all by letting out a laugh, his face full of wonder. "You truly are my youngling and the first female Guard. Tell me, what did you think would happen if you used the Warden's Dellatrax and bracelet together?"

"I wasn't really thinking. So, where are my powers? What's happening to me? And what is a Transformation? Why…"

Gabriel raised a hand to stop her. "Slow down! So many questions. Let's take our time. To answer your first question, you still have your powers, and much more. I have never met anyone who's Transformed and been less on the other side. If anything, they are the most powerful beings. Why is this happening? Like I said, a huge surge of power can sometimes trigger a transformation, but normally this only happens to select individuals. It's such an honour to know my youngling will transform." He looked like her dad when she'd won the egg and spoon race, aged six.

She was shocked by the contrast between his reaction and that of Zac. She'd lost her powers and Gabriel looked like he was going to take her out for a celebratory squirrel dinner. But that still didn't answer the question of when she would get her powers back. "You seem pleased, so I'm guessing this transformation is a good thing?"

"It's wonderful news. A transformation is a privilege, not a punishment. Hunter, when you return to the Prison you must take her to see the Tark. They will be your guides."

Zac took an uneasy step back and she noticed that he still didn't look anywhere near as enthusiastic as Gabriel. Actually he looked downright worried. "Gabriel, I have some bad news, the Tark are no more."

"What do you mean?" he asked, still a half smile on his face.

"They were removed from the Prison after a disagreement with the High Judges. Val has no guides and will receive no help. The Warden relieved her of her duty. If she is transforming in the way we know she is, then she is, as I suspected, in grave danger."

Now Gabriel became agitated. "What do you mean the Tark were removed? They are the Wise Ones, the ones that train the most powerful. What you're saying goes against the laws."

Val could see Zac was panicking. His eyes were shifting around and it was like the time they had faced the Collector. He did this whenever he thought he was going to get into trouble. "I really can't tell you any more, it would be wrong. I have already told you too much, but I think we need to keep a close eye on Val now."

"Hunter, you will tell me everything I need to know about the future of my Prison so I may protect and serve the laws I understand to be true." He advanced on Zac.

"What if those laws no longer exist?" Val stepped into his path. "I have no information on any Tark in the memories of the Prison's rules I received, and Zac - that's his name, not Hunter, has saved my life several times. I trust him and if he says he can't tell you any more, then that's it."

Zac responded. "I mean you no disrespect Gabriel, but you must trust in my honest word that the Tark are long gone. That anyone with enough power to pose a threat to the High Judges has, and will be, taken and dealt with as a threat to them. And Val is now a potential threat to them."

Zac was sad, she could tell that what he was saying hurt him as much as it was hurting Gabriel to hear it. Whoever these Tark were, they weren't an option. It was time they moved on to something they could deal with right here, right now. "Let's try and find answers to another puzzle. Where do you think my bracelet is? I know I didn't lose it."

"You can't have something your father still has in this time," Wendy said. They turned and looked at her in surprise. "What?" she shrugged. "I saw it on Dr Who!"

"Ok, so if that's true and I can't double things up, then does that mean that baby Val," she pointed to Wyetta's belly, "has my powers?"

Zac shook his head. "No, your powers lay dormant until you reached your age of initiation, eighteen. So now we know you are Transforming I can tell you what's happening to your powers. They are in a state of fluctuation, a bit like the insects on your planet called butterflies. You must not be tampered with until we understand how this will affect you. Please believe me, Val. Give us a little time to try and find out what you're transforming into."

"Transforming into! You mean like some of the creatures we've met? Tell me I'm not going to look like Bertha the snake woman?" Val was now really frightened. Zac was making it sound like she was going to grow horns or wings.

"No... well... I have no record of the outer appearance of a Transformer changing, but that's not to say you won't."

"Zac!" she exclaimed.

"Please." Gabriel interrupted Zac's failing attempt to keep things calm. "Val, I have met several individuals who have transformed and I can confirm that there was no physical change."

Wyetta waddled into the conversational crossfire, taking Val's hand. "Irrelevant of whatever my daughter is, will be, has or doesn't have, and whoever she needs to see to train, we need to rest. I don't have the energy to keep a conversation with no known outcome going all night. Will this transformation happen tonight?" she asked Zac.

"It's hard to tell." He shrugged.

"Then we will take it in turns to watch her," she replied.

"Do not concern yourself. I do not sleep, so I will keep an eye on her," Zac said.

"Very well. Then us mere mortals should get some sleep. We will make plans in the morning to free Brigit and to send you back to your time, but nothing will work if we are so tired that we have blocked and cloudy thoughts. There is only so much magic I can do."

Gabriel nodded, slipping his arm around Wyetta's waist. "Agreed. We will continue this conversation at sunrise. Hunter... sorry, Zac - keep a close eye on Val." Then he turned to Wyetta and smiling, placed his hand on her stomach. "How is my youngling?"

"Far too much like her father." Wyetta gave Val a warm smile. "And where is my meat?"

*

It took the group a good half an hour to settle back down after all the excitement. Val had to concede that there was nothing they could do until the sun was up. If she was going to sprout four arms in the night then it was out of her control. Yes, she was scared, but at least she had Gabriel and Wyetta to guide her. They had led her to safety before and she wouldn't doubt their commitment to her now. What a crazy day. She thought about all she had been through before this and it seemed to pale in comparison.

The group laid themselves down once more on the piles of straw. Val leant against the wall so she could see out of the small open window. As they all began to drift off, she noticed that Zac, as agreed, had positioned himself blocking the doorway where he sat, watching over her. He was a good Hunter, sometimes a little bit over-excitable, but loyal, though his reaction to her new tattoo had seemed exaggerated to say the least, compared to Gabriel's.

As she lay there thinking of possible ways to escape to the future, something caught her eye through the open window. Stars, brighter than she had ever seen before. She was almost sure she could see across the galaxy.

What would be going on in the Prison tonight? She had been expelled as soon as the Nyterians had been removed. The battle won. But how would everyone be coping with what had happened, with what she had done: bringing the Space to the surface? And everyone believed she was dead.

She imagined Taran and Alsom spinning their way around the Prison, laughing at the Guards and their inability to scale the walls. Enoch would be with Eswith, organising their move from the Space to the surface. Her Magrafe companions, Hadwyn and Boden, were probably fighting for the hell of it somewhere, and Sam... she saw him for a second, his dark eyes, soft olive skin, the way his hair just couldn't be tamed. Then she tore him out of her mind, replacing him with thoughts of her mum and dad. There had been no sign of them here. She wanted to believe that if the Warden had sent her to Wyetta and Gabriel, her parents were safe, still in the Space, the last place she had seen them, and not trapped behind the wall with Brigit.

She prayed silently for the safety of Brigit and her baby. Not just because in 1645 there were soldiers running all over, or people trying to kill witches at every opportunity, but as Fran had pointed out, there were so many other dangers in everyday life: Simple bacteria in food or water could kill them; a modest cut to your hand could cause a fatal infection. Things which would be minor in the future could easily end a life here. She was grateful she hadn't paid that much attention in history at school; the fear of what was out there would probably cripple her.

Tomorrow she would wake up, and go and save Brigit. Then she would find Sam and head back to her real home. She touched her uniform where her new tattoo was. So she was transforming. Well, only time would tell what she was transforming into. Thank goodness she had friends to stand by her and, from what she'd learnt, you didn't need much more in life. Her eyes wandered the stars as she took in the beauty of a night sky like none she had ever witnessed and her thoughts slipped back once again to Sam and the Prison.

CHAPTER 5

Sam's Future

The petite figure made her way down the corridor; there was urgency in her steps. She mumbled to herself, glancing again at the screen she was carrying. Up ahead, she saw the man she was looking for. He was with a group of Mechanics, pointing at walls that were broken, cell doors that were hanging off. They were still recovering from the Nyterian invasion. No matter how great the damage that had been inflicted on the Prison, mere broken objects couldn't compare with the broken morale that the news of Val's immediate extraction had caused. It was ironic how the Guards that had once mocked her were devastated by the news. The shock of the Prison's betrayal of one of their own was tangible, almost flavouring the air; it was something she'd never witnessed before.

"So, if you could work on this area first. We need ramps here and here, unless you want them riding the walls. Then we can arrange for the new accommodation to be built as soon as possible. I have a man who can help you with that. I'll bring him onto the surface next time I visit," he instructed.

She stood patiently at a respectful distance behind them, waiting to get his attention. She wanted to scream at him, 'LOOK AT ME' but that would be completely unacceptable. They were preparing the Prison for members of the Space to come to the surface. There wasn't room for them all to come at once, and some had even requested to stay in their homes, but the Prison had agreed to an open welcome for anyone who wanted to return.

As she waited, she reflected on the possibilities that Val had created by revealing the Space. It was personal for her: her very own youngling had been born with imperfections. For hundreds of years there had been frightening rumours about what happened to the ones who weren't perfect and she had tried her hardest in the short time they were together to hide her daughter from the Judges. Then Sam had arrived one night with a woman. She would never forget her face; it was so pale; her beauty exceeded anything she had ever seen. The woman's name was etched in her memory: Eswith. And she had taken her daughter, disappearing with her to a place of greater safety. Sam had instructed that she never ask any questions, and she had done as ordered; she never broke the law.

Just remembering her youngling's face, filled her with feelings of pain, as strong and deep as the day she had let her go. She took a deep breath and pushed them back. Sam had promised her it would all be alright and she trusted him above all others. She was too scared to ask if her daughter was in the Space, but what if she was?

At last he turned to acknowledge her. "Collector, how are you?" His smile was genuine and warm.

"I am well, Judge. May we speak?" she responded politely, giving no outward sign of her anxiety.

"Of course, please come this way." His relaxed tone masked his emotions. She knew he was desperate; the front, although good, could only last for so long. He opened a side door. "In here?"

"That will do fine." There was nothing to see but four bare walls.

She nervously checked that the door had closed before pulling her screen out to full size. "Are we alone?" she asked.

"Yes. This is a safe room, I made sure of it. Tell me, what news do you have for me?" He leaned over anxiously.

"I was reprimanded today." She tilted her head, a deep frown appearing. "Did you know I have never been reprimanded in over six hundred years?"

"I'm sorry." He looked confused. "But, what does that have to do with us finding Val?"

"I was given this paperwork." She levitated the screen with one hand and opened it wider with the other. "See this." Her tiny finger pointed to a red dot.

"Yes."

"That is an interaction that I did not register." She shook her head as if just saying the words was absurd.

"Can you tell me more?"

"I never forget to register interactions," she informed him, deep annoyance in her voice.

"Go on."

"This interaction belonged to my Guard at the time: Eleven."

He was instantly flustered. "Gabriel? When? What didn't you register?"

"He had an interaction back in 1645, during his final mission. It was a few days before his death, with a Transformer of unknown origin." As she finally said the words out loud she felt a welling of emotion. "Sam, I never forget to register anything. I'm renowned for my efficiency and this interaction was not there yesterday." She allowed herself a small smile.

"So what you're saying is that at this point in time," he touched the dot. "Gabriel came into contact with Val?"

She could see him starting to get breathless at the thought. "Sam, listen to me, this was a recorded interaction by Gabriel. It shows that he placed his Dellatrax on someone who was a Transformer. This never happened. I know what my Guards do, day in, day out. I write every report. I would remember something as important as this, especially after losing him. But be warned, this interaction was brought to my attention, and many questions were asked. I said I was guilty and that I hoped I could be forgiven for my inefficiency, particularly as it was a long time ago. But I know they doubted me, just as I know the information was not there yesterday."

"So what do I do? I need to get to her. If Gabriel has found her, at least she's safe for now."

"I wish it was that simple. They wanted to know why I hadn't registered a Transformer. They are going to trace her. If they can't find any evidence that she's been captured, then you know what will happen. They will go back to get her, and then you and the Warden who have risked so much, will be on the next extraction list. You need to get to her first and take her as far away as possible."

"I need my original time schedule for that visit. I can't cross over with myself."

She pulled a small disc of metal from her pocket. "On here is everywhere you went during your time in 1645. At the moment there is no information on your interacting with a Transformer, so I assume she still hasn't found you back then. Be warned, she's clever; you will be the first person she will look for."

"I'm counting on that." He placed the disk onto his bracelet, where three tiny gems touching his wrist lit up. "You're amazing." He patted her arm. When the transfer of information was complete, he returned the disc to her. "You should leave; I don't want anything to happen to you. Keep answering their questions, but do it as slowly as possible."

"What do you intend to do?" she asked.

"I'm going to find her; she needs me. If Gabriel has found her and she hasn't yet completed her transformation then she's powerless. But the minute she does, depending on her gifts, she will become a hunted animal. The quicker this information is spread through the ranks to the Judges, the more danger she's in. How long do you think you can stall them?"

"Well, I have admitted to my failure. Now there will be an investigation. They will be looking for her appearance again in the records. I can only delay them for a few days. Whatever they find, they will then hold a meeting of the Court, to document the latest news. After that, I can't do much."

"So..." Sam closed his eyes, organizing the information he had just downloaded from her. "...I have three windows of opportunity to see her in the next few days.

But have you taken into consideration that it's her day of birth in three days?"

"Then three days is all we have."

"I know where the village is. I just have to hope she's stuck around. If you get any more news on her please bring it to me as soon as I return."

"I will. Sam, you know they'll pick up your teleports? You can't go back in time without them knowing."

"I know, but it's a risk I'm willing to take. It's not like it's the first time I've bent the rules."

"I hope this risk you're prepared to take will be powerful enough to time-travel them all back here. She won't leave anyone behind; you know how stubborn she is."

"It will be. Don't worry, we have friends in 1645."

The Collector bowed her head. As Sam opened the door for her to exit, she placed her tiny hand on his. "Take care and may courage, honour and wisdom guide you to justice." She was genuinely concerned for him. It wasn't her job to be: no emotions - that was the law.

"It will." He exited the door behind her. Looking at his watch, he had a few hours before his first window to go back. He would use them to collect some equipment and a few friends. "I'm coming Val," he said to himself. "Just stay out of trouble."

CHAPTER 6

Sugar Coating

The light came far too quickly. It must have been four in the morning and Val could already hear movement outside. She realised how annoying it was to have no curtains, when she was greeted by Tom the Dirty, who was staring right in at her. "Mornin'," he saluted her. "Is Gabe here?"

Val pulled herself up and observed the bodies scattered on the floor around her. She could only imagine that 'Gabe' was her father. "Seems not, sorry." The warm smell of straw filled her nose, making her sneeze loudly several times.

"Bless you girl. May it take you quickly," Tom said solemnly.

"What will take me?" Val asked.

"The plague. Those who sneeze are normally goners." He shook his head mournfully.

"Oh, no, I don't have the plague; I have straw up my nose," she attempted to explain.

"Tom!" A distant voice called and he instantly lost interest in her excuse for survival.

"Gabe." Tom smiled and sidestepped, allowing a harsh beam of light to strike her directly in the eyes.

"Morning. Did you sleep well?" Wyetta greeted her from across the room.

Val felt the shooting pains from the cold hard floor run down her back. "Yes, great thanks," she lied, standing stiffly and counting heads. Jason, Fran, Wendy, Belinda, Wyetta... and Gabriel was outside. She looked around again, checking. Where was her Hunter, Mr Efron? "Have you seen Zac?"

"I think he's outside with your father. I'm just making a drink. Would you like one?"

Val flashed back to the last time they'd met and the drink she had been given, "You know, I'm not that thirsty, but thank you. I'm just going to see what the plan of attack is for today." She stepped over Jason and made her way towards the pond where Zac and the others had gathered.

"Morning," she greeted them, trying to comb her hair into some semblance of normality with her fingers.

"Hello." Zac stepped aside to allow her into the group. He was holding a stick, which he'd been using to write symbols in the dirt.

Val observed his drawings. There were four symbols in a line. It only took her a few seconds to realise they were her tattoos. "What's going on?"

"Val, we need a better understanding of what's happening to you," Gabriel said. "Please don't be alarmed. We just want to make sense of why your powers are changing. You are so unique that we literally just have to make an educated guess at what's coming next."

"Fine, but you said you knew what was happening: I'm transforming." The worries of the night before came flooding back.

"Yes, you are, but it's the speed at which these things are happening to you. Your Hunter has told me a little more today and it seems that you have changed four times in less than four weeks."

"So, what's wrong with that?" She wasn't keen on the direction this was taking.

"It took me three hundred years to become a Magrafe."

"I know it's weird, but I was told you'd given me the Magrafe Symbol, and that it wouldn't work until I was ready. That's why it happened so fast. The Prison needed me," she reasoned.

"And I'm sure that's true," he tried to reassure her, "but to be ready in only a few weeks... well it's just never happened before. But neither has there been a female Guard. Now, I'm not saying there's a problem, we just need to understand what's causing it. The symbol you have now only comes to those with great powers."

"Do you know anyone else who has one?" she asked.

"The Warden," Zac told her, frowning.

"Right, well he's ok." She hadn't expected that answer. "Anyone else?"

"From what Zac has told me, no one who's still alive." Gabriel's response was sobering, like a bucket of cold water in her face.

"Any particular reason why they aren't alive?" she asked.

"It seems that in the future, after the Tark were disbanded, the ones who transformed were like trophies. Their powers were so unique and so highly prized that with the lack of training, and no protection from the Tark, they became vulnerable. The villainous and corrupt hunted them, transferring their powers to amulets, so they in turn wouldn't then be murdered for the powers," Gabriel answered.

"Why didn't you tell us this yesterday, Zac?" she snapped.

"I interpreted the expression you taught me," Zac replied.

"What expression?" Val was confused.

"The last time we were in this much danger you told me to *sugar coat* the data. You said too much bad information at once is sometimes not beneficial."

"Great time to start listening to me, Zac." God, she wanted to be mad at him right now, but she knew he was genuinely concerned for her. "Well, we've made it this far and it's not the first time my life's been in danger, is it? We'll make it out ok." She tried to raise a smile. "Anyway, I think I'd look good as a necklace." She gave him a nudge, attempting to make light of their predicament.

"Val, this is no time for your stupid Earth humour!" Zac yelled at her, his face scrunched in anger, flushing red. He pulled away from her, his hands in tight tense balls, fighting for control of these unfamiliar emotions. She'd never seen him like this. He took a long moment to breathe, composing himself, before turning back to her. "I am sorry. I should not have spoken to you like that, but you don't understand how much danger you are in. The only place you will be safe from attack is back on the Prison. And now Gabriel knows too much about the future, and it's all my fault. I should never have let you go off and save the Prison." He turned away from her.

"Now you listen to me, Zac. You aren't responsible for my actions. You're here to tell me who to arrest and you do that perfectly. I chose to save the Prison and if saving all those Guards was wrong, then I will do things wrong forever, so get used to it buddy. But I won't go back to that place; I don't care what you say."

He glared at the ground. "We may have no choice." He struck through the symbols with his stick.

"You know what they'll do to me!" She wouldn't accept this option. "They'll have me extracted before I get through passport control! You said the High Judges don't want anything more powerful than them on the Prison... You said that!"

"They will want to see your powers. You may actually have a value to them," Zac responded.

Gabriel sighed. "I'm sorry, Zac, but I have to agree with Val. If the High Judges are capable of obliterating the Tark, a harmless civilisation, through fear of their power, then we can't risk sending her back there. We need another option."

Val needed an idea and fast. "Correct me if I'm wrong, but as long as I don't have my powers I'm still a nobody?"

"Yes. Go on," Gabriel encouraged her.

"So, what if I don't try to use my powers? Could that stop the transformation?"

'Ummm...' Gabriel looked at her thoughtfully for a moment. "If you have no powers, they can't pick up your signal. It's a risk, but it's an option."

"So I just stop trying to use them?" she quizzed.

Zac seemed more despondent that Gabriel. "I'm not sure that will work, but what choice do we have? At least it might give us more time to find a safe place for you to hide."

Val reached out for his hand. "Please don't give up on me, Zac."

"Val, only your death will make me give up on you."

Her eyebrows lifted and she gave him a crooked smile. "That's nice to know. I think."

"Well, you were relieved of duty, and I'm still here, so I can only imagine death is the only option left," he informed her matter-of-factly.

Gabriel knelt, rubbing the symbols out with his hand. "We need to carry on with our plan and not draw any unwanted attention to ourselves. The most important thing right now is to find a way to get you home before you're born."

She had another mission on her mind. "Gabriel, do you know Brigit the Writer has been captured?"

"Yes, Wyetta explained it all to me last night."

"Then you will understand that our first job is to save her and the baby. Surely you know that if her power falls into the wrong hands, it will be the end of us all. Our problems will pale into insignificance if someone gets to use her as a weapon." She wasn't going to be turned away from this mission; this was one of those moments where, once again, she was happy to do the wrong thing.

"I agree, but you won't be the one to do it. I'm here now. Let me take care of Brigit." Gabriel stood, patting her on the shoulder as he passed.

Zac followed closely behind him then paused. "Are you coming?" he asked Val.

"I will in five. I just need a little alone time."

"Fine." He carried on, giving Gabriel his version of the events from the previous day's encounter with Brigit, leaving her by the pond, alone.

She stood contemplating her reflection in the pond. The cut over her eye was healing, but then Eva popped into her head, followed by Daniel. She prayed once again that her mum and dad were with him, safe in the Space. She sighed. It was clear that Gabriel and Zac were going to be over-protective of her now that she was Transforming. She could hardly say the word without bursting into inappropriate nervous laughter; she pictured herself 'transforming' into Wendy's car and driving away with Bumble Bee and Optimus Prime.

Still wondering if she could rely on Gabriel to rescue Brigit and whether she could hope to escape from Earth before Wyetta gave birth, she realised she was thirsty. Last night's rainfall had left little pools of water on the leaves of some of the bigger plants around the pond. Gently she tipped the water into her cupped hand and then drank greedily. It was time-consuming, but she was confident that this water was safe to drink. So absorbed was she in her task that she didn't see Jason striding out to join her.

She jumped when he asked, "What going on, mate? Zac seems even more highly-strung than usual."

"I'm in enough danger without you trying to frighten me to death!" She grinned, softening the words. "Seems he kept a little bit of information back yesterday."

"Really?"

"Yes, he actually listened to me for once and sugar-coated the data!" She rolled her eyes. "Seems I won't be able to use my powers ever again, or I'll be hunted and killed, or alternatively, turned into some magical piece of jewellery, possibly a necklace. Or, even more interesting, I could be a test tube alien on the Prison. Sleep well?"

"Slept like a rock. And that stinks. You're much more of a bracelet type," Jason joked and she was glad there was at least one person who understood inappropriate humour in 1645. "But seriously, Val, can't this Brigit woman just write you a new story?" He asked, raising a small ceramic cup to his lips and taking a sip.

Val held her breath, waiting for him to spit it out, but he just sipped and waited for a response. "You seriously have the stomach of an alien."

"Focus, mate. Brigit?"

"Sorry. Well, I guess if she was here now then yes, that would be a solution, but she's not here, and I can't go get her on my own with no powers. You should have seen the eyeless nuns. They were terrible, a real force to be reckoned with. Even if I'd had my powers I would have struggled to take them out. Gabriel says he will rescue her."

"So those nuns recognised you as a witch?" She nodded. "What if I went to get her? I'm just a human so they wouldn't see me as a threat." He sipped again. "Like your Mum with the Novelia?"

"It would be too dangerous. Those soldiers were more than happy to strike a woman and I'm guessing they'd have no problem with killing you." Val was worried. Jason seemed to be using her as a sounding board for his own plan rather than as a companion on a journey.

"I dealt with those other guys, why not these?" he continued.

"With Wyetta and her magic," she pointed out. "Listen, you're not thinking of doing anything stupid are you?"

"Now why would I do that, mate?" He grinned and put his arm around her shoulder. "But I won't let anything happen to you or anyone else."

"I know that." She let it go, but she was going to have to keep an eye on him. Jason had just lost his dad. They hadn't really had time to accept the loss, but she was missing Shane so much that it hurt to even think about him, so she couldn't imagine how much worse Jason must be feeling.

She'd noticed that he'd been a little over-protective since they'd arrived and had put that down to being somewhere new, but listening to him now she was genuinely concerned at the lengths he might go to, to keep them all safe. She really hoped they would find Sam soon.

"Hey, you guys." Fran's soft tone brought a smile to Jason's face. "Stealing my boyfriend so early in the morning?" She kissed his cheek and Val felt his arm leave her and wrap around Fran. "Are you seriously drinking that stuff?" she complained.

"Glad you feel the same way," Val agreed.

"Wussies!" He tipped back the cup and finished it off.

"Well don't complain when you start to get red blotches all over your body." Fran pushed him away playfully. "So Val, what's the plan for day one of two, before your birthday?"

"I'm not sure yet. Gabriel seems to be in charge."

"We're going to save Brigit," Jason replied adamantly, turning abruptly and walking away.

Fran glanced at Val, reflecting her expression of concern. "Is that the plan?"

"Seems it's his."

*

Breakfast was another interesting event: more porridge-type food with a little bread and some yellow-tinged water to wash it down. As she ate, Val started to reflect on her options. One thing was starting to bother her: If she couldn't get them back to their time, if she disappeared at the time of her own birth, could the others survive without her? Would they be able to wait and meet the earlier version of Val, when she visited Earth to whup Excariot's butt, and then hitch a ride back home to the future? Well, if Delta could manage to get back to the future, she was sure Jason and the others could.

So Plan B was: tell Zac that if she didn't make it through this experience, they should follow the coven into the woods on the night of her initiation, when future Val would be able to take them back with her.

"Penny for your thoughts?" Belinda interrupted her planning.

"Just trying to find a way out of here," she sighed.

"I'm sure we'll make it out," she reassured Val, rubbing her arm affectionately.

"Wendy!" Fran shouted, making them all jump. Wendy, who'd been crossing the room with her plate of food, had dropped suddenly and silently, heading face first towards the floor. Jason just managed to grab her before her head struck the bench. Her body was limp in his grasp, her food splattered around them.

"She's going to do that thing that she does," Fran mumbled as Wendy's eyes opened. White eyes that had no depth and no reflection looked up into Jason's and he caught his breath.

"Move back," Belinda ordered. "Support her." She instructed Jason.

Jason pulled her up and they gathered round and waited.

It felt like they'd been watching in silence for hours, but it was only a couple of minutes before Wendy spoke. "He's coming back in time for her." There was a pause and she breathed deeply. "He will take her away," she hissed.

"Who's coming? Who's being taken away?" Jason asked, but there was no response.

Wendy's hand slowly rose into the air. Extending her index finger, she pointed at Val. "You, you must save the children. Stop the Lady. Kill the witch." The sound in her throat was like a snake, as it rattled to a halt. Wendy's body dropped limply back into Jason's waiting arms.

Val looked at the others for some sort of assistance. "I'm not killing a witch, and we've heard about the Lady, but children? What children do I need to save? Did you notice she never mentioned getting home?"

"I don't know, but that was creepy." Fran rubbed her arms, trying to stop the goose-bumps becoming even more prominent.

Wendy slowly opened her eyes which were now back to her usual green. "Was that good for you, Fran?" she asked, attempting a smile.

Fran flung her arms around her neck. "The best one yet, psycho," she cried, relief gushing out.

"So, any visuals?" Val asked. "Because that was kind of cryptic."

"No, I'm sorry to say that words and images don't always to come together. If they did, I would have known that you would never have worn a pink wedding dress, unless you were marrying a blue dictator."

Wyetta, looking thoroughly confused, passed her a drink.

"That was most impressive," Gabriel complimented her. "So, we know a male is coming for 'her' from the future, but who is she? Who is he? What children must Val save? And kill which witch?" he asked, tapping enthusiastically on his Dellatrax. Then they all heard it beep, and he tapped one more time. "I'm sorry, but I've received a faint signal from two alien life forms arriving in the nearby town. I have to go and investigate. After all, I'm still here to make an arrest. If I don't report anything questions will be asked and we don't need any more problems at the moment. Would you like to come with me?" he asked.

"Yes, that would be great. I really need to get out," Val replied enthusiastically.

"Sorry Val, I meant Zac. He will be of more use to me. You need to stay here. We'll return as soon as we can. Work with Wyetta to look for ways to get you all home."

She moved to one side, wanting to say 'ouch - that hurt' but she held back. "Of course," she said with deceptive meekness.

Zac's eyes were suddenly the size of saucers, gleaming with adoration and excitement. "Yes! That would be such an honour... If you think Val will be safe?" he said, looking first at Gabriel, then at Val, clearly torn between duty and hero worship.

She knew he really wanted this, to be with a real Guard again, even if it was just for one trip into town. "Listen Zac, we have three witches, one Judge in training and Jason, who can actually fight better than anyone I know. Plus me and Fran as back-up. I think we'll be just fine." She pushed him towards the door.

"I agree, she has adequate protection. Let's go." Gabriel headed out.

"Watch over her. Don't let her try anything stupid," Zac instructed Jason as they headed for the door.

"Leave," she ordered, pushing the door firmly shut behind them.

She watched through the window as they walked off into the distance. It wasn't fun having no powers, but she didn't have to ruin it for everyone.

After they'd left, Belinda and Wendy busied themselves chatting with Wyetta about the different spells the coven could use to enhance their powers. Meanwhile, Fran dissected her breakfast, showing Jason something that might be moving in her porridge and Val wandered around the room aimlessly, three, four, then five times. On trip six, it suddenly became unbearably claustrophobic.

She headed for the door, promising to go no further than the pond, where she proceeded to pace around its murky green edges in the same stir-crazed manner. After her fourth lap she headed back to the house. "Hey, Jason!" she called into the window.

"What?" He glanced up from where he was now sitting at the table with Wyetta, inspecting a small pile of colourful stones.

"Fancy going for a walk? I need someone to protect me," she asked, in the hope they would let her go. There had to be something for her to do, apart from collecting wood and water. They might even find Sam nearby, or her parents.

"Where are you going?" Belinda enquired.

"Just around the trees and stuff, nowhere far away, within shouting distance," she reassured her. "I just didn't want to go alone."

"Yeah that's fine." Jason stood, making his way out to her.

"Don't be long," Wyetta called to them from the window.

"We won't." She waved goodbye.

*

Val finally broke the silence after they had been walking for a few minutes. "So how's it going?"

Jason took her wrist, "Great, because you and I are going to get Brigit back. That's if you're still up for it?"

Val faltered. "You know I want to, but after Wendy's little turn and the arrival of two aliens only two days before my birth, don't you think we should wait for Gabriel and Zac to get back?"

"No, it's me and you or I go alone. Brigit is our only way out of here and you know it. If there was another way, we would've already left. The clock is ticking; we have less than two days and everyone seems to be sitting around doing nothing. That's not what my Dad would have done. He'd be out there now, looking for Brigit. No one else is going to die."

She could say *no* to him, but in her gut she knew he was going to go anyway. He had just used her as a window of opportunity to escape. She wasn't so sure that Shane would have run into this without a definite plan... or Sam at his side, but Jason needed her to believe in him and he had no-one else because of her. "Right then," she agreed, "let's go get us a witch."

CHAPTER 7

The Wall

They'd been walking for close to an hour and Val was most impressed that she'd remembered the direction in which the soldiers had dragged her the previous day. They'd stayed under cover by following the edge of the woods, but as the fortress loomed closer, they saw that they would now need to move away from the shelter of the trees and cross the open ground between them and the wall.

Val looked at the stretch of grass doubtfully. "So you're sure this is what you want to do?" she asked Jason for the fifth time in as many minutes.

"Yes! Brigit is behind that wall and, from what you told me she's pregnant."

"I'm guessing she's minutes away from giving birth."

"That baby isn't going to be born in a cell, surrounded by vicious nuns and soldiers," Jason declared.

"I agree." She would remember to tell the others that to justify what she and Jason were doing; they were going to be very angry when they realised what they were up to.

"So, if that's the place, what's our plan? Any input welcome. It looks well-guarded to me." They watched carefully, observing the bustle of people at the gate in the wall.

Val shivered. She was getting the same feeling she'd had when she'd seen Brigit for the first time. Something odd was afoot; a gut instinct was warning her to be very, very careful. She surveyed her surroundings again. "Duck!" she whispered, grabbing Jason by the arm of his t-shirt.

On a nearby dirt-road, a horse drawn cart was approaching. They both rose fractionally in the undergrowth until they could get a decent view without being detected. On the cart was a group of ten women, heavy metal chains binding them together. They were wearing a variety of different outfits of the time and appeared to represent a wide spectrum of classes, all clutching at each other for support. Some were sobbing, others looking slightly more resilient, but they all had one thing in common: they'd all had their hair hacked off; their heads were mostly bald.

"Who are they?" Jason whispered.

"I don't know, but I don't appreciate the whole 'women in chains' routine. These people seem to have serious disrespect for females, pregnant or otherwise," Val responded.

Jason took Val's hand, and as his wrapped around hers, she realised that it was clenched tight. "We need to sort them out, free those women and get Brigit."

Val was feeling more concerned than ever now. Jason seemed so blindly determined to get in there to rescue Brigit, but the most they had ever done on their own had landed Jason in hospital with concussion, and that was when she'd actually had powers. "So what would your Dad do?" She hoped he would say get the hell out of here – or at least get back-up.

"He wouldn't stand idly by while all those women were being tortured, that's for sure."

"Right." Not exactly the response she was looking for, but she had to agree with him. And it was true, the women in the carts had just added to the mixture of horror and persecution that was surely waiting for them behind the wall.

Jason was now staring in the opposite direction. "Look." He pointed and, there in the distance, coming down an opposing track, was a group of five more carts, a whole procession of the things, each carrying a huge wooden crate. "Looks like they're expecting a lot of guests." Jason stared at Val as the carts headed for the gates.

Val gaped at him. "You think there are more women in those crates?"

He nodded grimly. "What else could it be?"

Attempting to save Brigit on their own was beginning to feel like a bad idea. "Jason, look at how many people are going in there! I agree, we need to see what's behind that wall, but I think we should make this a reconnaissance trip. Let's just get an idea what we're up against and then go back and tell the others. You can't be crazy enough to think we can take on a fortress without my powers, with no weapons, no witches, and no Zac." Val knew how important her reconnaissance trip with Sam and Zac had been to the overall success of their mission to reclaim the Prison from the Nyterians. It would certainly be a wise option here too.

He shrugged, resignation in his response. "Ok, fine. This is a reconnaissance mission, unless we see an opportunity. So how do we get in?"

"We're going to need a disguise to get in there. We need to go for the peasant look. Just like that one." Val pointed at a figure approaching through the woods.

"Lie low." Jason pushed her down. A peaty smell filled her nostrils; ferns tickled her cheeks. She could feel Jason lying next to her, not moving. Then, as the figure closed in on them he jerked, like a snake snapping out at its prey. He was so fast! The next thing Val heard was a muffled cry as a body hit the ground hard. He dragged it between them.

"It's me! Please... stop," the figure cried.

Jason paused, fist in mid-air, his leg wrapped around the waist of whoever was under the cloak. "Wendy?"

"Yes! Get... off...me." The pressure from his grip was expressed in her gasps. Jason rolled back releasing her.

"What do you think you're doing?" Val crawled to her side.

She pulled back the hood of her cloak. "I could ask you the same thing," she retaliated.

"We're just trying to find out some more about what's behind the wall and where they've taken Brigit. Sorry we didn't tell you. Did you tell the others we'd gone?"

She shook her head. "No, I said I was going to look for some herbs. Wyetta and my Mum were showing Fran the joys of magic for the non-magical. She'll know how to cast a basic spell by the time we get back." She brushed the dirt off the cheek that Jason had crushed into the ground.

Jason grinned at her. "Fran and magic. I need to live to see that. How did you find us?"

"Please! Give me some credit. I'm a trainee Judge." She shook her cloak.

"Magic then?" Jason persisted.

"No. You two are really predictable; well you are to me. I knew the second you disappeared that you'd be getting into trouble."

Val lifted up onto her elbows. "Okay, let's fill you in on what we've seen. A cartload of women has just gone through that gate." Val pointed towards the fortress. "The women were all chained together like animals, their hair had been cut off and I'm guessing they weren't the hired help. That cart was closely followed by five more enclosed carts."

"It makes sense. They'll have cut the hair from their heads to find the mark of the Devil."

"What?" Val was shocked.

Wendy shrugged. "In 1645, the idiots believed that witches were licked by Satan and he left a mark on them. So they shaved their bodies to find any hidden symbols."

"That's the stupidest thing ever. Licked by Satan! God, this time in history was seriously messed up," Jason muttered.

"We need to get into the fortress to see what we're going to have to deal with to free Brigit, and to do that we need to find a disguise like yours, without attracting too much attention. Any ideas?"

Wendy's face lit-up. "Lucky I stole three of these then." She pulled back her cloak to reveal two more garments, wrapped tightly into bundles and tied around her waist.

"And there was me thinking you had some serious pie-eating issues." Jason took one and Val grabbed the other.

"So now we have a disguise, what's our plan?" Wendy enquired.

"Get in, find out where they're keeping Brigit, and get out without being captured. I would also really like to know what was in the enclosed carts. I get a feeling they were full of witches, but surely there can't be that many in this area?" Val signalled for them to follow her and crawled off in the direction of the fortress.

Jason grabbed her ankle. "Don't forget we said we would save Brigit if we could?"

"Yes... well... we'll make that decision when we find her, I promise," she assured him.

He released her. "Fine, then let's go."

Skulking through the last of the long grass at the edge of the woods, they got as close as possible to the gatehouse. Val raised her hand to bring them to a halt. She could hear some soldiers chatting loudly in the distance. "Listen," she whispered.

"Evil I tell you, all of 'em, need burning. Don't know why we keep them on the move," a deep voice protested.

"Well, it pays a wage, and if you're not a King's man or Parliamentarian then there's not much else that does pay."

The other one mumbled in agreement. "Have you seen those nuns? I'm sure they've come up from the guts of hell. Someone said they get served vermin three times a day."

"I heard they bring the dead back to life," his companion added.

Val rose cautiously and saw the two of them standing with their hands placed strategically over their weapons.

"Nah, fibble-fabble," the stouter soldier said and they both laughed at the audacity of the accusation before moving back towards another two soldiers.

Wendy shuddered.

Val felt physical repulsion at their words. A vision of the eyeless nuns feasting on rats and mice wasn't that hard to conjure up. "Any ideas on how to get past them?" she whispered to her companions.

"That's how we get in." Jason pointed towards a group of men and women moving along the road towards the gates with a small cart, pulled by an aging horse. It was carrying what they could best guess were supplies of food for the fortress. "Let's go. Dad always said that you could think yourself out of a situation before you were even in it. I think we need to make a move and they're our opening." He stood up, pulling the hood over his head.

Wendy quickly joined him.

"If it was good enough for Shane, it's good enough for me." Val pulled up her hood, its harsh material scratching at her cheek. "Ah, sackcloth, how I've missed you." She grimaced as they walked towards the group.

Standing guard at the gatehouse were four bearded men, watching as the convoy of enclosed carts entered. Each was dressed identically with knee-high leather boots, colourful loose fitting shirts and leather sashes, with a pistol and sword placed prominently on their belts. "About time!" one yelled over the bustle, slapping the horse's rear with his leather glove.

Jason pushed Val into the group of merchants. Wendy followed, quickly mingling until they were simply a part of the procession. The four soldiers at the gate called them all to a halt and Val could feel her stress levels rising. The 'what am I doing?' moment she'd had several times recently didn't feel any less powerful. Her skin itched with the sweat running down her cheek against the cloth of her hood. The guard questioned two hooded individuals leading the group. They readily opened bags, revealing bread and dead animals to the satisfaction of the soldiers.

"Come on then, hurry up," they ordered as the group were ushered in. Val and the others stayed in the middle of the melee.

They kept up with the merchants until they started to disperse in the centre of what looked like a small town square. The cart they had seen entering was now on the far side of the square where it was being pushed into position with several others, making a perfect circle around an imposing raised stone table. Val looked closely and saw it was decorated with deep black grooves in swirls and patterns all down its side.

Each cart contained ten women and was exactly the same as the one they had seen outside. The women were chained together, although their hair varied in length. She could only guess that was a sign of how long each group had been there. Val paused to take it all in. As she pivoted on the spot she could see the vastness of the fortress.

"Val," Wendy pulled urgently at her arm. "They're all witches, I can sense it, and if they have a way of capturing them," she pointed at the carts, "then you and I are in serious trouble."

She knew Wendy was right, but now wasn't the time to panic. They were inside enemy territory. "At what point aren't we in serious trouble?" she replied, squeezing Wendy's hand reassuringly. "Answer this

Wendy. If they're all witches, why aren't they doing anything to break free? I don't understand."

"Move on!" A man pushed Jason. "No loitering. You know no one's allowed contact with the heathens. Get back to whatever your duty is." He shoved him one more time for good measure.

"Sorry," Jason mumbled without lifting his head. "We need to get under cover, Val. We don't want to attract their attention."

She hadn't imagined the place would be so full of life. The fortress was bustling with traders, apparently oblivious to the captive women, and there were far too many soldiers for them to even consider saving anyone without some serious help. They huddled together under a small archway. "I have no idea what's going on here guys. We have a hundred or more witches tied down to carts in the centre of an enclosed fortress. And Brigit isn't one of them."

"I've read so many books over the years, Val. I've covered this period in history a hundred times or more. I know who the villains of the piece are, and who died, but I can tell you this, I've never read anything about this event or Lady Eleanor," Wendy said.

"I wonder why not?" Jason asked. "Is this happening because we're here, and we've changed things? Or is it because no one witnessed this happening at the time, so it's not been recorded?"

Val shook her head in disagreement. "I don't think our presence here has caused this." As she spoke, a woman cried out. Val's heart began to race. The cry had come from one of the carts where the woman were all shuffling backwards, as if trying to get away from something. Val gasped when she spotted what was causing them so much distress. "Wallace!" she forced the name through gritted teeth.

"What?" Jason asked.

She raised her finger and aimed it towards a well-dressed, elderly man in the crowd. "No wonder Gabriel didn't capture him. He was looking for Excariot. I bet this is how he managed to catch my father out and kill him." Val felt nothing but contempt. Inside she wanted to strike him down now, to end the suffering he would cause so many people over the next four hundred years until she managed to stop and arrest him.

"What's he doing here?" Wendy asked, equal agitation in her voice.

Jason took both Val and Wendy by the arms. "Ok ladies, I don't want to sound like grumpy old Zac, but we aren't here to change the past. I hate him as much as you do, but we've already dealt with him. You need to focus. Remember why we came. We're looking for the all-powerful Brigit - our ticket home."

Val took a deep breath. He was right. Just then, like the icing covering a mouldy cake, a beautifully dressed, golden-locked child made her way over to the elderly excuse for a body that Excariot was using. He stroked her hair. Val shuddered. "Seriously creepy. Well, at least we know Flo's here, so we can expect devastation wherever she goes." At that moment she felt relieved she didn't have her powers because the urge to kick Flo's backside into the next century was almost overwhelming.

She was also glad that Jason hadn't overheard her conversation with Excariot back on the Prison. If he knew that Excariot had killed his mother, Elizabeth, Val knew where he would be right now. She felt Jason's grip loosen.

Excariot and Flo chatted with the soldiers, pointed at the women and seemed unimpressed. Then another soldier joined them, waving a set of keys, and beckoned them to leave with him. "Wherever he's going, I bet that's where the closed carts are." Val stepped forward, but Jason stopped her.

"Look, as much as I'm enjoying standing in the middle of enemy territory watching a psycho and a dead girl enjoying themselves, I think we need to get the job we came here to do, done. Let's stay focused."

"Yeah, you're right,' Val agreed. "But this place is a lot bigger than I thought. We need to split up so we can cover more ground." They all looked at the surrounding buildings. "Wendy, you go check what's down that corridor." Val pointed to a passage. "Jason, look, there seems to be a much higher concentration of soldiers over there. Can you find out why? You're not a witch so they won't pick up on your presence. Finally, she pointed to the other side of the square and the carts. "I'm going to try and speak to one of those women."

"Sounds good to me," Wendy said.

"Back here as soon as you've done. Take care," Jason instructed.

*

Val watched as Wendy darted to the corridor's entrance. God she could run. Jason was more controlled with his movement, simply walking away from her as if it was just completely natural. Val moved with more caution, slinking between obstacles. Though there was a large number of soldiers loitering around the carts;

they seemed extremely relaxed for people surrounded by suspected witches, and this made her feel even more on edge. She noticed that the soldiers were all armed, some with swords that were heavy and cumbersome looking, rusty even, not like hers. The odd one had a pistol.

Her feet squelched in the mud as she homed in on a woman who was sitting on the edge of a cart, facing her. Her expression was blank, and she was dirty and visibly sleep deprived. The woman's hair had clearly been cut by a butcher's knife, simply hacked away. Her dress was filthy with a mixture of wet and dry mud. There were also a few splashes of dried blood, though the woman had no visible wounds. As Val got closer to the carts, the stench was overpowering. The urge to vomit almost overwhelmed her and she gagged. Taking care to breathe through her mouth as much as possible, she made a determined effort to ignore the smell and looked around carefully to make sure she was still going unnoticed. Everything seemed ok. "Hello," she called to the woman, not sure how to introduce herself.

The woman's eyes were fixed on the distance and she had to blink several times to refocus them onto Val. "What do you want?" she rasped, devoid of any emotion, her mouth parched.

"I want to help you. Please listen to me. My name is Val. I'm the daughter of Wyetta of Manningtree." She couldn't think of anything else she might say to make this woman trust her. To her relief the name visibly rang a very loud bell.

"Are you the daughter of the Star Man and Moon Mother?" She blinked now with more fluidity, moving her eyes as if waking from a nightmare.

Star Man: that must be Gabriel; it made sense. "Yes I am. Listen carefully. I don't know how long I can stay here. I want to help you, but I don't understand why you're not helping yourselves. You are all witches, aren't you?"

She nodded. "We are, but they have us trapped, bound to the spot." She lifted her hand to show Val the thick metal shackles. "Somehow these stop us from using our magic. We have no way of escaping whilst we have them on."

"Magic handcuffs, that's new."

Their little chat was abruptly cut short when a woman's voice bellowed, "WHAT DO YOU MEAN, SHE WON'T?" The witch with whom she'd been conversing shifted her position to cover Val, who moved as close as possible to the cart and peered through a gap between the women to see who was causing the commotion. Well, well! It was the man with the scar, the one who had ever-so kindly spat on her the previous day. He was clearly trying to appease some woman. Val watched until she came into view. This wasn't just any woman! For a start, her clothes were unlike anyone else's. They were stunning; like the Prada or Dior of 1645. Covering the woman's shoulders and reaching all the way down to her hips was a mane of strawberry-blond curls. A gold bodice made her waist look as narrow as Barbie's. How on earth could she breathe? Surely she would need to get some serious oxygen into her lungs to shout like she had.

"My apologies, Lady Eleanor, but the writer would not concede, even after torture. Please be patient. The baby is coming and we will take it from her as soon as it's born."

What a snivelling scum-bag! Val wanted to set his beard on fire, then blast him across the courtyard. They had tortured a pregnant woman and now they were going to steal her baby. What next?

The woman's expression was thunderous and Val watched as she flicked her hair back over her shoulder, allowing her profile to become completely visible. As Val watched in horrified fascination, Lady Eleanor grabbed the man's face with one hand and shoved her fingers deep into his scar. He winced and a thin trickle of blood started to roll down his cheek.

"She will lift the curse, do you understand?" The Lady waited for him to nod. "And you will do whatever is necessary to make it happen." Her hand uncurled and she slowly wiped her bloodied fingers down his jacket. Then she walked past him.

The woman was now heading directly towards Val, who finally got to see her head-on. Her chest grew tight with fear, sensing she was in great danger, that she was utterly defenceless. But she stayed where she was, her eyes transfixed by the figure who was getting closer and closer. The Lady's dress was a mixture of creams and golds that gave the illusion of moving like an angelica apparition through all the mud and dirt, but it was her face that was the most overwhelming, her mesmerising beauty. Val stared. The witch she'd been speaking to started to become nervous, fidgeting, trying to get Val's attention, but it was too late.

"What are you looking at, peasant?" Lady Eleanor yelled at Val, waking her from her frozen stare.

Quickly she bent her head, coving her face with her hood. "Nothing. I'm sorry," she apologised.

"Get out of my sight, vermin," The woman bellowed into Val's face, making her curl backward towards the cart. "Take me to her now, Durwood! I will torture her myself!" she shrieked. The soldier, blood trickling down his face, was once again at her side, guiding her into the passageway, the very passageway Val had sent Wendy down.

"Damn it!" Val hissed. They were going to catch Wendy. Think Val, what would Sam or Zac do? Firstly, don't panic. Even if they do see Wendy, she's smart, she'll think of something to say. Or will she? "Double damn it."

At that moment, Wendy emerged, standing for a moment in the archway that led to the passage, before scurrying towards a group of merchants and quickly mingling with them.

Val felt weak with relief then turned quickly back to the woman who was shackled to the cart. She reached for her hand, gently picking it up with its heavy metal burden. "I'll come back for you, I promise, but I need to go and talk to my friend, she may have news."

The woman used the little strength she had to grip Val's hand. "Listen to me daughter of the Moon Mother. Run, leave this place and don't return, and when you see your mother tell her Sara says we did our best."

"Don't give up, Sara. I promise we'll get you out." Val reached up and touched her face; it was so cold. She wanted to scream with frustration, she felt so helpless.

"Go to your friend." A tear streaked through the dirt, leaving a single clean line down her cheek. "Witches live forever; I have no fear of death." She lifted her chains and gave Val a smile.

"That's not an option," Val replied. From the corner of her eye she saw movement. Some soldiers were now paying her attention. She needed to become part of the scenery and quickly.

She darted across the yard, forcing her way between two horses. Wendy spotted her and was approaching at speed, head still covered by her hood. "We have a big problem." She sounded panicked and Val could see her hands were trembling as she pushed the horses aside.

"I know. I can't believe you got out that easily. Did you see her?"

"Who?" Wendy asked.

"Lady Eleanor and scar face. They just walked down the passage you came out of."

"No, no one came down the passage." She shook her head adamantly.

"I don't understand. I watched her walk in there. Where did she go? And if *she's* not the problem, which I'm pretty sure she is, what was down there? And why is it a big problem?"

"It's all much worse than we could've imagined. These witches…" she pointed to the women tied to the carts, "are just scratching the surface of the evil that lurks here, Val."

"What do you mean? Have you found what they have in the closed carts?" The tension was killing her.

"No, but I think it's best you see this with your own eyes." Wendy led the way back underground and Val followed.

Chapter 8

Symbols

As they moved under the archway and into the passage, the path became an eerie shade of blood-red washed with grey, the glow of flickering torches hanging on the walls the only light. Their shadows loomed larger than life. Val had this feeling before: the claustrophobia of being trapped underground. The sensation didn't get better with time. Her mind was spinning. How could Lady Eleanor have come down here and not crossed paths with Wendy? "Are you sure you didn't see anyone come down here?"

"Honestly, I didn't."

There was a sound. Val grabbed Wendy, pulling her close. "Did you hear that?"

"Yes," Wendy whispered as they stood motionless.

"There." A mouse scurried past Val's foot. She exhaled in relief. "OK, what are we looking for?"

"This." Wendy lifted a torch from the wall and held it up, revealing a symbol engraved on the wall. It resembled a number eight lying on its side. "That's the symbol for infinity," she told Val. Then she lowered the torch slightly. Below it was what looked like an odd knot with three points. "This is a Triquetra. It represents

the three phases of life: maiden, mother and crone."
Wendy flashed the flaming torch in Val's face to see if
she was listening.

"OK. Hurry up." She nodded, pushing the torch back
towards the wall.

"Pentagram, the symbol of the elements: earth,
fire, air, water and spirit," Wendy explained the symbol
that had been revealed. "It's literally oneness with
everything."

"I recognise that, your Mum wears one."

Below that was a snake wrapped around a tall pole.
"I'm not sure about this."

"I am," Val answered. "That's the staff of Moses.
He used it to part the Red Sea and stuff."

Wendy frowned. "And stuff...?"

Val shrugged. "What? So my Mum made me go to
Sunday school."

Then, at the bottom, there was a plain circle with
a small mark in the centre.

"So what's that?" Val asked.

"I don't know. I've never seen it before, but there are
so many symbols... This... it could be from any religion.
Val, bypassing the meaning of these symbols, the point
I need to make is I've seen this type of alignment
before."

"Why does your voice sound like you're going to
tell me something really bad? If you hadn't noticed,
we're already in a heap of trouble."

Wendy pulled the torch away from the wall and lit up
their faces. "It's a magical trial."

"What like a prison trial?" Val asked.

"No, more of a deterrent, a magical lock and key that
require a great deal of knowledge to open." She moved

the torch over to the far side where it illuminated a dark hole in the wall. "See that entrance?" Val nodded. "That's the way in. The symbols have been left by its creator as a guide, but only for people who know what they mean. The fact no one is here guarding it means they're either not worried about anyone getting in, or they're too scared to come near it."

"A bit like an Indian burial ground?"

"Yes, exactly."

"So what could be that precious?"

"My bet would be Brigit. I think she's down there." Wendy pointed at the entrance beyond the symbols. "If she's as valuable as you and I know she is, there's no way they're going to leave her unprotected."

Val knew she was right. Brigit had told her that once they had her underground she would be dead. "We need the others. We need to get Jason and we need to get the hell out of here."

"So you need me?" A familiar voice made them both jump.

"Jason you...!" Val embraced him, her heart pounding.

He squeezed back. "Nice to see you're safe as well, but I'm not bringing good news. I think you need to see something."

"Don't tell me it's another trial?"

"A what?"

"We can explain later when we're out of here. Let's go."

"Just follow me. Keep your hoods over your faces and your heads down," Jason instructed.

Walking in procession across the court yard, Val felt the sweat pouring down her back. Were they really stupid enough to have walked into the lion's den? Zac was going to kill her... if one of these soldiers didn't get them first. They edged around the chained women and she felt so vulnerable, so useless. How could she carry on with no powers, no magic? How could she save all these women from whatever horrific fate awaited them?

They reached the far side of the courtyard and the imposing wall made Val once again feel small and trapped. There were armed soldiers evenly spaced along the top of the wall, and a large group stood together, surrounding a perfectly square stone building. Considering the place they had just come from had not had one single soldier guarding, it appeared Wendy's concerns about the power of the trial were well founded. She could now see a large wooden door up ahead with several soldiers protecting it. "How do we get past all of them?" she whispered to Jason. "We have no weapons."

"We don't. Walk along the edge and keep quiet," Jason instructed.

They carried on moving, keeping a healthy distance from the men. Then Val heard a faint whimpering sound. "Can you hear that? What is that noise? Jason, what is that?" she demanded. He shook his head and raised a finger to his lips, which she understood to mean 'shut up'.

They reached a section of the wall which was free of soldiers, but was sheltering a row of horses, each one tethered to a stake in the ground. Val counted twenty, all in different colours and in various states of health. Jason squeezed up to the wall behind the hind legs of the first horse and signalled for them to follow him. Val groaned.

If she didn't get shot by a soldier or killed by Zac, she was going to be trampled by horses.

When they had joined him, Jason turned, careful not to startle the horses, and crouched down, facing the wall.

"Look in there." He pointed to a small grating, the size of a shoebox.

Val and Wendy squashed together, trying to see what he was looking at.

Val sighed. There was no way she was going to be able to see in there without lying down. "I'm going to be trampled to death." she whispered.

"Get down, Wendy and I will stand over you." He pushed her down.

Val lowered herself flat on the floor while Wendy and Jason straddled her. She could hear them soothing the horses that were starting to get spooked by the strange people invading their space. She pulled herself closer and peered through the grate. It was dark inside, but the noise she had heard was much louder. She waited for her eyes to adjust to the dim light. As they did she could make out movement, and a lot of it. It was like she'd switched on a horror film. Huddled in a metal cell were a group of small children, probably five or six years old. They were dirty and crying. With them was one older girl of about sixteen, who was desperately trying to keep them all subdued. "Wendy, I think we've found the children I'm meant to save," Val whispered.

That was just the beginning. As Val's eyes adjusted to the dim light she saw the full extent of the horror. Past the group huddled in the cell by the grating, were more cells filled with children. There must be at least ten cells, all containing at least eight to ten children. A husky male voice caught her attention, causing her to gasp loudly.

"That one over there, we got her especially for you from a family of gypsies. I think they came from over the sea. She's feisty mind." Val peered in the direction of the voice and could just see a soldier. He was accompanied by Excariot in Wallace guise, with Flo in tow.

Wendy nudged Val with her foot. "Hurry up, we're going to draw attention sooner rather than later."

Val pinched her ankle in return. They would have to wait; she needed to see this.

"She looks perfect," Excariot enthused. Val felt deeply distressed. She knew what he really looked like. Using this crumpled body of an old man as a disguise made her want to send him packing across the galaxy right there and then. The group came into view, moving into the cell directly below the grating. The children started to scream. Val's stomach ached with the pain of impotence. Just hearing their cries was enough to drive her insane. The poor things were petrified!

"Little sod bit me!" The soldier yelled, grabbing hold of a small olive-skinned girl, who wasn't going to make it easy for him. He shoved her towards Excariot and Flo.

Flo stepped forward. "Hello. We won't hurt you," she smiled. Her beautiful porcelain face looked so angelic; Val wanted to punch it. The child had now thrown herself to the ground. Flo knelt down, stroking her hair. "If you come with us we will make sure you get back to your family," she soothed.

It was as if she had said a magic word. The child's body instantly went limp on the ground, all her anger and fear gone. Val wondered for a moment if she was dead, but then her back seemed to move and she looked up at Flo. "Mi familiar, por favor?" she said, tears in her eyes.

Val recognised her accent. She'd heard it before. "Eva!" she gasped.

"What? Are you saying you can see Eva, here in 1645?" Wendy snapped.

"No, this isn't Eva, but I think we're witnessing the start of her family attachment to all things Excariot." Val pulled back onto her knees. "Jason, this is what they were bringing in, in the closed carts. They're selling children. But why? Nothing makes sense."

"I can tell you why they have the children," Wendy said, her eyes icy cold. She had an expression on her face that Val hadn't seen before, but she recognised pure hatred when she saw it.

"Please tell us?"

"*If* that is Eva's ancestor, then these people are trafficking in magical children."

"Magical children?" Jason probed.

"Yes, back in 1645 it was common practice for witches' children to be kept in ignorance of the family magic until they came of age. It was believed that it was far too dangerous to tell children about their heritage until they could be trusted to keep the secret. Then, at the age of eighteen, they were initiated and given their full powers. You have to remember this is one of the most turbulent times in history for witches."

"So when I came back in time to my Mum and they initiated me, they switched on my magic?" Val asked.

"Yes. You already had your Prison Guard abilities, and whatever dormant magical powers you had were awakened at that point. So, if these children are all the descendants of magical parents, like the witches in the courtyard, it's like they're living weapons, just waiting to be switched on. In the wrong hands that could be catastrophic."

"So we don't have to worry until they all reach eighteen, right?" Jason asked.

Wendy shook her head. "No, I wish it was that simple. I was initiated at the age of five because my mother knew I could be trusted, and she needed me to be ready to protect Val at any time."

Val always felt so guilty when Wendy spoke of her Guardian childhood. "I'm so sorry."

"Don't be. It's fun being magical at five. Didn't you ever notice I always got the best school lunches? It's acceptable to have magic, as long as you have the right teacher. Imagine what would happen to these children if they fell in to the wrong hands."

Jason searched their faces. "Excariot is about to take Eva's great, great, great grandmother on a road trip? I think that's probably the wrong hands. If we stop him, we could change her future."

Wendy reached out her hand to him. "We can't do anything to change history. Zac's right. We have to let her go. We know Eva's destiny is with Excariot. If you remember, she helped to save us from him when he had us in cages, and she's Daniel's mother." Wendy took a deep breath, as if just the mention of his name was painful.

"But what if that saves my Dad's life?" Jason asked. "Wouldn't you want him to live?"

Val knew this was a possibility, just as she knew she could save Gabriel by pointing out the old decrepit Excariot she had just seen, but they all understood the possible ramifications. "Jason, you know we can't do this. We need to leave now."

Wendy started to push past the horses. "We need to get the others. Your mother's coven will know what to do. We have to leave them Jason."

"Let's just focus on getting back to the future or just staying alive for now." Val took his hand. "We need you Jason. You have my promise that if I ever find a way to bring him back I will." Jason shook his head, his shoulders slumped. "I know you would, mate. Magic and time travel isn't as good as you imagine it would be when you're a child, and I get that. As much as I want to save Eva's ancestor and undo what was done to my Dad right now, we can't do anything with all these soldiers. We need to go back and get the others."

"Thanks for understand... Ow!" Val exclaimed, throwing her hand into the air as a mouse flew past Wendy. "It bit me!"

"Hey! What are you doing over there?" A large bearded soldier heard her scream and headed towards them, reaching down for a pistol strapped to his belt. "Answer me now!"

"Move!" Jason grabbed Val and Wendy's hands surging forward between the horses.

"Stop!" the soldier ordered.

"No!" Jason exhaled, but as they struggled to free themselves from the animals the soldier grabbed at Wendy.

"Not so fast!" He pulled at her bringing them to a standstill.

Wendy span, raising her hand giving a sharp order, "OPRI!" direct into the soldier's face. The soldier froze where he stood, his panicked pupils still flickering left and right, but the rest of him absolutely motionless.

"What have you done?" Jason exclaimed.

"I froze him. It could last a minute or less. It's new. Sam showed me it and thank the Goddess it worked!" She pulled her cloak from the soldier's stationary hand.

"Can you do it to them all?" Val asked, as another soldier noticed the commotion and started to make his way towards them.

"No," Wendy squeaked.

"Then let's get out of here," Jason encouraged them.

"Follow me." Val led the way as they moved hastily towards the exit. Her head began to pound as they skirted the soldiers. She was too scared to even breathe and the tension was making her feel faint with lack of oxygen. A group were now gathering around Wendy's victim and a ripple of alarm was starting to form as the other soldiers prodded they're comrade suspiciously with the ends of their swords.

Their pace quickened as they reached the gatekeepers. Luckily for them, they were distracted by several large wooden wine barrels, which were on a cart in the entrance and were drawing a lot of interest.

"Go," she instructed as they moved swiftly through the gate and out towards the road. Glancing back momentarily to check they weren't being followed, she finally took a deep breath. They had made it.

As soon as they were safely out of sight of the soldiers at the gate, they picked up their pace, jogging down the road and trying to put as much distance as possible between them and the fortress before the soldier Wendy had frozen, recovered.

Wendy pulled down her hood. "We need a miracle. This is one massive magical mash-up. No disrespect, but with you out of action, Val, no Sam and no Brigit, it's going to be a real job to defeat all those people. And someone has to face the trial," she panted, slowing to a walk.

"What's this trial?" Jason asked.

"We'll fill you in on the way," Wendy said.

"A miracle would be good," Val agreed. "Let's get back to the village.

***

Jarrad stood by an ageing oak tree at the top of a hill overlooking the fortress below, waiting patiently as a tiny mouse scurried over to join him. "Lovac, what do you have for me?" He waited as the creature shook his head, bringing itself to full size.

"Well, you won't believe it." Lovac straightened his whiskers. "It really was such a sight and of all the things…" he twisted his muzzle.

"Speak faster, before I cut off your tail," Jarrad reprimanded him, impatient of delay. A swirling symbol shifted slowly over the length of his cheek and onto his head.

"Sorry Master. The mark you search for is on the hand of a young woman, someone you know very well." He smirked, resting his paws on his furry belly.

"What, someone from the future is here as well?" Jarrad frowned. Lovac watched as another black circular symbol slid from Jarrad's lips and down his neck until it was hidden by his top. "LOVAC! WHO?" Jarrad screamed.

He froze as a blow struck him across the snout. "The Warden," he cried out in pain.

Jarrad raised his hand once more. "You lying, wretched rodent."

Lovac cowered. "No, no, it's true; I saw her with my own eyes." He pointed with his claws to each of his eyes. "But Master, I don't think she knows who she is." He rubbed the wounds vigorously.

"Tell me everything, now!" Jarrad barked.

"She's here with others and they have found magical children. I went down into where they are being held. They could become a magical army if they were initiated. That's what I heard them saying."

"What of the Writer? Where's she?"

"Deep underground. A woman called Lady Eleanor has her behind some form of magical trial. They were looking at symbols on a wall. I think something's wrong..." He twitched.

"What do you mean?"

"You know as well as I do that the Warden is unstoppable; she has made your life impossible. For all the searching we have done, we have never found her weakness, but here she seems to have no powers. They said she had to go... for help." He shrugged.

Jarrad started at the creature. Lovac braced once more, then Jarrad laughed. "She's not the Warden then."

"Oh yes! I remember her face. She even has the scar over her eye." His nod was painfully energetic.

"Did you mark her?"

"Yes, I placed it in her hand. We will know her every move master."

"Good." He stroked the oversized mouse on the head. "You know, Lovac, everyone has to be someone before they become the king of their destiny. Not only do we have the Writer, but we have the future Warden and an army of magical children. Just as my mother said before I cut off her head: 'It was worth the wait'." He patted the little beast. "Go follow them; let us see who else is here; it can only get better. We must take our time and strike at the perfect moment. There is far more at risk than I could have ever suspected, and so much more to gain if we win."

CHAPTER 9

The Visitor

Two figures ran down the stark white corridor of the Prison, their figures towering over the others. "We're going to be late. You just *had* to stun that Valangar!" Boden growled.

"She said I had the fighting skills of a Hunter. That's worse than calling me a Ranswar," Hadwyn replied, knocking a Guard out of the way. "We can make it, don't worry."

"That door." Boden pointed.

"Got it." Hadwyn slammed his bracelet against the wall. "We're here!" he announced bursting in.

Enoch, the leader of the Space, was standing alone in the middle of the room. "Sorry, but you're too late. Sam told me to tell you the next trip is in four hours and he *will* need you."

"Why didn't he wait?" Hadwyn demanded, slamming his hand on the wall.

"He has a fifteen minute window to see her. He'll be back here before you can blink. Just make sure you're here for the next teleportation."

"We will be." Boden thanked Enoch. "Come, there's

nothing we can do now; we will see her soon. She'll be fine."

"She'd better be," Hadwyn snarled at Enoch.

Boden stepped in, grabbing his friend by the arm. "Brother, we're lucky she's still alive. Until now we thought that, like everyone else, she'd been extracted. Now we've got a chance to get her back. Take deep breaths. I'll take you to the teleportation room; you can stun a few prisoners."

*

Val and the others travelled quickly, aware that they'd been very lucky to escape. Grateful for Wendy's ingenious use of magic, they chuckled as Jason did a boyish impression of the frozen soldier, but Val couldn't shake the sense that they were being followed. She took up position behind the other two and found herself looking back at regular intervals.

Wendy was explaining the trial in great detail to Jason when Val started to feel something odd in the atmosphere. She stopped, trying to work out what was happening. Something was definitely changing; it was as if each breath was taking longer than the last, as though the oxygen was becoming thicker, harder to draw in. She turned, taking stock of her surroundings, but there didn't seem to be anything out of the ordinary for a woodland path in 1645.

Then Wendy abruptly stopped her explanation in mid-sentence. Val, who had been checking behind her, pivoted and was met by a shocking vision. Jason and Wendy were frozen to the spot, mid-stride like lifeless statues. "Oh my God, Jason!" Val dashed forward and gazed into his eyes. There was nothing, his pupils simply mirrored her reflection.

Afraid to make physical contact with him in case she suffered the same fate, her eyes darted around. Who had done this? Had Wendy said the spell she'd used on the soldier and frozen them by mistake? No, this was different, she thought. Just then, a magpie landed on Jason's shoulder, as if he were a perch. She shooed it away. At least that confirmed that time hadn't stopped for everything but her. All at once Val knew who was behind this; it reeked of Excariot. She must think fast. She had no weapons, no powers. What could she do if he attacked? Left hook, upper cut seemed a little lame compared to his powers and, she knew from her own experience in battle with him in 1645, that he was at his most dangerous right now. And she was at her most vulnerable.

She had two choices: confront whoever had done this or run away. Running away wasn't an option; she wasn't leaving her friends. "What do you want? Show yourself!" she shouted, circling her rocklike friends. Her eyes darted from one tree to another, waiting for something or someone to leap out. She flexed her hands and stretched her arms readying for a fist fight. "If that's you, Excariot, I'm super powerful right now. Or should I call you Wallace? I've come from the future and I just destroyed your friend Nathan Akar, paralysed your girlfriend Lailah, and kicked the Nyterians off the Prison, so don't doubt that I'll go all blue ninja on your face!" Her fear of what was coming was causing her to shake. She must keep moving so it didn't show.

"Blue ninja?" The words exploded in a fit of laughter from some branches several feet above her.

She jumped back in surprise and strained her neck to see who was there. "Who are you? And what do you want?" she called up.

"You," the voice responded. The branches parted and Val saw his face.

"Sam! Oh my God, it's you." Her defences lowered as relief washed over her.

He jumped down and pulled her into his arms. "So you thought you could lose me?"

Before she could answer him there was a kiss on her lips, a reminder of everything she had lost. It was enough to make her realise that what they had was worth fighting for. Tears welled in her eyes as she touched his hair. Placing her hand on his cheek she whispered, "Hello," and kissed him again. "I thought I would never see you again, well not my Sam, Sam from the future - if that makes sense. You are my Sam aren't you?"

He smiled. "What if I'm not?"

"That's not funny." She thumped his chest. "Anyway, I'm just so glad you found me. It's all going wrong and we're in real trouble. Zac's watch doesn't work and my real Dad, Gabriel, is here, and you need to help me find my Mum and Dad. And look at Jason and Wendy."

He placed his finger on her jabbering lips. "I did that to Wendy and Jason. Zac probably has no signal. I know Gabriel is here and I thought your parents would be with you."

"No, we haven't seen them, or Daniel, but if you found us then surely you can find them?"

"It's not that simple. We didn't actually find you. Your Collector made an error in her paperwork."

Val frowned. "What? That doesn't sound like her. I didn't think Collectors could make mistakes; like Hunters can't lie."

"Exactly. I can only assume Gabriel scanned the symbol on your arm?"

"Yes, he did."

"Well, it created an alert. It was brought to her attention that he'd made contact with a Transformer that she hadn't recorded in his records from 1645. We guessed it was you."

"How did you know it was me that was transforming?" she asked.

"I saw it happen to you back on the Prison, when you were messing with the Warden's Dellatrax. Quite impressive. Where's Zac?" He looked around.

"He went off with Gabriel. My father's Dellatrax picked up the signal of two aliens arriving nearby."

His eyes narrowed. "Val, you need him with you at all times. He's your Hunter. Take control."

She wasn't prepared to admit that Zac didn't even know the three of them were out here because they had actually sneaked out from the village and were going to be in serious trouble when they returned. "I wish it was that easy," she replied.

Moving away from her, he fiddled with Jason's cloak. "Nothing is easy, but everything is necessary. Don't worry about these two, they won't remember a thing when I release them. Right, now we need to get you out of here."

"We can't leave yet." Val shook her head.

"Why not?" Sam enquired.

"Wyetta says the coven isn't strong enough. I have no powers and we agreed I can't attempt to get them back because if I do, Zac says someone, will come and hunt me, take my powers and make them into jewellery. Plus, I don't have a Tark, whatever they are, which really upset Gabriel."

"That's true, they will hunt you and the longer you can survive without transforming, the better; I agree. But just remember something; Val, you may not have powers, but that doesn't mean you're not powerful. Plus we have someone else here who will help us as soon as you find her, she..."

She raised a hand, "Wait, I've not finished. We can't leave yet. We have an even bigger problem if you can believe that! I met this witch called Brigit who helped me escape from some soldiers, and now she's being held prisoner..."

Sam interrupted. "Brigit... The Writer?" His expression became uneasy.

"Yes. How do you know her?"

"She's the one who I'm relying on to help me get you out of here. Where are they holding her? We have to get her back."

"Well, they have her about half a mile from here, trapped behind a magical trial, and to add to that, there are about a hundred witches shackled to carts. Oh, and don't let me forget to mention the eighty or ninety magical children in underground cells being trafficked as magical weapons." She exhaled. Sam attempted to speak, but Val pushed her hand forward to stop him. "And then there's the fact I'm going to be born in about, oh... one and a half days, at which point I will cease to exist."

He looked her straight in the eyes, his head shaking. "I can't save you *all* without Brigit."

This must be a joke, Val thought. "What do you mean, you can't save us all?"

He gave a solemn reply. "Jason, Fran, Belinda and Zac they're not like you. Without Brigit, time travel would kill them."

"So how did they get here?" she demanded, unable to believe what he'd just said.

"The Warden. He used magic to help you escape the Prison, something the Judges wouldn't detect. It wasn't the same as a straight forward teleportation through time. He delivered you here; you didn't time travel as such."

"So let's just do that again, because leaving without them isn't an option."

"I wish we could, but we have to get you from here to there, and the Warden can't help us this time. The centre of the magic has to be where you are. I'm afraid the only option has to come from here and now, and that means a very large dose of magic, provided by a pretty amazing collection of witches."

Val knew what was coming. "So Brigit is our only ticket home?"

Sam nodded. "Exactly: Brigit with Wyetta's coven. You must get Brigit back; it's imperative."

"I wish it was that easy. There's a lot going on behind the fortress walls." She fidgeted with her cloak.

"She must be freed; it would change everything. Brigit was the one who helped us send you to the future the first time. With her unique skills and your mother's coven, we created the spell, which no one has ever been able to trace or replicate." Sam glanced down at his bracelet which had just started flashing. "I need to leave you, but I'll come back."

Val shook her head. "No, you can't leave! You just arrived. I need you. We all need you."

"I'm sorry, but I can only be here when the past *me* isn't. You understand that we can't be in the same place at the same time, and I'm about to arrive just outside your village with Beth. I'll be back in..." He pressed a few buttons on his Dellatrax. "...four hours. Take this." He handed her a familiar silver tube, her trusty sword. "Val, don't tell the others I've been here, not yet. I can't afford for them to change anything. I need the old Sam to arrive and leave at exactly the same moment as before."

"Ok," she agreed.

"I'll see them all very soon. Just be careful what you do. They have you on record back at the Prison now, so there are more than one set of eyes watching. Keep your heads down and don't do anything, just for four hours."

"I'll do my best, but this gets more complicated by the minute. I preferred the 'go in, set it on fire and get out' times." She smiled weakly.

"Don't give up on me, Val." He reached out for her, but he was already slipping into a portal. "I'll come back for you, just hang on in there."

She watched him fade away. What was she going to do? She now knew, without a doubt, that she needed Brigit to get them home. There was no way she would let her friends die. She grunted and stumbled forward as Wendy suddenly collided with her.

"Val..."

"Sorry." Val reached out to balance them both.

"Weren't you behind us? How did you get there?" She turned around in bewilderment.

"I... I wanted to catch up, my fault, sorry. Let's get back. We're going to be in some serious trouble." She linked arms with Wendy and pulled her on, carefully slipping her sword into her cloak pocket. At least she had a weapon now.

"So, you say the last symbol is a circle with a dot in the centre?" Jason added, completely unaware of their moments of immobility.

"Yes," Wendy enthused.

Val moved them along. She knew Sam would be back in four hours and the original Sam was about to arrive somewhere close by with Elizabeth, Jason's long-dead mother. Wrapped in the complexity of their situation, she could just see a single glimmer of hope – Sam.

*

As they reached Wyetta's village, Val saw Zac pacing outside the cottage. He looked profoundly unhappy. Waving for his attention, she braced herself for a good telling off. Better get it over and done with, she thought.

"Thirteen! Val" He marched towards her. "Do you realise the complications you have caused by leaving and taking Wendy and Jason with you?" He was opening and closing his fists in a bid to control himself.

Wow, he was mad enough to call her by her number. "I'm sorry. I know it was wrong, but you should know me by now." She shrugged.

"I thought I did." He flapped around her, flustered and frustrated. "You can't be trusted. You have obligations."

Remember what Sam said, she thought. He should have been with her, she was still his Guard. "Fine, but look at you," she pointed at his chest, "so eager to run off with Gabriel. Maybe if you'd done your job and stuck with me, this conversation wouldn't be happening. Now, if you're not too busy to *do your job*, follow me while I tell the others what's going on," she ordered. The others watched in amazement.

She felt sick; she'd never pulled rank on him before. She had always treated him as her equal, but right now he was infuriating her. She marched towards Wyetta's house to tell them everything that had happened and was still to happen, but before they could reach the front door, Fran came out, running past her and up to Jason, embracing him.

"What did you think you were doing?" she agonised, scolding him with a punch in the chest.

He wrapped her in his arms. "Don't be cross Fran, please. We found this place with kids in prison cells." He pulled her fringe back and kissed her forehead. "Little helpless children who need us."

Belinda and Wyetta joined them. "You had better have a good answer to why you went out," Belinda scolded Wendy.

"Yes, you had us so worried." Wyetta backed her up.

Val paused, waiting for everyone to settle. "You know what, I'm really disappointed. You all seem to have forgotten what I'm capable of. I've saved Earth from an alien invasion – *twice*; saved your coven and taken down an alien dictator. Yet here you all are openly doubting me. Powers or no powers, I'm the same person. We have a mission and if you're all going to treat me like a child then expect childish results." She walked past them to Gabriel who was watching from the doorway. "And Father, no disrespect, but don't take my Hunter again; he's *my* Hunter for a reason." She looked back at the stunned group. "If you'd like to know how we're going to get home, then you can join me in here. If you're looking to point fingers and moan, then please stay outside."

She needed to make them believe she was still capable of pulling them through this. She didn't want to talk to them in this way, but the moment demanded that she take control, a control that she had allowed to slip since she'd been here. Yes, she was young, but Sam had once told her that one of Earth's biggest flaws was that they didn't believe in their children. She was starting to understand what he meant.

She walked into the room and stood nervously waiting. She *would* get them home, and then she would deal with her transformation, but she needed them to be behind her one hundred percent. Standing next to the fire, she let out a sigh of relief as Jason and Fran joined her, taking a seat at the table. They were followed closely by Wendy, Belinda, Wyetta and Gabriel. Val could feel the tense knot in her stomach beginning to ease, but still no Zac.

The door pushed open and he stood in the entrance, neither in, nor out. "You are correct." He nodded. "I was overwhelmed by meeting your father who is a legend on the Prison. And yes, I am your Hunter. You're right I should be by your side. But Valerie Saunders, everything you have done, you have done with these people by your side, not alone. Do not forget where you come from, and I will stand forever by your side."

Val swallowed back an emotional lump in her throat. "Deal! Come in." She beckoned him. "Zac, no one knows better than me that I need you all." He sat next to Wendy, who couldn't help but squeeze his hand. "Let's get to work. What happened with your signal Gabriel?"

"It led us to an empty field. We were late and just picked up the residuals of some new arrivals. Two alien forms, but they had gone and without Zac's device working, we couldn't pin point what they were."

Val wondered if it was Sam and Elizabeth. "Well, we'll find out I'm sure. We have a lot to fill you in on, so let's get a cup of that lovely... stuff you make." She smiled kindly at Wyetta. "It's time we saved a few witches."

CHAPTER 10

Elizabeth

"So from what you've told us, there are three parts to our mission: save the witches, release the children and free Brigit?" Gabriel tapped on his Dellatrax.

"What are you doing?" Val asked. She knew, from the little Sam had told her, that the Prison was picking up her signal because of his Dellatrax.

"I'm making calculations, don't worry. The question you need to ask is: how does this help you get back to the future?"

"Well I'm guessing that if Brigit can write the future, maybe she can write us back to our time." Val shrugged, trying to look as if she was really having this original idea, and hadn't been told by Sam that they couldn't leave without Brigit's help. There was no need for anyone else to panic. "With the coven's help, I'm sure it's possible." She smiled uneasily. "Anyone else got any other suggestions?" The group shook their heads. Val was relieved. If they didn't have an alternative plan then she wouldn't have to discredit it.

Gabriel stopped tapping. "As we are so few in number, we should move in strategic groups, strike from different vantage points, all at the same time. How many soldiers did you see?"

Jason replied, "There were four on the gate, Gabriel, but none by the trial. The girls think they may have been afraid of it. There were at least a couple of hundred scattered around on the walls and surrounding the children. I can't say if there were more underground or inside the main building. Their weapons are primitive; I saw single shot pistols and swords."

Gabriel stopped tapping. "Good, that gives us an idea of what we're facing. If we break into three groups, using the coven's powers to conceal us, it could work. I will take Wendy to the trial. Belinda and Fran can go with Wyetta and free the witches. Val, you Jason and Zac can free the children." Gabriel paused. "If that sounds feasible to you?"

"I think that sounds like an excellent plan," Val thanked him.

Wyetta pushed herself upright. "We'll need the cover of night to move such a large amount of people successfully. I will send a message for the coven to join us when the sun begins to set. Belinda, if they're in magical shackles what spell would you recommend?" The two of them moved over to the fireplace to look at an array of herbs hanging on the wall. "Fran, come and join us," Wyetta called to her.

"Sorry, time to work." Fran kissed Jason on the cheek. "Magic to be done."

He grabbed her hand. "Hey, you didn't tell me what spell they were teaching you while we were breaking the rules?"

She blushed. "Well, Mr Walker, that's a trade secret." She giggled and walked away.

Wendy smiled. "She's learning quickly. A witch's greatest asset is discretion. Gabriel, let me show you the placement of the symbols, see if you can see any way to get in." Gabriel agreed, leading her outside.

Val led her group's planning with trepidation. "That just leaves us. We know there are a lot of soldiers surrounding the children and Zac doesn't fight, so how many do you think we can take out?"

Zac responded curtly. "The object, Val, is not to have to 'take out' all the opposition. I once went with my previous Guard to an arrest where we were clearly outnumbered. With wise, well thought out moves, we didn't need to 'take out' any of the unwanted intruders, and merely captured our prisoner."

"Good, I would prefer no one got hurt. Jason, can you start putting together layouts of the area for Zac? Let him see everything we saw when we were there. He may find an opening we didn't." She patted him on the back and stood.

"Where are you going?" Jason asked, as he manoeuvred the cups and a plate into what Val imagined was his version of the fortress.

"I need a little fresh air. I promise I'm not going anywhere far."

"Ok," Jason agreed. "Back soon though. We need to work. Zac, this is the main entrance." He pointed at an upturned cup with his spoon.

By Val's calculations, and they were pretty rough at the moment, considering that no-one had a working watch, Sam and Elizabeth couldn't be far away. She needed to make sure that if they made it this far, they came and left without any hitches. Val estimated that she had been back in the village for a couple of hours, and if she could make sure they didn't make contact with the group for just a little longer, then her Sam from the future would return for sure. She sat down beside the pond, using a stick to draw the symbols she remembered from the trial on the ground.

"Hello!" A distant, yet familiar voice called to her and two figures in matching cloaks approached from the other side of the pond. It was Sam and a woman in a floor length emerald green dress who must be Elizabeth. Right, damage limitation, she thought to herself, standing up and making her way towards them.

Unluckily for her, Gabriel had also spotted them. "Sam!" he greeted them as he jogged past Val. "What are you doing here? It's so good to see you, Beth." He came to a halt, bowing his head in respect. She laughed pulling down her hood and hugging him.

"We picked up your signal and thought you might be able to give us some assistance. But firstly old friend, how are you doing? It feels like such a long time since we last met." Sam embraced Gabriel warmly. "I heard about your unexpected departure from the Prison. I hope things are going well for you."

"They could be better. I'm still looking for Twelve. If my memory serves me correctly, I was working with him the last time we met, when he fell for that two headed woman on Medora. How things change." His eyes wrinkled, cringing at the memory.

"Those were good days, days before that Ranswar, Lailah, led him astray." They both became sombre at the mere mention of her name.

"Times change and so do people." He shrugged. "Did you know the Warden gave me a name? It's Gabriel, and since I have arrived, my priorities have changed direction, just a little." He sidestepped, revealing Val. "Let me introduce you to my youngling, Thirteen, the first ever female Guard." To Val's surprise he gushed with pride. "You can call her Val; she prefers that."

Sam looked perplexed. "I'm sorry, did you just say first ever female Guard? How can we not know about this?" His glance met Val's and she blushed.

"And, she's…"

Val cut Gabriel mid-sentence. "You don't actually know about me yet. The truth is I'm visiting from the future and I am obliged to remind you both of regulation 747707," she responded, looking hard at Gabriel, who she was sure was about to tell Sam about her transformation.

Sam measured her with his eyes. "You clearly know your regulations, but forgive my shock. You are the first of a new breed. I think I at least deserve to know how you got here?"

"Long story and one I'm actually not prepared to share… changing future events and everything. My Hunter has very strict rules," she apologised.

"You have a Hunter, here?"

"Yes."

"Well, I will speak to him in due course I'm sure, and as much as I want to know about your unique situation, I have a more pressing mission and limited time." He turned his attention back to her father. "Eleven - sorry - Gabriel, reference the assistance we need, we're actually passing through looking for someone who was supposed to meet us here. I wonder if you've heard of a woman called Brigit?"

"Yes, we do know of Brigit. We're actually preparing to free her now. She's been captured and is being held in a fortress approximately one mile from here. Your expertise would be most welcome. We have quite a dangerous mission ahead of us."

The atmosphere changed with this insight, the focus moving fully to Brigit's peril. Val listened to them verbally compare notes on the Writer's powers. Sam seemed very concerned about Brigit's safe recovery, but Val had her own concerns – mainly about them pushing off and not staying to help.

While Elizabeth focused on the men's conversation, Val observed her, noting how stunning she was. Shane's paintings of her were striking, but her real-life beauty was far greater. There was something really special about her, she was… radiant. Val suddenly felt guilty for all that she knew. Elizabeth had no idea that she would miss her son growing up, or about Shane's death. So many secrets! They were beginning to weigh heavily on her.

"So Val, is it just you and your Hunter?" Elizabeth asked, snapping her out of her daydream.

"No, I've been sent here with some of my friends."

"Well, let's meet them," she enthused.

Sam nodded his agreement and continued exchanging data with Gabriel as they headed towards the house, but Val stood, feet rooted to the ground. This wasn't good. If they all started to chat then she stood no chance of them leaving in an hour or less, and the more information they gathered on her and sent back to the Prison, the more the risk grew of someone coming to arrest or extract her.

"Coming, Val?" Gabriel signalled for her to follow.

Think Val, how can you stop them from meeting the others? If Wyetta got hold of them Val wouldn't be able to get them away; they would have to have pottage and dirty water. God, she was just like her Mum in the future. She wanted to call out and stop them, but what if this was what originally happened? Should she just go with the flow? So many questions, so little time to work out the answer to even one. Her head pounded. Reluctantly she caught up with the group.

Wendy was waiting by the house for Gabriel. "Goodness me, a trainee Judge. Is your mentor here?" Sam greeted her.

Wendy's jaw dropped and for a moment they all stood awkwardly. Her eye flickered to Val who nodded. "No," she finally responded, lowering her head in respect.

"I see. I won't question you more, as I assume you will cite regulation 747707 as well?" Wendy nodded, and Sam gave her a crooked smile of approval and moved past her towards the door with Gabriel, thankfully not pressing the issue.

"A trainee Judge and a witch, I believe? Merry Meet." Elizabeth offered her hand to Wendy. "You can call me Beth or Elizabeth, either is good."

Val could see realisation and recognition dawning on Wendy face. "Merry Meet. It's such an honour."

"Really?" Elizabeth replied. "You say that like I'm someone of note and yet we've never met."

"I've heard of all the wonderful things you're doing," Wendy managed to recoup the situation neatly.

"Beth!" Sam called to her.

"Duty calls. Shall we?" She allowed them to go into the room first. Wendy was noticeably nervous and Val knew why. She felt the same.

"Val, look; Sam's here," Zac announced awkwardly as they walked in. She interpreted his oddly rigid body language as extreme stress with a subliminal, *don't say anything about the future, but let's try and get a ticket home*, written in the sweat across his forehead.

She walked over and whispered in his ear, "Don't panic. I used the 747707 card on him and that's the least of your worries. In about five seconds, Jason's going to see his dead mother. How do you deal with that one?" Jason was now the centre of their attention. He was so pleased to see Sam and had been busy re-introducing himself. As he pivoted towards the door to see who else was coming to the 17th century reunion, Val saw that Elizabeth was just two feet away from him, her raven hair flowing down her back just like in Shane's paintings. Jason's eyes met hers. For a moment it was as if time had stood still. Val couldn't breathe, but only watch as the penny dropped.

Jason froze, his eyes fixed on Elizabeth, yet she seemed confused. Val guessed that this was a boy she had last seen aged seven. Val desperately wanted to talk, break the ice, but Sam beat her. "Everything ok?" he asked. Everyone was just watching them.

Jason's mouth opened and the word, "Mum?" escaped.

"Jason?" Her eyes welled up. "You're so... so grown up. What are you doing here?"

He had already crossed the room and his arms were around her and his head burrowed deep into her neck. Val swallowed hard. She mustn't cry, it would just fuel the emotions flying around the room.

"Hey, hey." Beth pulled up the grown man's face. "Baby, what's going on? Where's your Dad?" she asked, looking around the crowd.

Jason's eyes shot across to Val. She shook her head. Elizabeth mustn't know about Shane. It could be a disaster. "He's at home," he croaked through the pain.

"You must have tied him to a chair," she smiled. "Now explain to me why I'm meeting my son, who I left in bed yesterday in his batman pyjamas, here in 1645? How old are you?"

"I'm eighteen, Mum."

Val needed to support him. "Elizabeth I'm sorry, but Jason can't tell you anymore. We have to keep ourselves safe. Your son is one of us now and a very important part of our team. The more we tell you, the more we risk you changing our futures." Funny how she was starting to understand Zac's need to keep all information under wraps. "All I will say is that you *must* carry on with your mission." She could feel the clock ticking in her head. She needed them out of here. It must be nearly four hours since Sam had left her. "You need to trust me. I will have your son back to the future in less than a day. Please believe that we know what we're doing."

Elizabeth stiffened. "I'm sorry, but you want me to trust you, a stranger, with my son's life? I'm guessing you're no older than him?"

Jason took his mum's hand. "Mum, listen, she's right, we mustn't change the past. I promise you can trust Val a hundred percent. Dad..." he paused. "Dad does, he trusts her."

Thankfully Wyetta stepped in. "I hate to break up this reunion, but we have plans to make, a coven to meet and a very short amount of time. You're welcome to stay, but you will have to join us, or move out of our way, because I need to save *my* daughter's life." She waddled into the middle of the group.

Sam pulled back his sleeve, observing his bracelet as it started to flash. "It seems our options are limited and we must leave. Gabriel, our mission is a perilous one, but we will return. You must free Brigit, she's very important to us. Keep in touch and don't forget why you're here. Twelve is still a huge threat. He could be planning anything."

Val noticed Zac glaring at her. He seemed even more rigid if that was possible. "What's up?"

"I fear they will go back to the Prison and tell them about you," he whispered.

Val wanted to tell him the truth, that she knew what was happening and that it was too late, they already knew about her transformation, but she had promised Sam she would keep it a secret until he returned. "It's going to be ok. Trust me."

Gabriel guided Sam towards the door. "Please tell my Collector I'm well and I will be back soon," he requested.

Sam nodded. "I will. She informed me as we left that Princess Lailah was extracted this morning."

"So soon?" Gabriel seemed shocked.

"They couldn't risk her escaping as well. She's going to see out her days on the Prison."

"Well, if they think that's the answer, then it must be." But Val could see Gabriel didn't seem so convinced.

"Elizabeth, it's time to leave," Sam instructed.

She agreed, then took Jason's hand, turning it over and observing the lines, running her finger down his palm. "Your life line is strong, but your head line is weak. Don't do anything your Dad wouldn't do, do you hear me?"

"Yes, Mum."

"We'll return soon, I promise," she said, placing a kiss on his forehead. Val watched as he emotionally transformed into the seven year old boy Elizabeth had left in bed one night, never to return. She cupped his face in her hands, holding it close to hers. "Whatever the future has brought you, son, you look like a wonderful young man. I'm so proud. We'll talk later."

He wrapped his arms around her. "Mum," he whispered into her ear. "I love you." The words caught on the pain that stabbed at his throat.

"Ditto." She kissed his cheek one last time and went to join Sam.

*

They seemed to leave as swiftly as they'd arrived. Gabriel offered to walk them to the edge of the village and, as the door closed, Val felt instant relief, then immense pain, not for her, but for Jason, who just seemed to crumble. Fran held him in her arms as his tears began to fall. Val couldn't imagine how much it must have hurt him to see his mum, knowing she would never come home again, and that Elizabeth's true love, Shane, his dad, was also dead.

They were all subdued. Even Zac looked despondent. "Jason," he said, "you did the right thing, not telling her."

His retaliation was instant and hard. "*Really*? I could have saved my Mum and Dad's lives, right there, just now." He punched the air, anger pouring out in his tears. "Zac, you may not know what it means to have family, but I feel like I just sentenced mine to death." He stared at the floor. "Anyone else here feel like sentencing their parents to death?" He slumped onto the bench, placing his head in his hands.

No one spoke for what seemed like ages. What could they say? It was as if their reason for fighting was gone. Val wanted to get to the future, but at what cost? Jason had lost his parents; Fran's sister, Yassmin's soul was trapped in the Interspace. Zac would probably be punished for helping her. That's if they didn't all die during the journey.

Then she saw Shane's face, knew what he would have said just then. Elizabeth had summed it up: don't do anything Shane wouldn't. He would have told her that now was the time she had to dig deep, and keep them going. This was what she had learnt from him. With his dying breaths he had told her to keep fighting, to be a soldier who protected those who couldn't protect themselves; people like the witches and Brigit.

She spoke, breaking the despondant silence. "Look, we can't change our families' futures, and that tears me up inside, more than you could imagine, Jason, but the truth is we're survivors. We've come this far and hey, who knows what the future has in store for us. Maybe one day, we'll save someone who goes on to change the world. Or maybe we save a couple of hundred witches in 1645? So, we don't belong in the mainstream anymore, but we belong together, we're family. What you did was beyond brave and, by not changing the future, you allowed Shane to be in my life. He would have done the same and you know it."

Jason looked up. "Val, sometimes you talk too much." She held her breath. "Other times you make me want to go on fighting. You're right. I'm sorry Zac. You're my family, mate, like a weird cousin from another galaxy. I have you lot and that's enough." He kissed Fran on the cheek.

"Am I included in that?" A familiar voice asked from the doorway.

"Sam?" Jason rose.

"How's it going?" He wrapped an arm around Jason's shoulder. "Just to make it clear I'm not the Sam you just met, that was 1645 me, and this is me now, or future me; whichever. I'm the Sam that knows you all too well." He grinned at them.

"Nice to see a familiar face," Wendy beamed.

His grin broadened. "I have a little bit of back up if you want it?"

"Yes, please." Val stood back, allowing the others to greet him; she'd had her moment earlier.

Suddenly, two huge figures filled the doorway, blocking out all the light. "Well, I see you just can't get by without me." one said in a deep throaty tone.

"Hadwyn!" Val dashed towards him then paused, she knew better than to hug him, "Hi."

"Arh, come here." Hadwyn grabbed her in a bear hug as she snuggled into his armour.

When he released her she turned to the other towering figure. "Boden!"

He gladly reciprocated her embrace. "Nice to see you're alive."

"What's going on?" Gabriel asked, joining the large group congregating in the single room.

"Eleven!" Hadwyn exploded, lifting Gabriel off the floor like a rag doll. "Good to see you my old friend."

"Hadwyn, good to see you as well." Hadwyn dropped him. "What brings you here? Sam?" He looked back at the doorway he'd just entered, as if puzzled. "I just said goodbye to you at the edge of the village." He scratched his head in confusion, looking out the door once more then back at Sam.

"You did, but it was me a very long time ago, my friend. I don't have much time to explain, but I'm from the same time as Val and the others, and I'm only here to drop off these two into your care. I need you all to work together to get back to the future. I know you have just met me and Elizabeth in the past, but please understand you mustn't see my past-self again. Any more contact with Sam in 1645 could be disastrous. He has enough to deal with without you lot distracting him." Jason pulled away from him. "But that means I won't see my Mum again?"

"I'm sorry Jason, but you would risk the future for yourself and Val. Please, just trust me."

"You know I trust you, but it sucks." Jason walked out, pushing past the others. Fran went to follow him, but Sam stopped her.

"Give him some space. I've known Jason for a long time and, if he's anything like his Dad, he just needs time to think." Fran sighed. Sam turned to Val. "Do you have a plan?" She nodded. "Then let's get to work, we don't have long."

"So, who do I get to stun?" Hadwyn laughed as he spun his gun proudly.

CHAPTER 11

The Plan

Val watched as they all confirmed plans. So many of them in such a confined space had become a problem for Hadwyn, demonstrating with great enthusiasm, how they should deal with soldiers who kept small children as prisoners. The way that he was pointing and waving his gun, it was a miracle that he hadn't managed to stun anyone yet.

"You ok?" Sam asked her.

"Just observing." She reached out for his hand. Touching him felt like home. The one constant in her life at the moment was this man. He seemed to always be there for her, whatever time in history. "Tell me; how do you know Brigit? And why had you come for her? You hadn't even met me yet and you seemed desperate to get her back?" she asked.

"You always know how to ask the most complicated questions, Val." His eyes looked tired, like this was all getting to him. "On Alchany we received news of a unique being who could create the future. So, Elizabeth and I were sent to collect her. She wasn't hard to find; just a young woman living on a small planet of farmers called Satnus. She'd ended up there because her own people feared her."

"You know she's Nyterian, don't you?"

"Yes. Nyteria has such a strange history. The Nyterians seem to reject everything that could help them. I wonder sometimes if they're destined to destroy themselves, to leave room for new life. When we found Brigit, she greeted us with such warmth and seemed to make an instant bond with Beth. Then we saw what she could do. Her power is breathtaking. To write something and watch it unfold in front of your eyes is a gift that should be treasured. Think of all the good Brigit could do. So, I told Beth we should leave her alone. We agreed to tell the Prison that she wasn't what they thought she was, but they weren't happy with my report and sent another Judge, Jarrad, to find her. He arrested her and delivered her to the High Judges. Once they saw her powers, they wanted to use her to make the Prison more powerful."

"So they're corrupt?"

"No," he warned. "Mistaken; mistaken in how much power they should have. They have made many errors, and Brigit was one of them. She was so scared! They locked her away and I knew I had to free her, but I couldn't be seen to be doing it myself, plus I was busy enough with the Space, so someone else took the risk."

"Elizabeth?" Val was now intrigued.

"Yes. She risked everything to save her, took her to Enoch in the Space. Finally, Beth brought her to Earth, to a time we thought would be safe, and until now, she was. But something's gone wrong. I don't understand how, after all this time, anyone could know she was here, or realise how powerful she is."

"Well, it seems a lot of people do."

"I know." His eyes shifted to his bracelet. "I have to leave again, and so do you. Everyone, can I have your attention?!" They all stopped what they were doing and the ones who'd ventured outside, returned. "I have to go. My past self and Beth are returning and you need to move Jason, Fran and the others out of here. Wyetta, the sun is setting. Will the coven be in position soon?"

She nodded. "Yes."

"Good. You will have to rely on the woods for cover from here on in. If everything goes to plan, this will all be over by sunrise and you'll be back in time."

Val could see that his bracelet was flashing intermittently, just like it had when he'd left her last time. She didn't want him to go, but that was out of their control. Just like their relationship. Her hand slipped from his. She wanted him to go with the knowledge that she would do everything in her power to get Brigit back. "Ok guys, let's make a move," she called, picking up her cloak and heading towards the door. They all needed to know she was in charge and ready, even without her powers.

"Remember, no walls." He pulled her close as he passed, placing a kiss on her cheek. Her body filled with pain. This was never going to get any easier. The more time they spent together, the more she understood what *soul mate* actually meant: that one person who could rip your very soul out every time they left you.

Sam reached Jason, embracing him like a parent would a small child. "I'm sorry, I know this is hard. Your Dad was the best friend I ever had, and Elizabeth was like my sister, so don't think for one second that my heart isn't breaking right now."

Jason shook his head. "Uhuh," was all he could muster.

They watched as Sam shimmered into the night. Then he was gone.

*

Val led the group into the cover of the dense woods. She was starting to know the area better than she'd hoped. They'd been moving for a while when Boden caught up with her. "I have to speak with you."

"OK. What's up?" She asked.

"When Sam brought us here, he withheld one very important piece of information. I hear from the others that you are transforming. Do understand how vulnerable this makes us?"

"No, but I don't intend to use my powers." His comment made her feel uneasy and she tried to reassure him.

"Val, I don't think you should come with us into battle - for your own safety." He placed a hand on her shoulder, bringing her to a halt.

"No! You're insane if you think I'm not coming with you." She could feel her chest restricting. "These are my friends."

"I know, but I have been a Magrafe for hundreds of years and you must trust me. I'm thinking of the collective and so should you."

This was crazy! She wouldn't leave them. What were they thinking? "Does anyone else agree with you?"

"Yes. They realise that this is our safest option, and in battle, that's all that counts."

"Is this true?" She rounded on the others who concertinaed behind her. "Is it true that you don't want me to come with you?" She stared at them, trying to gauge their reactions, to see what they really felt, but their features were partially cloaked by the dusk.

"It is," Hadwyn finally answered. "Val, you are a powerful Guard and Magrafe, but right now you have to consider that you could come into your new powers at any moment. We don't know what they will be, or even if you will be able to control them. Imagine how dangerous that could be... for all of us."

"And exactly what am I expected to do while you all go and save Brigit and the witches?" She couldn't believe what she was hearing.

"We want you to stay with Wyetta and the coven." Boden informed her of their new plan. "Hadwyn will go with Jason to free the children. Belinda, Fran and Zac will free the witches. Wendy, Gabriel and I will face the trial."

She turned her back on him, her head shaking. "You seriously want me to stay here? Surely I can do something? I'm responsible for you all."

Wyetta approached her. "Daughter, no one person is responsible for everyone. Like the birds, we have the ability to fly free and re-join our flock at any time, if it is for the greater good. I agree with your friends. We will have ample to do here when the coven arrives." She glanced down at her protruding belly. "Do you not believe it would be a good idea to keep me out of harm's way?"

"You could run circles around me, even as heavily pregnant as you are. But thanks for trying to make me feel better."

Jason tried to rationalize with her. "Val, Boden said you could transform without warning. Imagine if you burst into flames and that stopped us saving those women. You saw the children. Would you risk getting us all captured? Mate, this is bigger than you."

She wanted to rip her cloak off, stamp on it and scream in frustration, but as mad as she was, she knew they were making sense, just not the sense she wanted to hear. Jason took her shoulders and turned her around to face them again. Damn them all for being so grown up, she thought. "Fine, I get it. I'm a risk." She pointed at Hadwyn. "If anything happens to any of my friends or family I will transform and go all blue flames on you until every one of your blonde hairs is gone."

He bowed his head. "Val, my life for theirs, you have my word. They are my brothers in battle."

She was calmed by the depth of sincerity in his words; she knew he would do anything to keep his own safe. She took a step back, away from them. "Just go."

"You are making the right decision." Boden pulled a small silver bracelet from his pocket. "I would like you to have this." It was a simple silver band; on the join were four little gems.

He placed it in her hand. "Where's it from?" She had learnt from Zac that these portal keys were precious and people didn't just walk around with them in their pockets.

"It belonged to a great Magrafe. I guessed that your father would have his and you may need one. It will tell us if you are near."

She placed it on her wrist and, as her father's had, it shrank to fit her perfectly. "Thank you." She gave him a shaky smile. "You'd better go and get us a ticket home. I'll stay here and try not to transform or suffer from spontaneous combustion." Making an effort to disguise the emotion, that had suddenly glazed her eyes with unshed tears, she called, "Hey, Zac."

He mooched over, head down. "I know I'm abandoning you again, but if you want me to stay with you I will," he offered.

"No, go, make me proud. They need you more than I do right now. What's the weather?" She teased, winking at him.

"Signs are of rain in approximately two hours and thirty-three minutes."

"You're getting really good at this." She placed a kiss on his cheek and he stepped back in shock. "Relax, Hunter. You've been here long enough to understand that a kiss on the cheek means I care. Make sure you come back in one piece. Now go." She pushed him away.

They gathered together and Val instantly felt left out, anxious because she wouldn't be part of what was about to happen. Her father came to join her and Wyetta. "Val, I haven't known you long, but it gives me great pride to know that you are my youngling. Now I must ask one more thing of you."

"Anything."

"Take care of your mother and the coven. I know you have no powers, but I see how great you really are. Stay safe and let me find a way to get you home."

"I won't take my eyes off her, or me for that matter." She pointed at Wyetta's belly. "See you soon," she sighed.

Wyetta cupped Gabriel's face in her hands and placed a gentle kiss on his lips. "Return swiftly and with victory in your wings. Our daughter needs you."

"Come on Eleven," Hadwyn called. "We need to deal with these animals."

"My name is Gabriel," he chided.

"Yes, of course it is." Hadwyn laughed, as he ruffled Gabriel's hair.

They left her with a silent wave. As they walked away, she could hear her father trying to convince Hadwyn that the Warden really had given him his new name.

"Come." Wyetta led the way. "We must collect wood and light a fire. It will be a very long and cold night."

"Sounds like a plan." What choice did she have? She shrugged, resigning herself to the position of wood collector.

"Don't be too hard on yourself, daughter. You must learn that, sometimes to win a battle, you must not enter into it."

"How can you win if you're not there?" Val chuckled, amused at the idea.

"If you aren't there, who is there to fight?" Wyetta bent down and picked up a twig whilst Val stood opened-mouthed, not sure what to say. "Your friends will have success. Your companions from the Prison seem very able warriors, although Hadwyn seems eager to place his pistol in the face of anyone who will give him the time."

Val now laughed openly, God she needed that. "Yes, he's very proud of his gun." She grabbed a stick from the ground. The light was disappearing quickly now and it was getting cold. They needed to make the fire soon.

***

Val and Wyetta busied themselves collecting wood, but Val's thoughts constantly returned to the others. Would

Wendy be able to cast a spell quickly enough to help Gabriel? Would Zac be of any use to anyone? Would Jason remember how they got there in the first place?

"Val," Wyetta interrupted her thoughts, "inside your mind you can ask as many questions as you like, but they alone can prove themselves."

"Can you read minds?" She tried to clear her thoughts, which wasn't that easy.

"No, but your face is an open book. Have faith."

Wyetta was right. It was unfair of her to doubt her friends; they were all more than capable of finding Brigit. "Fine, so how do we light this thing?" she asked as she dropped a pile at Wyetta's feet.

"Be silent!" Wyetta's head twisted from left to right.

Val strained to hear whatever it was that had caught Wyetta's attention, but there was nothing more than the bird's chirping. "What?" Then it hit her. It wasn't a sound, it was a vibration. It was coming through the air towards them and it seemed to be speeding up.

"Run away," Wyetta ordered.

"Not without you," she protested. "I promised I would take care of you, anyway that's me in there."

"Leave me. I'll be fine." But it was already too late. The vibration had become a definite shaking.

As Val tried to work out where on earth it was coming from, the ground began to tremble under their feet. To Wyetta's surprise Val pulled her sword from her pocket and extended it. "Sorry, but I'm not leaving," She apologised and braced to protect her mother.

Then it arrived, shooting out of the ground literally feet away. Val gasped. A rodent the size of Flo landed on its hind legs in front of her, shook off the mud that covered its brown fur and gave them a maniacal grin. "Hello ladies. I'm Lovac and this is my master, Jarrad."

"Val, is this creature from your world?" Wyetta whispered in her ear.

"Possibly." There was a loud bang, and there he was, just a few feet away, next to his oversized pet. Val braced again, putting one arm in front of Wyetta extending her sword in their direction.

The first thing she noticed was that the man's flesh was covered in tattoos. Some Val recognised; others she hadn't seen before. To her horror, they were moving, crawling through his skin. "Don't tell me," she called to him, "you've come here for world domination?"

His eyes danced up and down her body, and then he grinned. "It is you! And no, world domination is so over-rated. Ruling the unruly is for simpletons."

At least he wasn't trying to blow them up - yet. Val needed him to talk; villains always liked to talk. "Seems logical. Do you have a girlfriend you want to free, or a grudge that needs settling? Because when people cross me they tend to fail," she informed him. She needed to convince him that he shouldn't mess with her, and just hope he didn't call her bluff.

"No." He advanced. Val caught her breath. As he got closer, his presence became overwhelming. There was something different about him, something dark. She had the uncomfortable feeling that he was very much aware of her, that he was in control of this situation. It felt like he already knew her. "I want something really simple," he grinned.

"Don't get any closer, I'm warning you." She pointed the tip of her sword at him.

Jarrad pulled up his sleeve to show a forearm that matched the rest of his visible body. He placed his fingers on it and then dug in. Val gasped; it was stomach churning to watch. His fingers probed inside the flesh, and then he seemed to catch something, pinching it between his thumb and index finger. Slowly he pulled out one of the tattoos. He held it between his fingers, his eyes widening with delight as it floated, a transparent form, in his hand. And then, without warning, it detonated. A thunderous clap and a single red flame materialised in thin air, making her jump. He tilted his head towards Val, a crooked grin spreading across his face. "You burn with the purest fire and yet you gasp at this silly little parlour trick?"

"Look, stop the games. What do you want?" she demanded as the mouse dived back into the hole it had emerged from.

He stepped in closer, raising his hand to her eye level. "Just your help, that's what I want." His breath caught Val's cheek and she held steady. "And that's what I'm going to get."

At that moment the flame he held exploded into Val's face in a ball of burning red ash. Her eyes blurred and she couldn't see. Through her disorientation she felt rumbling under her feet. Her sword escaped her hand as she fumbled, trying to clear her sight. Then she heard a scream behind her. "Wyetta," she called, spinning around, but it was too late. The ground burst open, unbalancing her and she stumbled helplessly. She could just make out a dark silhouette shooting up. Then she heard a sound, a crunch, and her mother became silent. She fumbled around, her hands reaching out in all directions, but there was nothing to hold onto.

"Stop what you're doing now!" she screamed, rubbing her eyes. But by the time her vision had started to clear, Wyetta had been taken by Lovac, the oversized talking mouse. "Give me back my mother." She grabbed her sword from the ground and lunged clumsily at Jarrad.

He was far quicker this time, pulling a black angular tattoo from his flesh and sending it flying towards her. It caught her around the throat and she was thrown to the ground, gasping for breath, losing her sword again.

He scolded her. "Now... now... You need to play nicely with me, Thirteen. I have waited a long time for this moment." He straddled her body.

Val tried desperately to lift herself up, but to no avail. "Ok, you have me. Tell me what else you want," she wheezed.

"Yes, yes I do have you, and now you are going to get me the Writer."

Val shook her head. "What Writer? I don't know what you're talking about."

He moved swiftly, crushing the breath from her with his knee, his hand grasping her throat, he began to squeeze. "You have caused me lots of problems, Thirteen." His fingers tightened as Val struggled in vain. "You know who she is and you know what she can do, so don't bother lying to me." He leaned even closer and pressed his nose against Val's cheek. She could feel his icy cold flesh. "Now go and fetch her and deliver her to me. When you've done that, my friend Lovac will release your mother. He bit her you know, and I'm not sure how long someone can survive with his venom in their blood." He sat back, loosening his grip a little.

She groaned and gasped for air. "I don't have any powers," she coughed, "but others have already gone for her."

Stroking her hair from her forehead he grinned. "They don't know you like I do."

"Then you're making a mistake. I've never met you."

He tapped her cheek firmly, "I don't care what your memories have to offer you right now. I know that even without powers you were clever enough to trick the bravest and most feared Candar warriors. I've seen you destroy your enemies with simple gadgets and trinkets. Your friends are fools to doubt you and leave you here. You have until sunrise to get the Writer and deliver her to me, or you and your precious Wyetta will no longer exist in any time. I believe it's your birthday tomorrow morning so you should get going." He released her throat, pulling another symbol from his hand. He held it steady in front of her, then slammed it forcefully against the ground. It flashed, momentarily blinding her. The weight lifted from her body and he was gone, leaving her lying there, choking and writhing on the ground.

Chapter 12

Journey

Val pulled herself up and spent the next few minutes running what had just happened through her head, trying to work out her next move, whilst rummaging through the foliage trying to find her sword. Eventually, she spotted it protruding from a thick green fern. Grabbing it, she shoved it into her boot. A line of glowing red torch lights came into view heading towards her. She watched them warily. What now?

"Hello," a woman's friendly voice greeted her.

There was just enough light left for Val to realise that this was the coven.

"Thanks goodness! I need your help!" she called out, pushing through the ferns towards them. It was instantly clear to them that all wasn't well, and they hurried towards her. Val recognised most of them from her previous trip back in time, and her dreams. Face to face with them again, it felt a little surreal. "I'm Wyetta's daughter, Val."

"Merry Meet. I am Knox. Where is she? We were expecting to see her here," an elderly man inquired.

"You're not going to believe me, but a very large alien mouse took her."

The group of men and women that had gathered around her looked bemused by her statement. "A mouse?" the man probed.

"Yup. It was the size of a child and it was accompanied by some crazy, tattooed guy who seems to know me too well, but I can promise you I've never met him. He said that I had to go and fetch Brigit. What's more, this mouse, he called it Lovac, has bitten her, and if I don't get Brigit, the venom will kill Wyetta, and me."

There was a long moment of silence while the witches assimilated this tide of unwelcome information. At last Knox asked, "Where are the others? We were told there were more than just one."

"There were. They left me and Wyetta here to wait for you while they went to rescue Brigit, the captive witches and the children. I'm certain they'll already be at the fortress, so I need to move quickly. I have to warn them what's happening."

Knox shook his head. "The woods are full of soldiers; you'll not be safe to travel."

"There's no choice. That man wants Brigit and he insists I go for her. So I need your help. Do you think you can make me invisible or something, so I can get to the fortress without being spotted?"

He nodded. "Yes, we can make you as dark as the night and as silent as the moon, but are you sure this is the path to follow?"

"Knox, there is no other way unless you have a mobile phone inside your cloak?"

"A what?"

"Exactly. We're running out of time. Let's do this." What had felt like a lifetime three days ago, was now winding down into just one night left to save her.

"Go. We will work as quickly as we can to protect you. Get Brigit and we will be here awaiting your return." He signalled for Val to leave.

"I'll be back." She thanked him as the other members of the coven started pulling dried sprigs and crystal wands from their cloaks, and handing around items, discussing how to keep her undetected as she headed back towards the fortress.

*

The wall of the fortress was illuminated by the glow of torches moving in the background. The main gate by which they'd entered the previous day had been lowered and there was a group of soldiers positioned at the guard house. Val crept cautiously through the undergrowth towards the place she and Jason had occupied earlier. As she got closer she heard a voice. Keeping as low as possible, she strained to hear.

"I'm telling you, we can't take them by force, there are too many of them."

"I say we stun the lot and go home."

Val felt a wave of relief wash over her. Only one person would say that – Hadwyn. She rose slowly, checking her surroundings and soon spotted her friends. They were low on the ground, near some large bushes. She made her way over cautiously, not wanting to make them reveal their position.

She reached Wendy first, but she didn't want to cause her to jump in surprise, so she decided a firm welcome would work best. "Wendy," she gave a confident whisper. Wendy didn't move an inch. "Pst! Wendy," she said again moving in a little closer.

They all continued speaking. Val was now only a few feet away. "PSSST WENDY!" she whispered more forcefully. She was going to have to make her get her ears tested, this was ridiculous.

Boden picked up a stick. "Val's birth is close, we really don't have the luxury of delaying much longer and, Hadwyn, we don't have enough information about the inside of this structure to go in guns blazing." He handed the stick to Jason. "Mark out a map from the entrance here. Give us as much detail as possible, then we will make a decision."

"Ok." Jason started to draw lines in the dirt.

"We're wasting our time with drawings in the dirt." Hadwyn huffed, folding his arms in annoyance.

Val crawled closer. She was now just a foot away from Hadwyn's back. She was sure he wouldn't jump like a girl; however, there was a much higher chance he would shoot her. 'Maybe not the best choice,' she thought. She crawled on a little more, towards Zac, who for some odd reason, was looking back towards the dirt track, in the complete opposite direction to all the others.

"Zac," she said his name as loudly as she dared. Nervousness making the word sound a little high pitched.

His head turned to face her. At last, someone had heard her. "Do you think Val is ok?" he asked the others. "I'm not sure I should have left her. She does tend to get into trouble without me." He glanced down at his watch. "In exactly one minute and fifteen seconds there will be a temporary downpour. Maybe we should take shelter."

What was going on? Why couldn't he see her? Or hear her? Val stood up and got within touching distance of Zac. "Hey, mate, it's me, Val." She waved her hands in front of his face, but he continued to stare through her.

"Let's move further into that wooded area." Boden pointed towards the area Jason, Wendy and Val had hidden in the previous day.

"Zac!" Val snapped, her tone even louder. She froze, realising just how loud she'd been. Holding her breath, she waited to see if the soldiers had heard her.

"Come on, move quicker," Gabriel encouraged, grabbing Fran's arm.

This was crazy. She shifted hastily towards Jason. "Hey," she called, but he didn't react. Then it dawned on her: the coven had done their job, just a little too well. She was officially as black as the night and annoyingly, as silent as the moon. She watched in stunned, unwanted silence as they all moved away from her. "Think, Val," she grumbled. 'They can't see me, or hear me, but maybe they can still feel my presence,' she thought. Grabbing a stone from the ground, she ran towards the front of the group where Gabriel and Boden were leading them towards the tree line. Taking careful aim, she threw the stone directly at Gabriel. It struck him on the arm. His response was swift. "Down!" He gave a signal and they all lay on the ground, Hadwyn yanking Zac to the floor beside him.

She ran around the group, positioning herself in front of Gabriel. Rain started to fall, exactly as Zac had predicted, the drops bouncing off their bodies. Gabriel rose, looking to see if it was clear. His expression changed, his eyes narrowed, and he squinted right at her. Val suddenly realised what he was looking at. If she could see the rain bouncing off of them, then surely they could see the rain bouncing off her. Invisible or not, she was still a solid object.

He looked to Boden, who nodded at him. They were both seeing her. "Fire," he ordered.

"No, please don't!" she pleaded. But they couldn't hear her.

Boden shifted his weight onto his front knee pulling back his bow, which created an arc of light. Val knew he wouldn't miss. She held her breath waiting for the shot as the rain came down even more heavily. "Please, Boden," she implored, as a voice in the distance rang out.

"Oy, who goes there?" a soldier yelled from the gatehouse. Four more men popped into view on the top wall, all armed with muskets. Then, everything changed. Boden's upper body pivoted as he fired a shot over his shoulder towards the wall, lighting the whole area with a single blinding arrow.

"Run!" Hadwyn was instantly on his feet, lifting Wendy and Belinda, one with each hand. Val was momentarily forgotten as several shots rang out. This was going to be her only opportunity to escape her own friends. She wouldn't escape Boden's bow a second time.

As she ran, she recognised that because of her, they had given away their position. The soldiers now knew someone was out there. She had to get into the fortress whilst she was still invisible. The others might not make it now that the fortress had been alerted to them, and she hadn't even managed to tell them about Wyetta.

Sprinting across the field away from them, the cold rain bounced off her body. Glancing back, she could just see them running towards the trees, with soldiers dashing out of the gatehouse in pursuit. She threw down her soaked cloak, its weight was slowing her down, and pulled her sword from her boot.

As she reached the bridge, her body jumped started at the reverberation of shots. She would recognise that sound anywhere: it was Hadwyn's gun. The few soldiers in pursuit stood no chance against them, but she'd left them vulnerable and at risk. How could she help them? She had to draw attention away from them somehow.

The gatehouse was just feet away, but was filling quickly with soldiers. Looking for another way in, she ran toward a small side door. It was wide open with just one soldier watching the goings on. She stopped, the rain finally no longer pounding on her back. "Can you see what's going on?" a voice called to the man, who was filling the entrance with his barrel-like form.

"They've called the men! Let's hope they don't get those evil looking nuns out, they make me sick to the stomach," he replied.

She felt panicked. What would the Sora do to her friends? The man turned, his belly was within inches of her. She dropped to the ground, rain water and dirt covering her front and face.

"Come on, get a move on," he called.

Out of the corner of her eye, Val spotted a large group of armed soldiers gathering and moving towards the gatehouse. She had to distract them.

Lying on the ground, Val felt another body moving closer. She pushed her body deeper into the mud, trying to stay as still as possible, praying they wouldn't hear her heart pounding.

"What's going on?" the man enquired. She recognised his voice and, turning her head a little, she peeked up at his scarred face. The one man she really could do without seeing right now; the man who had spat on her; the one the Lady had called Durwood. The barrel-like man stiffened to attention and suddenly Val was trapped, lying face down in the mud between their feet. One step in the wrong direction and she would have a foot in her face or on her backside.

"We saw a light coming from the woods. We think there are some witches attacking, and you know what those vermin are like, all sparks and show."

"And you're still standing here because...?" Durwood's tone was agitated.

"I don't know," the soldier replied nervously.

"GET OUT THERE!" Durwood yelled.

The soldier stepped back and Val got her break. She saw a gap and started to crawl towards it, using her arms to pull herself through the waterlogged entrance. She was inside. Now to get their attention. As she reached out her hand, she noticed the bracelet Boden had given her. How did it work? Would it let them know where she was? Grabbing at it she rubbed the gems, trying to turn it on her wrist. It did nothing, and she was just about to try and think it into action, like she did her uniform, when she stopped. Could she risk using it and bringing her powers back? No. She needed to give her companion's some kind of sign that she was here. Get them thinking.

The main wooden entrance gate was being raised to allow the larger group of soldiers out. What if she could close it? That would get everyone's attention. Standing amidst all the commotion, she was grateful to be invisible. This would probably be her only chance to help them. She started to move guardedly between the moving soldiers, looking for the place where the gate lifting mechanism was housed.

Without warning, a man three paces to her left shouted at the top of his voice into her ear, almost deafening her with his scream. "GHOST!" She spun, looking for the ghost that seemed to have alarmed him. As she followed his line of sight she realised he was looking at her. The front of her uniform was covered in sludge, and as she reached up a hand she could feel the mud on her face. She had just become extremely visible.

"Shoot it!" another man yelled in response.

"Seriously? You want to shoot a ghost?" Val raged at the man, who was oblivious to her outburst. He pulled out his pistol. Looking around her, there was nowhere to hide. She could see that her presence was creating quite a stir and it dawned on her that she was getting their attention and drawing it away from the others. Maybe she wouldn't need to close the gate after all.

She needed to make a bigger impression so that they would all want a piece of her. She started to turn in circles waving her arms, wishing they could hear her shouting. This was working, but not enough. She wanted as many people as possible to look at her. Extending her sword she frantically waved it at them. One soldier stepped in too close and she struck at his chest. He dropped instantly. Now she had their attention. A shot was fired from the wall missing her and hitting the ground, causing an explosion of mud. She had goaded them and now it was time to run away before she got shot. She set off towards the witches who, like everyone else, were now very aware of her presence. She had definitely woken up the camp.

"Stop shooting you idiot." A soldier on the ground screamed to the wall. "You'll kill us. Capture it, call the men back and get the Sora!"

As she reached the witches, Val spotted the thick metal bar running the length of one of the carts they were in. She waved at the women to move backwards. Then with all her strength she struck the bar with her sword. An explosion of electric blue sparks flew into the air as gasps of fear and astonishment came from all who saw her. It was working. "Come on!" she screamed. A few more blows and she had the guards' full attention again, and they were closing in on her.

*

Gabriel and the others had managed to make it into the dense woods, where Hadwyn and Boden made quick work of the soldiers that had followed them. Now they were trying to work out their next move. They had been expecting the soldiers to attack them, but nothing seemed to be happening.

Hadwyn jumped down from his vantage point high in an oak tree. "I see no one approaching. Something isn't right."

Wendy, who had moved a little further away so she could see the fortress more clearly, called them. "Look!" she pointed towards it.

"Where?" Gabriel replied, glancing towards the wall. His eyes focused through a gap in the trees and he could just make out what had caught her attention. Clouds of sparks were appearing.

Hadwyn moved over to join him. "What is that? And why are the soldiers not coming for us?" He placed his gun back onto his uniform. The group of soldiers who'd been heading out of the fortress gate were now running back.

"I think I know what's causing that." Boden held his watch up for them to see.

"It's Val!" Gabriel exclaimed. "How did she get in there?"

Hadwyn pushed Gabriel aside and marched out into the clearing. "Why is she there? Why isn't she where we left her? She wouldn't break protocol unless she had to."

"What's happening?" Zac asked, as he reached the group. He and Jason had been tying up some soldiers.

"See that?" Hadwyn pointed to the sparks, Zac nodded. "That's your Guard. Not sure how she does it, but she's in the thick of it... again. Let's go."

"Wait!" Belinda shouted. "Listen to me. She's clearly drawing those soldiers back towards the fortress to take their attention away from us. She must have been the silhouette in the rain. I've seen that spell done before, and we probably couldn't hear her because of magic as well. If we go charging in, we'll surely ruin our chances of saving Brigit or anyone else." The men stood looking at her, bemused and made thoughtful by her outburst.

"She's right," Gabriel nodded.

Jason barged forward. "No, she's not. We have to go and get her. She's all alone in there. I've seen what's behind that wall."

"I agree, we must go now." Zac joined him. Together they stepped out from the cover of the woods and started to run towards the wall.

"Hadwyn, stop them. NOW!" Gabriel ordered.

He pulled his gun and aimed. "No!" Fran screamed, leaping on his back, desperately trying to grab his gun, but she wasn't an issue for him. He fired two shots. Jason and Zac fell instantly. Then he pulled Fran off, lowering her respectfully to the ground. "Fran, they are only stunned. In ten minutes they will be awake, and I just saved Val's life."

CHAPTER 13

Down The Hole

Val was surrounded, her eyes darted, searching for a gap or a way out. A soldier slammed her body against the cart she'd been striking with her sword. The wet mud yanked them both off their feet and they sprawled on the ground. Scrambling frantically, kicking the man away, she rolled underneath the cart, still being pursued by the soldiers, with no idea how to escape. Then she saw a familiar face. "Sara," she called, but quickly remembered she couldn't be heard.

Sara's eyes were drawn between the mudded slats of her cart. "I see you," she said as their eyes met. "You must escape, run!"

'That would be lovely,' Val thought and rolled onto her chest. Mud filled her mouth as another soldier ran at the cart. The witches bravely lashed out at the soldiers, hissing and shaking their chains. Then Val heard a high-pitched scream. It was the Sora, she just knew it. They had come for her, with their disgusting, empty eye sockets.

She could see the witches cowering away from the Sora, huddling together. And who could blame them? Even she was petrified of the nuns.

"Get it out from under there!" a man's voice bellowed. Val watched from under the cart wheels as the long black gowns of the Sora drifted like sharks through the mud towards her. She shuffled backwards towards the centre of the carts and stood up. She needed to see her surroundings and plan her next move. Surveying her options, she spotted the archway leading to the magical trial. Luckily it was still unmanned.

Was it really that dangerous? Well, now was as good a time as any to find out. She twisted towards Sara, possibly for the last time. "I'm going in there," she mouthed, pointing towards the archway. Sara nodded, understanding from Val's hand signals what she was going to attempt.

"Sisters, we must distract the Sora so Wyetta's daughter can escape." The women on her cart gave a defiant cheer and passed the message on. Sara stood up and started to jump and scream like she had gone completely insane, shaking her dress and her head like a wild animal. The other woman followed suit until there was utter madness reigning down on the guards and the Sora who, faced with a hundred witches, seemed momentarily dazed and confused by the prospect of picking out just one. Val crawled back under the furthest cart, then dragged her sludge-covered body towards the archway. Sara was watching and turned to the others on her cart, giving a smile of satisfaction as Val slithered out of sight.

Val's hands reached for the solid stone flagstones then, pulling herself upright, she ran into the archway. At the far end of the passage she paused, looking back for her aggressors, as the gravity of her situation hit home with the daintiness of a sledge hammer. She was where

Gabriel was supposed to be and she now needed to weigh up her options. If she waited for the others to arrive and they couldn't get into the fortress, she would die. If she went into this stupid magical trial with no powers, she would die. As she hesitated, the sound of voices seemed to move a lot closer. If she did nothing, she and Wyetta would both die.

The only option was to go into the doorway Wendy had shown her, pass the magical trial, free Brigit, get the others, save Wyetta and head on back to the future before she was born. And not die trying. How hard could that be? She let out a small laugh, one of those inappropriate, yet uncontrollable laughs that came when faced with imminent death.

Grabbing a flaming torch, she headed towards the entrance, pausing one last time to look at the symbols on the wall. 'Infinity, weird witch's symbol, star, Moses and circle with a dot,' she recited. 'Note to self: bring pen and paper next time.' Hearing heavy footsteps behind her, she knew her time to choose was up as she stepped into the unknown.

*

It was darker than she'd expected and although her torch was giving off a great deal of heat, its ability to light her surroundings was diminished by the intense blackness. Then, slowly, as if someone was using a dimmer switch, she began to see light expanding at the end of a corridor ahead of her. "I'm pretty sure heading towards the light is not the best idea," she said to herself, but what other choice did she have? It was this or back into the hands of the Sora and the soldiers.

She inched forward. The floor seemed solid, though the walls appeared to be sloping in on her. The closer she got to the light, the narrower the passage became, until it was obvious that she was soon going to have to put her torch down or singe her eyebrows off. She abandoned it and kept moving.

"Welcome." A woman's voice greeted her.

"Hello," she called back. Why would someone be down here to greet her?

"You are in the trial. Please choose the correct paths," the voice instructed.

"Any advice about which paths are correct? I have no problem with cheating right at this moment. And who are you?" Val stood waiting for something to happen. Then the floor started to move. "Hello! Is this the right path?" she yelled in shock as the slabs began to disintegrate beneath her. Running towards the light was her only option, but she couldn't outrun the collapsing stones and, as the last slab disappeared, she began her sudden descent into the trial.

*

Zac sat on a rock rubbing his arm, the bruise from Hadwyn's shot was the size of a fried egg and shone for the others to see. "Tell me your plan quickly or I will go and get Val back myself," he demanded, still too dizzy to get up and walk.

Hadwyn placed his boot on the rock next to him and leaned in close. "You're either the craziest Hunter I have met, or the stupidest. I'm not sure which is worse. You're trained to Hunt, not go into battle."

"I am trained to stay with my Guard until death," he retaliated, "not hide in the woods."

"Enough!" Gabriel ordered. "I'm sorry we were forced to stun you, but Val was trying to distract the soldiers and you two would have sabotaged her efforts." He glanced over at Jason, who was sitting on the ground with Belinda, nursing his badly bruised leg.

Jason raised his head, his expression distorted by anger. "You're her Dad! My Dad would never have left me."

"I have not left her. I am going in, but let us do it with conscious thought, not emotional energy. Jason, you are a good friend to Val, but I have centuries of battle experience. There must be a reason Val did what she did. Think about the facts. We left her with Wyetta and then she's here, invisible, alone. Something's gone wrong."

Boden shimmered into view between them. "Did you see her?" Zac asked.

"She's not there anymore. There was a commotion around the women, who I assume are the witches, but it's all quiet now. There are a lot of soldiers in there, all armed. Some of them were talking about a ghost breaking in. I followed her signal into a corridor, but then it just disappeared..."

"She's gone into the trial!" Wendy exclaimed. "She must have been desperate. She has no powers and I believe I made it very clear it was extremely dangerous to navigate. Did you see an entrance?"

Boden shook his head. "No, it was a simple stone corridor."

"Then it's closed in on her. The only way she's getting out is by passing all the trials. We can't help her now."

Wendy slumped down next to Jason who instinctively put his arm around her shoulder.

Boden joined them. "Come now! You really believe that Val cannot defeat this trial? I thought you were her friends in arms?"

"We are, but this is a magical trial set to protect Brigit, a being so precious that it's going to be extremely dangerous," Wendy told him.

Boden shrugged. "So, she's up against a new challenge. I watched her take down the Nyterian Army. Have faith in her. And if we can't do anything to help her right now, let's at least free those witches and the children. Let's get in and send those measly soldiers on their way. That will make things easier for her when she gets out of the trial. Bickering amongst ourselves will help no one." He joined Hadwyn. "On the Prison we have a saying when a Guard goes on what seems an impossible arrest: May courage, honour and wisdom guide you to justice. So, let it guide us now on a path to save one of our own."

Wendy slowly lifted her face, her eyes wet from tears. She wiped at them with her cloak. "I like that. Val has all those things. May courage, honour and wisdom guide her to justice." She placed a hand on Jason's shoulder and started to rise. "Thank you." Boden nodded his acknowledgment.

Hadwyn spun his gun in her face. "And if that doesn't work, we'll stun them all."

CHAPTER 14

Infinity

As Val fell into the darkness, her mind spun with the fear of not knowing what was at the bottom. Would she smash into concrete, a landing that would surely break every bone in her body? Whatever was waiting for her at the bottom, it was taking a long time to reach it. The shaft must be hundreds of feet deep. She closed her eyes and hoped for a soft landing. When she finally arrived at the bottom of whatever this place was, the splash into deep water, although shocking, was a relief.

The temperature of the freezing water snatched her breath away and when she first burst to the surface she struggled to breathe. Her eyes stung as the mud she'd gathered on her journey across the fortress's floor washed off in a river of brown dirt around her. The light was poor, but she could just make out an arched stone ceiling above her. It must be the water system for the fortress. Bobbing in the dark, still gasping for breath, she felt alone and vulnerable. Swimming in the local pool with other people was fine, floating under a sixteenth century building with poor visibility wasn't so great.

She trod water, trying as hard as she could to make sense of it all, but the cold and the dark were confusing all of her senses. If she swam left, it could be the wrong direction and she could find herself exhausted before she found an exit; the same applied to the right. She splashed her face with the chilly water, trying to get some clarity. As she wiped her eyes, she spotted a shape in the distance moving towards her. How could she protect herself? Where could she go? There was only the opposite direction to the thing that was closing in on her. She pushed with her legs, but the figure was moving faster. There seemed to be no escaping it. Glancing back again she could now see it was a human form.

She swirled, ready to defend herself. The silhouette reached her and trod water beside her. "Hello, Val." Her mouth dropped open. Water filled it and she spluttered, "Shane?"

"How's it going?" He greeted her as he bobbed alongside. "I see you've got yourself into a bit of a mess." His face lit up with a smile that seemed to go on forever.

"Shane," she wept, grabbing him around the neck, "but you're dead."

He pulled back. "What? I'm what?" he exclaimed, a look of horror on his face.

"Oh my God, I'm so sorry. Well, I think you're dead, but how can you be here? Did you time travel as well?" she asked as they floated together in the dark water.

He grinned, splashing her. "Just kidding. I know I'm dead."

She let out a nervous laugh and then stopped herself. This was just too weird. Why was she floating in the dark with a dead man? "What are we doing here?" She grabbed his thick arm and held on. It felt so good having him close. "Am I dead too?" she asked. It seemed a likely explanation.

"No, you've arrived in the Infinity and I'm here because you wanted me to be here. By the way, next time you feel like manifesting me, could it be on a beach with a Bloody Mary?" He started to move backwards, pulling her along with him.

"What is this Infinity? I don't understand, and how did I manifest it?"

"You'll see soon enough." He rolled over and Val grabbed at his shoulder holding on as he continued to swim forwards in the darkness.

"Where are we going?"

"Nowhere, we'll just keep swimming. Isn't that a line from a film? I remember Jason watching it as a little boy. Blue fish something..."

"Finding Nemo?"

"Yes, that's the one. God, he watched it a million times or more." He laughed.

"Jason's coping really well." She wanted to reassure him, but as the words came out, a lump grew in her throat and another thought. Maybe she really was dead, but Shane didn't know it.

He slowed his pace. "Val, you're not dead. I won't tell you again."

"You can read my mind?"

"Yes, and I'm really dead. You also need to hear something about Jason. I can promise you he's not doing well at all; he's panicking about you. If you're not careful he's going to make a huge mistake."

"How do you know?"

"I watch over him from time to time, and you." He touched her cheek, his hand icy cold. "Val, I need you to promise me something."

"Anything."

"A time will come when you need to show him the truth. Don't let him run from his destiny the same way I didn't let you run."

"Ok," she agreed, not really understanding what she was agreeing to.

"But first we have to get you out of here so you can carry on your journey. So it's time to let go, Val."

Reluctantly she released his arm. "Now what?"

"No. You *need* to let go." His eyes grew sadder as he bobbed towards her.

"I did." She trod water, splashing her hands for him to see.

"I can promise you, you haven't. Listen to me. When you were face to face with that Nyterian dictator and he searched your soul, you saw Jason. Your love for him and me is overwhelming, and so is your guilt, which will keep you stuck here, literally for infinity. You need to let go."

"How do you know about Nathan?"

"Like I said, I'm watching over you, but if you keep holding onto me so tightly you can't escape this place. Life is about not looking back. The Infinity finds that special something your real world can't give you, the thing you want the most and makes it feel impossible to let go. I'm truly honoured it was me, but it's time to move on with your journey." He hugged her briefly, placing a kiss on her forehead. "Goodbye, Val."

She gazed into his eyes. God this was so painful all over again. It was impossible. Wendy was right. This trial was going to beat her; it had looked into her heart and found the one thing she never wanted to lose - again. She struggled to tread water whilst the pain washed over her. Tears started to fall down her cheeks and mingle with the endless watery abyss around her. "I don't want to let you go. I won't lose you again," she announced.

"I know, and that's what they're counting on. And they will keep you here forever. Val, you're stronger than this. The world needs you. Hell, the galaxy needs you, and your friends need you!"

She felt sick, but she knew this manifestation of Shane was telling her the truth. "How do I do it?"

"Close your eyes and trust."

"I can't. If I close my eyes I'll never see you again. I can't do it!" She was now crying and the water was getting choppy, splashing at her face.

"You have to move on. Let me go. I'll always be watching over you."

She stopped treading water and just floated. She couldn't let the others down. She closed her eyes, then quickly opened them again. Shane was still in front of her.

"Val, do it properly."

"I love you," she said.

"And I love you, my friend."

She closed her eyes, the tears still escaping. She wanted to open them, but in her heart she knew he was right. The minute she'd arrived in 1645, knowing they could time travel, she'd wanted to bring Shane back, to save him, to change what had happened. Her heart ached with the reality that she had held on so tightly to her guilt.

Then something grabbed her by the ankle. Her eyes shot open. Shane was gone. It tugged again, pulling her under the water. She pulled against it, frantically trying to break free, but it was stronger than her. It felt like hands grabbing her. She fought to get above the surface, gasping for air and kicking as hard as she could, but she was pulled violently under again. With a jerk she was completely submerged. She screamed and her lungs began to fill up with water. She was choking, being dragged deeper and deeper until she could no longer breathe. Her eyes closed and nothing hurt anymore.

CHAPTER 15

The Curse

"Wake up." The small oval face leant down, shaking the limp body. "Please wake up, Eleanor," the girl whispered.

A spray of water spurted out of Val's throat, the pain ripping though her chest as she vomited up the liquid. Coughing, she wheezed and rolled away from the pool of water as two small hands dragged her up into a sitting position. She gazed up at the face of a small blonde girl. Blinking and rubbing her eyes, she rasped through her sore throat, "Where am I?" She put her hands on the ground for support and she felt its soft texture, something like sand mixed with mud. Just a moment earlier she had been drowning, and now she was on dry land, but with no shoreline in sight.

The girl frowned, scrunching her blue eyes almost shut. "You're here," she reported matter-of-factly.

Val leant forward, smiling at the little girl, just grateful to be alive. "I see, I'm here," she nodded. "Does this place have a name? And who are you?" She observed the child's confident stance, her hands firmly on her tiny waist. Dark brown leather trousers and a cream shirt made her look like she'd stolen her outfit from a tiny pirate.

The little girl pulled back her mane of blonde hair. "You know my name's Kaliyah. Why are you acting so oddly?" She leant in, her tiny fingers inspecting Val's head for lumps and bumps.

Val heard a woman calling. Glancing over her shoulder she spotted an elderly figure trudging through the black sand towards them. This was the strangest of places. There was definitely natural light coming from somewhere, although there was no sun, only an open expanse that resembled the sky just before a storm. Was this another mirage?

"Welcome home," the woman greeted her as she reached them. Her face was pale and her long hair matched the child's, although it had a generous sprinkling of grey flecks. They looked uncannily alike. Perhaps grandmother and granddaughter Val wondered.

The little girl grew angry at the woman's presence. "I found her!" she snapped, as if Val was her toy.

"There is no need to be like that. She will think us rude." The woman smiled warmly at Val. "How was the journey?" she asked politely.

"Er...interesting, but I still don't know where I am."

The small child threw her arms in the air, clearly exasperated by Val's stupidity. "Is this what we've been waiting for?" she grumbled.

"Now, now, Kaliyah. She will remember us; we just need to help her," the elder woman who was, Val guessed, in her late sixties responded. "We will make you remember. We can tell you much."

"I can't help, I'm just a child," the girl sniped sarcastically. Then she crossed her arms and plopped onto the ground next to Val. "Just hurry her up old woman." Her frown was deep and oozed annoyance.

"It's about time you came to free us," she said to Val, her voice heavy with resentment.

Feeling more and more puzzled, Val reached for the child's hand. "I will set you free from this place, I promise." How could someone trap a child and a pensioner in this hell hole? There was nothing; it was just a barren landscape.

The woman reached forward, pushing Val's fringe away from her wet face. "Eleanor. Your name is Eleanor. You are 'the Lady' and as such you are to be treated with the upmost respect."

Val stiffened in horror. "No! You're mistaken. I'm not that woman," she protested, getting to her feet.

"It's fine," the older woman reassured her, patting her hand. "I will tell you everything you need to know; you will remember."

Val controlled her impulse to run, to get as far away from them as she could. Maybe she could learn something useful here. These people thought she was Lady Eleanor, the woman she'd seen in the fortress yard and, because of that the older woman was prepared to tell her everything. Maybe this was one of those times when she needed to shut up and listen. She took a deep breath and sat back on the ground. "Please help me remember. That would be wonderful. Thank you so much." She smiled.

The woman seemed over the moon with this new attitude. "How far back should I go?" she beamed.

Val shook her head. "The beginning if that's ok?"

"Pathetic!" Kaliyah turned her back on them both.

The woman was wearing a long thick, deep red dress that was made from a carpet-like material. It folded like a curtain as she lowered herself to Val's side, grimacing a little as she bent her knees. "You were such a beautiful child. Your hair shone like the sun and your eyes were the colour of gem stones." She looked wistfully into Val's face. Val felt a little uneasy; her hair was dark brown and her eyes matched - a sort of muddy brown, not at all gem-like. The older woman seemed too wrapped up in her daydream to care.

"You weren't that pretty," the little girl mumbled.

The older woman ignored her and continued, "Everyone loved you: the servants, the gardeners. You would play for hours in the gardens and then your mother and father would collect you. Oh, how they loved you. I loved you. You were so precious."

Val started to wonder just how long this story might take. She'd heard the World War II story from her Nan and that took days. "So what was I like as an adult?" she tried to move things along.

The woman's voice became deep and throaty. "You met him!"

"Him?" Val enquired.

"Lord James. He came to you and you fell head over heels in love. Some say you were besotted. I don't agree; I say that's stupid." She dragged her finger through the sand.

"So what happened to me and Lord James?"

"You were married and had a child." The woman paused, looking at Val, waiting to see if this comment jogged her memory.

"A child...? Ok. And my child's name?"

"Edward. That's when the troubles began. It was a dark moonless night and James had gone to the village for a drink. If he had just stayed with you and your child this would never have happened." She glanced at the little girl. "She gets so angry about him." She placed her fingertip gently onto the child's back, who wriggled in annoyance.

"He was such an idiot," Kaliyah mumbled as she drew circles with her finger in the sand.

"Well anyway, we can't change what happened. James met a woman there, as men do. A beautiful woman to be precise, who knew how wealthy James was. She knew he was a Lord and she wanted him. They say she gave him a potion, to make him fall in love with her, but his feelings for *you* and Edward were too strong, and it drove him insane." She linked her hands nervously.

"Feelings for me?" Then she remembered they were talking about Eleanor. "What happened to him?" she asked.

"The woman that he met was so angry with him for defying her spell that she placed an eternal curse on his loved ones." The old woman paused and when she went on her voice was little more than a whisper. "She cursed our family to never feel or give love again." She fell silent and Val took a moment to comprehend the gravity of that.

"So, you're saying Lady Eleanor can't feel or give love? That she's cursed. What about the baby?"

"Don't you mean you?" The little girl turned her head towards Val, her stare cold and unforgiving.

Val instantly corrected herself. "Yes me. I'll never feel or give love again. So what has happened to my child?"

"You sent him far away to the Americas in the hope that another's love would break the curse. How could you be around a baby you couldn't even hold without feeling disgust?"

"And James?"

"He disappeared within weeks of losing your love. Some say he killed himself. Others say his heart broke. But you, you have kept searching for a way to break the curse. A way to free yourself from the emptiness." She reached out for Val's hand.

"So who are you?" Val asked.

She smiled tenderly. "I'm your mother and Kaliyah is your little sister."

Val's face scrunched in confusion. "What?" Lady Eleanor had imprisoned her own mother and sister. "Why did I send you here?"

"You were angry. I was old and the curse didn't affect me, only the descendants. I still feel love. Kaliyah lost her ability to love or be loved, which is why she's so angry. You left us here, saying when the time was right you would come back. We've been waiting for you to set us free. That's why you're here, isn't it? We've been waiting for you here all this time; waiting for you to lift the curse, so you can love us again."

Val nodded. "Yes, I'm glad I arrived just in time. So, what now?" She needed to know how she could escape this place.

"We'll all go back to the fortress together and be happy at last. So many years of pain will be forgotten." The woman straightened her dress.

This was what she needed to know. "Great. So how do we get back to the fortress?"

The child stood up, turning finally to face them. "You're not Eleanor, are you?" She pointed at the old woman. "And you're as stupid as I am. We aren't getting out; she's never coming for us. Don't you get it? We are the parts of her life she didn't want. Too young to have power," she prodded herself in the chest, "and too old and weak with that ridiculous thing you call love." The old woman pushed her fingers into the child's hair, splitting it into pigtails and pulled hard. "She will come for us, she promised!" she screamed, launching herself at the child. They collapsed to the ground clawing at each other.

Val had never seen a pensioner and a child fight. It wasn't pretty. "Stop! Please stop." She shoved an arm around the woman's waist pulling her backwards with all her strength. "I will help you escape. Just stop," she pleaded.

The child kicked Val in the shin. "You're lying, just like the other woman they brought through. It's all lies."

Val released her hold on the older woman and grabbed the girl by the shoulders. "What woman? When?"

"Ow, you're hurting me." She wriggled.

"Tell me about the woman. Now!"

"Fine! She came here a few days ago. She was being led by some weird looking nuns with no eyeballs." The little girl gave a grotesque demonstration, pulling her eyelids back.

"Where did they take her?" Val put a little more pressure on the child.

The girl tried to pull away, but Val wasn't letting go. "They took her to the Elemental Woods," she relented at last.

"Which way?" Val surveyed her surroundings; there was nothing to see other than sand.

"Over the hill." The girl pointed to a mound.

"Look, that woman was Brigit; she was telling the truth. I'm here to get her out of this place, and we'll help you too. You don't deserve to be here anymore than I do. I promise I'll make this right."

"Get lost." The girl hissed, managing to pull herself free and sprint away.

The older woman wasn't in so much of a hurry to escape. She was sitting on the ground, rocking gently backwards and forwards. "Your sentiments are honourable, but we know our fate. Unless Eleanor feels love, we are prisoners here for eternity. Go find your friend. Make right what she has made so very wrong."

Val could hear the defeat in the old woman's voice. She knew it might not be possible to help them, but that didn't mean she shouldn't try. "I will do everything in my power to get you out of here, that's my promise to you."

"Others have said the same." The old woman pointed to the top of the mound. "This has been Eleanor's hiding place for a very long time. People go over the top and never return. I wish you luck. You just seem like such a nice young woman."

"Wait, you know I'm not Eleanor?"

"Life sometimes hands you a glimmer of hope in the eyes of a stranger. You gave me the spark. I just wanted to light a flame of possibility in your face. Now go and save your friend. We know our destiny."

"Is the next trial there?" Val asked.

The woman pointed. "It's with the others over the hill. That's all I know."

Val looked towards the mound. The elderly woman pulled herself up and went off in pursuit of the angry little girl.

Val started to walk towards the rise. "So, over the hill I go."

CHAPTER 16

Triquetra

As the sandy ground steepened, Val began to see the top of the bank; points of wooden posts jutting out like spikes became visible to the left and right. She wished Zac and the others were with her; she could really do with some help right now. Hadwyn's trigger-happy attitude would have been most welcome.

Nothing could have prepared her for the sight that greeted her at the top of the hill. She let out a wretched cry, which she quickly muffled by clamping her mouth tightly shut. On and between the wicked-looking spikes were a collection of scattered bones and body parts. From what she could tell, they were human remains. The stench filled her nostrils. She staggered sideways, taking an involuntary step away from them.

Turning away from the atrocity, she clambered up a higher mound of sand, putting her in a better position to survey her surroundings. Behind her, her two recent companions were gone. To her surprise, a couple of hundred yards in front of her was a wood. It looked oddly out of place; in contrast to the dark sand, the lush green looked almost luminous.

From the corner of her eye, she spotted something shining on the ground a few feet away. On inspection she found it was an axe, with a decorated double-head. It was an intimidating weapon, probably belonging to one of the skeletons who evidently didn't need it anymore. She had her sword, but another weapon might come in handy. She picked it up, wrapping her fingers around its wooden handle. It felt good. The weight of the head was perfectly proportioned and it rested comfortably in her hand. Hadwyn would love this, she thought as she set off towards the woods.

As she walked, she tried to remember the conversations she'd had with Wendy; how she'd warned her that the symbol, the one with the three points all connected, was something to do with maids, mothers and something else...something that sounded like cronies. God, why didn't she ever listen to the witch? She seriously knew what she was talking about.

At the edge of the wooded area Val sensed, a strange numbness in the air. The area in front of her seemed void of life, which made it creepy; a wood is a place that should be teeming with life. She stepped onto the mossy ground and a shiver ran down her spine. Now her suit wasn't working! The icy atmosphere was seeping into her bones and the cold was numbing her. This wasn't fun.

"Choo."

Val stopped. Three steps into the woods and she was already hearing things. She lifted the axe to the level of her head, its blade resting inches from her cheek.

"Choo."

There it was again. She edged forward. If something was going to attack her, it had better hurry up. She was losing patience with this trial. Then, just up ahead, she spotted an opening and in the centre was a small creature. She crept in its direction. Having seen all the human remains, she knew she needed to treat everything with the utmost care.

"Choo."

Val watched as the creature sneezed, sending a small flame popping out onto the ground. She almost wanted to giggle. It looked so silly. Like a baby with a cold, that had flames for mucus and... wings. From what she could see it had a cat-like body, the colour of fudge, with two tawny wings held firmly to its sides. Its head shook and as it rotated she could see its face. It looked familiar... Too familiar! The creature's head was human; a child's head to be precise. Her stomach flipped. She'd seen aliens before, but this was deeply disturbing. It sneezed again. The ball of fire flew from its mouth and rested on the damp moss for a moment before flickering out. Through all her repulsion and fear of the unknown, it still didn't look like a killer. But looks could be deceiving, she reminded herself as visions of Delta popped into her head.

She decided her best option was to skirt around it, avoiding confrontation. From what Wendy had told her about the Triquetra symbol, it was the three aspects of life; youth, middle age and old age. So if this creature was potentially youth that meant there could be two more of them out there. Knowing her luck, they doubled in size with age.

The creature suddenly froze. "Who goes there?" it challenged, rising onto its hind legs. Val could now see it wasn't any old cat's body, it was a young lion. It raised its human nose into the air, its head tilting from left to right, sniffing deeply. "I can smell you. Stop, wherever you are."

"Damn," she murmured. Cat's sense of smell. How was she supposed to avoid these things?

"I am the guardian of the woods. Show yourself, so I can eat you!" it announced, its feline body now slinked towards the edge of the opening, hackles risen in annoyance, its tail flicking aggressively. "Choo." It sneezed another ball of fire.

She could run, but her bet was that a lion, even a small one, would have her down in a blink. She could attack with her sword or even her newly acquired axe, but she had a problem: it was a child. Whatever creature it was, it looked too young for her to hurt it. She pulled her sword from her boot. "Ok guardian of the woods, I'm coming out. Please don't eat me. I don't want to hurt you." She stepped through the ferns to the clearing.

The child's face unexpectedly filled with fear. It had evidently not expected her to respond to its threat. "Puri daj, Puri daj!" it screamed.

"No, no! I don't want to hurt you." Val threw her weapons to the ground.

The creature curled backward, wrapping its wings around itself for protection. "Puri daj!" it yelled again.

She needed it to be quiet. "Please," she lowered herself onto her knees. "I really don't want to hurt you."

"Who are you? What are you doing here?" The creature started to prance in an awkward catlike manner sideways around her. "My Puri daj will come and eat you." A forked tongue flicked out at her.

"I'm Val Saunders and I don't want to be eaten, I just want to get out of here. Please, I'm looking for a woman.

Her name is Brigit and she came through here a few days ago with four creatures with no eyes. That's all I want. Can you help me?"

"Val Saunders." The creature's snout rose, then it extended its tongue, rhythmically tasting the air around her. "You tell the truth, I can tell. You smell of fear and only the fearful are too afraid to lie." It sat, hind legs bent like a pet dog, observing her.

"So, did you see her?"

The creature inhaled again, puffing out it's chest, opening the golden plumage of its wings as if to intimidate her with its stature. "I am Wiflin, the guardian, and yes I did see her with the creatures with no looking holes."

Val nodded. "Yep, that's them, crazy mad nuns with no looking holes."

"They made me sick. Then they took my Daj away."

"Daj?" Val asked.

Wiflin paused a moment in thought. "Mother?"

Val felt an odd sense of relief. If there was supposed to be three of them then this meant that at least one of the creatures was out of the equation. "I'm so sorry. Where did they take her?"

"Into the dark centre." He lifted a pad and pointed.

Val's eye's followed the direction of his paw. In the distance, between several old and twisted trees, she saw a doorway. "If they took your mother through there, are you alone?" 'Please say yes,' she thought.

"No, there's one more like me, my Puri daj," he hesitated. "Grandmother?"

"Yes, grandmother, that's right. So, is she really old?" Val crossed her fingers.

"Oh yes, she's very old."

"Where is she?"

"She's out hunting. She will return soon and eat you," Wiflin told her.

His ease in telling her her destiny was a big red flag; it was time to leave. But Val felt sorry for this child-like creature. No one should be separated from their mum, she knew that too well. However the idea of Wiflin keeping her prisoner till Grandma returned to eat her wasn't particularly appealing. "If you let me go, I will try to find your Daj and bring her back to you, I promise. I know how it feels to lose your parents."

"You can do that? Then can we go home?" Wiflin asked.

"Yes. Where is your home?" She started to rise, reaching for her weapons and the creature became rigid. "I promise I won't hurt you," Val reassured him.

"I will trust you for now." He extended his claws into the ground as a warning. "We are part of an ancient band of gypsies. We were visiting the island of Kyra when some men came hunting witches. They captured my family. When we arrived in this place evil magic was cast upon us."

"To keep you here?" Val asked.

"No, to make us look like this." Wiflin raised a paw.

"You know, now you say that, you look a lot like the sphinx I've seen in books. They're creatures from Greek and Egyptian mythology."

The child nodded. "The Lady wanted something to protect her doorway, and it seems she had heard of these things you call sphinx also, and so the man with the scar did this to us."

Val had that pit-of-your-stomach-hatred feeling rising into her chest. "Blonde hair?"

Wiflin nodded. "I want to go home, Val Saunders."

"Then my promise is to make sure that happens, as long as you help me get out of here."

"You swear you will find my Daj?"

"Yes, I swear." She needed to speed this process up. "So, I just need to go through the doorway?"

Wiflin's head snapped upwards sniffing the air. "Puri daj is coming now! You must escape. Run!"

Val sensed the urgency in his words and knew she had to get away, fast! She gripped her axe's aged wooden handle, set her sights on her destination and started to sprint, heading towards the doorway. She daren't look back. However, nothing Wiflin had said could have prepared her for the sound she heard. It was a lion's roar, deep and throaty. And far too close. Fear flushed adrenaline around her body as she pushed on, fear of becoming the prey making her legs shake as she scrabbled through several thorny bushes. "Run Val Saunders!" Wiflin called.

Her heart was beating so fast it felt like it might explode. Then she felt the thundering of the creature's heavy paws on the ground behind her. She couldn't look back; if she wasted a second she would be dead. The door was only a few feet away now. Then it appeared, leaping through the air and landing directly in front of the door. Its face was that of an old woman and a mane of long grey hair fell around her wrinkled face. Her eyes black with anger, she roared a deathly bellow directly into Val's face, causing her to skid and tumble to the ground. Val lay there for a second, taking in just how massive Grandma was. She was so much bigger than Wiflin that her wings looked the size of a Pterodactyl's.

Rolling over, Val pulled herself up and changed direction, running back towards Wiflin. Grandma wasted no time in following and Val could feel her hot animal breath down her neck. Off to her left she spotted a gap in the trees. Throwing herself through feet first, she skidded into the tiny opening. She hoped Grandma wouldn't be able to get through, and she was right. A roar of frustration rang out. Val leapt out on the other side and started running again, heading once more for the doorway as a blood curdling yelp filled the air.

"Wiflin, Stop!" She leapt over a bush and glanced over her shoulder to see Wiflin had sunk his teeth into his Grandmother's back. She was thrashing in anger. Val knew he'd done this for her and she wouldn't waste the opportunity. As she reached the doorway, there was another yelp of pain. This time it was Wiflin. She grabbed the handle and, to her surprise, it turned. She paused, this could be a trap, but facing Wiflin's Puri Daj was a much darker option. She pushed through the door and fell into the emptiness.

Chapter 17

Pentagram

Falling forward, Val instinctively reached out, planting her palms down to stop her body colliding with... the darkness. Her hands slid across something cold and hard. Taking a few controlled breaths, she tried to contain her rising panic. Her eyes desperately tried to adjust, but she couldn't even see the edge of her uniform. Then a distant crackle caught her attention.

"Welcome." A deep male voice greeted her and a small flame appeared floating in thin air. What was the next symbol? Val searched her memory frantically, lowering her body flat on the ground and holding her breath as the flame grew. Its glow allowed her to see the hand supporting it. Ok, so whoever was there had her powers. 'Assess your situation – you have a sword and an axe' she thought, trying to make herself think this through calmly.

"We can make this quick and painless if you want, but if you choose to fight, I will kill you." Another flame sparked. She assumed it came from his other hand. Then the flames skipped up his arms. The added luminosity didn't help Val, as the rest of her surroundings were still pitch black. One of her options was to crawl away, but to where? There could be a hundred foot drop, two inches in any direction.

"Not in the mood to talk?" he asked. The flames joined in the middle and now Val saw his face. He was a young man, wearing something she recognised instantly. He had a cloak like her mother's.

"I don't want to hurt you!" she called out. What else could she say - 'please, turn on the light?' She couldn't imagine him doing that.

His expression changed and she saw something that gave her hope; she'd confused him. "Then I pray you can forgive me." He raised one of his fire balls and aimed. Before she had time to call out again it was flying towards her. As it travelled, Val could see its reflection on the surface she was lying on. It was like a sea of black glass. The ball passed just inches from her head, singeing her hair. "There you are." He aimed the other ball directly at her. At that moment she realised he couldn't see any better than her. She rolled to the left. If she fell to her death at least she wouldn't be on fire at the same time. She cringed with the fear of falling, but after three rolls she came to a stop still flat on the glass floor. Come on Val, think! He doesn't want to kill you, but he's going to do it anyway. Why? If he was wearing the same cloak as her mother then maybe he knew Wyetta.

"I have an eternity to kill you!" he called out as the glass like surface she was lying on started to vibrate under her. There was nothing to hold onto and as it rumbled up, she was hurled uncontrollably backwards and forwards: two feet to the left, then two feet to the right. Then the rumbling got louder and she could feel the surface breaking up under her, splinters flying around her face.

'He's the Pentagram.' The realisation flashed into her head. 'The five pointed star.' Wendy had said it represented the elements: fire, earth, air, water and spirit. So this guy had the same powers as her, and clearly wanted to kill her with an earthquake. Val flipped over, slamming her axe hard into the surface, sparks flying into her eyes as the metal bit into the glass. She gripped the handle with all her strength while her aggressor continued to try and vibrate her to death.

"How's it going over there?" he shouted over the cracking sounds.

As her body slammed again on to the ground, she only just managed to maintain her grip on her axe. She knew she had to take a risk. He had the same style of cloak as her mother; it was the only lead she had and without her powers, talking was her only weapon. "I'm Wyetta's daughter!" she shouted over the cracking glass. Abruptly, as if the ground had listened to her, it stopped moving and there was moment of silence.

"Liar!" he yelled back. And then, from above, a torrent of freezing water smashed into her, propelling her across the floor and tossing the axe into the darkness. She gasped for breath, soaked from head to toe, trying to find some purchase on the glass.

"I'm not. My name's Val and I'm from the future. I'm the daughter of Gabriel, the Starman, and Wyetta, the Moon Mother. You have to believe me."

He clearly didn't. A gust of wind lifted her up, her arms and legs flying, unable to control the spinning.

Then it stopped and she knew what was coming next as she plummeted towards the ground. A deep groan escaped her, as her body hit the glass. He was going to kill her, there was no question. Why wouldn't he believe she was Wyetta's daughter? It was ridiculous.

"How dare you use my Priestess's name in vain? Now I will make sure you suffer, as I am; never seeing the light of day, or her, ever again, and never to escape this infernal prison."

Had he just called Wyetta his Priestess? So, was he was from the coven? Come on Val, think! Then remembered something. "Sorreoreoe," she screamed. 'No, that wasn't it'. What had her mother said when she was looking for Daisy? It was a call to find a sister witch.

"Are you ready to die?"

Val saw the flames again. "Sorry ad me." No, it still felt wrong. Then she heard her mother's words. "Sorores ad me!" she called out in vain. "Sorores ad me!" she cried, pleading, three times over. The words seemed to have no effect. She wrapped her arms around her head, trying to protect herself from another assault.

There was silence. Val lay on the ground, her heart pounding and everything ached from the drop. She wondered if she had broken any bones. Then a voice made her raise her head. "You really are Wyetta's daughter?"

She scrambled back, blind with in perpetual darkness and terrified. He was so close, but she still couldn't see him. "I am. My name is Val, please believe me." She spoke into the void.

A flame lit in front of her face and there he was. He seemed younger now they were so close. His dark eyes observed her. "How are you possible? When I was taken Wyetta was not with child. Have I been here that long?" He pulled back the hood of his cloak to reveal a mess of dark black hair.

"It's a long story, but she's pregnant right now, with me to be exact. I'm trapped here looking for Brigit the Writer. I have to free her because someone's kidnapped Wyetta. Brigit's the only way I can get her back, free the witches and the children, then return to my time. Did I tell you I'm from the future?"

He reached his fire-free hand out to her. "Goodness me."

"Yes, my sentiments exactly." She smiled at him through the amber glow.

"I'm Kez and I will help you free Brigit."

Val winced as he pulled her up. "Thanks, glad to have you on board. We're going to work great together. We have your fire power and all your other gifts. You can definitely fight." She complimented him, rubbing her sore back. "Let's go."

"No, you don't understand. I can't come with you. You must go alone," he told her.

Val frowned. "So how exactly are you going to help me?"

He took her hand and started to lead her through the darkness. "I can allow you safe passage."

Val shuffled behind him, like someone who'd just broken both their legs. Being in complete darkness all the time was making her feel unwell. "How? And why aren't you coming with me?"

He stopped. "Because the moment I let you pass to the next trial, the Lady will take away my spirit."

Val shook her head. "Sorry, that's not an option." She didn't know much about magic, but the idea of losing your spirit seemed a terrible thing. "Let's look for another option. You can't live without a spirit. Surely it's not possible."

He took both her arms, determination filling his words. "Daughter of Wyetta, I have been destined for eternal sleep since the day they captured me in this cursed trial. There is no escape for me. They told me when I arrived that if I failed to guard the darkness they would remove my spirit, and I have fought all this time because I had a reason to live. Yet I have learnt that even when I win I continue here. In my desperation and insanity I thought I might eventually escape." He pulled her closer. "But you, you are the daughter of Wyetta, and you have reached me. I believe you can make it through to Brigit and save her and the others. Do you believe you can?"

"I think so, but we should maybe take a few moments to think about our options." She tried again.

"No, there's no time." He put pressure on her arms. "You will survive, and then you have to do something for me. I came to the fortress looking for my little sister. I was trying to free her when the Sora trapped me in here."

"I've seen the children, Kez."

"Good, then she will still be here." Val noted a glimmer of hopefulness in his voice. "I know of Brigit's power and I have loved your mother, Wyetta, as my mother. I will give you access to the next trial, but you must promise me you will save my sister, free her from this place or die trying. Do you promise?"

"Of course I will, but there has to be another way out of here. No one has to lose their spirit. I bet there's a backdoor; they always have them. And I have very powerful friends here... well, outside. We can do this together." She could feel herself becoming tense with the sense that something bad was going to happen. She strained to watch as Kez bent down. He rose, her axe in his hand.

"You will need this. You're not out of trouble yet." He turned the axe's handle towards her. "Remember this, Val, my sister's name is Claudia and she's gifted with the power of lootus."

"Lootus?" she asked, taking the axe.

"Yes. You may call it hope. Although she's too young to be initiated, one day she will help many people see the truth of their inner strength. It's her destiny."

"I'll save her. We'll save her! How does that sound?" she pleaded. "I can save us all. They can't stop you coming with me." Val reached out for Kez's arm. She gripped it with a trembling hand, but in her heart she already knew there was no stopping him.

"Val, have you not learnt that a witch's soul lives forever?" He stepped towards her and she nodded. "Save Claudia. Tell her I tried my best to get back to her, that I was brave till the end and I never gave up trying." He wrapped Val in an embrace.

She could feel his heartbeat through her uniform. "Please, Kez, help me find another way," she whispered as the tears began to roll down her face. "Please don't."

"Surra," he whispered. Val grabbed him as he started to go weak in her arms.

"Please God, no." She wept as she felt his heart slowing. His body started to sag and she couldn't hold his weight. They both sank to the floor; the flame in his hand that had illuminated their faces faded. She leant over his chest and sobbed, her face pushed into his cloak. She couldn't do this anymore. No one should lose their spirit for someone else. But she knew he hadn't done it for her: he'd done it for Claudia. "I'll save her, I promise. Then I'm coming back for you," she whispered.

After a few moments, Val noticed that nothing in her surroundings had changed. They were still in the dark. Where was the light? Where was the way out? So he'd done this for nothing. "You have to give me light!" she screamed into the darkness just as a blunt object struck her across the head and she was rendered unconscious.

CHAPTER 18

The Assault

Wendy's heart pounded as she ran with Boden and Gabriel. They'd cloaked her with invisibility so they could enter the fortress through the side gate. It wasn't possible to cloak them all so the others had been sent with Hadwyn into the sewer. Zac had openly complained about that, saying he should have gone with her for Val, but they all knew he would have been as useful as a piece of wet lettuce. The plan was to save the children and the witches, and her job was to reveal the Sora so they could be disabled, in the hope it would allow them to find Val, if she was still alive. Boden still had no signal for her.

"Where now?" Gabriel asked. Wendy pointed towards the entrance to the trial. "I'm guessing the Sora are somewhere around this area here?"

Boden nodded. "I agree. I also sensed a malevolent presence here when I followed Val."

"I presume that's why no one is coming closer. If we start a fire under the actual entrance we should be able to flush them out, and we'll have more time for the fire to take hold."

Gabriel grabbed her unexpectedly, shoving her against a wall as a large group of heavily-armed soldiers marched in their direction. As the last rank passed, he removed his arm from her flattened body and apologised. "Sorry, but it was necessary."

Wendy wheezed, flushing red. "It's fine."

"Boden, I need to find out where they're going. It's too large a number to ignore. I'll follow them, they may lead me to Val. Wendy, as agreed, burn this place to the ground," he instructed.

Boden bowed. "Be safe." Gabriel patted his arm and was off running in the direction of the marching soldiers.

As they passed the witches, still firmly attached to the carts, Wendy wanted to scream in anger and disgust. All her life she'd known about the witch trials of 1645, and how so many innocent men, woman and children had been murdered, but to be here now and see them strapped down like animals was too much to stomach.

Boden caught her attention, showing her the screen of his Dellatrax. "They're inside the fortress," he enthused. Thankfully, Hadwyn, Gabriel and Boden could still communicate, unlike Zac, who was now the trusted weatherman. They moved under the arch as Gabriel had instructed. The entrance to the trial was gone, replaced by a solid wall that definitely hadn't been there before. How could a wall just appear? She reached out, putting her hand against its cold, rough surface. "May courage, honour and wisdom guide you to justice, Val, and back to us."

"Are you ready?" Boden asked.

"Yes." She pulled a small blue flower out of her pocket.

Boden frowned, his huge frame leaning over it. "You are going to start a great fire with this?"

"Uhuh." She lifted it up for him to see. "It's a forget-me-not, a symbol of remembrance for all the tortured witches."

Boden tilted his head. "And this will help us how?"

Wendy took the flower and crushed it in her palm whispering into the broken petals, "Let the fire now be free; bring the spirit of the witches back to me." A spark lit in the middle of the crushed petals, at first barely visible. The broken petals jumped into life on Wendy's hand and the spark rose until it was floating in mid-air. Wendy gently blew on it, then its tiny form lifted towards the ceiling.

"I am concerned that this will be of little use. I believe Gabriel's order was to burn the place down." Boden was still frowning as the spark reached the upper limit. Then it held in place and, after a moment, started to grow, spreading like a fiery weed, reaching its tendrils out, further and further.

Wendy smiled at Boden, who was mesmerized. "What were you saying?"

"I wish to have some of this forget-me-not." He grinned back at her.

She patted his arm. "Maybe, one day. Now let's go get the others."

*

Jason slipped in behind Hadwyn, their entrance into the fortress so far undetected. However, there was now a good chance they would be discovered, simply because they all now reeked of excrement. Entering through the sewer had been a good plan, but the rats and, what he could only imagine were random body parts and other indescribably gruesome things floating in the water, had caused Fran to vomit several times. She had definitely won Hadwyn's respect by simply smiling and carrying on.

They surfaced through a large iron grate in what Jason recognised as the wall furthest from the entrance to the fortress. He pointed out the area where the children were being held. Belinda found seeing the witches in the courtyard in such dishevelment most distressing, and Zac awkwardly placed an arm around her, in a clumsy attempt at support.

Luckily, Hadwyn had advised they all carry the cloaks they had taken from the village, tied to their waists in bundles. The warmth they now gave them was much appreciated.

They'd started to move forward when Hadwyn suddenly held his hand in a closed-fist level with his temple, bringing them to an abrupt stop. He pointed ahead to where a group of soldiers was chatting loudly. He signalled for them to lower themselves to the ground. "Jason, you come with me. Zac, go with Brigit and Fran to the witches. They will need you to be as brave as a Hunter can be, to free them." He squeezed Zac's shoulder firmly.

"I will make my Guard proud."

"I'm sure you will," he agreed. "We will deal with the soldiers."

This was it; it was time for them to separate. "Fran." Jason grabbed at her hand as she turned to follow Brigit. Her eyes moved longingly up his face. "Survive." His voice choked. He wouldn't let anyone else leave without knowing how he felt.

She gave him a sweet smile, placing her hands on his chest. "I will. I'd kiss you, but I just chucked, so you'll have to survive to take me home so I can brush my teeth. Plus you smell really bad."

Jason ignored her request and pulled her close, kissing her cheek. "I will take you home, I promise."

"We need to go," Zac interrupted.

Fran turned to leave and Jason could see the tears in her eyes. He'd known her long enough to know the joking and confident exterior was all a front, she was as scared as he was. And who wouldn't be scared right now? He would have preferred her to be with the skilled Hadwyn rather than the non-fighting, Zac, but they had a big job ahead of them and Hadwyn was the only one crazy enough to attempt it, and *he* was clearly the only one stupid enough to follow. "Ok, let's go deal with some soldiers." He glanced back to see the other three making their way towards the witches in the centre, mingling as he, Wendy and Val had, amongst the horses and abandoned carts.

Suddenly, calls of "FIRE! FIRE!" echoed around through the court yard. "Wendy's done her part," he said.

"Yes, it's time." Hadwyn agreed, a disturbing twinkle in his eye, clearly enjoying himself. Pulling a gun from his uniform, he offered it to Jason. "Here, this is my backup, but be aware, once you pull the trigger, you will never want to use a silly sword again."

Jason shook his head. "No thanks. Dad's number one rule was no guns." He showed Hadwyn his fists. "I think these will have to be enough in 1645."

Hadwyn frowned. "I wish I had met this 'Dad'. He sounds strange, but I respect that."

As the calls bellowed back and forth across the fortress, the flames and smoke became visible to them all. Wendy really had gone to town. Jason followed Hadwyn closely as they sprinted around the corner catching the unsuspecting soldiers completely by surprise. Hadwyn smashed the first to approach him with the butt of his gun. Jason grabbed the next one and it was a straight forward knock-out.

Hadwyn moved through the group with brutal efficiency. "Where are the younglings?" he called as he stunned two more soldiers point blank.

"There," Jason pointed and they crashed towards the entrance to the underground cells, obliterating anything standing in their way. The fire had caused chaos, just as they'd hoped. Everyone should be free in no time. Then the only problem would be getting Val out.

Jason fought with all his might. He'd never been outnumbered in this way before. In the training Shane had insisted he had as a youngster, it was always in controlled environments, but this was pure adrenaline driven and the danger was very real. He was fighting for his, and the lives of what was left of his family: the only people he truly cared about.

Glancing across at his companion, he saw that Hadwyn was unstoppable. He realised why Boden tolerated Hadwyn's macabre enthusiasm for battle. He was utterly ferocious, tearing through the soldiers with no fear. Although his size was imposing, he moved with an easy speed through the bodies. They cleared the opposition and had almost reached the children, but he was very aware that reinforcements could arrive at any moment. Turning the corner, they were faced by a passage heading underground. Jason sprinted down the steps to the main set of heavy metal bars separating them from all the cells. He grabbed them with both hands, pulling hard but they were locked. The children were screaming and crying, distressed already by the oncoming attack and threat of an unknown fire. Tiny hands reached out, pleading with Jason to free them. "Can you...," he yelled over the noise, but before he had time to finish his sentence, Hadwyn was blasting at the bars. Three, four, five times he fired, sparks flew around them, but nothing happened. Then Jason spotted a young woman waving her arms frantically.

"Stop!" she hollered at them.

Jason grabbed Hadwyn's gun, to stop him firing again, then called to the girl, "How do we get you out?"

She pulled her body to the bars of her cell, her matted hair falling around her eyes, her nails covered in dry blood. Jason could only imagine from failed attempts at escape. "They're magical. You need the Gatekeeper."

"Who is the Gatekeeper? How will we recognise him?" Hadwyn demanded.

"He's out there." She pointed toward the entrance. "He has a scar on his face and long yellow hair. They call him Durwood."

"We will free you, small people," Hadwyn reassured them before they both turned to head back up the stairs. A clanking sound greeted them and the main cell door that they'd passed through on the way in slammed shut. A soldier stood on the other side, greeting them with a dirt-stained snarl. It was wiped off his face as he realised he was facing the end of Hadwyn's gun. He turned and ran. Unflinching, Hadwyn aimed and fired.

Jason grabbed the bars, shaking them with all his strength. "Damn!" he yelled. The children's hysterical cries were ringing all around them and panic was spreading, the smell of burning beginning to permeate the cells. "We're trapped. What are we going to do?" Jason demanded.

Hadwyn tapped on his Dellatrax then leaned his back casually against the wall. "We wait. Boden knows I'm here. He will come."

Jason threw his arms into the air. "That's it? That's your plan? Wait?" He paced around him like a caged animal, mumbling. "They're going to come and shoot us!"

Hadwyn watched him. "Please relax, Jason. When you're trapped you must not waste the energy you will need to escape. Stop moving. Maybe you should sit." He pointed to the ground.

"I can't sit," Jason moaned.

Hadwyn calmly aimed his gun at Jason, its cold metal resting on his nose. "Sit! Your spinning is unpleasant to me." He flicked the butt of the gun downwards, the whizzing sound of energy building up in the barrel a stark reminder to Jason of how painful its shot was. He plopped onto the ground. Being shot once by Hadwyn was once too many times in his opinion.

*

"Do you think it's enough?" Wendy asked as she darted towards the carts following Boden.

"I am sure your fire will smoke them out." He directed her towards one of the carts and she crawled underneath as the soldiers attacked.

"BEHIND YOU!" she screamed as a large figure seemed to appear like a picture book apparition over

Boden's shoulder. Instantly his bow was out, glowing with energy. He shifted, blocking the sword that was smashing down towards his head with killer force. Wendy crawled forward grabbing the attacking soldier's leg as Boden knocked him over with a swift kick to the chest, stunning him where he lay on the ground.

"Thank you." He acknowledged her, then his attention was drawn skyward. "I sense the nuns are coming."

Wendy scrabbled into the centre of the carts among the captive witches and saw the spreading panic. As the flames consumed the roofs, spreading an amber glow over the fortress she spotted him. "Zac!" she called out. His head bobbed between the women, looking for the source of her voice. Then she saw him, and her mum and Fran holding hands behind him. Belinda gave her a wave and made her way to the centre of the carts to join her, wrapping Wendy in her arms. "Impressive fire!" she complimented her.

"You smell terrible!" Wendy kissed her cheek quickly then gently pushed her away.

"Thank you," Belinda shrugged. "Let's focus. It's time to set the witches free. How long do you think it will take to flush out the Sora?"

They didn't have to wait. In a deafening crash and splintering of burning wood, a nearby roof exploded, shattering into a thousand pieces and showering them all with hot soot and embers. "Not as long as I'd hoped," Wendy groaned.

Belinda and the others watched in horror as the four nuns floated out of the hole they'd created, chanting loudly.

"Wow, Val was right! They are some scary looking nuns," Fran said, revolted by the vision.

"They can fly!" Wendy gasped.

"Look at their lips, Daughter. We need to shut them up. There are several types of magic: some are seasonal, some are elemental and some are vibrational. That means that they are using the vibration of the atoms in the ether to fly, but also to contain Brigit's powers and stop anyone reaching her. It's like a barrier made by their voices breaking up and joining the air."

Zac nodded. "I understand what you are implying, but how do we stop them creating this barrier?"

"We stop them chanting," Belinda responded with resolve.

With the appearance of the Sora, the soldiers that had been trying to overwhelm Boden had begun pulling back and he had the opportunity to join the others. As he entered the circle of carts, he began firing at the four floating nightmares, but each arrow was effortlessly shattered to dust by their shrill, screeching chants.

"Do quickly what you need to do to stop these things," he ordered.

Belinda was frantically pulling herbs and stones from her cloak pockets when Zac interrupted. "We have a problem."

Wendy stared at him. "Seriously stating the obvious, Zac. We all know we're under attack."

"No." He shook his head. "It's more than that."

"Tell us," Belinda demanded, throwing four petrified frog's leg's on the ground.

"I see it will rain in exactly three minutes and seven seconds." He showed them his screen.

Wendy looked at the dots on his watch, then the spreading fire, which had flushed the Sora out and was keeping the majority of the soldiers busy. "How bad?"

"Bad enough," he responded.

"Mum, what do we do now?" Wendy asked.

"We need to free the witches fast. An unravelling spell should work for the chains." She handed Wendy a bunch of dried herbs.

Boden barged through, walking backwards into the middle of the group, firing repeatedly at the Sora who were nearly on top of them. "You must work alone. Hadwyn and Jason have been captured." He waved his Dellatrax.

Fran gasped. "Are they ok?"

"They are well, but I must go and assist them. I will draw these hags away. Do your magic." He moved past them leading the Sora, who were drawn to him, to the edge of the carts.

Zac watched as Boden leapt the links holding two carts together. The Sora stayed with him like bees attracted to a potent flower. "I have observed something, Belinda." He tapped on her arm.

"Wait." she raised a finger to silence him as she sprinkled the crushed flowers onto a circle Wendy had created in the wet mud. "Abrumpat." She stepped on a dried frog's leg and it snapped. "Abrumpat. Abrumpat," She repeated with another two and then paused, waiting for a sign that the witches were free. Instead the women started to scream out in sudden agony. In horror Belinda observed that the shackles that held them were glowing lava red. "Para! Para!" she shouted at the top of her voice and the helpless witches' screams changed to moans of relief.

"It's not working, Mum." Wendy shook her head. "Something's blocking you, twisting your magic."

"May I speak now?" Zac interrupted a second time.

"Quickly." Belinda said, kicking the remains of her failed spell into the mud in frustration.

"I believe the formation of the Sora gives us vital information we may have been missing. They are moving as one, a collective, a hive. This could be important. Pack formations like this normally indicate a leader. Someone the others are protecting. Maybe they aren't our main adversary at all."

"Elaborate?" Belinda encouraged, as they left the failed magical concoction on the ground and crawled under one of the carts.

"On earth, the lion stays at home while the lionesses kill. I believe there is something stronger than them here, and we are going to have to deal with *it* in order to defeat the Sora and save Val."

Wendy asked, "So what you're saying is that there's a bigger baddy than the nuns, and we can't win until we find it, which we didn't plan for?"

He nodded.

"Wait, let me just add to that; Boden has gone running off to save Jason and Hadwyn, who are now captured. Gabriel went after a load of soldiers and hasn't returned, and we don't know how to free Val. We don't even know where she actually is." Wendy's voice rose as she realised how desperate their situation was.

"Yes, and it will now rain in exactly one minute and seventeen seconds, extinguishing the fire that is keeping so many busy," he added.

Wendy turned to her mum and Fran. "Any ideas?"

"We need to find out who's in charge fast," Fran insisted. "We need to make them reveal themselves, but how? If they're more powerful than the Sora, how do we do that?"

Wendy agreed. "Sam taught me that in the face of an unseen adversary, you need to show your power, real power, something they haven't shown you. He told me most criminals are naturally drawn to show-off their strengths and will reveal themselves to face the competition, irrelevant of the risk. That's why they get caught. Criminals are show offs. But without Val and her powers, what can we do?"

Suddenly, Zac darted towards the stone table at the centre of the carts. "Zac!" Belinda called out, but he wasn't listening, or didn't choose to listen.

Leaping onto the table he raised his hands above his head. "Halt! Halt!" he shouted. "Look at me!" he shouted at the top of his voice. It was the oddest thing. Zac just stood there in full view.

Wendy held her breath. What was he thinking? "Mum, he's gone mad."

Belinda pulled a small sprig of pink flowers out of her pocket. "Just wait." She raised a hand. "He's been around a couple of hundred years; he may just have an idea. Let's hope whoever stopped my spell, was only working on the shackles," she said as she mumbled into the petals. "Stop this violence; help bring Zac silence." Blowing the petals into the atmosphere as he called out again, she smiled as an odd hush came over the soldiers left trying to extinguish the fire.

A skinny, red-headed soldier made his way to the outer edge of the carts. "What are you doing idiot?" he cried. "Do you want to die?" he aimed a flintlock pistol directly at Zac.

"Do you?" he called back, pointing at the soldier as more of his companions gathered round.

The soldier looked confused at his response. "No," he grumbled miserably.

"Then be silent," Zac ordered, raising his hands. "I am the most powerful witch that has ever lived and I can change the way the ground beneath your feet turns." He waved his hands in circles over his head. "I can make this place you call England, flood with the anger of the Gods, so a little respect will go a long way." He raised an eyebrow at the soldier who quickly lowered his pistol.

Zac noticed a disturbance in the background and then a woman's voice rang out. "Who are you?"

He looked around, pausing as he spotted her. Expanding his chest, growing in stature he introduced himself. "I am the great God, Zac Efron." From under the cart the others could see the woman approaching from the left. Lifting her heavy, gilded gown she casually made her way down some steps, which swept down from a small wooden door, well away from where Wendy had lit the fire.

"Really, Zac Efron, and what exactly are you the God of?" she jeered as she walked towards the cart. The soldiers closed in, careful not to get too close to her. "The God of the skies," he goaded her. "Can you make the heavens cry?"

Her expression changed to one of intrigue, before she let out a little laugh. "Such power would be impossible. No one controls Mother Nature in such a way." She reached the carts. "Show me this power so I may see it for myself," she demanded. "And when you can't, my men will kill you and post your body parts on pikes around my fortress."

Zac made eye contact with Wendy, and nodded. She suddenly realised what he was trying to do. She knew he had drawn out the pack leader, but what to do with her? Wendy whispered to her mum. "How can we help him?"

"Wait." Belinda was almost grinning. "He has a plan."

Zac raised his arms up towards the sky. "Oh weak God of the skies, bow down before me and cry tears of fear!"

Everyone watching shifted their gaze to the clouds. It was like a miracle. As the last word escaped his lips, the drops began to fall, like splashes of victory. Zac stood, allowing the rain to land on his closed eyes, as they all gasped. Within moments the rain was pounding down on his upturned face. It was as if he had turned on the deluge. It was genius.

Suddenly there was a huge crack of thunder; it couldn't have been more imposing. "Impressive." The woman who was now standing by Zac, seemed most excited. She reached out her hand and Zac took it, helping her onto the table. "I am overwhelmed. You have put out the fire that was ravaging my fortress." Her sapphire blue eyes now looked deep into his. "Zac Efron you are a God."

"And who are you?" he asked, keeping his voice calm and wrapping his arm around her waist to stop her from falling.

"I am Lady Eleanor Troughton."

Wendy gasped out loud. "Mum, she said Troughton. That's Delta name!"

*

Boden had been in many battles, but these malevolent beings were destroying his arrows before he could even get to them. He was following the signal Hadwyn had sent him across the fortress, knowing his companion's capture would be infuriating him.

"Hadwyn!" he called, leaping over several unconscious soldiers and spinning athletically around the stone corner of the entrance to the cells, to find his friend standing waiting patiently with Jason sitting on the ground at his feet, both imprisoned behind a cell door. He frowned. "What are you doing? We have no time to play with these people."

"Magic," Hadwyn responded shooting at the cell lock.

Boden covered his eyes against the exploding cascade of sparks. When they had died away he immediately saw that the shot had had absolutely no effect on the metal. "So brother, you're trapped, again, just like the time on…"

Hadwyn raised a hand. "I don't need a reminder," he grumbled. He pointed to the girl he'd befriended. "This youngling says a yellow haired man with a scar is the Gatekeeper. Find him and release us."

Boden heard the screeching of the Sora closing in on them. "I am a little occupied at this moment." He leaned back, pulling back his bow, and fired a warning shot through the doorway. "Any clues on how to defeat flying creatures with no eyes?" he called to the children who were gathering at their doors.

"So your attempt to burn them failed." Hadwyn shook his head in disapproval.

Boden snorted a laugh. "You are in no position to criticise as you have plainly allowed yourself to be captured."

Jason interrupted their bickering. "Wendy and the others know how to do magic. Can't you go back and get them?"

"They have enough to do trying to free the witches." Boden fired two more ineffective shots. "Hadwyn, I have observed that these creatures they call nuns seem to need one another to function, very much like the Grindary. I can't get close enough to split them up." He fired again at the creatures, then at a soldier who'd been stupid enough to stray into his path out of misguided bravery.

"What's happening when you shoot at them?" Jason asked. "I've never seen you miss."

"The arrows disintegrate before they reach them. This vibration magic they seem to be using breaks up anything in its path, and at this moment it's allowing them to hover over us." Boden glanced out once again. "They're here."

Hadwyn lifted his gun as Boden backed towards the cell bars. As soon as the Sora entered, Hadwyn began firing on them. Two of them turned in unison, their hollow sockets facing the men. Their dry lips mumbling in anger, they vaporised the bullets. Boden fired his bow, but knew he stood little chance against them. Their constant chanting mixed with the children's screams of fear was deafening. The Sora were advancing steadily and it was clear that Boden couldn't possibly defend himself against them. The nuns had now surrounded him, their chanting causing his huge frame to curl into an agonised ball on the ground, his hands thrust over his ears trying desperately to block them out.

Hadwyn acknowledged that his shots were in vain. "Boden, fight!" he called out to his companion. Then he turned his gaze onto the nearest nun. "I'll kill you all!" he bellowed, desperately shaking the bars with all his strength. The Sora continued, oblivious to his threats, directing their chanting at Boden. Jason watched helplessly as blood oozed through the gaps in Boden's fingers.

Then, all of a sudden, Hadwyn felt static building in the air. The hairs on his arms were rising; it felt like a thunder storm was coming. The energy grew rapidly into a surge of electricity, which made their bodies tingle. The Sora closest to Boden unexpectedly yelped in pain, sounding like a wounded animal. Then beams of pure white light emanated from her eye sockets. It was as if someone had switched on a light inside her head. Her mouth gaped open, revealing several rows of rotten teeth and a light shot out through them aiming directly at him. The other three Sora instantly became disorientated, unable to continue without the fourth. Hadwyn's centuries of training made him grasp the opportunity. Three shots rang out and the remaining Sora dropped to the ground, stunned into submission. The fourth reeled in pain, then became still. Then a light as bright as the sun exploded around them. Forcing his hands over his eyes, Hadwyn waited. Sensing the retreat of the light he looked up and the Sora were nowhere to be seen.

Jason looked around for the cause of the explosion, of light, expecting to find Wendy, but it was someone else who had come to their rescue. "Sam!" he called out in relief.

CHAPTER 19

Illusionist

The pain in the back of Val's head was excruciating. Why would someone whack her like that? She could actually feel the lump that was forming from the stretching of her scalp. Then suddenly it dawned on her that she could see. There was light, but no Kez. She reached up tentatively to find a damp piece of cloth stuck to her head, blood and hair matted around it. Turning, she groaned with the pain. In her line of sight, an elderly, bearded man was kneeling next to a narrow stream. Leaning on his wooden staff, he pulled himself up. Val watched as he walked over to her with a pottery cup in his hand. He was wearing a black robe, which shimmered as he walked. His wispy white beard reached his waist.

"Hello." He smiled warmly, his face full of kindness.

"Are you the person who knocked me out?" she asked, checking his stick for visible traces of blood and hair.

"Goodness me, no. I wouldn't do something like that." He offered the cup to Val. She took just a small sip. She was very thirsty and this water tasted... well, like water.

Very gently he removed the bandage. She winced.

"So, who are you and where is Kez?" The words caught painfully in her throat.

"I don't know anyone called Kez and you, young lady, are in my garden," he said shuffling away.

Val looked around. He seemed to be telling the truth; she was in a garden. Whether it was his or not was another matter. Her mind switched to the reason she was there, searching her memory for the next symbols in the trial. It was the one after the star. It had been a stick with what looked like snakes wrapped around it. As she sipped the water, she observed the man picking what she surmised was some form of herb. His manner was gentle and he seemed to speak to the plants before he pulled them out, as if guilty for taking their lives. The symbol was the one she had recognised. "Are you Moses?" she asked tentatively.

He paused, looking directly at her. "What, THE Moses?"

"Yes." She nodded.

He then let out a hearty guffaw. "Goodness me, no!" He exclaimed, placing the herbs into a pot at her feet and heading off again. Val watched him. He didn't venture far, but slowly collected some firewood, then once again returned and set it down near her. "Are you cold?" he enquired.

She thought for a moment. "I'm not sure."

He seemed pleased with this response and went off to collect some larger pieces of wood. "Call me if you want anything," he told her.

"Ok." He seemed like a nice man. She knew someone with a white beard. She could see him in her mind, but his name eluded her. She sipped again from the cup. It tasted so nice; she thought it was actually the nicest water she had ever drunk. Glancing down, she observed her clothes. They were odd, all black and clingy. Why did she wear this stuff? She took another sip.

The man came back and knelt, with a groan of old age, to light the fire. "So, what's your name?" he asked.

Her head felt so fuzzy, like the snow on a TV screen. "I don't know... Do you?" Who was she, and why was she here?

"I think I will call you Edith; seems like a nice name." He tapped her cup with his staff. "Drink up," he insisted.

"I'm Edith?" He nodded and smiled warmly. "Ok." She smiled back, a sense of peace washing over her. This place was nice. She sipped again. The flowers smelt so wonderful. She could spend her life here with no worries. She was sure she'd had worries before, but now they were all gone and in their place was a warm blanket of nothingness.

"Edith, would you like me to light a fire?"

"Would I?"

"Yes, you would." Laughing heartily, the bearded man sat and poured another drink as he set the fire.

Her head was beginning to ache. She was Edith, if she remembered correctly, and she liked being here. They were going to pick some mushrooms after another drink. "I'm happy here aren't I?" He nodded as the flames started to rise and the smell of burning oaky wood filled her nostrils.

"Val..." She heard a distant voice calling. Her ears pricked up to the unfamiliar voice invading their perfect little sanctuary. She pulled her hair back, tying it loosely with a chain made of some sweetly scented flowers. She didn't know what they were called, just that they looked like sunshine with clouds around the edges. "Val!" This time it was louder, harsher, more urgent and her head twitched enough to draw the attention of her friend.

"Edith, is everything all right?" His face seemed to be distorted. She scrunched her eyes shut, then opened them again. "Edith." His voice seemed deeper, throatier.

"I feel a little odd. Maybe a walk would help." She stood and on the edge of her line-of-sight she saw a small group of trees shimmering. It was both annoying and distracting to her. Why was this happening? They had been so settled, yet now something appeared to be calling to her. The trees continued to change shades, from bright greens and warm ochre's to a dirty black with splashes of grey.

"Edith, you must have another drink and stay right here!" he ordered, annoyance growing in his voice.

"Just a minute." She walked away, thinking how sick of drinking she was. It made her want to wee. Did he have any idea how hard it was getting this outfit up and down? Her instinct was driving her now. Then, as if by magic, the silhouette of a woman appeared in the distance, between the shimmering trees. As she moved forward, feeling suddenly uneasy, she realised that the woman was some sort of captive. Her hands were strapped to the ground inside aged metal boxes, with heavy chains laid across on her back, weighing her down. She wore a soiled black cloak and, as she moved closer to the prisoner, it became very apparent that the woman was heavily pregnant.

As she got nearer to her, it was as if someone had taken a sword and cut a clear tear in the fabric of the woods, like a painting that had been slashed down the middle, and the gash was growing by the second.

"Edith!" the sharpness of the request made her spin round in surprise. What she saw made her gasp in horror and she only just managed to hold down the instant flux of vomit that surged up her throat. The thing she had learnt to recognise as her friend, the man who resembled Moses, was now standing just feet away. His face mutated before her horrified eyes, becoming disfigured beyond recognition as a putrid stench of rotting flesh washed over her. His bulging head had a stream of buttery puss dripping from one of his ears, and his body was no longer covered in his sparkling robe, but was naked, except for a beige cloth hanging around his waist.

"What are you?!" she screamed, stumbling backwards.

It was obvious from his reaction that he realised she was seeing his true appearance and he screamed in anger, then whispered something to the staff in his hand. He held it out in front of him and it started to change, transforming in his grasp into something she recognised all too well: a snake, and a very large one at that.

"Val!" She heard the name again. It felt different this time, familiar, like home. She looked towards the woman who had now managed to lift her head. Her face was bruised and beaten, her bottom lip bloodied.

Val turned back to face the revolting creature that was now setting a large black, writhing snake down on the ground. The woodlands faded into darkness and filth wherever the snake touched on its twisted journey through the undergrowth towards her. Her head was still fuzzy. What should she do? She was so scared; she didn't know how to stop a snake. She crouched low, curling up into a ball and waited for the end to come.

"Edith! Come back to me and it will all be alright." The creature's voice bubbled horribly in its throat. It held out a large, crooked hand, reaching out for her.

"Val, you must remember," the woman's voice cried out to her.

She lifted her eyes in the woman's direction. As the two worlds continued to merge and the tear moved around her, the ground under her feet was not lush green grass anymore, but dirty grey flagstones. Without moving, she had shifted to the woman's side, and the woodland's constant disintegration was making it easier to see that they were actually all in the same space, that this was all just an elaborate illusion.

"Val, come here." The woman spoke again and, strangly, she felt like she belonged with this person. She'd called her Val, it sounded so odd, but genuine. She scrambled frantically over the cool, hard floor towards the cloaked woman. "Val," she whispered to herself, feeling the familiarity of the name.

"Yes, that's you. He's not real, Val. His aim was to make you believe, to have faith in him, but he's been drugging you." The woman now had tears of relief welling in her eyes.

She glanced back at the creature. The reality that she'd slipped through to the woman's world was making it very angry. "I gave you a chance!" The creature spat. It drew its deformed head back and cried out, "Kill her!"

The snake now started to move in to the attack, slithering across the ground at greater speed.

"Val, please try to remember who you are." The woman pleaded. "Remember the Sora, the Prison, Alchany, your home... Sam. Do you remember Sam?"

"Sam."

"Yes, Sam. I bet you know him, he's a Judge on Alchany. You're from a prison a long way away. I knew as soon as we met that you were a Guard. Sam brought me here. I'm sure you must know him."

She knew that name. Her body filled with emotion at the mere mention of Sam. Then, in her mind, she saw him; his dark hair, his eyes looking at her, a smile, a touch, a kiss. And then she remembered the nuns walking towards her screaming, 'Witch', and Shane in the water, Kaliyah, Wiflin and then Kez. How could she have forgotten them? Memories came flooding back, her friends and her family. The snake was halfway over the threshold between her and the creature who was now pulling chunks of hair out of its mutilated, blood covered scalp.

She lifted herself up, standing protectively in front of the chained woman. She knew who she was now, and she knew what she had to do. "Hey," she called out. "I'm Val, not Edith. Prison Guard Twenty-three Thirteen from the planet Alchany and *you* just messed with the wrong girl."

There was a painful moment when the creature stopped its screaming and just glared out of its uneven bulging eyes at her, like she'd shot it through the heart. Its agitation at her recovering memory was visible and, after the initial silent acceptance, very audible. It scrambled over the break in realities that was still growing, uniting the two environments, screaming in its desperation to get at her.

Val looked around. How long had she been here? And where was her axe?

"Val! Run! You must protect yourself!" the woman screamed.

She turned to see Brigit strapped to the floor. "Hello, I've been looking for you," she said, reaching down to pull her sword from her boot. "Back in a second." Extending it she spun and without fear, sprinted at the creature.

She leapt over the oncoming snake, but it lifted its body up to strike at her. Its fangs flew towards her leg as the tip of her weapon struck it on the head. Sparks showered it's body and it fell shuddering to the ground. Her heart pounded, adrenaline rushing into her body as she kept moving towards the being that had taken her memories.

A look of confusion mixed with panic flashed across its grotesque face. It changed direction and started to lollop away from her, bending down to scoop up something, something she couldn't see.

She was on top of him in a blink, her sword above her head ready to switch his lights off with one huge jolt. But the creature stopped dead, something she hadn't been expecting, and as it pivoted towards her she saw a glimmer of what it was holding; her axe. The blade sliced her across her stomach. The sensation as the edge cut through her uniform was odd. She could feel the wound; it was smooth, precise. There was no pain... yet, but shock made her collapse onto all fours. Her hand reached down, blood gushed out hard red over the soft green grass. As she lifted her extended fingers into view, her hand was shaking, the red liquid oozing between her fingers.

"Edith, I told you not to go." The creature leant down next to her, puss dripping out of its ear. "We can try again, if you want to live." The head of the axe was now resting on the ground next to Val's face. "Just place the water on your wound, like before, and your pain and memories will go away."

"I'd rather die," she responded.

He stamped his foot in anger. "I don't want to be alone." He raised the axe above her head ready, she thought, for her execution. "There will be no more talking," he announced, bringing the blade down forcefully. Val only had one chance. She dropped, rolling onto her back, lifting her sword and blocking the blade. The bolt of electricity from her weapon shot through his, throwing the creature backwards. He stumbled, backwards over an embankment. The one which only minutes earlier had been covered in glorious multi-coloured flowers. She watched from the ground as he fell, rolling head over heels, two, three, four times before he came to rest.

She waited a moment in the silence, her hand holding her wound, breathing deeply as the pain started. Knowing she couldn't stay like this forever, that he would be back to finish her off, she crawled to the edge of the bank, trying to think how she would continue to fight when he got back up. However, as she got a full view, she realised that he would no longer be a problem. His body lay motionless, half in and half out of the stream, her axe protruding from his motionless chest. She turned away. It was painful. She hadn't seen death like this before.

"Val." Brigit called to her. She stood holding her stomach as tightly as possible. There seemed to be a lot of blood and, although there was still minimal pain, a feeling of tiredness was starting to wash over her.

Stepping over the motionless snake towards Brigit, she pleaded, "Help me." Holding out her hand she showed Brigit the blood.

"Oh Val, I'm so sorry. You need to escape. Something must be happening in the fortress, for you to have been able to see me. I can only imagine the Sora are dead or wounded."

Val slumped at Brigit's feet. "I need to free you. There's one more symbol. What is it?"

Brigit pointed to the floor in front of her. There, in a stone slab was the circle with the dot in the centre. "It's The Awakening. But forget it, you just need to leave," she commanded.

"What's The Awakening?" Val ignored the order.

"It doesn't matter, please just do as I say."

"No, I'm not leaving without you, after everything I've been through. I need you. A man called Jarrad has taken Wyetta."

Brigit shook her head. "Val, you can save Wyetta. You don't need me."

She shook her head. "Just tell me what The Awakening is and let's get going, before I bleed to death."

Brigit's voice was soft and controlled. "You are a great warrior and you have been warned. If you break this seal to free me, a dark magic will be awakened, power over life and death." She shook her head.

"What do you mean by awakened?"

"When Lady Eleanor put me here, she told me that if someone was skilled enough to free me, then she would need an army to stop that individual. An army to deal with someone like you." Val wanted to laugh; she had no powers at all, and was in the process of bleeding to death. "So her final test in the trial was this seal. To make sure that if someone was insane enough to take the risk of breaking it, after I had warned them of the consequences, a power so dark and commanding would be released that they would be destroyed. That's why you're not going to do it," she insisted.

"Can't you stop them? You're the Writer?"

"If I was free I might be able to channel the seal's power, split it between good and evil, but what good would it do? It's aimed at enhancing magic. Even if I could mutate it, how many people do you have with you with magic powers? You would have to face an army of evil, alone."

Val actually smiled through her pain and dizziness. "At our last count a couple of hundred witches just above our heads." She pointed to the ceiling of the cell.

Brigit tilted her head in question. "What?"

"Above us are approximately a hundred witches tied to carts, and another eighty novice witches are being held in cells."

Brigit suddenly looked more positive. "That could work. I can use them. But it's still risky."

"That's my life. Just hurry, ok."

"Val as the seal breaks I will be released and so will the dark magic." Brigit pushed herself onto her knees.

"Then the witches will get their powers back, yes?" Val asked. Brigit nodded. "All the witches?" she added.

"Yes. I'm ready. Break the seal, we need to get you some help," Brigit said.

Val had one thought. She was a witch. She was about to get her powers back and become the most hunted freak in the galaxy, but the other option was unthinkable.

She knew if she didn't make it out of here, that Brigit was powerful enough to make this right and free Wyetta. She crawled, retrieving a loose slab that was lying on the floor of Brigit's cell and made her way to the concrete seal in the floor. "You ready?" she looked at Brigit who nodded. "Then let's do this." She raised the slab above her head and with the last of her strength, she slammed it down on the seal.

The centre folded in. Val scrambled backwards as a black oozing smoke began to seep out. She glanced back to see Brigit's hands were free of the boxes, and she was scribbling frantically in the ground with her fingers. The smoke was rising around Val's head and choking her. She coughed and tried to crawl to Brigit who looked up momentarily to give Val a nod as she sat back onto her heels. "It's done," she said as Val closed her eyes.

Chapter 20

Brigit

The cold stone floor against her cheek was a welcome relief. She recognised the corridor. It was the place she'd entered to begin the trial. She pulled herself up to see Brigit lying on the floor next to her, her pregnant belly bulging out of her cloak. She crawled over to shake her. "Brigit, we're back," she whispered.

Brigit lifted her head and pulled her hood down. "Then the battle has begun." She rose unsteadily, made awkward by her bulk. Val wanted to join her, but it wasn't going to happen. She really didn't have the strength to move. "Brigit you need to escape. Find the others, they were outside the gate the last time I saw them. Get them back to the woods where the coven is hiding, save Wyetta." Pain ripped through her stomach.

Brigit was now standing. "You said there were a hundred witches. One of them will surely be a healer. Stay still. Conserve your energy." Brigit knelt down next to Val, placing her finger on Val's forehead, she drew what felt to Val like a small swirl. "Sleep," she said, and, as much as Val tried to fight it, she drifted off.

Brigit left the stone corridor and made her way, for the first time in days, into the fresh night air. Pulling her hood up, she made her way across the courtyard. There in the centre, as Val had promised, were approximately a hundred women strapped to carts. There were only a few soldiers outside, which surprised her. What had happened? They seemed exhausted and confused by what looked like the remains of an aggressive fire, but luckily they were too busy to pay her any attention. She walked with small steps through the squelching mud. There must have been a recent downpour as the ground was extremely wet and she slipped several times, wrapping her arms protectively around her bulging stomach.

"Hey," a voice, sharp but not too loud called to her.

She looked around. There was no one other than three soldiers who seemed occupied with guarding a doorway.

"Brigit." The voice called out again. She crouched placing her finger into the wet mud, ready to write. She wouldn't be captured again. However as she lowered herself she spotted three women under the cart. "Are you sister witches of Val?" she started to make a swirling motion with her finger.

"Yes, and you're Brigit. I saw you in a vision," Wendy reassured her.

Brigit allowed her hand to rest. "She needs a healer, she's been wounded." She stood and scanned the women on one of the carts.

"Brigit." One of the women lifted her head, her teeth looking bright in contrast to the black muddy streaks on her face. "Is that you?"

"Yes, Sara." She moved to her side, embracing the woman. "Wyetta's daughter has freed me and you should have your powers again."

The woman flexed her hands. "Fire." She spoke into her palm, but nothing happened. "No, I have nothing."

"I don't understand." Brigit was bemused.

The women under the cart crawled out. "I'm Wendy. This is my mother, Belinda, and friend, Fran. We were trying to find Val. Where is she?"

"I have left her in a slumber. She broke the seal. These witches should have all their powers - I don't understand." She frowned and looked from one cart to the other. "These women are witches, but none seem able to even stand."

"The chains are magical." Sara shook her heavy metal shackles at them.

"Where are the children? Val said there were magical children?" she asked. Wendy pointed towards the building on the other side of the courtyard. Brigit knelt down making a symbol in the mud, paused as if listening, and then she moved quickly away.

"Wait." Wendy followed her. "They're over there, but so are our other friends who are trapped and we've just lost our Hunter, Zac, to Lady Eleanor. I don't know where Val's Dad, Gabriel is, and it's all getting a little confusing. We need to make a plan." She grabbed Brigit's arm.

Brigit's hand was swift. A simple tick on Wendy's hand left her stunned, crying out in pain.

Belinda stepped out to block her way. "Stop!"

"Move!" Brigit ordered.

"No, we've all risked our lives to save you. How dare you hurt my daughter?"

She paused, taking a deep breath. "I need a healer. I'm sorry, but this must not be delayed. I know you are here to help, but you are slowing my progress. I sense there is one over there." She pointed toward the area that held the children. "Come with me, but if you stop me again the consequences will be severe." She stepped around Belinda and kept moving, with the three women now behind her, Wendy rubbing vigorously at her sore hand.

*

Sam helped Boden up, placing a small square of material from his pocket onto his bleeding ear. "Well, I see everything is going to plan." He grinned.

"Which Sam are you?" Boden croaked.

"The one that's not really supposed to be here - yet has the pleasure of saving you once again."

"Oh good! You're the one who's four hundred years more sarcastic." Boden wrapped his arm over Sam's shoulder, leaning on him for support. "Thank you."

They moved away from the place that had seen the Sora's demise. "Can you release us?" Hadwyn called for their attention. "I'm bored." He rattled his gun along the bars idly.

"I can!" A girl's voice called from behind him.

Hadwyn turned to see a young girl. She seemed to be the carer of a few smaller children, who she reassured, before stepping forward. Her aura was glowing the colour of the sun about to set; deep warm reds and oranges. "Well, well, seems we have a new friend." He gave her a friendly look. "And when were you thinking of telling us about this ability to free us?"

She looked down at her palms. "I just got my powers. I didn't have them before, but I know what I can do. My mother told me that one day this would happen - I just didn't expect it to be today." She grinned sweetly.

Hadwyn nodded respectfully. "Then show us, small one, what your inner warrior can do."

The girl moved towards her cell door. She was so slight; lack of food had left her emaciated. Her skin was dark with dirt and her rags were soiled, but the glow around her was transforming her into a divine form and within seconds it mirrored the brightness of the first star in the night sky. Her eyes changed from green to dark brown as she placed her hand onto the cell's lock. Her glow engulfed the bars. There was a tense pause, then they all exhaled with approval as it clicked open. She looked at Hadwyn and smiled. "See."

He mirrored her expression. "Mighty warrior, I think maybe my door will be next." He coaxed her over. "Tell me, my friend, what is your name and where did you and this power come from?"

The girl moved towards Hadwyn and Jason "My name is Rhianna and I am a fifth generation witch from the East. I was taken from my home and brought here by the Lady and my power," she took hold of the lock on Hadwyn's cell, "is to undo dark magic, like my mother before me promised." She glowed bright and as previously, the door clicked open.

Hadwyn looked at the children around them. Something had changed. "How many of you now have powers that you did not have before?" he asked. At the back, in the far corner, they saw a glow and then a small boy stepped forward, engulfed in flames. "Good, good." Hadwyn slapped his hand on Jason's back as their door finally opened.

Jason was first out, wrapping his hands around Sam's shoulders. "We need to get Fran and the others," he insisted.

"Looking for me?"

Jason looked over Sam's shoulder and saw, in the doorway, Wendy, Fran, Belinda and a very pregnant woman. His relief was enormous.

"Brigit." Sam greeted her enthusiastically.

"Sam." She bowed her head respectfully. "I will explain soon, but for now I need him." She pointed behind him.

They all looked around. "Who? And can anyone tell me where Val is?" Sam asked.

She ignored him and marched over to Jason, grabbing his hand. "Val is wounded, and I need the healer! We can speak later."

"No! You're mistaken. Look at the children, they're witches. You must be picking up on someone else's magical abilities." He frowned, pulling away from her.

She pulled up his sleeve, quickly drawing a circle with a dot in the centre onto his arm. Jason dropped to his knees. With a cry of distress, Fran leapt forward, but Sam stopped her. "Wait," he said holding her around the waist. 'Look,' he said softly. Fran watched as the place on Jason's arm where Brigit had drawn her symbol began to glow, softly at first and then more brightly. Jason's eyes closed; he was ashen with the pain.

"You are the healer," Brigit whispered in Jason's ear. "Come, save your friend." She pulled him up.

Jason's arm stopped glowing, but the symbol remained. "Where is she?" he asked, no longer doubting her.

Brigit smiled at him. "We must go to her now." She turned to Sam. "The children have awoken. Val broke the seal to release me, and they are ready to fight. The witches are still prisoners. You must prepare for a great battle. We have released an evil that will take all we have to defeat it. I will take this boy now."

"You can't be seriously letting her take Jason?" Fran complained as he meekly allowed Brigit to lead him away. Wendy and Belinda watched in bewilderment.

"Fran, Brigit is the most powerful being I've ever met in the whole galaxy. Trust me, if she says Jason is a healer, he is, and if she says there's evil on the way, you had better be ready. Now, let's get prepared. Children," Sam addressed the waiting youngsters, "come here and tell us your powers."

*

Val coughed. A warm hand touched her forehead. She opened her eyes once more. The last thing she remembered was having a dream that she'd gone home for tea; her favourite, Hawaiian burger. Her mum had been there to greet her, smelling of home cooking, and her dad had given her a hug, telling her to hold on just a little longer. Now she was back to the harsh reality of pain and the cold stone floor, wet with her blood.

"Val." A voice caught her attention. She opened her eyes as her vision gradually cleared and saw Brigit and then Jason. Her heart filled with joy.

"Hello mate." Her voice was frail and didn't reflect her relief and joy at seeing him.

"Jason has come to heal you," Brigit told her.

She laughed, which caused a painful cough, making her wince in pain. "Seriously? If he has a laptop, possibly!"

"Jason, place your hands on Val," Brigit instructed.

He knelt down beside her. Val started to feel worried. She couldn't be serious. Jason wasn't a witch. He was just Jason, son of Shane the tattoo artist and Elizabeth the psychic witch; map-creating, time-travelling assistant to Sam. As the thought rested in her fuzzy head she felt a shiver rush down her spine. She had awakened *all* the witches' powers. Was Jason really a witch? Was he a healer? Could it be true?

"What should I do?" he asked.

"Remove her pain. See the healing process. This is your power. Let your true abilities take over."

Jason looked at Val, who was slumped against the wall, a pool of blood by her side. He placed his hands on her. "Val."

"Yes, mate?" She nodded unsure what was about to happen. Jason seemed different. He definitely wasn't himself.

"I think this might hurt." His eyes locked onto hers as a ripping sensation pushed her hard against the wall. Her midriff exploded with pain. The flesh across her stomach and under Jason's hands stretched and pulled and intertwined as the damaged layers knitted themselves together. Deep within her something wrenched and twisted before settling. She screamed in agony, unable to stop herself, despite the need for secrecy.

He pulled back, flexing his hands as if they ached, staring at them as though he couldn't quite believe what he had just done. Val slumped limply on the floor panting in pain.

"Oi, you!"

She tilted her head to see three soldiers coming at them fast. 'No!' she thought. 'Not now.' She summoned all her courage against the expected onslaught of pain, then rolled onto her knees before using the wall to push herself upright. To her amazement there was no pain. She could feel the strength returning to her limbs, feel her head clearing.

Jason was still in a state of shock. "What just happened?" he asked.

One of the soldiers pulled a pistol. "You just got a death warrant my friend."

Now Val could feel her powers. They rumbled in the pit of her stomach, moving up, spinning and fizzing through her like live wires exploding onto the surface. Her powers were back. In the blink of an eye she aimed a fire ball at the soldier, her body alight. The next one to approach she threw back down the corridor with a gust of air, his body smashing against the wall and dropping unconscious to the floor. The third stood motionless, jaw hanging as she aimed at him, her body glowing a deep blue, flames skipping up and down her uniform. As he turned to make his escape, Val called out, "Run, and tell the Lady I'm coming!"

CHAPTER 21

Lady Eleanor

Zac had observed Lady Eleanor as she made her way through the corridors, soldiers opening doors as if she were a High Judge, bowing their scruffy heads and removing their hats to reveal their greasy hair.

He'd been waiting patiently for several minutes in a sumptuous dining room while she had talked with her soldiers. Finally she addressed him. "So," she smiled, "you've been a God for how long?" She made it sound as if it was something that had just come upon him one morning.

"Well, I came to this country only a few short days ago." He paused to think. "I realised that on this soil, British soil, I was special." He gave her a feeble grin.

She patted the chair next to hers, inviting Zac to be seated. He had barely sat down before the main door flew open, causing them all to start. In staggered a soldier, dirty and long-haired. But that just about described them all.

"Lady Eleanor!" he spat at them through a mouth with no teeth.

"What!" Her expression was thunderous, visibly unhappy that she had been interrupted with her new 'God'.

"Things have gone wrong, very wrong." The soldier pulled off his hat shoving it down by his side.

"What? What is the problem?" she asked, striding towards the soldier who was starting to cower. The other men in the room fidgeted from one foot to the other, trying to avoid eye contact with her.

"The Writer has escaped the trial and I was attacked by a woman on fire, blue fire," he said, his head now bowed so low he could no longer see her.

"Where are the SORA?!" she screamed at him, her hands clenching her thick gown so hard her knuckles turned white.

"We think they're dead," the soldier muttered.

She shook her head as if disbelieving him. "A woman on fire, my Writer gone and the Sora dead? Do you have any other news for me?" She bent and whispered in his ear, "Before I kill you." Her hand shot out, grabbing him by the throat.

Zac inhaled sharply. Surely a woman of her physical stature couldn't hurt a fully grown man?

"Please," the man wheezed as she lifted his head, her fingers biting into the flesh of his throat. Zac could see his skin bulging through her fingers as if it might pop.

"Where is this woman now?" She spoke directly into his petrified face.

His voice became weaker. "By the trial, with the Writer and a man." He coughed, wheezing between each syllable. Zac had seen prisoners die, but not at the hands of such a petite woman. To his relief she released him, allowing his body to drop to the floor where he writhed, gasping for air. He also felt elated. The man had seen a woman on fire, blue fire. That could only be Val. But that must also mean that she had regained her powers. His elation turned to irritation. Why couldn't she stay out of trouble? She was now in more danger than ever. He glanced at this watch; still no signal.

Lady Eleanor wiped her hands on a silk napkin that lay on the long wooden table in the centre of the room, then she turned to Zac. "Well, if this 'fire' woman wants a war, and she's stupid enough to have freed Brigit, then she'll get one." She gave him a sweet and slightly unbalanced grin. Throwing her arms into the air she turned to address the soldiers who were standing around, waiting for her orders.

Before she had a chance to speak, a blonde-haired soldier came marching confidently towards them. "Lady Eleanor," he greeted her, kicking the soldier on the ground in disgust.

Zac noticed how pleased she seemed to see him, but this new arrival could only spell disaster. The blonde hair and the deep blood red scar on his face made the man instantly recognisable. This was the man who'd knocked him out in the woods. He, in turn, would be bound to recognise Zac and would surely connect him with Val. And that would be his demise; the end of his time as a Hunter. At least he had stopped this crazy woman from killing Wendy and the others. He braced himself for death as the man approached.

"Durwood, tell me the news. It seems someone was deranged enough to break the seal to release the Writer. Is everything in place?"

He nodded. "When I knew the seal had been broken I sent out the guardian just to warm things up a little. The army have been awakened and are ready for your orders. Whoever did this will be dead before dawn. Your word will draw them all here to us." He bowed then rose slowly, his eyes tracking Zac from toe to head. "How did he get in here?"

Lady Eleanor defended her new acquaintance. "He's the God of the skies. He made rain fall. With all your power I have never seen you do such things. Do you know him?"

The man let out a patronising laugh. "I knocked your God out with the butt of my rifle. He's no God." His lip curled up in a snarl. "He is the weak follower of your enemy. Make it rain fool," he demanded.

Lady Eleanor changed direction, all her attention now on Zac. "Prove you're a God!" she demanded.

Zac was desperate. What could he do? He had no powers, no information on his screen. This was it. He stood proudly. He had always known this day would come. "I have no powers. I am Thirty-Three Twenty-Seven, Hunter to Twenty-three Thirteen, Val Saunders, Guard from the Prison planet of Alchany, and she will stop you." He held his head high, waiting for them to end his existence.

Eleanor's hand was fast, her nails dug into his throat. "You have made a fool of me!" she bellowed squeezing hard.

Durwood interrupted. "My Lady!"

She had already lifted Zac a foot clear of the ground. "What?" she snapped, unbothered by Zac's body writhing.

"We should keep him alive, just until this issue has resolved itself. If he is connected to this Val Saunders then we can use him." Durwood moved to her side. "Let him down." His hand hovered over her arm, but he didn't attempt to touch her.

"If this plan doesn't work, I will take pleasure in killing you both," she said, flicking back her hair and dropping Zac to the floor. His hands grabbed the bloody marks on his throat as he lay choking.

"Say the word, my Lady, and your army will deal with all the infiltrators." Durwood said.

She turned to face the room of men; her followers, her soldiers. "Awaken," she commanded.

*

Val's heart was pounding. She needed to blow something up. She had so much trapped emotion: anger for Kez, pain for Kaliyah's imprisonment and fear of Wiflin's grandmother. She'd made it through the trial without any powers and the thought of it made her stomach churn. She could have died at any moment, but she hadn't and to her surprise, she had just been healed by one of her best friends.

Jason was still dazed and Brigit was calmly trying to explain what had happened. "No, I don't bloody understand," he responded.

"Hey! Language, Walker," Val scolded him. "Whatever you just did saved my life, mate." She reached out her hand for him. "Come on, magic boy. Let's go find the others and get out of here."

Jason grabbed it. "I'm sorry," he apologised to Brigit. "But Val, look what she did to me." He lifted his sleeve to reveal the symbol of the awakening, angrily red on the raised flesh of his arm. "I don't see how you can be this calm about what I just did. It was like something was inside me making me see you were better, but why now? Why me?"

"Jason your apology is accepted," Brigit told him. "And why you? Well your mother was a witch. Why now? Val had to break the seal releasing a dark magic to free me. All I could do to moderate the spell that was keeping me prisoner was to split it evenly: good versus evil. What you need to be aware of is who cast the spell. That was a dark and evil witch. I believe they call him Durwood. He has yellow hair and a scar." She pointed to her cheek.

"Oh, yes," Val muttered. "Me and him are going to have a little chat."

"So this is your fault?" Jason poked her in the arm. "We'll get Wendy to get rid of this 'witchy first aid kit' weirdness when we get home." Then without warning he wrapped Val in one of his arms, pulling her close. "I missed you." He planted a kiss on her forehead.

"We must join the others." Brigit hurried them along.

"Now that we have awoken the evil magic, Brigit, what do you think is coming?" Val asked.

"I have no idea." She shrugged. "This spell was directly connected to my power. The moment the seal was broken, I could only alter the spell, not cancel it out completely."

"So we're still in some serious trouble?" Jason's eyes met Val's.

"Yes, in trouble as always. Listen mate, we can talk about your magical power when we get home - come on Tinkerbell."

*

As they re-entered the main body of the fortress, Val saw the devastation her friends had caused. Burnt wood was splintered across the court yard, unconscious soldiers were strewn where Hadwyn or Boden had stunned them and there, in the centre of it all, were Wendy and Belinda, trying desperately to free the witches. "Hey!" she yelled, bolting over one of the links connecting the carts, in the urgency to see her friends.

Wendy's face lit up. "You're here." Her arms locked around Val's neck. "I was so worried."

"That makes two of us," she agreed.

Wendy began inspecting her. "Are you ok? We were so scared for you."

"I'm fine." Val gently nudged her back. "The trial was ... er... interesting. But thanks to all of your hints I made it out. It's not all good news though. The last symbol, the circle with the dot in it, was a booby trap, set so that anyone trying to free Brigit would have to unleash dark magic."

"So what did you do?"

"I had to break it. We had no choice. But Brigit managed to split the outcome, fifty-fifty. She has awoken the powers of good as well as evil, so anyone with magical powers is ready for battle." Val raised her hand, on it rested a ball of blue fire.

Wendy's expression changed. "I thought if you got your powers back people would come to hunt you?"

Val theatrically blew out the fire ball. "Yup, but it was the only way; Wyetta's been kidnapped and I need Brigit to free her. It's a long story, but a man and a mouse have her."

"Wyetta's been kidnapped? Oh my goodness!" Wendy began to pace anxiously. "That means you, well, baby Val, has been kidnapped. This is terrible news. And a mouse!"

"Guard!"

Val swivelled, her sword extending effortlessly from her uniform. But there was no reason to worry, it was just Hadwyn.

"Decided to show up for duty have you?" He patted her firmly on the arm.

"Well, being invisible and being shot at by my Magrafe companions didn't really work for me!" She allowed him to push her around a little, knowing this was his way of showing his relief. They were joined by Boden and Fran and, as they all gathered in the square, she had a feeling they would be getting Wyetta back very soon.

"Val." She heard Sam's voice before she saw him. "You had us worried." She tensed as he appeared at Boden's side. These moments were always confusing. Her connection with Sam was something she couldn't escape, but they never seemed to get five minutes alone. It seemed the gathering crowd didn't bother him, as he wrapped her in his arms. "I don't have long," he whispered into her ear, then his lips pressed softly on hers and she allowed him, as always, one kiss.

Pulling away, she gazed into his dark eyes "Well, at least I know which Sam you are." He took her hand and she felt his soft skin warm against hers feeling safety in his touch.

It was impossible to not notice the children spilling out of the entrance to the cells and the obvious lack of soldiers. "I see you've been busy." She raised an inquisitive eyebrow.

"Yes, and they're magical younglings, most impressive," Hadwyn informed her.

"Well, I hate to ruin the party, but to get Brigit out I had to release a big bad something and Brigit doesn't know how it will manifest." Val paused. Someone was missing. "Where's Zac?"

"Oh Val," Wendy said, "Zac was so brave. Lady Eleanor came for us and he used his watch to predict the weather, telling her he was a God who could make the sky weep. She was so impressed she took him away."

Val could feel her chest restricting. "Where... did... she go?" she asked, in as restrained a manner as possible.

Sam released her hand as her body became engulfed in flames. "Val, we will find him, but first we must free all these people. There are more pressing issues at stake here, trust me."

"Val says that a man and a mouse have Wyetta, and not to be the bearer of bad tidings, but we're running out of time." Wendy stepped away from Val who was now burning too intensely for anyone to get close.

"You do what you need to do to free the witches and the children. I want Zac and I want him now." Her teeth were gritted.

Hadwyn quizzed. "The Hunter gave himself over?"

"Yes, he was extremely brave," Belinda confirmed.

"Most odd. We must save him, I agree." He pulled his gun.

Val looked around. "Which way did they go?" she pointed towards several possible exits.

Wendy directed her towards the door. "Lady Eleanor took him in there with the few soldiers she had left but, before you go rushing off, there's something you need to know about her."

"What?" Val asked, as a single blood curdling scream caught them all by surprise. They froze, the children who were still spilling out into the square becoming still. Then it came again. Val had already spotted the source of the screams, which were coming from a petite red-head at the front of one of the carts. She was crouched into a terrified ball. Still on fire and unable to switch it off, Val went to the woman. "Hey, what's wrong?" she called up to her.

The woman's eyes met with hers, terror shifting her pupils rapidly left and right. "Up there." She lifted a thin finger towards the sky.

Val followed its direction and there, coming through the night sky, was Wiflin's very large and very angry mother.

CHAPTER 22

Escape

Lady Eleanor and her follower, Durwood, had left to make plans for the arrival of the Awakening and, having stood patiently for a few minutes, a soldier had decided it was time to secure Zac. As he was pushed roughly onto, then bound to a high-back chair, with a rope lashed around his wrists for good measure, Zac could hear the sounds of commotion and panic growing outside. He wouldn't fight to escape; he was trained to follow his captor's instructions. This was normal protocol for a Hunter. He would now have to sit and wait to be rescued or terminated.

He did just that until a familiar voice whispered into his ear. "You were lucky there."

"Gabriel?" He looked sideways, yet saw nothing.

"Correct. Seems we have a big problem, Hunter. How many soldiers have you monitored?"

Zac ran his journey through his mind. "Here; twelve, outer room; ten more; three on the door. Gabriel, I believe Val is free."

"Never doubted her."

Zac felt pressure pushing down onto his shoulder as an unseen body leant against him, pulling at the ropes that bound him to the chair. The soldiers were taking advantage of the fact that Durwood and Lady Eleanor had left and were stuffing themselves with the food on the table. The roasted carcass of a large animal in the centre was quickly being devoured. They themselves reminded him of animals, he thought, as they pulled and tore at it, laughing raucously, seemingly unconcerned by what their leader had released by pronouncing the word "Awaken". But Zac was worried. He knew how powerful she and her scarfaced friend were.

"You're free," Gabriel whispered.

Zac felt the ropes loosen. He grabbed them. If they fell to the floor the soldiers would know he was free. He must stay alert. He knew that Gabriel would have to become visible to fight. "What now?" he asked, surveying the room, looking for the best way out.

"This." Just as he'd expected, Gabriel appeared standing to his left. He caught the soldiers completely by surprise and they fumbled to draw their pistols and swords. Zac had never witnessed Gabriel's fighting skills at first hand, but he had read about his success rate in the archives. He'd witnessed Hadwyn and Boden in battle, so he knew to expect something impressive from a Magrafe, but nothing could have prepared him for Gabriel's incredible skills.

Gabriel stretched his arms out at his sides; extending from each one was a glowing, foot long pole. He moved towards the flabbergasted soldiers, his attack swift and unforgiving. A shot was fired. He deflected the bullet with one flick. "Move," he ordered Zac and with sweeping motions he struck down two soldiers. Leaping into the air, he used the back of one solider to project himself feet first towards another.

Zac followed. For a moment it felt like he had slipped back to a time when he had served his previous Guard. Gabriel swung left and took out the remaining three soldiers. The noise of the brief skirmish had drawn unwanted attention, and the large wooden doors to the room burst open, revealing a further ten soldiers. They hesitated, absorbing the devastation around them. Gabriel took that as the perfect time to attack. There was no hesitation, no questions, and no reassuring conversation, like Zac would have had with Val; it was the way it should be; arrest or be killed.

Gabriel beckoned Zac to follow. "Let's go. After listening to Lady Eleanor and her witch Durwood, I can only imagine what we might be heading into. We need to warn the others."

*

The group stood frozen, a ripple of fear spreading through the courtyard as the witches looked skyward at the huge creature circling them.

"Sam, I've met her baby," Val informed him. "I promised I would re-unite them, so no killing the sphinx, ok."

Sam's sword extended. "You have a really strange way of working." He frowned.

"Listen, Wiflin took on his grandmother to help me escape and Lady Eleanor took his mother." She pointed towards the sphinx. "Her. They're prisoners, the same as the witches; gypsies who got the magical whammy from someone evil. Everyone in the trial was a prisoner of some sort." Val had to make this right. Plus, her gut-instinct was telling her that this wasn't the Awakening.

A small boy, whose body was covered in a soft green light, screamed, "Look! Look over there!"

The group's attention was drawn away from the flying creature towards the main gate. Past his tiny frame, in the distance, coming out from the woods was a wall of soldiers, marching in unison; the thud of their feet striking the ground soon had everyone's attention. It was eerie watching them emerge between the gaps in the trees like ghosts, then joining together, with military precision, to form perfect ranks.

But Val noticed there was something very different about these soldiers. They looked shoddy, bedraggled, their swords rusted and their pistols rotten, yet their steps were firm and in unison, like an army heading into battle. The small child turned, his face filled with fear as he ran towards an older girl who embraced him protectively. "They're dead, all of them, dead," he cried, shoving his face into her tattered dress.

"I'm guessing this is your doing?" Hadwyn goaded Val, gun at the ready, pushing some of the children behind him.

"Dead soldiers, *really* my fault Hadwyn?" she protested. Then, to her horror, she spotted Lady Eleanor and Durwood leaving the main building. She wasn't sure which way to turn. Outside the fortress, inside it, or above it, there was no escape.

Wendy grabbed her arm. "Val, I need to tell you something."

"That the approaching army is dead?"

"No worse."

"Worse?" she groaned.

"That woman..." Wendy signalled towards Lady Eleanor, "her surname is... *Troughton*!" she exaggerated the surname in a way Val imagined only Wendy could.

"What?" She hissed. "So Lady Eleanor could be a distant relative of Delta's?" 'How much could one person impact on your life?' she wondered. This explained so much. If Lady Eleanor really was related to Delta, that meant Delta couldn't give or feel love, which actually explained a lot about her personality. But now wasn't the time to fill in the branches of the Troughton family tree. "Listen to me, we need to forget about Delta. She's in the future. What's important is that you know that Lady Eleanor has been cursed."

"Cursed?" Sam asked, his head cocking in bemusement.

"Yes, I met her mother and she told me that Lady Eleanor was cursed by an evil witch. She wants someone to lift the curse, and Brigit here was supposed to be that someone. What I don't understand is how she's getting all this power.

Shots rang out from the distance and the children screamed. The soldiers weren't close enough yet to hit anyone, but that wasn't deterring them from trying. Brigit grabbed Val's arm. "She got her powers directly from the witch that cursed her husband," she said.

"How?" Wendy asked, as she helped guide a few confused children into a group. "If the witch was powerful enough to create a curse to take away love, why would she then dish out that sort of power to a stranger?"

"Lady Eleanor wasn't given the magic. She killed the witch; the rules of magic state that a curse binds a witch to her victim. Eleanor couldn't be freed once she'd consumed the soul of the witch, and the more evil she does, the further she gets from being free."

"Surely you can do something?" Jason asked Brigit.

She shook her head. "No, I have already divided this magic equally between good and evil; I have no more power here."

Val heard snorting sounds in the distance where she could see a group of military horses pulling cannons towards the entrance of the fortress. 'Dead horses! Was nothing sacred?' she thought. "Is there any way to save Eleanor? Or a way to delay this lot?" she asked, as she watched Lady Eleanor making her way with her scar-faced follower across the courtyard, going towards the approaching army.

Brigit nodded. "There is only one way; she can pass the curse onto a more powerful witch."

"Great, that at least gives us an option," Val enthused.

Brigit scolded her sharply. "Tell me, Val, who would *you* choose to give this curse to? Would you cause me or my unborn child to never feel love? Because we are the only ones on Earth powerful enough to take on the curse."

Val shook her head, feeling the heat of the rebuke rising in her cheeks. Brigit was right. How could you wish something like that on someone? It would make you as guilty as Lady Eleanor. "I'm sorry, you're right."

Boden pushed between the women. "This conversation of curses and witches will have to wait, we need to close the gate and someone needs to deal with that thing up there. Come on Val." He pointed to the sphinx that was still circling overhead. She stepped aside as he passed her, leaping the links between the carts with ease, Hadwyn and Sam following. She followed, running towards the gate and the oncoming army.

Hadwyn was quick to start firing with Boden in support. He shot anything on the ground that came in range, while Boden used his arrows to finish off the last few soldiers on the fortress wall, the dead army surged fearlessly towards the gate.

"They're closing in fast Val, we need to lower the gate," Sam said.

She nodded. They may be dead, and a little slower than your average live soldier, but they looked by far more menacing. The front row dropped to their knees as the large cannons were pulled into place by the bullet-ridden horses. Their dead eyes stared at her as they prepared to fire on the fortress. It was a haunting image that would never leave her.

"Fire!"

Val turned to flee the cannon's shot. "Duck!" she yelled at the women and children, signalling for them to crouch, as the echo of the cannon's shot ricocheted inside the fortress walls and the gatehouse was partially destroyed. Debris showered them and a cloud of dust choked them, clogging their throats. They would never be able to lower the gate now.

"They're reloading." Hadwyn called to her. "Protect the children." He fired at the front line. Three horses dropped, their large carcasses crushing several soldiers. "We'll have to find another way to close the gate."

She had no time to think about that because Brigit let out a blood curdling cry and collapsed to the ground.

Jason grabbed her. "Brigit, are you ok?"

"I think my baby has very ill timing." She let out another hiss of agonising pain.

Belinda held her hand. "Val, she's in labour, magical labour. I don't know how long we have before this baby is born. We need to get her out of here. You have your powers. Can you teleport?"

"I don't know. I haven't tried." She looked around her desperately. They were in so much danger. The army was moving relentlessly forward; they were being pounded by cannon fire, and the first ragged soldiers were only moments away from the gateway, which was still wide open. They needed her here. But Brigit needed her too.

"Well, now would be a good time," Belinda encouraged her.

"What if I take you out of the fortress and I can't get back to the others?"

"Arghh!" Brigit screamed again, doubling over as Jason supported her weight.

"Just take us into the cells," Belinda suggested. "Better locked in, than out here in the open."

"OK," Val agreed.

"Wendy, Fran and I will protect her. Let's go." Belinda herded the women around Brigit.

Jason yelled, "Wait. What if teleporting hurts the baby?"

Belinda pointed at the oncoming aggressors. "They're going to curse it, set it on fire or kill it. Which do you think presents the clearer danger?"

In the middle of their birthing argument, Val realised that Lady Eleanor had noticed them. She screamed the order, "Get my witch!" To the few soldiers she had left inside the fortress.

Val grabbed Wendy's hands and turned to Jason. "We don't have a choice. Wait here for me?" Brigit let out another cry.

She took a deep breath. This was it. She knew for a fact that this one act would start the chain reaction Zac had warned her about. As soon as she disappeared, a definite blip would appear on a screen somewhere on the Prison, a report would be rushed to the Collectors, then to a Judge, and they would have her whereabouts. But without Brigit, who was going to help save Wyetta? She really couldn't win. "Ready?" The group agreed and she braced for whatever was about to happen. Closing her eyes, she silently pleaded that they arrive in one piece.

It was slow to start with. For a few seconds nothing seemed to be happening, but then she felt a fluttering in her stomach, that drawing sensation she had grown accustomed to. Her thoughts flashed to their destination; the cells where the children had been held. The stench filled her nostrils as she relived the vision of degradation and suffering. Her insides started to pull, a feeling so familiar it was almost reassuring. It was working. She knew it was time and she gripped Wendy tighter. Fran gasped. They disappeared and all she could do was hope the baby arrived safely.

They all materialised in the cells and Val took a moment to feel relief. A groan interrupted her thoughts. Brigit was still very pregnant and clearly in agony, but delivering a child was definitely not on her list of skills.

"Val, go help the others. I can protect them from here," Wendy instructed waving her silver wand, "a gift from Sam." She grinned.

"Nice. See you soon."

"Val, keep Jason safe," Fran added, visibly unsettled from the teleport, reaching for a wall for support. "Go!"

"Will do," she replied setting off again. Irrelevant of it being dangerous or wrong to teleport, it felt so good, and gave her a sense of power and control. Her landing was precise; shame no-one from the Prison was there to appreciate it. She arrived inches away from Jason. "What did I miss?" she said into his astonished face.

"That." Grabbing her cheeks between his thumb and forefinger he turned her face. The army was now almost at the gate where Sam, Hadwyn and Boden were still frantically attempting to break the chain that held it open. The children watched in horror.

To her left, Lady Eleanor was heading towards them, Durwood, her loyal crony, at her side. "We need to free these witches," Val said, as a ball of fire the size of a cannon ball hit the ground just feet from her and Jason. Mud and fiery saliva exploded around them. Instinctively she shielded him with her body; she was fireproof after all.

"Thanks, mate," he said, as she released him.

Winking, she wiped a large gobbet of mud from his cheek. "It's the least I can do. I don't suppose your new first-aid ability gave you the magic to open those shackles?"

He groaned. "No and I'm not using it again, but I think I know a girl who can help. Rhianna's her name, small but powerful. Rhianna!" He shouted into the air, as another fiery cannon ball of saliva struck the ground next to them. Val looked skyward to see the sphinx preparing to dive, her face full of anger.

A young, mousy-haired girl came running over towards them. "Yes, Jason?"

Jason pointed at the witches' shackles. "Do you think you could open these like you opened the cells?"

She shrugged. "I can try."

"Great, I'll leave that with you." Val needed to stop the sphinx before it incinerated someone. She jumped up onto one of the carts as a bullet whizzed past her head. She faltered but the women helped her keep her balance.

"Get her attention," she yelled at the women as they all began frantically waving their arms, trying to get the sphinx's attention.

"Hey! Hey!" she yelled at it. "Please, listen!" But it was too late. The sphinx had already tilted, her wings pulled back against her lion's body and was diving straight at them.

"Down," Val ordered. The witches did as she said, huddling together. Her job was to protect them at any cost, but also to keep her promise to Wiflin. She lifted her hands high above her head, grabbing the air as if it were putty in her hands. She could feel it swirling between her fingers, felt its tingling vibration, its power. Then she lifted the vortex of air and aimed at it the creature, projecting it forward hard. The gust caught the sphinx under its wings, flipping it over, and throwing it temporarily off course. It roared in anger, flapping desperately, trying to regain its balance.

The sound of clashing metal made her look back at the gate. The army had forged forward. Sam and her Magrafe companions had been unable to break the heavy chain that held the large wooden gate aloft and were scrapping with the vanguard of the soldiers.

"Val!" Jason yelled. He pointed at the young girl, who was trying to free the witches. "We need more time." Then he shouted a warning and pointed skyward just as an angry screech announced that the sphinx was coming round again.

"Keep trying," she called back.

When the Nyterians had attacked the Prison, it had felt like nothing could ever equal it. No aggressor could top Nathan Akar; nothing could be as frightening as being told that she was going to be extracted. And yet, here she was, in an enemy's fortress surrounded by deep dark things from history books and mythology, creatures that wanted to kill them all. Her parents and Daniel were still missing, although she considered it a blessing that they weren't with them at this moment, and she was not at all sure she was going to be able to save Wyetta.

And then, as if it couldn't get worse, in the midst of the madness, a spine chilling voice called out. "EDITH!"

She froze. It couldn't be. But it was. Over by the entrance to the trial stood the creature, the thing that had left her without a memory of who she was, or why she was here. As it staggered out into full view, its appearance caused everyone who could see it to react in exactly the way she had. Even the dead soldiers were avoiding it. A mixture of fear and repulsion echoed in their gasps. Val could see her axe, still protruding from its chest.

"What the hell's that?" Jason yelled.

"I'm not sure it has a name, but I definitely thought I'd killed it!" she called back.

"You killed someone?" Jason's horror was apparent.

She shook her head. "Well no, it fell on my axe." Which she consided didn't sound much better in all honesty.

"What axe?" Jason quizzed her.

She shook her head. "Long story; keep working."

Val saw Lady Eleanor changing direction again, moving quickly towards the children's cells and Brigit. She also noticed her glancing back several times at the creature from the trial - as if afraid. It was becoming apparent that everyone was scared of it, but why? Why *was* the Lady so afraid? Surely she controlled everything in the trial? How had it escaped?

All thoughts of the Lady vanished when she heard Boden giving the instruction to fall back. The army was about to overwhelm them and the gate was still open.

She jumped down from the cart. "Children, quickly!" She hurried them. "Does anyone have the ability to create a force field, a barrier of protection, or something?" A mass of blank young faces stared back.

Then two identical twin boys stepped forward. They spoke in unison. "We should be able to, but not big enough for everyone."

"Ok. Listen, I want you to get everyone inside this circle of carts, and you *will* protect them all. Do you understand? I'm counting on you." She gave them a fierce look and they nodded. She felt a little guilty at being so stern with them, but now wasn't the time for hugs and reassurances that everything was ok, because the reality was everything most certainly wasn't. "Everyone inside the circle!" She instructed the children, who moved swiftly. Shots were now cracking over their heads as she just caught her name being called over the noise of the cannon fire.

The first wave of the assault moved into the fortress. Sam's bellowed instructions were past urgent. Hadwyn and Boden were being forced back. She sprinted across the courtyard, leaving the twins to set up their barrier. As she fought through the sea of bodies, several balls of fire rained down from the sphinx, missing her, yet colliding with the soldiers, blowing some of their rotten carcases flying, knocking down others like skittles.

"Keep them busy," she instructed as she ran past Sam.

"That's going to be harder said than done," he called after her lunging at one, his sword catching in its ribcage. He struggled to remove it, with his foot placed firmly in the soldier's chest, as it continued to swipe at him with its half mangled fist.

Hadwyn and Boden had been cornered and were shooting the soldiers at close range. But stunning the dead was useless. Its only effect was to slow them down. They fell but rose again covered in scorch marks which filled the air with the stench of burnt flesh. A bolt of fire flew from her hand and the remains of the gatehouse door exploded.

She bounded up the steps that the cannons had missed and was soon standing at the highest point on the fortress wall. Her fear of heights made her feel dizzy and she crouched, grabbing onto the thick wooden gate. Keeping low, she pulled herself to the centre, not daring to look down at the army entering underneath her.

Pushing herself up into a seated position, she perched on the gateway's arch. Placing both hands on its main support to steady herself, she grabbed the rusting iron chain. She could see everything from up here. The volume of soldiers still piling out of the woods was terrifying. She could see the barrier that the twins had formed to protect themselves from the approaching battle and the sphinx, which had just spotted her, was sure to attack. Just below her, her companions were desperately trying to keep back the living dead.

She knew she needed to focus if she was going to close the gate. Closing her eyes she began to block out the noises. "Focus," she instructed herself. She took a deep breath as her hands began to vibrate. Her fingers gripped the chain as hard as she could. She had to block the entrance. The metal was cold under her grasp, but as her focus grew, she started to feel the energy surging through her arms and the metal became warmer. She had dislocated a rollercoaster for heaven's sake; surely she could break a chain.

CHAPTER 23

Living Dead

The decomposing army continued surging forward. There was little Sam and the others could do to stop them. They concentrated on deflecting their blows and dodging their bullets. Then a noise from above made them all look up. Val's attempt to break the chain was causing it to vibrate and groan loudly. The metal lurched and moaned.

Deep within herself she summoned the last of her energy, "COME ON!" She screamed, as the chain began to crack under the pressure. Sam and the others could see what was coming and moved hastily back. The dead soldiers seemed unaware and kept surging forward.

"Val, do it now!" Sam called to her.

The massive wooden gate plummeted to the ground, flattening the bodies of the risen dead soldiers, who struggled under the weight of the crushing object. One soldier, whose legs had been severed, continued to crawl towards them moaning, his compulsion to attack undiminished.

The sheer number of dead soldiers attacking the gate made it obvious that it would only be a matter of time before they broke through. There was no use in looking back. She knew the gate would fall, so it was time to deal with the dangers inside the fortress.

Swinging her legs over the top of the gate, Val scrambled to the ground, to be met by Boden, Hadwyn and Sam. They had joined together in a triangle and she was in the centre. "What now?" she asked breathlessly, as they continued to fire on the enemy on their side of the gate.

"Magic. It's all we have. Our skills are of no use here," Boden said, drawing a triple arrow and firing.

Hadwyn fired repeatedly. "I agree. We must free the witches, and fight fire with fire."

Val lit up. "Then let's do it. It's time we showed them some Prison hospitality." The group moved away from her intense heat and she led them back towards the witches like a beacon of light.

When they reached the courtyard, Val saw at first hand the high, straight wall of energy that the twins had created surrounding the carts. Val could see Jason and the young girl still desperately trying to undo the shackled witches within. On the outside, a group of the few remaining living soldiers were standing protectively around Durwood. Lady Eleanor was nowhere to be seen. This was her chance to show him how it felt to be on the other end of the prisoner fence. "Take out those soldiers, he's mine," she instructed her companions.

Val couldn't control her emotions as her flames grew in ferocity. Anything that attempted to come near her recoiled, or was duly set on fire. It seemed the longer you were dead the less you remembered just how flammable clothes were. As she closed in on Durwood, the man who'd degraded her and imprisoned all these people, Hadwyn and the others dispatched the soldiers surrounding him, giving her the chance to concentrate solely on Durwood.

She was only a few steps from him now and could see he had placed the palm of his hand directly onto the force field. His fingers were spread wide and where he was making contact thick black veins of dark energy were spreading out, like tendrils of venom, moving quickly and wrapping those inside in darkness. Val looked at the two small boys who were holding onto each other's hands fighting to keep the field intact, and knew they were too young and lacked the stamina to hold it for much longer, even with the desperate screams of encouragement from the other children. She needed to move fast.

She would strike him from behind, light him up.

"EDITH!"

Val turned, but it was too late. Something slammed into her from the side. The violence of the impact hurled her sideways like a ragdoll. She stopped only when she collided with a solid stone wall. Winded, she slid to the ground, her flames extinguished. She sat there for a moment shaking her head, unsure what had happened. As she attempted to pull herself up, a misshapen foot stamped her in the stomach.

"Edith, why did you leave me?" The creature leaned his full weight onto her, making her gasp for breath.

"You're dead," she choked, unable to move.

"I know I'm dead. Look at this." His deformed hand pointed to the axe protruding from his chest.

Val saw her chance. Grabbing the axe handle, she yanked hard. The creature screamed as she pulled at it. Then the shots started. Hadwyn was blasting the creature. Its hand flailed in an attempt to reach the Magrafe, but Val had a firm hold of the handle and wasn't going to let go. Though Hadwyn was unable to stop the creature completely, his consistent fire was enough of a distraction to cause it to stumble. Its foot lifted off Val's body for a second and she took her chance, pulling herself up by the axe's handle. Jerking it upwards as hard as she could, she ripped it from his chest, to the sound of cracking ribs. She swiftly extended her sword directly into the open wound. "Get him out of my way!" She yelled at Hadwyn, who was a step ahead of her, as always. With a hefty blow he knocked the creature sideways.

Val looked past the soldiers at the children and witches. The wall was almost completely black now, a seething mass of sinuous energy coming directly from Durwood's hand. The children were hardly visible and Jason was trying valiantly to keep them calm inside. She ran toward them, her axed poised to strike. Sam and Boden helped her through, but as a soldier fell, another rose in this endless battle. She extended her sword and flames exploded off her once more. Her arm raised over her head, she lunged forward with her weapon. The blade came down towards Durwood's head; another moment and it would be over. But it wasn't; her blade struck something solid. Instead of striking him it had been blocked by another weapon. An explosion of sparks dazzled her.

"Val, no!"

Electricity exploded around her head and she was once again on the ground, thrown backwards, bringing several soldiers to the ground with her. She pulled herself up, undeterred, ready to surge forward once more, striking out at the ones in her way when she came face to face with Gabriel.

"Oh my God, it's you!" Her flames abated.

Gabriel grabbed her arm, guiding her towards the wall and away from her target. "I'm sorry I had to do that, Val. You were rushing in without all the facts."

"Val." Zac's voice made her turn to see her Hunter.

"Oh Zac, I've missed you," she enthused, watching as Gabriel quickly absorbed his surroundings, his eyes flitting from one situation to another. "Is your mother safe with the coven?" he asked.

"No, she was taken by a man called Jarrad. He's really powerful, Gabriel – like alien powerful. He said if I didn't deliver Brigit to him by the morning he would kill her, and that's the last I saw of him."

"Jarrad!" Gabriel's face became thunderous. He looked at his Dellatrax for a moment.

"Is he registered?" Zac asked.

"Not anymore. We've met in battle before. His powers were strong, but he was taken by the Warden for punishment, and that's the last I heard of him. Clearly he's after Brigit's book of Vari."

Just then a fiery cannon ball landed a foot to the left of Val. "Sorry, no time to chat. Let's focus on getting out of here alive. We still need to stop Durwood from getting to the witches. So what's this information I was missing?"

"I stopped your attack because Zac recognised the virus he's spreading." Gabriel told her.

Zac stepped forward. "He's not trying to get in, Val. He's trying to stop *you* getting in and *them* getting out."

She was confused. "Why would he do that and not protect himself?"

"He needs to keep something in there safe," said Gabriel, glancing over his shoulder. "The magic to create an army of dead soldiers would take a lot of power, more than just one witch could supply. Zac, do you think Durwood is pulling his energy from all the witches?"

Just then, another barrage of cannon fire struck the fortress, but the gate was still managing to hold the rest of the army outside. Hadwyn, Sam and Boden were simply repeatedly beating back the dead soldiers that were on the inside.

Zac looked shocked by the force of the cannons' fire, but once the noise subsided he continued. "That would explain why he's trying to stop us getting to them."

"So, what do we do? The gates won't hold forever. Easiest target first; let's attack Durwood." Val started move towards him again.

"Wait." Zac grabbed her arm. "I believe that if he's connected to all the witches, and he's left himself outside of the wall, he won't have left himself vulnerable. He could have a greater connection to them than you think; one that could harm them if you harm him."

Gabriel nodded. "I agree. We can't take the risk."

Val waved her arms in frustration. "Tell me what to do then. We need to do something quickly."

"Is there something that connects the witches?" Gabriel enquired.

Val shrugged. "Well, it's not their coven. They're from all over the world. Some are from Wyetta's coven and others were taken from as far away as Egypt."

Zac interrupted. "The shackles! They're all connected; they must be magical shackles to drain the witches' powers."

"Then that's the link." Gabriel patted Zac on the arm.

"Jason's in there with a young girl trying to break them now," Val said.

"I think we'll need more than the power of a child's magic. What about the trainee Judge?"

Val shook her head. "Wendy's busy protecting Brigit, who conveniently went into labour." As she finished her sentence, they noticed an unnatural quiet. It became apparent that the fighting had come to a standstill. They looked to see what had caused the lull in the battle. To their horror, they saw that Wiflin's mother had given up circling and hurling fiery balls at them, and was now standing, all four paws firmly on the ground, between Sam, Boden, Hadwyn and the gate.

"Have you met our resident sphinx? Get many of them on the Prison?" Val asked, as the creature stalked the group. But instead of attacking them, Wiflin's mother turned towards the gate and with one large explosion of her fiery breath, the whole thing was afire. "Did I tell you she can spit fire?" Val shrugged.

"Someone needs to get her out of the way and we must break the witches' chains. Sam!" Gabriel called, waving an arm to draw the attention of the others, who backed towards them, putting down covering fire as they withdrew. "Nice to see you again. We have a plan, that starts with freeing the witches."

"Gabriel thinks Durwood is connected directly to the witches, and he's taking their power through the shackles, but he may also have connected himself to them magically. Zac thinks Durwood isn't trying to get to them, but is keeping them trapped under the force field," Val said, noticing that Sam's bracelet was flashing its usual signal, indicating that he was going to leave them. Surely he wasn't going to abandon them now when the situation was so serious?

"Have you found the child, Rhianna?" Hadwyn asked. "She's gifted with the anti-magic. She opened our locks."

"Jason's in there with her now," Val said. "Sam, anything you need to tell us?"

His eyes met hers and she could see the concern in them. "It's the Collector; she's been arrested. I'm being summoned. Seems some female Prison Guard called Thirteen, who's supposed to have been extracted, has been teleporting in 1645 no less, and we're being called in. Forgive me, this is out of my control," he pleaded. Then his lips met hers, and in all the madness, she felt his love for her rushing through her body. "I will come back. Look after her." Then in a flash of light, he was gone, the warmth of his lips still on hers.

"Well that was poor timing." Hadwyn frowned.

Val was once again left behind. He'd gone so quickly, not even giving her time to plead for him to stay, but she knew he wouldn't leave her like this unless he really had to go. Now it fell on their shoulders to make this right, but the night was speeding past and she was going to be born in just a few hours. She had to get Wyetta back by morning.

She stood in the midst of chaos, knowing she had to take control. She closed her eyes and suddenly, her mind cleared and she knew what they had to do. "Gabriel, go and tell Jason what's going on. Boden and Hadwyn, cover my father. Zac, you must go to the cells and make sure Brigit is safe. Lady Eleanor was heading over there, but she'll have met resistance from Wendy. I'm going to deal with her." Val pointed at the sphinx that was still prowling around the gate, blowing flames onto the wood as it crackled and burnt.

"But..." Zac protested.

She touched his hand. "Zac, I'm sick of this place and I want to go home. Please do as I ask."

"Very well," he agreed.

*

Val sprinted across the courtyard toward the sphinx. The army of putrid soldiers were now trying to clamber through the burning gate. The ones that succeeded in squeezing their bodies through the gaps were alight as they stumbled into the court yard, burning like human torches. The sphinx spotted her approach. Rising into the air she rained a cascade of fire balls down on Val. To its obvious surprise, Val walked straight through them, untouched by the flames. But it had cleared a path for her. Soldiers lay strewn in the wake of if its attack.

Val raised both hands, throwing her axe to the ground. "Listen to me. I know your child, Wiflin!" she called out.

The sphinx's cat-like eyes widened at the mention of his name. She flicked her tail in agitation, "How? And why don't you burn?" She snarled at Val, her lip curling, revealing black gums in a human mouth full of canine teeth.

Val came to a stop. "Because I'm different, like you. I went through the trial and met him there." A soldier lurched towards her and she blew him away with a gust of wind. The sphinx watched him collapse several feet away. "He's just a child and he's scared. He needs you; you're his Daj. I can help you get him back, but you have to stop attacking us and help. We aren't the enemy." Another body lurched towards her. She lowered onto one knee, grabbed her axe and slashed at it. With one blow she brought the decomposing soldier to his knees.

"This cannot be true. My child is dead. The Lady told me he was killed by the one they call the Writer."

Val rose. "That's a lie. I was with him and your mother and they are both very much alive."

The sphinx sniffed the air, her forked tongue flickered in and out. "If you're telling the truth…" she extended her wings and shook her head as if shaking off a bad dream, "…tell me what I truly am."

"You're a gypsy and you were captured on an island with your son and mother, sent here and transformed by that scumbag Durwood." Val pulled a finger down her cheek to show where his scar was. "And the Lady tricked you."

"You know a lot." The sphinx now hovered over Val and she could see the creature's tail relaxing, falling onto her haunches.

"I know your child, what more matters?"

"Nothing." She shook her head and her mane of golden hair cascaded like a river. "Stranger, my name is Urania and you have met Vertina, my mother, and Wiflin, my only child. If you're telling the truth, you have turned a lie that tore out my heart into a truth that will restore my faith."

"I'm Val, and I promise I'm telling you the truth, the same as I did when I promised Wiflin that I would get you back to him. I have the Writer, she will free you all and return you to your home, but you have to help me now." Val could sense the gate was going to fall, and she braced to meet the horde.

The sphinx turned at a loud cracking sound that was followed by the moans from a hundred mangled throats as the walking dead toppled like dominoes into the court yard, were crushed by the falling gate. Val and the sphinx leapt away from the falling debris.

"What do you want from me?" Urania asked, landing beside Val who quickly brushed hot ashes off the fur on her back.

She pointed at the soldiers. "Keep them busy. I'll do the rest."

"Very well, but if you lie, I will eat you and your friends," she warned.

Val realised this was no empty threat; she'd seen the remains of the other bodies, so she knew Urania meant it. "You have my word."

Urania acknowledged the agreement with a curt nod and let out a roar that sent chills down Val's spine as she leapt onto two of the soldiers and tore them appart.

*

Val needed to regroup with the others. Coursing across the fortress, she was soon at the barrier that was protecting the witches. She really wanted to deal with Durwood, but knew better. Every time his name popped into her head she could feel the flames growing inside her and had to consciously stop herself lighting up.

However, that didn't stop her watching him, preparing herself for the moment when she would finally be able to put an end to his evil. There was, she realised, something odd about him. She stared at him. He hadn't moved; hadn't changed his position by so much as an inch. Hadwyn and Boden had dealt with the soldiers surrounding him in a matter of minutes, they were human after all. So he stood alone, attached to the barrier by just the palm of one hand. She made her way along the edge of the protective wall, as close as she dared, to get a better look. His face was still; she couldn't even tell if he was actually breathing. She edged a little further. It was too far.

Durwood's head snapped towards her and she caught her breath in surprise. This wasn't the movement of a human, there was no natural flow; and there it was, something she had seen before. His pupils were as black as the night, void of human conscience, just like Eva's. Slowly his head recoiled as if on a controlled spring. She stumbled backwards. Durwood was joined with the witches and there was nothing she could do to him.... yet!

"Val!" Gabriel called for her attention.

Leaving Durwood she went to her father who was on the opposite side of the force-field, out of Durwood's sight. He was busy peering through one of the few gaps left in the barrier through which he was speaking to Jason.

She popped her head in front of the hole. "Hey, we have one problem solved; the sphinx is on our side for now, but she *will* eat us if we don't free her mother and child."

"So we will assist the creature," Boden said.

Hadwyn pulled out his weapon. "Yes, I have never fought alongside an animal like that. Let's go." He grinned, tapping his forehead with the barrel of his gun in a salute before heading back into the melee.

"I must join them." Gabriel extended his fighting sticks. "Free the witches as quickly as you can," he said as he followed his companions into battle.

"Mate, what's going on?" Jason's questioned her. His face was as close to the blackness as he could get it.

"We have a sphinx on the team now. How's it going with the children?" In her mind, she was punching a hole through to him and then a similar hole in Durwood's face.

He shook his head. "Not good. The twins are finished and Rhianna hasn't stopped trying to open the shackles since you left us here, but she's just not strong enough. They've lost their faith, Val. They need you in here, not me. You remember what Nathan called you?"

"What?" She was bemused for a moment.

"He called you The Bringer of Hope. These children need to feel that hope too. They can't do this alone. They're scared; half of them don't even know what their powers are. The women aren't much better. The darker the wall gets, the weaker they get. Gabriel believes Durwood's bleeding them of every last drop of magic. I just don't know how much more they can take."

"Hope! That's it. Jason, find me a girl called Claudia, quickly. Tell her I was sent by Kez." She glanced over her shoulder to monitor the fight. Even with the three Magrafe and Urania burning anything in their path, she guessed they had only minutes before they were overwhelmed.

Jason had disappeared from view, but she heard him calling out the name. The children chattered amongst themselves and then, though the hole, Val saw her. She was so tiny, yet in comparison to the other children she simply shone. Val found herself in awe of the child's presence. She had a mane of hair that ran the length of her back, as yellow as a buttercup reflecting the sun. Her little blue dress almost reached the floor, clearly a hand-me-down from one of the bigger girls, but its colour was still strong. In that instant, Val knew what was special about her. It was like staring into the eyes of an angel.

Like Val, Jason seemed unable to stop himself staring at her. "I'm Claudia, sister of Kez." the child said in a soft, composed tone. Her eyes, as they searched Val's face, were like crystal pools of water. Even the dirt on her couldn't detract from her beauty.

"I'm Val, a friend of Kez. He told me just how special you are. He said that when you were all grown up and initiated, that you would have the power of lootus." The child nodded. She was no more than six or seven years old. This was crazy. How could Val put this sort of resposability on such small shoulders?

"Have you seen Kez?" Claudia asked, her eyes widening.

In her mind's eye, Val saw him, as she had left him, limp, and apparently lifeless. She swallowed, made herself smile gently. "Yes, and he sent me to get you, but I need you to do something for me first. You have your powers now, did you know that?"

The little girl shook her head. "No, but Mother told me not to use them until I came of age, and I'm not yet there." She glanced down at her palms, shaking her head.

"Trust me, Claudia, you have your powers and Kez needs you to use them right now. Have you been told how they work?" Val was talking, but also listening to the sounds of battle ringing out around the fortress. Trying to keep herself steady, so as not to alarm the children was a battle in itself.

"Yes, Mother was teaching me, before they took her."

"Is she here?" Jason asked.

"No." She shook her head.

"Claudia, I need you to help us." Val kept her voice soft. The girl's head bobbed in agreement.

"Good girl. See Rhianna over there?" She pointed at the girl whose glow was dimming. "I need you to go over to her and make her believe she can do this. I want you to give her hope… lootus, ok? Then I want you to spread that hope through all the witches. Claudia, do you understand how important this is?" Val's voice cracked with tension, and she paused, taking a deep breath. Her hands were twitching with the stress. She knew this was a huge request for someone who had never used her powers before, but Claudia simply nodded. Nothing seemed to be fazing this child.

"Val, we need you!" Gabriel called.

"Just a minute. Jason, I know she can do this," she insisted, closing her mind to the sound of the approaching militia.

Claudia stepped towards the others, her tiny feet bare, no socks or shoes to protect them from the harsh ground. Yet her step was regal. She reached out for Rhianna's hand. It had been wrapped around the shackles for so long that her knuckles were white, her fingers lifeless. Claudia placed her tiny hand gently on top of it. Rhianna's eyes dropped to the hand and they all held their breath. And then Claudia spoke. Her tiny voice saying just one word, "Usk," she whispered. Then her face broke into a radiant smile and she gave Rhianna a nod, to confirm that it was done. When she lifted her hand, Val saw a tiny flash of light pass between them, like static. Rhianna had tears in her eyes. Val felt a strong urge to get in there and feel the magic of Claudia as well. This must be it; the shackles would be broken now.

Val was about to join Gabriel when Claudia did something she hadn't expected. She watched through the peephole as Claudia walked towards the edge of the black wall that now held the children prisoners, only just visible to those on the outside.

"Stop her!" Val screamed. But it was too late. Claudia had placed her hand onto the blackness. Val yelled and Jason roared his warning, dashing towards her, as the women on the carts screamed for her to stop, but she just stood there.

Val had to do something to protect her from Durwood's dark magic. She ran towards him, determined to stop him now, racing around the circumference of the force field, but what she saw when she reached him brought her to an abrupt halt. Durwood's palm was still on the barrier, but his body was jolting, like he was receiving an electric shock. Gradually the jolting stopped. His head shook, as if he was waking from a dream, and then he looked directly as her. His eyes were back to normal. Val realised the true strength of Claudia's power. Claudia had placed her hand directly opposite his and he was getting the full force of her lootus. The man they couldn't touch through fear of harming the other witches was now being confronted by the little girl.

Val stepped back from the sinister black prison that Durwood had created and watched as the man himself began to realise the significance of what was happening. "It's time to give them their hope back." Claudia told him. It was clear that the sense of hope he had taken from the witches, which had empowered him was now being removed. His eyes flickered from her to his hand and Val could see panic on his face. She had never considered the fact that someone as brutal as Durwood could be as hopeful as her.

Then there was a clicking sound and Rhianna let out a cry of relief. The first lock was open and Jason was dashing to help pull out the chains. As the witches were released, Durwood seemed to crumble. Val was poised ready to leap on him, but she would still have to wait till they were all free. She couldn't risk attacking him and causing a single witch to be injured by her action.

In her obsession with watching Durwood she'd completely lost her focus and was oblivious to everything else. Suddenly an arm shoved her to the left, deflecting a sword hurtling towards her head.

"Watch yourself!" Gabriel called as he struck out at another soldier.

She was shaken. Her preoccupation with Durwood had caused her to lose focus. They were in danger of being overrun by an army of the dead which, despite Urania, Boden and Hadwyn's best efforts, was forcing them back. But now it was time for them to release *their* magical army against the macabre horde. With a hundred now fully-functioning witches, things were about to get interesting.

CHAPTER 24

The Army

In an instant the battle was upon them all. Val wrestled with a soldier whose decayed half-eaten face was far too close for comfort. She threw him off just in time to see Durwood break his hold on the wall. The blackness evaporated to reveal Claudia standing on the other side. Val's chest constricted with the fear of what he would do to her. She slammed the next soldier who was already closing on her with her full body weight, sinking an elbow into what was left of his chin, then broke away, not even waiting to check that he went down.

Durwood was staring down at the little girl, but she simply stood where she was, gazing serenely back at him. He was the first to look away, a look of pure horror flashing across his eyes, as if, Val thought, he'd understood the pain he'd caused. His hands rose to cover his face and he stumbled away, grabbing at his hair as though trying to pull whatever he had witnessed out of his head. Then he turned and made a dash towards the children's cells.

"Sisters!" A voice made them all turn to see Sara, the witch Val had spoken to earlier, who was standing on one of the carts. As soon as the chains had been removed, the witches' magic had been transferred back to them and they were looking pretty fierce. "Three fold magic return. These demons are dead and must respectfully go back to their graves. We must protect our own." A cheer rang out. "These children," she continued, "now need us to repay their bravery." She raised a fist that Val could see was glowing deep blue. The witches cheered again and it was as if she'd stepped into some surreal dream.

Val stepped back into the battle and took down another putrefying body. She was astonished at the speed at which the witches were recovering and ready to fight. From the corner of her eye she could see Claudia, Rhianna and the rest of the children being grouped together. A very tall woman, with sharp features and piercing emerald green eyes that seemed luminescent, had taken control, creating a circle in the soil around them. Val could tell from her expression that she meant business. No one was going to get close to the children who'd freed the witches from their torture.

The rage that had been contained by shackles was now spilling out, making the very atmosphere crackle, causing Val's skin to prickle under her uniform. Bodies were flying through the air; they were making short work of the soldiers. However despite their best efforts, the piles of bodies continued to rise. Worse, they were still pouring into the fortress, row after row, oozing in like sardines being packed into a can.

As she battled, trying to make her way across the courtyard to link up with Boden and Hadwyn, a bright light exploded, causing her to throw her arm up to cover her eyes as it grew in intensity. What was it? She needed to know if this light was being caused by something good or something evil. She climbed onto the nearest cart to get a better view. There, in the centre of the battle, was Urania, the light shooting out from her torso. Everyone around her was forced to move away.

Attempting to shield her eyes with her arm Val could see that Urania's body was contorting. Her wings extended as if she was about to take off and then each individual feather started to vibrate like a bee's wing in flight. Her head tilted skyward and her mouth opened to reveal her dog-like teeth. And then she roared. The sound was immense, coming from deep within her chest, making the ground tremble. As it gradually reduced to a grumble, the feathers dropped to the ground, exposing a pair of human arms. Val blinked, rubbing her eyes as Urania's battle with her body continued. Her lion-like form jerked, backwards and forwards in sharp movements. The sound of crunching bones was stomach churning.

Val realised that now Durwood had lost his witches; his magic was being undone. To master the power of so many he must have had to do unspeakable things and Urania and her family were his victims, made to suffer terrible pain and loss. To Val, the release from his evil magic was almost as painful as the spells he had cast. Urania endured more painful twists of bone and rips of flesh, before a light, too bright to withstand, engulfed the half human, half creature that howled in pain.

Val felt everything in the fortress pause; even the dead couldn't withstand the light. Then it stopped and with the darkness came the inability to see more than silhouettes and shadows. When Val regained her vision, there standing before her was an exhausted woman. She pulled her long brown hair away from her face, revealing dark olive skin that contrasted strongly with her bright multi-coloured dress. She reminded Val of pictures she'd seen of gypsies standing by brightly decorated wagons. Urania glanced down at her hands, absorbing everything, as if it was the first time she'd seen them. Then she looked up at Val on the cart and smiled. They both knew this meant that she was free from Durwood's hold and Val would like to bet that Wiflin was as well. But Urania wasn't out of the woods yet. A soldier lunged at her. But now she had a reason to survive and before Val could reach her, she had dodged his blow. Pulling a sword from the chest of another who was within reach, Urania began to fight for her life and that of her family.

Suddenly Gabriel was grabbing Val's arm, pulling her down from the cart. "Val, go and make sure Brigit and the others are safe. Now Durwood has gone, we can cope here."

She looked across to see Jason fighting alongside Hadwyn and agreed. "Ok, but keep my friends safe."

"Hurry!"

"I'm gone," she said and teleported out. This time there was no pause, no need to concentrate on how to teleport. She knew that her last teleport had caused the arrest of her Collector and the summoning of Sam. It was too late to take back what she'd started.

*

As she reappeared, a shot struck her directly in the chest and pain ripped through her body. Unable to focus she collapsed onto the ground.

Val could hear Wendy screaming to her left. "No! NO!"

She lay on the ground for a moment, eyes closed, reaching for the spot where the shot had struck her. Luckily, it seemed that since she'd been awoken by Brigit, her uniform was once again functional and had done its job. Although she'd had the wind knocked out of her and was bruised, she was otherwise uninjured. As she opened her eyes, she saw a pair of feet hanging over her in mid-air. Then she heard a woman's voice.

"You would kill him?!" Lady Eleanor bellowed in annoyance.

Annoyance flared in Val, along with the intense urge to reassure her she was definitely not a HIM, but a girl, even with this stupid uniform on. Then it dawned on her that she was talking about the person who owned the boots floating over her. Getting to her knees she could see the boots belonged to, Zac, who was turning blue under the grip of Lady Eleanor's delicate hand. Her body exploded in aggressive blue flames. "I'm only going to say this once. Put my Hunter down," she growled.

"Entertaining," Lady Eleanor laughed.

Val rose, flipping her axe into the upright position, its silver head reflecting her flames. She knew there wasn't time to talk. A ball of flames formed in her hand and she pointed it towards Eleanor. She was sick and tired of talking. But to her surprise, Wendy beat her to it. A ball of energy rocketed past her head, aimed directly at the Lady. It didn't even get close.

"Arch!" Eleanor roared, flicking her wrist and sending the shot ricocheting against one of the walls.

So, the Lady had powerful magic, but could she take on two at once? Val leapt for Zac's body. Grabbing him around the waist she tried to pull him away, but it was as if Lady Eleanor was rooted like an oak tree to the ground. Val was wondering what to do when a spine-chilling cry rang out.

"Wonderful." Lady Eleanor rejoiced, dropping Zac's limp body to the ground like an unwanted toy.

Val scrambled to his side, forcing his sleeve up to check he had a pulse. "What are you playing at?" she scolded his still body. There. It was there. She could feel a pulse - weak, but definitely there.

"Val!" Wendy screamed.

Lady Eleanor was now at the bars of the cell. In the background, Val saw Fran wrapping her arms around a weakened Brigit while Belinda desperately covered Brigit's newly born baby in Wendy's cloak. They cowered against the back wall. Val stood. Zac would survive, but no Troughton, Lady or otherwise, was going to take another baby away from her. She'd abandoned Daniel and she would die before she let that happen again. Without thinking, she teleported into the cell, wrapped her arms around Belinda and the baby and teleported them out.

*

They arrived inside the corridor to the trial. Belinda stepped backwards in confusion, still clutching the child.

"Are you ok?" Val asked.

Belinda pulled the cloak tighter around the child. "Yes. Now go, save the others."

Val didn't waste a second and was soon back in the cell with Wendy and Brigit. "Miss me?" she nudged Wendy.

"Something's wrong." Wendy didn't move an inch. Her face was pale and Val noticed that Lady Eleanor now had her back turned to them.

"What's going on?" Val asked.

Wendy continued to respond in monotone. "Something screamed. I think it was a man. Val, I think someone's dead."

She grabbed Wendy's arm. "Who? One of us?" she demanded.

"I don't know."

Val had no choice. She teleported through the bars and arrived only a few feet from her previous destination, coming face to chest with the creature who had taken her memories. Still spewing green puss from his wounds and completely unconcerned by her sudden appearance, he shoved her out of the way.

"YOU!" his wretched voice screamed at Lady Eleanor. Behind him Val could see the body of Durwood, twisted and broken, on the ground. It was sickening, but at least it wasn't one of hers.

"Please James, I can fix this," Lady Eleanor pleaded.

Val recognised fear, she'd heard it in her own tone often enough, and for some reason Lady Eleanor was very scared. And had she just called that abominable creature James? Wasn't that her dead husband's name?

"No, you can't," he said, as drool dripped from his mangled chin down onto his bare chest where the hole from the axe allowed it to enter his body again.

Her face filled with pain, Lady Eleanor screamed at him. "You, you cursed me and Edward. It's your fault this has all happened. If you had just stayed with us and not gone out drinking... I don't even feel love for my own child! Do you understand?" She still didn't move, yet the creature advanced.

"James!" Val called abruptly.

The creature turned his head. "Edith." His eyes flickered with recognition. "I'm sorry for what I did to you, but the control they had over me is gone. Stay out of this. There is only one way to stop the army of soldiers and rid this world of her venom."

"Then tell me how and we can do this together," Val said, stepping in closer.

His crooked index finger pointed towards Eleanor. "Her death. So do you want to kill her, or shall I save you the trouble and do it myself?"

Val shook her head. "No, no one has to die," she said firmly, taking another step forward. Her sword tip began to extend from her uniform.

"You can't kill me, you love me," Lady Eleanor reminded him. "Don't forget, James, the curse I placed on you was to love me until the day you died. That's why you haven't killed me before." Val genuinely wanted to slap her face. How could she have cursed him in this way? But Lady Eleanor was missing something vital.

James took great pleasure in enlightening her. "Well my love, if you haven't noticed, I'm dead, so the curse no longer applies." He laughed in her face, the sound gurgling in the back of his throat, then he threw his head backward in a howl of pain and lunged forward, grabbing her.

She screamed and before Val could get to him, he had her body in the air over his head, holding her like she was weightless. Val struck him with her sword, but he didn't move. He was focused on only one thing: his wife. Val swung again, slicing at him from the side this times with her axe. "James, stop!" she yelled at him.

"Stop!" Wendy shouted, firing at him with her wand, but to no avail. Val could see Brigit, supported by Fran, frantically writing in the dirt of her cell floor, but even their combined effort didn't seem to touch him. He was beyond magic.

When it happened, it seemed to play out in slow motion. Her axe was still protruding from his side and Wendy had struck him once again in the chest with what should have been a disabling blow. His head tipped back, looking up at the struggling body he held in his arms.

"Brigit, do something!" Wendy screamed, but the Writer just shook her head.

How could they stop this creature, created from a curse and made of hatred and anger? Val saw his knee rising and Lady Eleanor's body dropping. She flamed up in one last desperate attempt to stop him, the explosion rippling out in waves of intense focused heat, the intense brightness of which caused them all to cover their eyes. The creature was now completely engulfed in her flames, but it was too late. He smashed Lady Eleanor's body down onto his knee. They all heard the dreadful sound of her back snapping. Their cries of horror filled the air.

He held her for a second, cradling her in his arms like a child, as if unsure what to do with her. Then his twisted hands opened and her broken body slumped to the floor. The creature allowed a smile to cross his warped mouth then he too slumped forward across her motionless body.

Val grabbed frantically at him, pulling his smouldering carcass off the broken figure. "Stay with me," she pleaded, lifting Lady Eleanor's head onto her lap. It really didn't matter what had happened, this woman had been cursed like so many others.

Lady Eleanor let out a weak laugh. "You cannot fix this," she murmured, as blood flowed down her cheek from a wound on her head. "I know what you are, Alien." She took a rasping breath. "My family will curse your existence until the sun in the sky stops burning. That is my promise to you." She exhaled slowly and her battered and broken body gave out it's last breath of life and took on the first stillness of death.

CHAPTER 25

The Swap

"Did she just curse you?" Fran called from the cell.

Val laid her hand over Lady Eleanor's face and closed her cold dead eyes. She was surprised that they seemed void of life so quickly. Lifting her head, she saw Fran was waiting for an answer. "Yes, I believe she did." Her forehead was wrinkled in annoyance.

Brigit interrupted. "Listen."

Val focused, and quickly realised what had caught Brigit's attention; there was no noise; everything had become quiet. "Wendy, come look after Zac. I'll be back," she said, placing Lady Eleanor's head on the ground and teleporting out.

*

There in the centre of the fortress, stood the witches, bloodied and exhausted, still surrounding the children. Hadwyn, Boden, Gabriel and Jason had joined them. Looking around her, Val beheld an apocalyptic scene. All of the dead soldiers had simply dropped where they stood and now, in the stillness, the stench of putrefied flesh was rising into the air. She had to step over the carcasses to reach the others.

"What happened?" Gabriel asked, pushing a lifeless soldier aside with one of his sticks.

Val didn't want to relive it, but they would need to know. "Seems the creature we met was actually James, Lady Eleanor's husband."

"Jesus!" Jason exclaimed.

"Yes, well, she cursed him to love her and never harm her. The only way he could do that was if he died. Seems watertight if you think about it."

"So when you killed him, and he came back with the Awakening, she had no power over him anymore?" Boden said.

She nodded. "Looks like it, but I didn't kill him. It was an accident." She frowned at Jason who was clearly the rumour spreader. "And he, in revenge, has just killed her, and it appears that her life force was connected to all these soldiers. He snapped her like a twig..." The words caught in her throat. She closed her eyes; wanting it not to be real, but it was one of those memories that burnt into your mind in 3D multicolour. She shivered at the remembered sound of Lady Eleanor's back breaking.

"So you're saying that when she died they ceased also?" Hadwyn asked, bringing her back to the present.

"Yes, well that's the only answer I have. The creature seemed to pass away with her."

Boden surveyed the women and children. "We need to move them to safety. The living soldiers that have escaped could come back at any time."

Val seemed to be the only one who didn't agree with his assessment. "Gabriel, we still need to work out how to get Wyetta back."

"Yes, we should split up. Val, where is she and how do we find her?" Gabriel asked.

Val shook her head. "I don't..." But before she could finish the sentence, she heard her mother's name ring out.

"WYETTA!" A woman's voice, full of joy, called from the group of witches. And there she was, standing amongst the rubble in the entrance to the fortress. But she wasn't alone. Jarrad had her by the arm and Lovac had his tail wrapped firmly around her waist.

"I'll deal with this." Val was just about to teleport when Gabriel grabbed her arm. "Don't do anything. Do you understand?" his voice was as firm as his grip.

Hadwyn pushed forward. "Tell me that's not Jarrad." he growled.

"I take it you know him as well?" Val asked.

"We all do, Val." Boden replied, already drawing his bow.

"Don't. Not yet. Not till we have her safe," Gabriel ordered.

Val could see Boden's teeth clench, his jaw muscle twitching as he reluctantly lowered his weapon.

Jarrad walked towards them, leaving Lovac holding Val's mother. The witches started to gather around the four of them. It seemed almost unbelievable, one hundred witches and four Magrafe and yet no one could make a move.

"Gabriel, surely we can take him?" She felt the urge to ignore him.

"Jarrad, give me Wyetta!" he demanded, striding forward.

She couldn't believe him. "Everyone stay calm, everyone stay here," she mimicked. "Subtle-much, huh?" she shrugged at Jason who was just watching like the rest of them.

"Look at her," Jason whispered. "She looks odd, as if she doesn't know where she is."

Val looked more closely. It was true. Wyetta's face was completely expressionless; she was hardly blinking.

"Eleven! What a pleasure to see you again. It's such a small universe, and well, with time travel and all, there really is nowhere left to hide anymore," Jarrad smirked. "And your youngling, she's got a future ahead of her, unlike you I'm afraid."

Gabriel extended his poles. Val tensed. This was seriously double standard. She stepped forward and Hadwyn grabbed her arm. "No, this is his fight."

Boden growled in a way she'd never heard. He was always the voice of reason, but right now his hands were clenched into tight fists.

"Please, someone tell me what's going on before the freak kills my father?" Val demanded.

"He tortured and murdered our Tark," Boden said through gritted teeth. "We were chosen for Magrafe duty together and were designated a Tark leader for our initial training. Jarrad killed her."

"Why? When? Her?" But it was too late, Gabriel was advancing and Jarrad was reaching for a symbol on his arm.

"Stop!" Brigit called, moving slowly across the courtyard towards Jarrad.

"No!" Val ran towards her, grabbing her around the waist to support her. "Keep away. We can deal with him. We need you here," she ordered, but Brigit ignored her. Her finger touched Val's hand, a small tick and Val dropped to the ground, pain shooting up her arm. It was excruciating, like a hundred bee stings. "Gabriel, don't move," Brigit ordered. Kneeling carefully, visibly still in pain after the birth of her son, she allowed her finger to drag into the soil. Slowly she wrote a backwards Y and Gabriel was also brought to his knees, where he stayed, silently battling the pain. Jarrad laughed, then took the opportunity to swiftly kick Gabriel in the chest, making him fall onto his back, unable to retaliate. "Touch him again Jarrad, and I will kill you," Brigit warned. Jarrad stepped away, like a scolded child. "No one interferes. Hadwyn, that means you as well," she warned, pointing at him. He raised both hands into the air in submission. "Release Wyetta, Jarrad, and I will come willingly."

Jarrad glanced back at his rodent companion, waving a hand, and Lovac removed his tail from Wyetta's torso. She remained by his side, though clearly in some sort of trance. Val thought it was probably the effect of the poison Lovac had put into her when he bit her. Lovac reached up and sniffed Wyetta's neck and Val found herself holding her breath. She was terrified of what he might do, but a simple scratch of his paw and Wyetta seemed to wake. She looked around, clearly confused, then, spotting Gabriel on the ground, she went to him as fast as her legs could carry her.

Lovac now dropped to all fours and galloped to Jarrad's side; as always his loyal pet.

"You will come with me!" Jarrad ordered Brigit.

She nodded.

Val couldn't understand why she was doing this. Surely they could have beaten him? But then if Jarrad had killed Gabriel's Tark, maybe he was more dangerous than she thought. She just couldn't understand why Brigit would give herself over so freely, seeing how powerful she was, knowing how hard they had fought to free her and how important she was to their survival.

Brigit reached Jarrad and the world seemed to come to a standstill. "Brigit, no!" the women cried out. They were all so helpless. Jarrad held them at bay. No, Brigit had done that by crippling her and Gabriel. Whose side was she on, after all?

Brigit turned and Val could see the tears in her eyes. "It's best this way," she said, looking directly at Val. There was no waiting, no big '*I've won, you've lost*' speech from Jarrad, he just grabbed her and they were gone. Val started to sob.

Wyetta had reached Gabriel and she struck him in the chest with the open palm of her hand. "Solvo," she commanded and the relief on his face was instant. She knelt down over her large bump and, grabbing his face, she kissed him three times repeating the words, "I love you," between each one.

This made Val cry even more. What Wyetta didn't know and she did, was that in the next fourteen days Gabriel was going to be killed. Jason grabbed Val around the shoulders. "It's going to be ok," he reassured her.

"No, it's never going to be ok," she cried. "Never. I miss Shane so much." She looked up into his eyes and saw him filling up.

"I know, and I'm sure he misses us as well." He allowed the corner of his mouth to lift.

With somewhat less force than she had used on Gabriel, Wyetta removed Val's pain and then wrapped her arms around her neck, breathing her in and placed a kiss on her forehead. Val struggled to compose herself.

The witches that knew Wyetta had waited patiently, but now they surged forward greeting the woman who, to some, was their High Priestess and to others just a good friend and mentor. She greeted them all with the same energy and enthusiasm.

"Val." She saw Hadwyn's hand reaching out for her and grabbed it. He lifted her up. "I have a question."

"Ok, what is it?" She wondered why he looked so confused.

He shrugged. "How did that woman know my name?"

"What?" Val frowned at him, as if he was speaking a foreign language.

"She said my name. I've never met her before." He seemed genuinely bemused.

Val felt her knees buckling. It was true; Brigit had never met Hadwyn. So how did she know him, and know him well enough to realise that he would be the one most likely to ignore any order not to attack and shoot anyway? The only way was if it hadn't actually been Brigit who'd given herself over so freely and gone with Jarrad to God knows where.

"Jason, we have a problem." She grabbed his hand and, without giving him the chance to ask what, she teleported them out.

*

Their arrival caused the others to jump. Fran was kneeling at Brigit's side, her face wet with tears. Zac had been moved and covered in a dirty blanket and a cloak had been placed under his head. "Where is she?" Val demanded.

"She said you'd be angry." Fran sobbed. "Get us out of here," she pleaded.

Val marched up to the cell and grabbed the lock of the door. With one swift move the metal melted under her fiery hand. "Fran, tell me. Where's Wendy?"

Fran's misery was without depth, and her words escaped between gasps for air. "Val, she knew you would stop her. Please listen to what I have to tell you. When you left, she had a vision. She told us that this was her time; that all her life she'd been preparing for this one moment."

Jason stepped forward, scooping Brigit into his arms. It was clear she was unable to walk. Val should have known that giving birth in a prison cell in 1645 would leave you on your back for a day or two. Why hadn't she seen the signs? Damn Wendy.

"Val, what Wendy did was extremely brave and I owe you and her, my own and my son's life." Brigit's voice was unwavering. She wasn't apologising for what Wendy had done, just reminding Val why.

"Not enough," Val retorted. "I need Wendy. You know she's risked her life for me before and I won't let this go. Tell me where they've gone. I can get her back." She was so angry. Why hadn't she realised that Wendy had taken on Brigit's appearance, exactly the same way she'd swapped places with her on the Prison when she'd been captured by Nathan?

Brigit shook her head. "I don't know where this man has taken her. And Wendy's wish was that you not follow her."

Val ignored what Brigit said. Wendy would need her. "Tell me who can give me the information I need?" she demanded. "My mother said you were *so* powerful." She moved closer to Jason and Brigit, the anger building inside her stomach, causing knots of pain to wave through her. The floor started to shake under their feet. "Well, now it's time to prove it. The man that took her, Jarrad, wanted you. Where would he take you?" Val wanted to explode with frustration. It was getting harder to control her emotions and flames were starting to form on her arms.

"Val, enough!" Jason snapped at her, steadying himself as one of the slabs cracked under him. "We all want Wendy back safe, but this isn't the way to do it. Get a grip of yourself right now."

She had never been scolded by Jason before and the tone of his voice left her feeling stupid and out of control, which was about right. She stepped back, taking a deep breath. The floor settled. "I'm sorry."

"Val, I am powerful, that's true, but sometimes power isn't enough. Sometimes being small and still is the greatest answer." She reached out her hand and took Val's "It's time to awaken the alien in you." Brigit's eyes fixed onto Val's, as she pressed her forefinger into her wrist. It didn't hurt like last time, but she couldn't stop Brigit either. Her eyes followed Brigit's finger as it moved over her flesh. As her hand pulled away, there on her wrist, was the same symbol she'd marked Jason with: a perfect circle, with a dot in the centre. "It's time for you to face your destiny," she said. "Jason, please take me to my son."

"Yes of course. Val, can you just check on Zac." He tipped his head in the direction of her Hunter.

She shook her hand, it was still tingling. "Ok." She felt dizzy as she knelt at Zac's side. "Go, I'll join you when I'm sure he's ok," she said, wanting to be angry with Brigit, but finding it impossible to muster the emotion. What had she done to her? And what did she mean *awaken the alien*?

"I can stay." Fran offered.

"No, it's ok, we're fine." Val took Zac's hand in hers. His pulse was much stronger than before.

She waited till they had all left. "Zac." She spoke to his still body. "What am I going to do? What's my destiny and where did Wendy go? Why does that stick-thin crazy witch always have to be so brave? What's Jarrad going to do when he realises she's not Brigit?" But Val knew what he would do. He would kill her and then just come back for the real Brigit.

A croaky voice interrupted her chain of thought. "Val…"

"Zac." She couldn't help but smile. Before he could complain she kissed his forehead. "You're such a trouble maker."

Lifting his head he looked around, his eyes resting on Lady Eleanor's body. "Is she dead?" His asked, his voice weak.

"Yes. It turns out the creature was her husband and he knew that if he killed her, her magic would be cancelled out."

He shook his head. "Bad choice of husband."

Val laughed. "I guess he was. Not that I can talk about marital choices. Thanks to him the army has gone, and now so has Wendy."

Zac's brow creased. "Wendy's gone?"

"She took Brigit's place and Jarrad took her."

"Jarrad…? Has this whole experience taken my memory?" He scratched his head.

She hugged him. "No, mate. You missed out on the amazing Jarrad who, it turns out, killed Boden, Hadwyn and Gabriel's Tark trainer. He now has Wendy instead of Brigit and has disappeared off the face of the planet with his oversized mouse." Val slumped back onto her bottom, pulling her legs up. "What are we going to do? I seem to live in a crazy world where nothing ever ends happily. When's it going to go my way?"

"I believe life, as you humans see it, is for living. If you were not living, then you would be dead. So from my analysis this is normal. You are simply living."

She pushed her fingers through her hair and winced as they snagged on the tangles. "I don't know. I just thought getting the sack would leave me a little down time."

"I thought that being relieved of duty, being jobless, for humans was a most stressful time indeed." Then the smallest beep caught their attention. It was Zac's watch. His face lit up. "I have a signal." This was the first one since they'd arrived.

"Is it my parents?" she asked.

He tapped the screen, the expression on his face becoming concerned. "No, two alien forms are coming in," he warned, trying to pull himself up, but it was too late, they'd already arrived.

CHAPTER 26

Tark

Val stared, mouth gaping, as two forms shimmered before them and slowly became fully visible. Zac let out a gasp and she shared the sentiment. What were these things? Their bodies glowed and towered over her by a couple of feet at least. She had to tilt her head up to see their faces. Their skin was a creamy white, like marshmallow, and one had deep purple, circular markings across one side of its face. The other had green swirls that went from the peak of its brow as far down as she could see. Both were wrapped in deep blue outfits that covered them from the neck down to the floor; the material shimmered like water.

Zac had now pulled himself up from the floor and she watched dumbfounded as he proceeded to kneel. "Welcome," he greeted them, not lifting his face.

"What's going on?" she asked him.

"Val," he snapped, indicating that she should join him on the floor.

She knelt, knowing Zac was normally right about this kind of stuff, encouraged that he didn't seem scared, more in awe. Then she saw that the new arrivals had begun to change. They were reducing in size and the glow that had surrounded them was gone. And then there stood a young man and a woman.

She peeked up at them. His face was pretty, almost too pretty for Val's liking, and she would actually have called him beautiful, which felt wrong on so many levels.

"Hunter, you have done your job, we are pleased. The Warden chose well." The man spoke first.

Although he was still looking at the floor, Zac's face lit up with pride. He raised his head slightly. "Did the Warden send me here?" he asked.

"No, that was the action of a Judge who warned us about the girl. We were only to observe her, but the strong signal we just received led us to believe her transformation was complete. But you have always been the one to stand by Val."

"How do you know my name?" Val asked.

The woman answered. "We are time, we are everything. We are Tark," she said. Val dared to lift her head now that she was being engaged directly. Half of the man's face was still covered in the purple circles, although his golden hair seemed to blend into the markings perfectly. Next to him the woman's green swirls poked out from a mane of dark brown hair, falling in jagged, harsh layers. She reached out a hand to Val. "I am Fiora and this is Beck. We have come for you, Val Saunders."

Val respectfully took her hand, it was colder than she expected, but she allowed Fiora to assist her in rising. "What do you mean?" Although they looked human now, she knew they weren't.

"It's time. You have been transformed and you must begin your training." She smiled warmly.

The man placed his hand on Zac's shoulder. "She will be well skilled on her return." Zac nodded, as thought he was satisfied.

Val glared at him. Not even an 'I'll miss her'. She shook her head. "Well thanks for the invite. Sorry about the wasted trip, but I don't want to go 'train' with you. I have to rescue my guardian, Wendy."

Zac now stood, his hand reaching for her. "You have no choice. When the Tark come you have to go," he said, an edge of concern in his tone. Not because she was going to leave him here, but because he was clearly worried that she was going to refuse to go.

She stepped away from them. "You're missing the point. I don't want to train. I have no reason to train. I no longer belong to the Prison or the Warden or you. I have to get Wendy back; she's the one who needs training. She's a Judge."

"We understand that this Wendy is important, but it is you who needs us. We are here to help you complete your journey. We don't want to hurt you or your friends. Please trust that we can help you survive. Right now you are like the creature from your planet called the Dodo. Do you know this bird?" Fiora asked.

"Well I haven't seen one – they're extinct."

"Exactly," Beck said. "Our kind are also following the path of this bird. We too are on the edge of extinction due to hunting. The Tark were once the most respected and wisest of them all, and then a way to extract our powers was found and even those among our own species turned on us. We fled our home and settled on the Prison, but they too grew uncomfortable with our power and made the mistake of banishing us. Now, we take only the ones who are truly powerful souls and in need of our guidance. You are one of those, Val Saunders. Like this or not, you are now ready, and must be trained. If you are not, you will be hunted to extinction."

"I can look after myself," she insisted.

Fiora shook her head. "You think you have faced aggressors in Excariot, Lailah, Nathan; Lady Eleanor? You know nothing of danger. The group that will come for you is greater than anything you can imagine. That is why the Judge told us about you."

Val felt that, from Fiora's open expression that the woman was telling the truth; there was something so simple, so honest in her face. She really cared about what they were telling her, but it wasn't enough for her to abandon Wendy. She raised her hands. "Well I'm sorry, but either you help me rescue Wendy or I will go get her myself. There's no other option."

The man took the female's hand and she nodded. It seemed that they didn't have any need to speak to each other verbally. "We understand," she said.

"Good. Look it's not personal and thanks for coming all the way here for me. I hope you enjoy your trip home." She smiled as Zac tutted in open shame in the background.

The man's mouth lifted at the corner. He seemed almost amused with her. "No, we are not leaving, Val Saunders. We will show you where she is, but on one condition."

They definitely had her attention now. "You know where she is?" Her heart was beating faster, given a surge of adrenaline just from the mere thought that they could tell her where Wendy was.

"Yes. On the condition that when you have freed her, you must come with us."

"Where to and for how long?"

Beck tilted his head quizzically as if her question was ridiculous. "Somewhere safe and for as long as it takes to train you. You need to understand, Val Saunders; you are a danger to everyone around you. You friends, family and companions are at risk every moment you don't take responsibility for your power, or what it could mean in the hands of another."

"They're right," Zac added.

She gazed at Zac. "Tell me, can they get me to where Wendy is? Yes or no."

He nodded. "They can, and you also need to think about your parents, Jason and the others. If you stay with them, when they come for you - whoever *they* are - we will all be in danger. Val, trust me, the Tark are yours and Wendy's best chance of survival."

She always hated it when people made sense on a grown-up level, and Hunters never lied. "Fine, I'll come with you to find Wendy. But if I fail and Wendy doesn't come back safely, the deal's off." She reached out her hand.

"Val!" Zac snapped. "You don't deal with the Tark."

Beck looked at her outstretched hand then offered his.

"Do we have a deal?" she said, grabbing it, exaggerating her words and ignoring Zac's complaints. They needed to know she meant business.

"Yes," he said.

Val shook his hand vigorously. "On Earth this means if you don't keep your side of the bargain, bad things will happen." She couldn't think of anything big enough to threaten them with.

He nodded. "We should go."

"Wait." She pivoted, reaching out for Zac and pulling him close. Her cheek rested against his. "Listen to me, Zac. Find my parents. Get Jason and the others home. Brigit can do it. Then get the hell back to the Prison with Hadwyn and Boden. Sam and the Collector are in trouble and I need eyes on the ground. Do you understand?"

"Yes, but Sam is more than capable of looking after himself," he said in her ear.

"I know, but better to be safe. And for God's sake keep yourself alive until I come back. I'll come for you - you're my Hunter." She kissed his cheek. Funny, this time he didn't perform his usual disgusted recoil at her open show of affection, but stood very still, looking into her eyes until she stepped away. "Ok, I'm ready to go," she said.

"Good. Hunter, you have done well and she will be returned to you, but you must leave now," Fiora advised him. He bowed his head, took one last look at his Guard and walked away.

Val stood patiently waiting. "What now?"

Beck reached out a hand. "We take you to the time your friend is in."

"The time? Don't you mean the place?" She asked, a tremor of panic in her tone.

"No. Your friend is being held prisoner in the Earth year 2515." His hand took a firm grip of hers.

Val's head felt like she had just been struck with a hammer. "What? 2515? What are you talking about? That's hundreds of years in the future; it's not possible. Sam said that no one could travel to the future because we couldn't see where to go."

"That's true, and Sam hasn't travelled to the future, but he also told Wendy she was the Prison's best chance of survival. Those who see the future like Wendy can open the window."

"How do you know he said that to her?"

"We know everything." Fiora gave her a sweet, knowing smile.

Val could feel her brain starting to ache with the overload of this insanity information. "Well, I can't open that window. Wendy's the psychic, I'm just a Magrafe. I can't tell you what I had for breakfast a week ago, let alone tell you the future. So how do we get there?"

"Val, limitation is in the mind of the individual. Sam can travel to the past because he believes he can. You have to believe that if Wendy is in the future then you can reach her."

"It's time to leave. You are about to be born to Wyetta and you know what will happen if you are still here." Beck took Fiora's hand.

Val nodded. This was it. She was really going to have to leave; leave Wyetta, although she knew they would meet again; leave Gabriel to his fate at Excariot's hand; leave Jason and the others to go home; and leave Zac to try and make things stable on the Prison. Leave them all without a proper goodbye. "I guess there's no time for a farewell party?" she asked, trying not to let them see the tears that were filling her eyes.

Fiora shook her head. "We have no time left here," she said gently.

Val took a deep breath, blinked away the tears and straightened her back. "I'm ready to leave," she said. "If I can be here in 1645, then I can also go forward in time. I *will* find Wendy."

Beck smiled. "Exactly. You are worthy of your power, Val Saunders, don't forget that."

Despite the brave face she was showing the Tark, Val didn't feel worthy of anything. To her mind she was hopping off and leaving the others to deal with the mess she'd created, but she knew there was nothing she could do. She was sure that if she didn't agree to go with the Tark, they would take her anyway so, she should be grateful they were allowing her to go after Wendy.

She thought about the form that they had arrived in. They definitely weren't human, so what were they? And then there was the way Zac had behaved. He had clearly been in awe of them, confirming their importance and convincing her that theirs was the right choice. The Warden had sent Zac with her for her safety which was nice to know, and the Judge that had sent them for her must have been Sam, the only Judge she knew. No matter how much she learned about her strange new life, there were always more and more unanswered questions. Would she ever understand it all?

"Come." Beck squeezed her hand. His cold flesh creeped her out a little.

"Should I bring my axe?" she asked, unsure what was going to be acceptable.

Fiora let out a small laugh. "I think it has served its purpose; you can leave it here."

"I was getting quite attached to it." Val leant it up against the wall.

"When you're ready." Beck sounded just a little impatient.

Fiora nodded and they both tugged on her arms, pulling her towards them, the way children do in the playground, catapulting you into an oncoming boy. It wasn't gentle; it was like her arms were being pulled from their sockets. With a huge shock, she realised that she was literally being hurled into the future; she could feel the pressure of passing time, racing over her body. As the pressure reached her head, she saw darkness, closed her eyes, then everything was once again, gone.

*

When Zac reappeared in the courtyard, there was a palpable sense of relief passing between everyone. Wyetta was busy caring for some of the injured. Belinda, Fran, Jason and Brigit, now holding her new born baby in her arms, were all emerging from the entrance to the trial. Then there was a sudden squeal and the girl they had called Claudia ran past him to meet a young man in a cloak who was coming out of the entrance behind them. "Kez," she cried repeatedly until she reached him, throwing her arms around his neck and burying her face deep into his collar. With a sob he knelt and wrapped her in his arms.

Then an elderly woman appeared, holding hands with a young boy, their clothes more brightly coloured than anything Zac had ever seen and their skin a deep brown to match their eyes. The boy sprinted through the crowd, leaping the bodies on the ground and threw himself into the open arms of the woman who had been a sphinx until a short while ago. Next to exit the trial was a white haired woman in a very elegant dress, holding hands with a small blonde girl who was just stared in open astonishment towards the new dawn. It was odd that they met no-one they knew Zac thought, as they left without drawing attention to themselves.

He wondered if they should have been stopped and questioned, but who was going to do that right now in the face of such a great victory? Anyway, they didn't look like criminals and what danger could an old woman and a small blonde girl possibly be to them? He made his way over to join the others. "Gabriel, we must speak."

"Hunter... Sorry, Zac," Gabriel patted him on the shoulder, then paused looking around him. "Where's Val?"

Zac took a deep breath. For the first time in his memory he couldn't control his emotions. Things that he had never noticed before seemed to be moving, stirring inside him. "The Tark came for her. They gave her little choice but to leave with them."

Gabriel grabbed Zac's arm, causing him to wince. "You said they were gone, that they no longer existed."

"What's wrong?" Boden asked.

"The Tark have taken Val." Gabriel replied not taking his eyes off Zac.

"Gabriel, let him go," Boden said gently, placing a soothing hand on Gabriel's shoulder. "He's Val's Hunter and we have both witnessed him risk his life for her. You know that he wouldn't have been able to stop this. Tell us Zac, what are your instructions?"

Zac waited for Gabriel to release his arm. "She instructed me to make sure that Brigit sends her friends back home. I am to return to the Prison with you and Hadwyn to make sure Sam and the Collector are safe." He would keep the search for her real parents to himself for fear of agitating Gabriel further.

Boden nodded. "Then we will do as she has requested."

"No, that's not enough. I need to know why they would take her now. Where did they go?" Gabriel shook his head.

"They said she was ready for training; that she had transformed. A Judge told them of her existence and that her signal had drawn them to her. She made a deal with them."

By now, the others were joining them.

"Where is my daughter?" Wyetta asked.

"Zac was just telling us the Tark have taken her," Gabriel said. "Apparently she made a bargain with them, but no one bargains with the Tark."

All eyes rested on Zac. "She insisted they take her to Wendy; they agreed, on the condition that she goes with them for training as soon as Wendy is safe."

Fran became frantic at this, yelling that Val had done enough. "Wendy knew what she was doing when she took Brigit's place," she cried. "I watched her have the vision. She was calm, like it was her path. Val shouldn't go; we need to stop her."

"It's too late. She will have gone by now." Zac shook his head.

It seemed like they all started ranting at once: Wyetta at Gabriel; Fran at Jason; Belinda at Boden. The only person not screaming in anyone's face was Brigit, who was calmly nursing her new-born.

A series of shots cracking in the air brought an abrupt end to their arguments. Everyone ducked. The silence that followed allowed Hadwyn to speak. "She's gone with the Tark! Do you not understand? They will train her to stay alive, in the way of the warrior. They teach only the chosen to succeed. The Tark are older than time itself and their kind are under great threat. They risked everything when they revealed themselves to fetch her. Their orders will have come from someone in great power. The other option is for Val to live her life in constant danger; to be hunted for her powers. Stop reaching inside yourselves for your own pain. Val has been chosen to be powerful, to be a beacon and you are squabbling over you own selfish desires. She has asked Zac to give you her instructions and gone to save her friend. Now do as she asked. Gabriel, clearly not all Tark were murdered like ours was. She won't suffer the way we did. And if I remember correctly, you pushed our Tark to the limit of her patience most of the time."

Gabriel cringed at the memories. They had all been shamed by the one member of the group who normally said nothing that didn't include the word *attack* or *shoot*. Yet he was now their voice of reason.

"It is time for me to send you home," Brigit interrupted.

"But you're still weak," Wyetta objected, sucking in air sharply as the pain of her first contraction hit.

"I think maybe Val is ready to arrive," Brigit placed a hand on Wyetta's belly, "and look around you, we have a coven of a hundred full witches. I think we can get them back to their future."

"So, what was Wendy's vision?" Belinda asked.

Fran put her arm through Belinda's. "Wendy had a vision that told her to take Brigit's place and she left because she believed she had to. That's all she would say."

Zac added. "If it helps, Val made the Tark do the Earth promise." He took Belinda's hand and shook it. "And I promise you, Val will get Wendy back. She wouldn't move an inch until they said she could. I believe Wendy will come back to you wherever you are."

Belinda held his hand. "Thank you, Zac; that's good to know. Val's lucky to have you. Wendy's job is to guard Val's welfare and if she had a vision, then I must trust that this was her true path."

He nodded then turned to address the group. "Hadwyn, Boden we must return to the Prison. Sam and the Collector need us."

"We will, and we'll make things right," Boden assured him.

"Gabriel, you still have a job to do," Zac reminded him. "And a youngling to protect."

"I'll have to wait until she gets older to tell her about her adventures and all the worry she caused us," Gabriel said, oblivious to his own fate that was moving closer with each passing minute.

Boden saw the anguished expression that crossed Hadwyn's face and caught his arm. "Remember, change nothing," he reminded him softly.

"Please, it's time to leave; a baby is arriving," Brigit told them. The sun was rising as they stood huddled in the middle of what had been a battlefield. An army of the dead had been defeated, a baby born and disaster averted. Brigit passed her baby over to Wyetta who kissed its forehead and passed it on to Sara who was waiting in line.

"What's his name?" she asked, kissing the tiny fingers that popped out of the top of the cloak that Belinda had bundled him in.

"His name is Flynn." Brigit smiled. "Now go and rest."

Wyetta agreed and then she flushed with another contraction. Sara and a few other women led her off to someplace quieter so she could deliver the daughter she had already met.

Brigit addressed the gathering witches. "My magical sisters, let us raise some energy. I can't do this alone." A roar of approval rang out.

"Is it true? Can you really change the future?" Zac asked her.

She tilted her head thoughtfully. "I can, but I won't, and if you're going to ask me to save Gabriel, you have to understand that his loss drove many people to fight harder than ever before." She placed her hand on his cheek. "You will learn very soon that loss and lack is the greatest motivator."

The witches were forming a large circle and the children made two smaller ones inside it. Brigit led Zac to one of the smaller circles where Boden and Hadwyn were bidding farewell to Gabriel.

"Thank you, Zac, for looking after Val," he said.

Zac bowed his head in respect. "I won't say she has been an easy Guard to work with, but she is by far the greatest… and Hunters never lie."

Gabriel smiled. "I must go and welcome my youngling into the world," he said moving away, leaving the Hunter and the two Magrafe inside the circle of children.

Jason, Fran and Belinda were guided into the other circle. "Hey Zac, see you soon." Jason called.

Zac's eyes met Jason's. He had no idea when they would meet again. It was dawning on him that this could be the end for them all. "I hope so. It has been an honour to be part of your family," he called back.

"Sisters," Brigit interrupted. "Merry we meet. Thanks be to these people that we have our freedom to fight for others that will be persecuted." There was a cheer that seemed to rock the walls of the fortress. "Let us send our friends and saviours back to their homes with our love and protection." Yet another cheer rang out.

She moved into the circle and grabbed Hadwyn's hand. "Mighty warrior, your heart shows the true depth of your power. Many thanks for everything." She drew the shape of a bird into his flesh with the tip of her finger. Hadwyn didn't flinch, but thanked her. Then she moved to Boden. "You are the one who keeps all things moving; the turner of the impossible wheel. Thank you." She drew a wheel with six spokes on his wrist. "And finally you, loyal Hunter: the rock that gives her strength. Never doubt your own power." She drew a simple heart on his wrist. Zac flinched, but managed not to moan out loud. "It's all done, you may now leave."

Brigit's eyes softened with tears as they all began to disappear, shimmering into nothing until she was alone in the middle of the circle. "Blessed be," she whispered.

The children who had gathered around them now moved to join the others. Fran looked petrified; Jason held her close. "Sister witch," Brigit greeted Belinda, "I owe you the life of my son. Your daughter saved me and I promise that debt will be repaid. Have no fear for Wendy. She knew what path she had to follow." She placed a kiss on her cheek and drew a five pointed star on Belinda's wrist.

"Thank you," Belinda muttered through her tears.

"Fran." Brigit beckoned her. She nodded and moved forward nervously, still holding onto Jason. Brigit took Fran's hand. "Without any powers you have stood guard at my side and stepped into harm's way again and again. You are a force to be reckoned with and one day your choices will direct the changing tides." She drew three waves on Fran's arm. Fran winced and let out a small cry of pain.

Finally, Brigit took Jason's hand. "You, I have marked already." He still had the circle with the dot. "Be proud of your heritage. Your mother and father didn't give their lives for you to not be what you were meant to be."

"You know about my Mum and Dad?" His eyes flickered as tears rose.

"Yes, and they are so proud of you." She smiled sweetly at him. "Now go home and do the right thing. People will need your healing power in the future, so don't make the mistake of thinking the ability to heal is a curse, not a gift. It's your power, your path."

The three of them stood together. "Well, seems like we're on the move again," Jason quipped as they started to rise into the air. Then a light enveloped them. As the witches chanted together, its energy grew in intensity, and then the light dispersed and they were gone.

Brigit stood looking at the space they had filled as the sound of Wyetta's screams echoed through the fortress. Val was on her way and things would never be the same again.

Chapter 27

Where's Wendy?

Val felt the tapping on her face before her eyes opened. It wasn't harsh or aggressive, more of a gentle wake-up tap.

"Warden."

She forced back her lids and was greeted by the concerned face of a woman in a Guard's uniform. Val scrambled backward colliding with a wall.

"Warden, it's me, Thirteen Twenty-five. Alice." She raised her bracelet to show Val, as if it would make the difference.

Val took a deep breath. What was going on? Why had she called her Warden and why was this woman in a Guard's uniform? "Where am I?" she asked. Although just from looking around her she had a very good idea exactly where she was.

"You're on the Prison, a few feet from your office." She reached out a hand to help her up.

"Why are you here? You're... a woman?" Val asked, staring at the outstretched hand.

Alice cocked her head in confusion. "Maybe I should get a Mechanic. You have suffered a fall and you seem to have some memory loss." She went to speak into her

Dellatrax, but Val knew this would draw unwanted attention.

"No!" she snapped, then smiled. "Just help me up and back to work." She hoped that this female Guard would know where her place of work was.

"Of course." She took her hand, pulling her up onto shaky legs. Travelling to the past was a lot less taxing than the future. She felt weak, like she had flu or something. Alice led her across the corridor to the Warden's office door. "Do you want me to come in?" she asked.

Val already knew she'd need the Warden's bracelet to get in here, and when this Guard realised she didn't have it, she would surely raise the alarm. "No, it's fine. Please return to your duties," she said, shooing her away politely.

"Thank you, we are quite busy at the moment." She bowed to show Val respect and walked away.

Val waited until Alice was out of sight then placed her hand on the door for support. She would just wait here for a minute until the Warden arrived; he would know what to do. To her astonishment the door opened. She stumbled forward in surprise, expecting the Warden to come out. Instead, an assistant who was sitting behind a desk greeted her with a pleasant smile, "Good morning, Warden."

Val glanced behind her. There was no one there. "Morning," she said quizzically. expecting a sharp rebuff.

"Busy day?" The assistant responded, handing Val a transparent tablet. "May I ask why you're wearing your Magrafe uniform? I thought you would no longer be taking part in missions."

Val let out an odd grunt, which was about all she could muster.

"I will bring you a coffee," the assistant told her, closing the door behind her and leaving Val alone.

Coffee? On the Prison? What was happening? She walked around the Warden's office. It was almost exactly as she remembered it; plain white walls, glass desk. Why had she arrived here and why were people calling *her* the Warden? How was this supposed to help her find Wendy? What if those Tark people had been lying, Zac was wrong and Hadwyn had been right? She really was *always* in trouble.

To her annoyance, in her weakened state, the tablet felt quite heavy. She was just about to put it on the desk when somebody grabbed her from behind. Two strong arms wrapped around her waist, and the stranger's hands clasped together, squeezing her firmly. Someone was attacking her. She needed to protect herself. She squirmed, but a pair of lips touched her ear and the words, "Happy Birthday, Val," were whispered softly, followed by several kisses on her neck.

She turned inside the arms and came face to face with a man she had never set eyes on before. "Happy birthday!" She seethed, pushing his chest back with the little strength she could muster.

He stared at her, his blue eyes squinting in annoyance. Finally he released her, pushing his hand across his shaved head, scratching the inch of brown hair that covered it. "Did I get it wrong again?" he asked.

Now she was more confused than he was. "What?"

"It's your Birthday today. We do this every year, and I always get it wrong. It's the twenty-ninth of July on Earth today." He threw his arms in the air in submission.

"You know what, between your Christmas, Easter and Halloween, I can't keep this up."

"Yes that's it," she said, stopping him mid complaint. "It is my birthday." He was right, it was her birthday, and she was alive. She'd managed to leave before her birth. Strangly it seemed almost insignificant now. More importantly, who was he? And why was he nibbling her ear? She took a moment, trying to look more confident in her surroundings, moving towards her desk. "So what are we doing for my birthday?" She asked; any glimmer of information was going to be useful in her escape.

"Same as we do every year for your birthday, I hope?" He winked and the corner of his very attractive mouth lifted. Val wanted to panic and run.

"Right." She faltered, hitting the desk with her bottom, using its smooth edge to guide herself around it, putting a comfortable distance between them and plopping onto the seat that seemed a lot smaller that the Warden's. It actually felt... her size. "Well, I'll just get my work done here then I'll meet you later to celebrate, ok." Her lips parted in an awkward false grin.

But he wasn't going anywhere. His expression almost mirrored hers now. He was visibly confused by her behaviour. "Who are you?" he stepped towards her. "You look like my wife and you sound like my wife, but after three hundred years, I know you're not my wife."

Val choked. Her throat tightened. Three hundred years of marriage. "What?" Her voice came out as a high pitch squeak.

"I said, who are you?" He had now reached the desk, a mixture of fear and trepidation written on his face.

Val didn't want to make an enemy of someone who might be able to shed some light on her situation. She needed someone on her side and who better than her husband? "Fine. I'm Val Saunders, from the past, aged eighteen. I've been sent here by the Tark to save Wendy, my guardian. The last I knew, I was in 1645, fighting an army of dead soldiers with an army of witches, if you can believe that. And *you* don't look anything like the last man I married." She shrugged. "Oh yes, I have no idea why people are calling me Warden, or why I'm on the Prison. And I have never seen you before in my life. I don't doubt I'm the woman you married, but I just haven't done it yet, if that makes sense. Look I'll make it simple: I need to see Zac or Sam. Maybe you know Boden or Hadwyn?" Give names, she thought. Someone was going to be there for sure.

His expression became disturbed "What? Why are you saying those names?"

"I just left them. Well, Sam went off to help my Collector. She was arrested because I transformed and teleported... long story. If you're my husband, sorry second husband, you must know her. Small, smart looking woman, sharp tongue." She raised an eyebrow and smiled.

He leant over the desk, looking her directly in the eyes, as if searching for something. "What's your favourite film?" he asked.

She nearly choked. "Are you serious?"

"Tell me?" he ordered his voice sterner and his eyes narrowing.

"Star Wars," she replied.

"Which one?"

"A New Hope."

"Favourite character?"

"Han Solo. Is this leading anywhere?"

"Final question, what was your first job on Earth?"

Val's shoulders dropped, memories flooding in. "It was at Wallace Frederick Gallymore's antique and first edition bookshop."

His face seemed to relax. "It is you!"

She took a deep breath and sighed. "So, if I'm me, where am I, my body and stuff? And what's with the bank account application questions?"

"I have no idea what a bank account application is, but you told me that if ever you seemed odd or not yourself, to ask you those questions; that you would know the answer to them and no one else would. In answer to where *you* are, and your body? Please make the question a little clearer?"

"OK, I have just come from 1645, the year I was born. I had to leave before I was born because I couldn't be in the same time with myself. It would have completed my loop, crossing over my time-line, or that's what Zac said. So, if I'm here," she pointed to the floor, "then future me must be somewhere else in time. Oh dear God, I feel so confused."

To Val's surprise he actually smiled at her. "No, you're here and no one else is. You see from what you've learnt. Travelling to the future is very different to travelling to the past. If your body exists in a future time, you will step into that body automatically, as you are constantly creating a new universe and the future is yet to come, so there is no overlapping. Imagine the future is a straight line, there can be no crossing over."

"So right now I'm actually me, age five hundred and something?" He nodded and she managed a genuine smile. Looking down at her uniform, she poked her thighs and then her bottom. "Not bad for an old lady. So husband number two, what's your name?"

He was about to speak then he stopped and paused as if assessing whether to tell her or not, but he definitely wasn't as cautious as Zac. "I'm Flynn."

"Hello Flynn. I'd shake hands, but considering you just nibbled my neck it seems odd to go back to basics." Flynn's cheeks filled with colour. He was actually quite sweet. "You know Zac would have told you not to answer that question?" she said, trying to put him at ease. "So where is my loyal Hunter? Retired?" She grinned.

His eyes, that only a moment earlier had been sparkling blue pools, became a shadowed grey as they met hers. "You need to come with me. You made me promise that if you ever didn't remember the past, I should take you somewhere to remind you before we continue talking." He reached out his hand. "I have things you need to see."

She took it. If he was her husband and they had made a pact of questions *just in case,* then she had to trust he was sincere. Anyway, he was extremely attractive and she was impressed with her choice. But why wasn't she married to Sam? She knew that the chances of being with him were slim because of the lives they lived, but she would have taken the risk for him.

Flynn led her down familiar corridors. She received nods of respect from everyone they crossed, yet still there was not one single familiar face to be seen. Flynn paused next to a wall. It seemed just like all the others, but on the ground were a collection of palm-sized stones in mixed shades of red, purple and green. They contrasted so prettily against the stark white of the Prison.

"Place your hand there," he said, pointing at the wall. Her stomach tensed at his sombre tone. She guessed she wasn't going to like what she saw.

"Anywhere?" she asked. He nodded. She reached out tentatively and the wall seemed to come to life as her palm came to rest on it. At the very top were the words, *The Darkest Day in our History.* "What is this?" she asked.

"The worst day in the Prison's history. You put this here so no one would forget the atrocity. You need to read it, Val." He stepped back, leaving her to take it all in.

Her eyes scanned the top line.

On the first day of August in the first Earth year of the First Female Warden's rule, the lives of many brave friends were taken. Their names are here to remind us of what they gave up for friendship and for loyalty.

May courage, honour and wisdom guide you to justice.

Those extracted on the day:

Prison representatives:

Judge: Earth name, Sam Law.

First Warden.

Hunter: Thirty-three Twenty-seven, Earth name, Zac Efron.

Magrafe: Earth name, Boden Ekwall.

Magrafe: Earth name, Hadwyn Houte.

Collector: Earth name, Heather, given in respect by her daughter - survivor of the Space.

Val couldn't believe what she was looking at – it was too horrific for her to accept that it was true. She continued to read.

Supporters from the Space:

Susan Saunders, mother of Twenty-three Thirteen.

Mike Saunders, father of Twenty-three Thirteen,

"No..." she exhaled reaching out to touch her mum and dad's names. They had been here all the time. They'd never travelled to Earth.

Guard: Enoch.

Mechanic: Eswith.

Beloved children: Alsom, Taran....

She couldn't read another name. She turned into the chest of her husband, her head in her hands. "What happened?" she sobbed, her chest constricted. She'd seen the name of almost everyone she loved on that wall.

He wrapped his arms around her. "They were all found guilty of different crimes, unauthorised time-travel and aiding Sam and the Warden's cover-up of your survival. Your parents died simply because they were related to you and, after your union with Nathan Akar, it was believed all connections to you should be dealt with harshly. The High Judges were furious that you'd survived and every person remembered on that wall paid with their lives. They literally walked into a death trap."

"My Mum and Dad are really... dead." She retched. She was going to be sick. Waves of anguish racked her body; her heart felt like it was going to give out there and then.

He took her shoulders and held her firmly. "Listen to me. When this happened, you came back and punished them all, and because of you, everything changed. You changed the Prison, Val. You made it what it is today; a place where we live in equality. Female Guards working hand in hand with male; fair trials; no more extractions. Val, because of them, you have saved millions from injustice."

She didn't care what he was saying. They were all dead, her family, her friends; the people she loved. Zac, Sam and the children from the Space. "I'll go back to change it," she said, wiping her eyes. "I have time on my side. This won't happen, you'll see. I won't let it." She stepped away from him. She needed to complete her mission, she needed Wendy and then to get back as fast as possible. She would stop them; there was no other option. "Flynn, I've been sent here to find Wendy. Have I ever told you about her? She's not on the wall?"

"Yes of course you have, Val. I know Wendy as well as I know you. But she went missing about six weeks ago, on a mission."

He knew Wendy. This was good. No - this was great. This wall was a mistake. She would get Wendy and together they would make sure this so-called Dark Day never took place. "If you know her, then that means I've already saved her, in my past." She scratched her head. "But right now I need your help. I also need to find a man – he's called Jarrad. Sound familiar?"

He shook his head. "No."

"He's got to be here or they wouldn't have sent me." She searched in her head for something to jog Flynn's memory. "Tattoos, he's covered in them, and he has a pet rodent, like a large mouse."

"You mean the High Judge Twenty-Six Eleven?"

"Seriously? A High Judge? Where is he?" No wonder he was so powerful. But how had he got to the future? She was sure that Gabriel had told her the Warden had dealt with him. But if he was in possession of the spells from book of Vari, Brigit's book, that would answer the question, and with no one from the past here to remember him, this was the perfect place to hide. It made 'hide and seek' look a little pathetic. 'Close your eyes and count to five hundred years' was going to be a winner every time.

"Just use your Dellatrax." He pointed at his watch.

"That simple?" she said.

He nodded. "We're all connected. You can find any one of us at any time."

"Great." She glanced down at her wrist. There was nothing more than the bracelet Boden had given her. "Seems I don't have one."

He shook his head. "Clearly," he huffed, "you have lost it *again*. Well, future you. You know, I even put up a special shelf for you to leave it on," he complained. "You do have this really bad habit of losing it."

"Listen Flynn, forgetting my ability to misplace stuff in 2515, do I have anyone left; anyone I trust apart from you who might be able to help?"

"Daniel, he's your closest friend."

Val wanted to laugh. The person who'd killed Shane was now her closest friend. This really was a messed up future, but if anyone was going help her save Wendy, he would be the man. That was if he and Wendy were still an item. The list of questions was endless and her head hurt. "Take me to him please. I need to put this right. This isn't the future I had planned."

"Of course." He offered her his hand. "Val?"

She looked at it. "Yes?"

"Just so you know, even though the wall tells a very sad story, your life since I've been in it, has been amazing." Their eyes met and she felt the need to take the outstretched offer of connection.

Had she really just been that thoughtless? This man had been her husband for three hundred years and she had just torn out his heart, disrespecting their life together. "I'm so sorry, I'm sure we're great together." She squeezed his hand. "Now let's go get Daniel."

CHAPTER 28

Old Reliable

As they moved through the Prison, Val could see how different it was. The physical structure was the same, but the number of women now matched the men. Female Hunters and Guards moved around freely. But there was no-one she recognised. Her people had gone. "Flynn?"

"Yes."

"What are you?"

"I'm sorry?" he asked.

She didn't want to offend him, but she needed to know; not just who, but what, she'd married. "Are you a Hunter or a Mechanic?"

A grin spread across his face. "I'm a Ranswar. Surely you knew that?"

Val was the one blushing now and her cheeks burnt. "Well, it's a very good job to have." She coughed to cover her embarrassment.

"Don't worry, I'm half Nyterian on my mother's side. We were matched as I was the only male Ranswar left, so I guess we were both alone in the galaxy."

Now she wanted nothing more than to get to know this man. He had just explained why she had chosen him in a way that made her want to stay with him more than ever. They had been alone in the galaxy. He opened a doorway and they entered an area she recognised very well: the teleportation bay. And there in the centre, talking to another Guard, was Daniel, dishevelled from battle. Clearly he was still a hands-on type then.

"Hey, Val!" He waved, pushing his way through to her. "What's up with the uniform?" He grinned and slapped her on the back, as if she was one of his compatriots. "Want to come play for while with the big boys?"

She laughed at his comment. "Daniel, we need to have a chat."

"Ok. Put those in cells four, five and six for now!" He instructed the group of Guards, who were retaining a large cluster of fishlike creatures. "What's the matter?" he asked, as they walked out into a quieter corridor.

"Daniel, I'm just going to come out with it. The last time I saw you, I was defending the Prison from an attack by the Nyterians." There was no point in sugar coating this one. She had a husband as backup just in case.

He stared at her. "That was a very long time ago, Val. I'm not sure what you're implying." He shoved his hand through his hair, scratching his scalp, then rubbed his face as if it would make what she was suggesting disappear.

"I know. It's a long story. The situation right now is that I have been sent here, to my future, by the Tark. I'm here to find Wendy. I was in 1645, but really I'm from…"

Daniel raised his hand for her to stop. "You have news of Wendy?" His eyes became wide.

"So you two are still together then?" She allowed herself to feel a glimmer of hope. If they had made it, then surely there was a chance for her and Sam.

"Val, we have five younglings, but Wendy has been missing for six weeks now. Where is she?"

"I'm sorry, I really don't know where your Wendy is, but mine was taken by a High Judge, back in 1645. This Judge came back in time to find a super powerful witch, and Wendy being the crazy, brave person she is, saved her by swapping places. Then the Judge brought her here. So, here I am, ready to take her home, back to the 21st Century. But I'm not at full strength. Travelling into the future is quite draining."

"Don't worry, you'll get used to it," Daniel responded.

"Do we do it a lot?" she asked.

"I guess knowing anymore is a bad thing, sorry."

"Fine, but right now I need to get Wendy back home before Jarrad, the High Judge with the tattoos and the giant mouse Lovac, finds out she's not who he thinks she is."

"Where is he?" Daniel asked.

"I have no idea, and I don't have a Dellatrax."

Her husband gently tapped on her wrist. "She lost it again."

"Val!" Daniel sighed.

"I just got here; complain to the old Val when I'm gone."

Daniel looked at his Dellatrax. "If you don't have one, and mine doesn't allow me access to the Judges, we'll need to find another way."

"Well, actually you do have something a little different that might just work," Flynn told her.

"What and where?" Val asked him.

"Come with me."

They walked together to an area she hadn't been before. Flynn informed her that it was the Warden's private quarters. Although as they entered, she instantly felt like it was her home; her personality was splattered over every white wall. Fun images of her with Wendy and Daniel and their five red-headed children, projected onto the walls. Then more of her and her husband; they looked so happy. She was laughing and they were kissing, how could she ever have laughed again after losing her family and friends? It felt wrong, like a betrayal, but she couldn't deny the evidence of the pictures. Then, in the bedroom, there they were, on display over the bed; her very own Dellatrax. Not the instant access, techy-type Dellatrax that other Prison officials wore on their wrists, but the original powerful volumes that had seen her through her early days as a Guard. "Oh my God! The last time I saw these they were in a box and had been stolen by Flo in the body of David Beckham." She jumped onto the bed and stroked each spine as if touching a long-lost friend. They were worn, some burnt and torn on the edges. "How did I get them back?" she asked.

"Best we don't tell you about the past, Val," Daniel said.

"Right, well, when I see you again, I'll remember not to tell you stuff," she grumbled, pulling down a volume. "This is the healing one, I can feel it." She pulled it close to her chest and breathed deeply. In the odourless atmosphere of the 26th century Prison, the smell of the bookshop was strong and welcoming. She felt a wave of nostalgia, remembering when Zac had delivered them and how excited Wendy had been. "I may not be able to find *him* with these books, but they know Wendy as well as I do," she said, her voice just a whisper. She ran her finger once more across the spines. "Tell me old friends, where is she?" The tingle started at book four, and peaked at book six, where a small blue hologram jumped out at her. "Bingo."

"So what now?" Daniel asked, as the hologram grew in size.

Val shrugged. "I missed the Dellatrax class, but Zac taught me that it was alive, that I needed to listen to it. The book can tell me what I'm looking for or it wouldn't have given me the image."

Flynn stepped forward and raised his hand. "Look, it wants to show us where Wendy is." He opened his palm and the hologram dutifully drifted onto it. "I listened when I watched the future Wendy trying to teach you how to use it," he explained.

Looking at Flynn standing there, proving once again that her ability to retain information matched that of a goldfish, she felt a spark of affection for him. All at once she knew that he was *the one*; that if by some stroke of misfortune she had to choose a husband that wasn't Sam, he would be it.

"So what do we do now?" she asked, smiling at him.

"Show me Wendy," he said softly to the hologram.

The book Val was still holding started to vibrate in her arms. Hastily she lowered it onto the bed. It instantly flipped open, pages flashing past them. When it stopped, the three of them leaned over it, enthralled. There, on the page before them, a map was writing itself.

Daniel was the first to recognise it. "It's the Prison! She's here still."

Then the writing paused. "Is that it?" Val asked, thinking it wasn't giving them much of a clue, but it was as if it needed to think. After a moment it started a new drawing underneath the previous one, as if it was in a subterranean level. "Is that what I think it is?"

From Daniel's expression, he too knew exactly where it was. He nodded. "The Space. They're in the Space. Let's go." He was already heading towards the door.

"Wait. Maybe it's not finished," Val protested.

"There is only one way in and out of the Space, Val. Come on," Flynn urged her, as impatient as Daniel.

"OK." She joined them reluctant, wishing she was better prepared; wishing Zac, or Jason, or any of her friends were with her. Daniel was already well in front of her with Flynn close behind. She had to run to catch up.

"We can only get down there through the main entrance. It's changed a little since you were last here, Val," Daniel told her.

Flynn and Daniel led the way, discussing the underground layouts. Val followed, wondering how they would deal with Jarrad. He still had Wendy hostage and had all of Brigit's powers to help him. He'd already killed a Tark and then travelled to catch Wyetta. He was no fool and she needed to be ready. But she wasn't, and they were rushing her.

"Wait." She stalled as they reached the entrance. The last time she'd visited this place her mum and dad had been here. She shut her mind to the memories, knowing she needed to focus on the task in front of her. "Surely we need a proper plan?"

"Surprise," Daniel replied, and his whole body sparked and crackled with electrical energy.

She stepped back surprised by how powerful he appeared to have become in the past five hundred years.

"Well, that could work." She shook her head, trying to get her statically charged hair down again. To her wonder, what resembled two lift doors, opened in front of them. "You have a lift down to the Space?"

"Let's just say that the Space isn't what it was last time you were here, or we'll be picked off while we're giving you the guided tour," Daniel said, allowing his display of power to subside as they stepped into the elevator.

Val stood between the two men, tension building inside her. This was madness. They were travelling into an enclosed space where Jarrad, a power crazy High Judge, was probably expecting them. It felt wrong. Then Flynn began to hum the theme to Star Wars. She glanced across at him and he grinned awkwardly.

"What are you doing?" she asked, shaking her head in disbelief.

"Well you always hum this when we travel to the Space. You said that's what it's like on Earth." He shrugged. "It's your habit - not mine."

"Are we safe to take him with us?" she asked Daniel. "He has no powers."

Daniel let out a laugh. "Excuse me?" He turned to her husband. "Flynn, haven't you told her anything?"

"No, I haven't felt the need to show off yet, Daniel," he responded dryly.

"So not just a Ranswar then?" She nudged him. "I'll try not to let it influence me when I meet you for the first time, and I'm sorry for assuming you had no powers. Do you think I should know about them before we…" But it was too late, they'd arrived; the lift opened onto the Space.

CHAPTER 29

Expect The Unexpected

There wasn't time to find out what Flynn could do before she actually got to see him in action. The doors of the lift opened and there, standing right in front of them, were three dog-like animals, the like of which Val had never seen before.

"Can they see us?" she whispered to Daniel, which seemed silly as they had no eyes. Their tongues flicked out towards them like those of serpents, searching for their pray. The smell coming off them was like rotting meat.

Flynn put his arm across Val's body. "They're Viewers; they can sense things that can't be seen by the naked eye," he whispered.

The three hairless hound like creatures, swayed in unison with each other. Their skin was hard and crusty, covered in battle scars and, from their dribbling jaws, protruded fangs that could easily crush a human. Val shuddered.

"Flynn you're up," Daniel said through gritted teeth.

He nodded. Val wanted to stop whatever madness was about to happen, but she didn't have a voice; her throat was dry with fear. "Thought you would never ask." He smiled and stepped away from her, straight towards the Viewers. "Hello, fancy a bit of fun?" he goaded.

The first of the three leapt at him, its fangs slashing and snapping. Val wanted to scream, but Daniel quickly placed his hand firmly over her mouth. He shook his head. "Shh," he warned. "They sense movement, among other things."

Then the Viewer yelped. To Val's astonishment its jaws had clamped down on its own tongue, passing straight through Flynn's arm as he strode confidently through the animals, like a ghost. When he reached the other side he turned and winked at Val. "Come on, it's exercise time!" he called and started to run away from the lift. The Viewers circled around, their heads high, sensing and tasting with their tongues. As Flynn ran, they took up the chase.

Daniel slowly released her. "Let's find Wendy." He stepped out of the lift.

"What about Flynn? Those animals are after him... My husband's a ghost," she said, scratching her head.

He patted her on the back. "He's not a ghost, but he can change the vibration of his molecular structure. We call it phasing. He can pass through objects, and he can make himself so solid that nothing can penetrate him. It's very cool. I'm jealous, but don't tell him that. He's already far too aware that he married the Warden and has super-powers."

Val just nodded. "Ok, so my husband is pretty cool; that's better than being a ghost I guess."

Their conversation came to an abrupt end when they heard a man screaming. "That's not Flynn," Daniel answered her fear before she got a chance to voice it. He was instantly on the move and she followed. Her time in the Space had been limited to three visits and she wasn't sure of the layout, but Daniel moved with confidence, running up a staircase towards the platform she had stood on with Enoch and Eswith, calling on the inhabitants of the Space to fight the Nyterians. As they came close to the top, he signalled for her to wait. They crouched on the steps and Daniel cautiously raised himself to get a better view. "Wendy," he whispered. The name was sweet music to Val's ears.

"Let's go." Val stood as another blood curdling cry rang out.

Daniel wouldn't let her pass. "No, don't interfere," he ordered.

Was he crazy? She'd time-travelled to the future and had agreed to go train with some random aliens so that she could rescue Wendy. She wasn't going to *not* interfere. "I don't think so." She lit up, hoping it would distract him and give her time to get by him. She was right. Daniel covered his eyes against her bright flames.

She surged forward and, as she reached the top of the steps, she heard a man repeatedly pleading to be released. What she saw definitely wasn't what she'd expected. She had come here with every intention of saving Wendy from Jarrad, the man who'd kidnapped her mother and killed her biological father's Tark. However, from what she could see, Jarrad was the one who needed help.

Wendy had Jarrad on his knees with one of her hands firmly around his throat. Her other hand was raised high in the air holding a book. It wasn't a book Val recognised. It was plain black with a circular mark with a dot in the centre embossed in silver on the cover. The mark was the same as the ones Val and Jason had received from Brigit.

She could only surmise that this was Brigit's book and from the way Jarrad was screaming, it seemed that Wendy was taking back the magic he had stolen.

"You dared to steal from a witch," Wendy shouted into his upturned face. "Now you'll pay the price."

This wasn't a pretty scene and Val was shocked by Wendy's ferocity. Was it the book that was causing this, or Jarrad?

"Wendy!" She called to her. Wendy's eyes moved from her victim's face to Val's. Val gasped in horror. Wendy's face was covered in flickering images; even her eyes and hair were alive with symbols. Her skin looked as if it had a life of its own as they rushed through her, using her as a conduit and flowing back to the book.

"Why are you here?" She didn't seem at all pleased to see her. "I told them to tell you I could do this on my own."

"I know, I can see that, but this isn't right. We need to arrest him, not kill him."

Jarrad's eyes pleaded with her. He was shuddering with the pain as each image was ripped from his flesh and transposed onto Wendy's. "Help me," he beseeched his voice weakening as he slumped even further. Wendy's hand stayed firmly on his throat.

Just past them, Val could see the half-eaten carcass of Lovac. So, the Viewers weren't here in support of Jarrad, as she'd assumed, they were here... with Wendy? What the hell was going on?

"I need you to stop." She stepped closer.

"I will when I've finished," Wendy replied coldly.

"That's not what I wanted to hear." Another few steps and she could grab her. It all came down to what was right.

"I have instructions and I will follow them," Wendy said, bending to keep contact with Jarrad who had now collapsed.

Val stepped forward once more. "I think you're misinterpreting the orders, Wendy. Brigit would never kill anyone."

"Just stay out of my way. Go home. Be a good Guard and let the rest of us do what's necessary."

Val couldn't believe what she was hearing. This was Wendy, little, skinny, harmless Wendy Whitmore. "No, I won't let you go down a path that there's no return from. We, you and I, just watched Lady Eleanor being killed. We've lost Shane. That's enough, Wendy."

Val focused her energy, and a fiery ball formed in her palm. She aimed at the book blowing it out of Wendy's hand and sending it across the rocky ground.

Wendy screamed as it left her hand, then collapsed to the floor. Val ran to her friend's side. "I'm so sorry," she said.

"What have you done?" Wendy groaned and, as her hair fell back from her face, Val could see the tattoos had solidified in her skin.

"Oh my God, Wendy, I'm so sorry."

Daniel, who was now behind them was quick to paralyse the exhausted Jarrad with a bolt from his hand. "Thanks, Val." He grumbled.

"You should have stayed away." Wendy began to sob.

Val pulled her into her arms. "I'm sorry, but I'm never going to leave you alone."

"Well you may have no choice now. Unless you want to kill him yourself."

"What do you mean? Why are you talking like this?" Val asked.

Lifting her head, Wendy looked into Val's eyes. "He's going to kill me and the others. I saw it in a vision."

"What others?"

"Jason, Fran, my Mum. You've just stopped me fulfilling my destiny. I just pray that yours is to stop my fate from coming to pass."

"I'll make sure it is. I won't let anyone hurt you guys. But why do you have all these marks on you?" Val touched Wendy's cheek.

She took Val's hand gently and sighed, her voice shaky. "You stopped me transferring them back to the book. I was the conduit. We'll need to find a way to get them out of me, but not here, not now. We need to go home. The others are still at risk from him wherever they are."

"Wendy." Daniel reached out a hand for her. Her expression softened at seeing him. "I've missed you so much, Wendy," he said, pulling her to his side and wrapping her in an embrace that made Val feel envious of the love they had.

"Well, I'm not quite the Wendy you know." She blushed as he lifted her face and kissed her. Val looked away, blushing as well.

"I know, but if you've travelled here and I can see you, then my Wendy is alive and as well as you are."

"Hey!" A very out of breath Flynn arrived on the scene. "Wendy," he enthused, arrived at the perfect moment.

"Flynn." Val jumped up, greeting him with an embrace. "I was really worried about you."

"Don't be silly, we've made it this far. I managed to lock the Viewers in one of the few rooms with a door in this place." He grinned and kissed her cheek. "Val,

I know you don't know me yet, but I'm worth the wait."
His arms gripped around her waist and turned to what
felt like steel, "And now you know my powers."

There was an awkward cough in the background.
"Val Saunders."

She glanced around to see the Tark had arrived.

They all paused, Flynn's hold softened.

"Ah... there has been a slight change of plan. I would
really love to go train with you, but I need to get Wendy
back home," she said nervously.

Becks' expression didn't change at her attempt to get
out of their agreement. "Val Saunders, it's time. You
made a promise, an Earth promise. Do you not keep
those promises on your planet?"

"Yes, usually," she answered.

"Remember this training is for your safety, and that
of your loved ones."

Now she was angry. "Well, it's going to be a waste of
my time, isn't it? It's too late for that."

"Too late?" Becks repeated, looking faintly
surprised.

"Yes. Too late. I just saw a wall that's proof that my
parents and all the people I love are dead." Her throat
was constricting with grief and anger.

"What?" Wendy exclaimed.

She turned to Wendy. "Yes, dead, all of them in two
days' time, because of me."

Fiora spoke next. "Val, you have no choice. We are
trying to do this is in a way that feels right to you as a
human. We don't have to ask your permission; we don't
need to help you or your friends and family. We are Tark;
we are everything, everywhere."

"Look I get it, but I need to go home. Wendy has all these tattoos on her face that we need to get rid of. Plus, she's seen her own death, which I need to prevent."

Becks was taking no more of her stalling. "You will leave this place with us and we will return Wendy to an agreed spot in exactly sixty of your Earth seconds. The talking has finished."

"No!" she screamed at them exploding into flames.

Flynn reached out to her. She flinched, expecting him to burn, but he didn't, he just took her hand, his flesh solid like metal. "Val, from what I remember the Tark taught you everything you know. They weren't a negative force in your life. I think you should leave, with them, peacefully."

She shook her head at him and rushed over to Wendy. "Listen to me, you need to get to the Prison. They're all going to be extracted. Do you understand? On the first of August."

"Yes." She nodded.

"Val, you have thirty seconds. Where would you like us to send Wendy?" Fiora asked.

Val looked at her. "Send her back to the bookshop."

"But the bookshop no longer exists," Becks answered.

Val paused, taking a second before responding. She knew that right now they were the only chance she had to save her friends and family. "Please make it exist. Put it back the way it was. You are everything, everywhere, aren't you? Then I will come willingly."

"We are, and we can make it so. There are ten seconds." Becks demeanour lightened with her change of attitude.

She grabbed Wendy's wrist. "Save them. I'll be back for you. Daniel, lock up that scum bag, Jarrad, in the Interspace. Flynn, it's been fun and I look forward to the day we meet."

"Three."

She kissed him. It just felt right, like it would make him feel better.

"One."

She heard Fiora's voice and then felt Flynn's lips. Then Wendy and Daniel were gone.

Chapter 30

Look Who's Here

Wendy's last view of the future was Daniel, still her true love, which wasn't a shock; she'd seen him before in her own private visions of the future. The other man with him she'd never seen before, but she guessed from the way he'd treated Val, that he was important to her. Her mind was still spinning with the shock of what Val had said to her. Everyone was dead. But in *her* vision she had only seen herself Jason, Fran and her mother die at Jarrad's hands. Had that been because Sam and the others on the Prison were already dead? Whatever was happening, the last thing they needed right now was for Val to be taken away for training.

The journey home was beyond uncomfortable. She'd heard Val ask the Tark to take her back the bookshop, but why? What could be her reason? Everyone they wanted to avoid knew exactly where the bookshop was. For heaven's sake, it was slap bang in the middle of the High Street. She landed hard on the hard wooden floor and it hurt. She howled in pain and lay still for a moment, collecting her thoughts. Slowly she pulled herself up and dragged her matted hair away from her face. As she pulled her fringe back, she could see that the

Tark didn't mess around. She was sitting on the floor of the bookshop and there in front of her, was the battered water cooler, a victim of one of Val's battles, along with a few dirty coffee cups. The Tark really had put everything back as it was.

She could feel the tears pricking her eyes as she knelt and saw her reflection gazing back at her from the cooler's distorted metal. The shock of her reflection made her head reel. Her face was marked from her forehead all the way down her neck with stark black tattoos. Her mum was going to kill her.

"Wendy?" A voice called her name and she froze. Who was here? Who knew the shop was back?

She scrambled to her feet, but to her relief she realised that the voice was that of someone she recognised and loved. Jason stood behind the counter. The infamous door with the private sign, that had hidden the double personality of Excariot and his little crony Delta, was wide open and coming from it were her friends and mother.

"Wendy." Belinda pushed past Jason and ran to her daughter, wrapping her in an embrace. "What happened to you?" She stared in appalled fascination at her daughter's disfigured face.

"It's a long story."

"Do you think?" Fran greeted her. "We're standing in a bookshop that we watched burn down. I have time to listen to your story, Wendy. And where's Val?"

"She came looking for me. Oh Mum, I made a mistake. I tried to stop Jarrad on my own and look at me, look at my face. Then Val was taken by the Tark for training."

"Who are these Tark - I'm still not sure?" Belinda asked.

"They're teachers that were expelled from the Prison a very long time ago because they were considered too powerful. The Prison couldn't destroy them, so they were deemed dangerous, but when they were at their strongest they were a beacon of hope for many. They were loved by all who came into contact with them."

"How do you know all this?"

"Sam made me study them. He said it was an important part of our history. I even recognised the markings on the ones that came for Val. Sam showed me images of those two and explained their connection to the Prison. They hadn't been seen since they were banished from the Prison several centuries ago. I think they're called Fiora and Becks. Quite famous for their skills in battle. Funny how you remember stuff after the event. I wish I could have told Val that."

"So why come back now?" Jason asked, pouring a glass of water from the cooler and sniffing it.

"They came for Val. Seems that with great power comes a new training regime. The one thing that Sam kept repeating about them was that they were good, that they saved countless lives. They trained the greatest Guards the Prison ever saw, and so we have to trust that they have Val's best interests at heart, even though she didn't want to go with them."

"Typical Val," Jason said, taking the smallest sip of the water, as if it would poison him. Then, accepting it was safe, he gulped it down then poured one for Fran and the others. "So what's next for us?" he asked between swallows.

"This will decide," Fran replied walking back behind the counter and into the corridor. She picked up the receiver of the ancient telephone and dialled. They watched her as she waited. "Mum." The tears welled in her eyes, but she kept her voice steady. "Yes, I'm fine. No, what's in the news is not true. Please don't worry about me." There was another pause. "Yass is fine; she's staying at a friend's. I'll get her to call you as soon as I see her. Mum, I have to go; it's safer if I don't tell you any more. I'll call, ok. I love you." She replaced the receiver, tears streaming down her cheeks. "Looks like we're still Britain's most wanted."

Jason finished off another glass. "Great news. So much for a little time off."

Wendy touched her cheek. "There's definitely no time off. I had a vision Jason. It told me that I had to take Brigit's book of Vari and go with Jarrad, because he was going to kill us."

"Well, he hasn't and you stopped him. Didn't you?"

"Jarrad took me to the future, not a pleasant trip I have to say. But when we got there I realised the future me was still alive. I could only guess that was because I'd destroyed Jarrad, like I did in my vision. So I felt confident that I knew what I needed to do." Her eyes avoided making contact with the others; she wasn't proud of what she'd done.

"What does that mean?" Jason asked.

"It meant I had to kill Jarrad. It just so happens that in my future I have a very good relationship with an animal called a Viewer. I actually have a pack of the things."

"A Viewer? What's that?" Jason interrupted again.

Fran shoved him. "For heaven's sake let her talk."

"Sorry."

"It's fine. A Viewer is a creature they use on the Prison to control crowds, or hunt down special cases. But their speciality is to sense psychic powers, and other things that can't be seen by the naked eye, and they're really gross looking. But I have a very good relationship with them and when they sensed I was on the Prison they came looking for me. I have to say, both Jarrad and I were alarmed at first, but it was apparent quite quickly that they were on my side. I took advantage of the confusion to pull out the book Brigit had given me back in the cell and start a draining spell. The marks on Jarrad had to be removed from him and sent back into the book. It would have killed him if I'd taken them all."

Belinda pushed Wendy's hair behind her ear. "So what happened?"

"Val happened. She arrived with Daniel and stopped me. She cut me off before I could finish and these marks were left on me."

"Daniel was there? That's good news. So what did they do with Jarrad?" Jason asked.

"Val ordered that he be sent to the Interspace. But it's not enough. I know he'll still come for us. We haven't seen the last of him."

Fran was shaking her head "Wendy, please don't take this the wrong way, but I'd rather not make you a killer. Val did the right thing. She knew that if you'd killed Jarrad you would never be the same again. Now we know he's coming for us, if Val hasn't stopped that, we can get ready. But we don't kill people."

Wendy lifted her glance to meet theirs. "I know. I don't know what I was thinking. I just felt like we had lost so much already. Then Val told me something even more disturbing before I was sent back here."

"How unusual." Jason responded, sighing deeply.

"This is really bad," she warned them. "Because of our little trip to the past Sam, Zac, Sue, Mike... well everyone we know that's not here now, will be extracted on August the first. Val wanted us to go and stop it."

Jason's face was turning grey. "Sam left to go and help the Collector, she'd been arrested. So how do we get to the Prison without him and the others?"

Fran started to laugh. "Oh, my, she's so clever."

"Who?" Wendy asked.

"Val. She made them put the bookshop back. I really hope she got everything she wanted." Fran ran towards the private door. "Come on." She beckoned the others to follow her.

They all bounded up the stairs to the tiny flat that had been home to Val for the few days she'd been its owner and there, in the corner of the bedroom, was the cupboard door. It was closed.

"Of course! Do you think it's really still there?" Wendy said.

Jason stepped forward. "Only one way to find out." He grabbed the handle and looked up. "Dad, if you're watching over me, please make this an inter-dimensional portal to another galaxy, not a load of nasty tweed."

The handle turned; the anticipation was palpable. Then to their collective relief a shimmering portal to Alchany was revealed. Wendy let out a squeal. "We can do this. We can save them," she said, just as an explosion rocked the room.

The glass in the window smashed across the floor as a wave of energy came at them. They huddled together in shock. Then to their amazement, the glass that had one second earlier been shattering around them, rose up and hovered in mid-air. Then, as quickly as it had exploded over them, it reversed itself back into the window, reforming into a perfect pane of glass.

"Please tell me I wasn't the only one who saw that," Jason demanded.

Fran and the others just stared at him open mouthed. "Where did the explosion come from?" she asked.

"Outside I think," Belinda said, running to the window and pulling back the curtains. "Wendy, you need to see this."

On the street stood three figures and a fiercely burning car, which looked to have been the cause of the explosion. "Come out, Alien!" a voice screamed.

Wendy's voice was filled with hatred. "Delta!"

"What?" Jason exclaimed, heading towards the stairs.

Fran followed. "Jason, don't do anything." Then they were all on the move again.

As they reached the front door of the shop they realised who exactly, had come calling. Delta was joined by two figures. To her right was Flo, who'd taken the body of Fourteen, the Guard, so she could steal the Dellatrax. "Who's the blonde guy?" Jason asked Wendy.

Her eyes were fixed on him. "He's the new and improved version of Excariot."

Fran let out a cry. "What do we do?"

"Alien!" Delta hollered again at the top of her voice.

"Why is she saying that?" Fran asked, grabbing hold of Jason's hand.

"It's her pet name for Val. She must think she's in here," he replied.

Delta raised her hand. In the centre of her palm rested a ball of light. It was a perfect circle; its edges glowed with a pearly sheen.

"What's that?" Jason asked.

"Looks like she's finally got the power she wanted," Wendy said.

"Can you stop them?"

She shook her head. "I can't. Not all three of them. We need to leave."

"Where would you like us to go? I think the fact that the window just repaired itself is a good sign," Fran said. "I think we're safe in here."

"Yes, but I think Val wanted us to go to the Prison," Wendy said.

Belinda was pacing, "No! If all those who helped Val are to be extracted we'd be going to our deaths. I don't think Val wanted us to all go there. I think she meant it as an escape route for them. We need to keep the door to the prison open, and protected."

"I agree," Fran said.

"Protection spell?" Wendy looked at her mum, who nodded.

The trio was already heading for the front door, when a male voice from behind made them all jump. "Hello there. Sorry, I was sleeping." They turned and saw a young man who was standing by the bookcases. "I've been waiting for you," he grinned.

His clothes weren't current, but they all recognised his attire which was that worn by the people they had just left in the seventeenth century. His skin was tanned by the sun and he had clear blue eyes, looking out from under a mop of dark brown hair. A straight nose led to full lips and a square jaw.

"Who are you?" Jason demanded.

"Wait!" Wendy snapped at him. "I recognise you."

"Well that's good news. I'm sorry if I scared you. I've been waiting here a while."

Jason moved around him suspiciously. "It's not the best time for introductions. We're about to be attacked by a gang of demented psychos, with enough power to take out the High Street."

"Don't worry about them, they can't get in; they've been trying this for a few days now." He raised an eyebrow. "Let me explain before you start asking questions. I've been waiting for you to arrive. My mother sent me here. She said it was time for me to repay a favour, and since I arrived they've been visiting on a daily basis. The blonde girl who screams a lot doesn't understand that no one is going to let her in. She's not too bright."

"So," Fran prompted. "Who are you? Why can't they get in, and who's your mother?"

"I'm sorry that was rude of me. I used a protection barrier my mother gave me; it seems to be keeping them at bay. My mother's Brigit the Writer, and I'm her son, Flynn. So..." He looked at each of them in turn. "... which one of you lucky people is the Alien?"

The End

Special acknowledgement goes to:

Market Harborough Museum for letting me play with swords!
The gang at Market Harborough Starbucks,
who know me better as *Bob*.
All of the wonderful school children I met in 2012/13.
FACEBOOK fans; all 10 billion of you (we wish).
Adele and Jason for suffering my grammar.
and Chris, as always, for the magic.
I thank you all xx.

Lightning Source UK Ltd.
Milton Keynes UK
UKOW03f0734070314

227736UK00001B/5/P